The CRAVING

KAREN DEEN

Published by Karen Deen
Edited by Contagious Edits
Formatted by Lee Reyden
Cover Design by The Book Cover Boutique
Cover Photography by Wander Aguiar
Cover Model is Pau T

About the Author

Karen Deen is an author who loves to write stories that will stay with you long after you've finished reading them. Her stories are filled with spice and witty banter, while being full of emotion, comedy, suspense and twists and turns that you never see coming. All the time steering her characters to their happily ever after. Everything you need in a good love story.

Writing has become her career, which she is lucky to be doing in such a picturesque hometown near Sydney, Australia. Enjoying life over good meals with her childhood sweetheart husband, three adult children and their ever-growing family. Or a sneaky lunch or coffee date with friends that involve laughter until your sides hurt.

Contact

For all the news on upcoming books,
visit Karen at:
www.karendeen.com.au
contact@karendeen.com.au
Facebook: Karen Deen Author
Instagram: karendeen_author
TikTok: karendeenauthor

Dedication

To my husband, who helped me to step off the edge,
into a world of happiness.

THE CRAVING

KAREN DEEN

Prologue

RICHARD

I knew if I came back today, I would see her.

Walking along the beach, with her long, wavy blonde hair falling down her back, the breeze blowing it behind her, and the sun highlighting her face. Bronzed skin like she's ready for a photoshoot. But I doubt she'd be interested in that. From afar, she just doesn't seem like the kind of person who cares about how other people see her. All the primping and makeup they use, she doesn't need any of that to look attractive. To me, she is just an all-natural beauty and a product of living in this beautiful place.

When I left England wanting an adventure, looking to find myself before taking up my role in the family business, I never imagined what I would find in Australia. I have traveled widely over Europe with my parents and visited many beach resorts, but nothing compares. The beauty of the golden sand and the blue of the ocean waves is just like I'd heard about.

But no one told me about the Australian women.

From the moment I arrived, it was like a smorgasbord of

gorgeousness. And from that first night I spotted her, she captivated me.

The woman of my desires.

She's quiet and unassuming but radiates all the confidence of someone who takes life in stride. There's no sign of stress of what life brings her or the worries of a business empire hanging over her head.

She doesn't compare to any of the girls I grew up with in my stuffy lifestyle of money and the aristocracy all around me. I live in a world of glitz and glamor. God forbid one of those women should leave the house without a face full of makeup or hours on end spent at the hairdresser and nail salon.

They aren't real women… not even close.

Biding my time, I finally see her appear at the edge of the grass, stopping to slip her sandals off before stepping her bare feet onto the sand. It's like she is taking a moment to connect with nature, just sinking her feet into the sand. Her long loose skirt is blowing in the breeze, and today, she has a wide-brimmed straw hat on her head, containing her wavy hair around her face, but the rest is hanging down and moving with the gentle air blowing through it. The floral bikini top she has on is visible through a very thin white shirt that is only buttoned twice at the top, and the rest is scooped up and tied under her breasts, exposing her stomach that has been kissed by the sun and tanned to an olive tone that makes her blonde hair stand out even more.

I'm not about to let this opportunity pass me by today. Pushing up off the grass to my feet, I walk onto the sand. I'm not like the Aussie guys I've seen around on the beach, my feet are soft. Comes from always living in fine Italian leather shoes and my skin rarely touching the ground. Keeping the flipflops on my feet only lasts about ten steps before my feet get heavier and there's sand all over them. I feel like I'm dragging half the beach with me.

"Fucking useless shoes!" I slip my feet out of them and throw them behind me. Now my feet start to heat up, to the point of burning pain beginning to shoot up my legs.

"Who the fuck thought it was a good idea to make a beach

hotter than the ground in Hell!" I yell as I start into a full jog, heading toward the water. Reaching the packed sand at the edge of the waves, my feet are on fire, and all I can hear from behind me is sweet laughter that is now getting closer.

I'm still dancing on my toes until I finally hit the water, and it's like I can hear my feet hissing as the cold water runs over the hot surface of my skin.

"Your Pommy skin isn't designed to handle our beaches." Standing almost level with me, we both look out into the waves.

Great start, Richard. I'm almost too embarrassed to turn and face the woman I have been fantasizing about for days, since that first morning I spotted her. Instead of pulling myself together, my arrogance comes rising to the surface, and the words just blurt out of my mouth.

"Why in God's name do you Australians call us Poms? I mean, it doesn't even make sense. It's not like it has anything to do with the word English or British." Turning to look at her, I realize in the first few seconds that she is even more beautiful up close than I dreamed about.

Her giggle is already doing things to me, and I don't want to embarrass myself further by showing how much it affects me.

"History tells that us Aussies love to shorten names, words, anything really. So, the word British just wasn't going to cut it when they started shipping you Pommies here to work. The word Pom is short for pomegranate, which rhymes with immigrant. The word stuck, and Poms or Pommies it became. Makes perfect sense, don't you think." She kicks up the water each time a wave runs over her toes.

"No. Not an ounce of sense, really. And why the big thing about us being immigrants? We could really go back to you all being convicts that we stuck on a ship to send to some random island that wasn't worth living on." *What is wrong with me? Shut up, you idiot.*

The smile on her face gets brighter, and she spreads her arms out to her sides and starts spinning in a circle.

"Of course, nobody would want to live here. I mean, just look at it. What a punishment to be shipped here. Now you might understand why things turned around and the British started immigrating the first opportunity they got. Welcome to our horrible island." Still twirling in a circle, she looks up into the sky and soaks in the warm sun on her skin. The twirl now turns into a dance, swaying backwards and forwards, as she holds her skirt and swishes it side to side.

Nothing awful touches this woman. Her soul radiates purity.

Transfixed by her happiness, I'm taken aback when she reaches for my hand, the softness of her fingers running up my arm.

"Dance with me. It will help take away the grayness sitting on your mind."

Confused at what she's saying, I almost start to question her nonsense, but she reaches her other hand toward my face, with her finger touching my lips, shushing me.

No one ever shushes me!

But I can't stop from taking her in my arms, and we start moving to the imaginary music that is playing in her head.

At the edge of the water, with her head now lying on my chest over my heart, swaying together, I've just found what feels like love with my mystery woman.

I have no idea how I will ever let her go. I don't even know who she is. It's crazy, but in this moment, I know I will make sure she will never be tainted by my life.

The life I thought I wanted, that I was raised to live.

Now I just need to work out how I can change that path to keep my golden girl with me and as happy as she is today.

Crap, what have I done?

4 Weeks Later

"Sally, we need to talk." It's the worst sentence on the entire planet for a person in a relationship to say out loud.

I wrote my parents a letter a few days ago and posted it in the mail. By the time it reaches them, I'm hoping I'll be out of contact because I'll be traveling and can deal with the explosion after they've had a few days to simmer down.

I've known deep down for a while that taking my place in my

family's business was not my true calling. It was the reason I traveled to find out where my passion lies. I had never been allowed to find what I liked or to choose my own career. I was born into the Darby Hotel dynasty, worth billions of dollars and owned and managed by my father. Originally, he and his brother started a hotel together, but Uncle Lenny hated it and left, with my father happily buying out his share. Lenny spent his life being a painter and made a reasonable living from it. My dad was always hard on him, saying he could have had the world if he'd stayed in the business, but I know his art meant more to him than money.

That's a true passion.

This will kill my parents, but I hope they'll see what Sally means to me and why I can't bring her into that world. The vultures will eat her alive and kill her free soul. I have proposed that I take twelve months off, get married, and then maybe open a small version of one of our hotels in Australia. Something low-key that will provide a reasonable income for any future family we have. Uncle Lenny has a son and daughter, so maybe they can take on my role back home. I don't know the answer, but what I do know is that Sally is more important to me than anything else in this world. She is the passion I was destined to find.

Trying to describe her to them in words was hard because you need to be in her presence to fully understand her beauty. And to be honest, my mother is going to hate her. She won't fit into the society mold that she thinks is important. To me, I couldn't care less. But either way, it's too late now, the letter's written and mailed.

"Talking is overrated. Sex is so much better. Let's go for round three." Shimmying down my body, Sally's lips are just on the tip of my cock when I pull her back up toward me. My whole body is groaning at me, because I could definitely go another round. She is insatiable, and I fucking love it.

"As much as I want that, I'm serious. I need to tell you some-thing." It must be in the tone of my voice that has her head tilting to the side. She takes in my face and seems to understand that I don't want to talk about the weather.

"O…kay." Sally tries to pull away from me to sit up, but I'm not letting her leave my arms. I tighten them around her and hold her by my side, as we are now lying looking at each other.

"I have to leave for a few weeks and go home." The moment the words are out, her whole body stiffens in my arms. I don't think I've ever seen her tense, and I don't like that it's me that is causing it now. Usually, she's never short of words, but now, her silence scares me.

"Please don't panic, let me explain. It's not as bad as it seems. I'm coming back for you. Let's get that straight right from the beginning." Her tenseness eases slightly, but not as much as I want it to.

"I need to go home to explain to my parents that I don't want to go into the family business because I want to be here with you. We were meant to meet, I have no doubt of that. And from that first moment of dancing on the beach, I knew deep in my heart that I'll never let you go. When you find your soul mate, you marry her and live happily ever after, or so the fairy tales say. I know it's all too soon, but I want you to know I want all of that with you. Once I'm back and can tell you everything, then we can make plans."

I wish I could tell her more, but we have loved the sexiness of the mystery in our relationship. And I can look my mother in the eye and truthfully say that Sally is not after my fortune because she has no idea who I am. This just started as two young travelers who tried telling themselves they were just having fun. A holiday romance that we would look back on fondly one day.

But all that changed the moment I kissed her. I knew there was no going back.

I remember vividly the moonlight on the water and the sound of the waves crashing onto the shore, and that nothing could be more perfect.

Stopping at the edge of the water, I turned Sally so she was facing me, her eyes twinkling in the light of the night sky. Neither of us could hold back any longer. I'd used just about every ounce of gentlemanly restraint in my body the last few days since our dance on the sand.

"I'm about to kiss you. Tell me you want that too." I softly took her face and tilted it up to the perfect angle.

"More than I can put into words." As she rose onto her tippy-toes, I could feel the electricity when our lips finally touched. I wanted it to be the perfect romantic moment, but that went out the window in less than ten seconds. Our bodies were craving each other's touch, and nothing could hold us back.

The pure intensity of the lust carried us away, literally, all the way back to my hotel room. One that I made sure was not too fancy to give away my wealth but comfortable enough that I wasn't sleeping on the ground in a tent like Sally was. I wanted to give her the world but in the way that she wanted and not in the over-the-top life it could be.

Call me naïve, but I wasn't ready to fall for a woman so quickly and wasn't at all prepared. Laying Sally down ever so softly on my bed, I knew that I couldn't hold back even if I tried. I was going to be asking for her trust and for her to give it to me too.

Her hands were already moving, pushing my shirt up my chest, making sure she was touching my skin that was so much paler than hers.

"Please tell me we are going to have sex?" She looked up, her eyes pleading with me.

"Every part of my body wants that more than I know how to express, but I don't have a condom. I'm so sorry. Maybe we should wait?"

"Fuck that. I want you now, Richard. I'm on the pill and clean, I promise you." Her hands continued to push past the elastic of my shorts, and the moment she wrapped her hand around my hard cock, I knew I could never tell her no.

"I'm clean too. I haven't slept with anyone since I left home and was tested," I said, trying to make sure she knew she could trust me too.

"Richard… Just shut up and fuck me." Using her fist, she pulled up my cock with such firmness that I failed to hold in my moan. She stopped and traced her fingers around my rim, her thumb sliding over the precum that had been leaking since her first touch of my bare chest. The shudder she drew from my body was my breaking point.

"Oh Sally, I don't want to fuck you. Instead, I'm going to make sweet, passionate love to you. You deserve to be treated like a princess. And I intend to make every part of your body feel like you have been worshiped." I reluctantly took her hand from my body and pushed up onto my knees, hovering above her.

Pulling on the hem of her short little dress that had been taunting me all night, I slid it up her body and over her head. I'd seen her in a bikini on the beach, but her pretty pink lace lingerie took my breath away.

"Oh, this is perfect. You are perfect…" My words trailed off as I leaned down and took her nipple into my mouth, sucking it hard. Her body arched off the bed as I slid my hand down her stomach and under the top of her panties. Yes, she was so ready for me, the moisture on her sex, and I didn't waste any time rubbing her juices up and over her clit.

"Yes… more, oh more." Her sultry voice told me what she wanted. And my body was ready to give it to her.

Working my fingers inside her, up and down her folds and round and round on her clit, her body was like my puppet, and I was the puppeteer bringing her all the ecstasy. Writhing under me while I had her pinned, she threw her head back, and the scream of my name off her lips as her orgasm ripped through her body was a sight I will never forget. Nothing will take this vision from me.

I stripped her panties and bra from her as she came off her high and finally dropped my shorts to the floor. We were both naked, and all I wanted was to be joined with her like this forever.

"Are you sure?" I whispered to her as I nudged at her wet entrance. My lips were so close that her breath was mixed with mine.

"Yes, I don't just want you, I need you more than I need air." Our lips joined as our bodies became one. Pushing inside her bare was something I had only ever dreamed of. I was taking a risk, but the reward was worth more than I could describe.

I had all the visions of taking her slow and loving her, but our bodies took over, and before I could pull back, we were fucking, and I was pounding into her harder than I imagined I ever would. This woman brings out every carnal cell in my body I didn't even know existed. I want to completely control her body and make it mine. Sally screamed her pleasure with every thrust inside her. Her pussy took every inch of me, almost strangling my ramrod-hard cock with her tight muscles.

The orgasm that ravaged her body had her gripping me so tight I couldn't hold on any longer.

I released every drop of my cum inside her, until my body finally stopped quivering and I dropped on top of her, our sweat a sign of how intense that was.

Rolling onto my back and taking Sally with me, we stayed like this until she was fast asleep on top of me. And finally, I knew I had found my home.

. . .

Looking into her eyes, I know Sally is thinking back to that night too. We both knew there was no coming back after that. Giving our bodies to each other in such a way was the sign we both needed to confirm we are exactly where we are meant to be.

I could lie here and watch her forever, but we have more to talk about. Her voice brings me back to the present of the heavy conversation we are having.

"You are my soul mate, and I feel it too. But I don't even know your surname, and nor do you know mine, yet you are making plans to marry me. Maybe we should talk a bit more before you leave." Concern is hidden behind her smile, and she tries to cover up how worried she is.

"Let's not ruin what we have. I will tell you everything about me when I return, and you can tell me your deepest and darkest secrets too. I only have tonight. My flight leaves tomorrow, and I can't miss it. Let's spend the rest of the night making the memories that are important, and the only details you need to know are how every part of my body feels against yours."

Threading my fingers through her hair, I pull her face toward me, taking her lips with mine and kissing her with every bit of electricity that is burning inside me, just from being this close to her.

"So just lie back and do as I tell you like a good girl. Watching you give it all up for me is hot as fuck, but remember, you come when I say. I own your pleasure now." Her eyes tell me she is giving herself over for me to control in this moment.

The more I devour her, the quicker she softens in my arms. As both of us are swept up in our emotions and the sadness of being away from each other for a while, I can't stop claiming her. Pushing her onto her back, I drive inside her already-wet sex. I swallow her moan as I start pounding her harder. She loves to feel everything so intensely, and I'm making sure she doesn't forget who owns her body. Over and over again, I pound into her until I can't hold off any longer. Her pussy squeezes me so tightly as her orgasm wracks her body, and I let go, filling her with everything I have. Marking her, like a caveman, a savagery I never knew I was capable of feeling.

Sally is mine, and when I return, I won't ever leave her side again.

Not wanting the hard goodbye, I take one last look at her naked body, lying face down on her bed in the caravan she's now staying in, at my insistence. I want her safe while I'm not here to protect her.

I whisper into the room and hope she knows in her soul the words she isn't ready to hear out loud yet. "I love you, my ray of sunshine. Until we meet again."

I'm sitting on the plane and looking out the window as the wheels touch down on the runway. The weather is dull and raining.

"Welcome home," I whisper to myself.

I'm not sure that everything around me feels so dreary because it's normal English weather or if it's just because I already miss my ray of sunshine.

I take a deep breath, knowing what will be waiting for me when I get to the house. "You can do this, Richard. Stay strong and don't waver. The prize is too great to lose."

Gone is the calmness of the sun, sand, and waves I've left behind, and before me is the chaos of London.

Stepping out onto the street, I can't think of anything except Sally and getting back to her as quickly as possible. Telling her who I am and what I'm worth. I know it won't make a difference to her, but we need to start off our lives together with no secrets.

Having not told my mother what flight I was on, I know my driver won't be here to collect me, and I'm glad. Blending in is all I want to do today.

Climbing into the back of a black cab, we start driving off into the traffic on a rainy Friday afternoon. I know this is going to be the hardest day of my life.

I just need to get through today.

Chapter One

35 Years Later

NICHOLAS

I toss my phone onto the bathroom counter. "Mum, I can't talk now, I'm late for work." I nearly trip myself as I drop my shorts and scramble to get my shirt off.

The sweat running down my back plasters the shirt to my skin and doesn't make it easy. Running in the morning sun along Manly Beach will do that to you. Australian summers are relentless, and it doesn't matter how early you get up, it's hot all the time.

"Then why did you answer the call?" Her laugh comes through the hands-free speaker on my phone, making me smile as I finally peel my shirt off.

"Because if I don't, I know you will just keep ringing until I do!" I yell as the water starts spurting from the showerhead.

"Never... okay, well maybe, but otherwise, I don't get to talk to you. How often do you say I'll call you back in five, and I'm assuming you mean five minutes, not five days or five weeks, Nicholas!" Wow, my full name, she must be trying to make a point.

"Yeah, yeah. Well, unless you want to stay on the phone and listen to me washing my private parts, Mum, then I've got to go." My finger is hovering over the end call button on my phone.

"Nothing I haven't seen before, Son." Her laughing is not funny this time.

"Far out, Mum. I'm thirty-four years old. It's been a long time since you've seen me naked, and I'd prefer not to even think about that last time." My mind drifts back to that moment.

"Sex is natural, Nic, but, seeing your son balls deep in his girlfriend and hard at it wasn't what I was expecting that day, that's for sure."

"Mum, for fuck's sake, you had to go there, didn't you! That's it, I'm out. I need to get to work to make sure the prep for the lunch menu is right."

What is wrong with this woman? She is still laughing at the memory of walking in on me at the age of twenty, while I was pounding into my then girlfriend from behind. Not my finest hour. Actually, to be honest, if my memory serves me correctly, it was a damn fine hour of fucking we'd been having until Mum arrived home early and killed that within about zero-point-one seconds.

"Bye, Mum, love you." I can't help but chuckle to myself, pushing the button to cut her off and stepping under the steaming water. The fifteen minutes I planned for my shower is now ten, and that's stretching it.

Being the head chef at the Park Hyatt in Sydney does not allow me to be late. They expect the best from me, and I in turn expect the same from my staff. Never set a bad example for others. I've been where they are, grinding away, trying to climb the ladder in the kitchen. And I will never forget what my pop used to tell me when he was teaching me to cook all those years ago in the little kitchen of their small red-brick suburban house, that a good boss leads by example. If I ever want to make anything of my life, I need to work hard, love what I do, and show people respect, no matter what their position is in the company. I have always tried to live by that motto.

Pop was the cleaner in a big-city office tower. Sometimes on the school holidays he would take me with him at night and I would help him. But most of all, I loved staring out the window at the Sydney Harbour Bridge in all her glory, lit up like a piece of art on display for all the city to enjoy. Below us, from what felt like my tower, was the Opera House that also looked awesome, but the bridge fascinated me more.

Who would have guessed all those years ago that I would be managing the five-star restaurant in the hotel nestled right under that same bridge? It's like it was meant to be. If you believe in that shit.

Growing up with a mother who was a firm believer that everything happened for a reason, I got a little sick of hearing all the crap she would tell me about believing in the process and what the universe was or wasn't doing. But as I got older, I realized it was what got her through the tough years of raising me on her own. Well, technically, she was on her own, but my Nan and Pop were a huge part of my life too. They never turned their back on her when she turned up at their front door seven months pregnant after traveling on her gap year after high school. Not quite what her plans were, but if you ask her, that's what the universe had intended for her.

I call bullshit on that, but hey, I can't complain. I'm here, aren't I!

If only my asshole father had done as he promised and come back for her, then maybe things might have been different. Or if she wasn't so carefree, and actually asked for more details about him, like an address, phone number, or you know, even a date of birth would have been handy. She waited six months for him, but then knew it was time to come home. She was just a holiday fling to him, four weeks of happy endings and a promise of more as he left, taking Mum's heart with him and in turn leaving her with her own little surprise.

Mum was never bitter, but as I grew older and became a teenager, I was pissed as hell. After watching her struggle to put food on the table and keep a roof over our heads, I vowed that one day, if I ever met him, I would punch him square in the face and walk away, not even giving him the time of day.

As I've gotten older, that anger has not dissipated, but it has combined with the sadness of never knowing my father. In the end, it was him that missed out. Mum never married, and although she had some partners along the way, nothing ever made her eyes sparkle like they do when she talks about him. I often wonder if she has romanticized the memory of him over the years. I mean, she only knew him for four weeks, yet she never got over him. That sort of thing only happens in the movies.

Shutting off the water and stepping onto the white fluffy bathmat, I snap out of my daydream. I don't have time for these thoughts. Time's wasting, and I've got to make the ferry to get across the harbor, otherwise I'm screwed.

Traveling in a big city, it's easier most days to take public transport. The cost of driving a car and parking it for the long hours I work in a day is the killer of any extra money from my paycheck. Besides, it's become a habit. It gives me thirty minutes to get myself into the zone, to clear my head, and then the moment I walk into the kitchen, it's game on.

Time has gone so quickly since I got off the ferry this morning. The lunch serving was problem-free today, but dinner has just been a shitshow. We were booked to capacity all night in the restaurant, with more diners sitting in the bar. It's getting later in the night, but from all reports of the waitstaff, at least the party of eight in the bar are having a great night. Quite often we get the quiet, serious diners who have loads of money but can't seem to crack a smile. Or couples, where one partner is trying to impress the other by bringing them out to such a high-end venue. But this group in the bar tonight is loud, laughing and enjoying the food and a whole lot of margaritas. My idea of a night out.

Not that I get one often. I live to work, not intentionally, but that is just what happened. But over the years, it has gotten me to where I am today, at the top of my game. The harder I work, the easier living is. I started with nothing, and I don't want to go back there.

I'm not rich by any means, but I am comfortable, and I make sure my mum is too. She hates it when I do things for her, telling me she doesn't need it, but the satisfaction of seeing her driving a car that I know won't break down on her makes me worry less about her when I can't be there.

"I don't know what the drama is!" I hear one of my junior chefs mumbling under his breath with one of the waitstaff, standing there with food on the plate she has just brought back. One thing I pride myself on is having excellent hearing above the noise, so I've always got my finger on the pulse in my kitchen.

"Because you served her up a plate of pure fat, you dickhead. Not one piece of meat on that plate. No wonder she didn't eat it."

Feeling the hairs on the back of my neck start to rise, my fists are clenching.

I need to give him the chance to sort this out. It's the only way he'll learn.

"Well, sometimes you get that. It's just as tasty, so she missed out," he replies to her, making Brea, the waitress, huff as she slams the plate down in front of him and turns for the door.

"I'm not charging her for that meal, and that's on you," she calls over her shoulder, flicking her ponytail as she storms back out of the kitchen.

Stupid little shit.

"Dirk!" I call across the kitchen. You need a loud voice in here because things are never quiet, and if they are, you should worry. A noisy kitchen is a busy kitchen, which leads to a profitable kitchen, and that means I'm doing my job right.

"Yes, Chef?" He looks up from where he is plating up a steak. We are almost closed for orders for the night, so everyone is trying to push out the last meals on the lists.

"Since when do we serve up food that is not to my standard?" I walk closer to him, wanting to hear every part of his explanation.

"Never, Chef." I can see his pupils getting wider the closer I get to the plate that is sitting on the counter next to him.

"Correct." I poke the leftover food on the plate with a knife that was lying next to it. My muscles tense as I see what it is. "Then…

what... the fuck... is this?" I draw every word out, trying not to explode but loud enough that everyone in the kitchen gets quiet, listening to what is about to go down.

"Sorry, Chef, I didn't see that. I swear it had plenty of meat on it." The sweat now beading on his forehead is not from the hot plate he has been working over all night.

Wrong answer, buddy!

"Are you trying to tell me the customer is a liar?" I hiss, pushing the plate to the side, probably a little too forcefully, as it almost flies off the other side of the counter.

"No, Chef." He looks scared that I thought that, and he's dreading what I will say next.

"Get that meal plated and out of the kitchen now, before we have another upset diner who is out there spouting that the food in Nic Weston's restaurant is disgusting. Because it's not your name they will be using when they tell every friend they have what a bad meal they were served from my kitchen, is it?"

"Sorry, Chef." His hands work double speed to plate his meal and make it look perfect.

"Then when you're done, get your fucking ass out there and apologize to that customer and organize a free drink at the bar for her. I don't care how much you grovel, but she better be leaving here tonight happy and feeling satisfied. Understood?"

"Yes, Chef," is his reply, but he's a little less confident and quieter than before. He looks down, afraid to make eye contact. And so he fucking should!

I demand the best in my kitchen and nothing less. And I respect this kid enough to teach him that, otherwise he has no place working in a restaurant like this.

Turning back to check on the rest of the kitchen, all faces are on me, and as soon as I make eye contact, they are scrambling to look like they're busy and weren't watching me rant.

"Get the last dishes out now!" I shout, demanding their attention but also reminding them to keep their head in the game.

My kitchen is my domain. No one fucks with my place.

By the time we have finished with service and the clean-up routine is almost done, I'm checking on tomorrow's bookings, triple-checking the supplies on hand and the orders that are due in the morning.

"Well, that was an interesting night." Flynn, my sous chef, the man I trust to be in charge when I'm not here and my best friend for years, drops onto the stool next to me at the counter I'm doing my paperwork on.

"If by interesting you mean a shitshow, then yes, you're correct," I say, scribbling down in my order book to talk to the supplier of the lamb we had trouble with tonight. If they can't supply the highest quality I expect, then I'll find someone who can.

"Don't think that new junior chef is going to make the cut. Not exactly what we expected."

"Yeah, he's cocky and not afraid to push his point. Talented, but that's what's so frustrating. Drives me fucking crazy."

"Hmm, not like anyone I know when they started out. I mean, the lad I'm thinking of all those years ago was out to become the best of the best. Wonder what happened to him…" he rattles off at me with his smart mouth.

"He became your boss and can sack you on the spot for being such a jackass. Now let's get out of here. You up for a beer over at the Cruise Bar before I jump on the last ferry? I need to blow off some steam." Slamming my book closed and placing it back in my tray, I pull the tie on my apron. Once it slides off for the night, I'm done, and the staff know not to ask me anything. My late-night head chef who handles the room service during the night takes over, and I know he will handle anything that crops up.

"Only steam you want to blow? Well, I was thinking of finding a nice blonde who will turn this night around by blowing me instead." Flynn hangs his apron on the hook next to mine, knowing when we return tomorrow our clean fresh ones will be hanging there in their place.

"You wish. All the women in that place are about ten years younger than us, and that just sounds like too much hard work for me. Call me crazy, but I don't want a clinger." Grabbing my phone, keys, and wallet from my locker, I notice multiple missed calls from Mum.

"Shit," I can't help but say aloud as I read her messages. She never calls when I've told her I'm at work, not unless it's important.

> Mum: Nic, sorry I forgot you were working. I'm going to bed now. Not important. Call me in the morning.

Noticing the time is almost eleven pm, I don't want to call her, but something doesn't sound right about this. Mum isn't forgetful, and it's not like I didn't talk to her fourteen hours ago.

I can't help but worry about it.

"Everything all right?" Flynn is standing beside me now, after retrieving his phone as well.

"Don't know. Missed calls from Mum, but she says it's all good. Oh well, I'll have to wait until morning. Come on, your shout, on account of... ummm... oh yeah, you're a Pommie, and they say they are tight with their money. So, take this as a training exercise on how to be an Aussie." Slapping him on the shoulder, he just groans at my feeble excuse. I mean, it's not like he hasn't been in the country for over fourteen years or anything.

We have been friends since he walked into the restaurant where I was working as a second-year apprentice. He was straight off the plane from the UK, looking for work. He had no training whatso-ever, and it turned out to be his lucky day. The first-year apprentice had quit that morning, and Flynn slotted straight into his job. We have managed to continue working together ever since. He might be slightly older than me, but that doesn't mean anything in maturity levels. My mum tells me I'm an old soul, and Flynn hasn't ever grown up, but somehow, we work as friends.

Walking through the hotel's bar, I give a chin lift to the staff who are now cleaning up and serving drinks to the few couples still enjoying the quiet of the beautiful view outside. Hugo is on the side door tonight and smirks as he sees us coming toward him.

"Out on the town tonight, boys?" he asks, pushing the door open in front of us.

"Nah, heading home to bed like good little children," Flynn says, holding his hands under his chin like he's praying. He might have lived here for a long time, but he still has the broad English accent and some of the words that come out of his mouth make me laugh. You can take the man out of England, but you can't take the English out of the man.

"Right, and the sky ain't blue." Hugo chuckles.

"Crap, did you say blue balls? Don't jinx me, man!" Flynn thumps Hugo on the arm on the way past.

"Just watch the steps tonight. The wood's getting slippery after all the rain." Hugo points his flashlight at the stairway down to the boardwalk that runs around the rocks area. I love that the heritage of this place has been kept, and the buildings of yesteryear are still here and preserved.

"You think he would be a gentleman and help us down the stairs by holding our hands, wouldn't you, Nic?" Hugo rolls his eyes as Flynn holds his hand out for him to take it, like he would take a lady's hand to help her.

I'm still laughing at Flynn and his desperation to get laid tonight and worrying about his blue balls, that Hugo's reaction just makes me laugh harder. Flynn has had a few girlfriends since he took up residence here, but then a few he has scared away back to their own countries too. Well, at least that's what I tell him. It's a common thing in our line of work and where we socialize. It's a melting pot for overseas tourists who are here on a working holiday, just like he was in the beginning. He loves it, but for me, the thought of losing someone because they are going back home is a bit too close to real life.

"He's good value, old Hugo, isn't he? Always has a good come-back." Walking toward the Cruise Bar, I'm only vaguely aware of a man who appears in his mid-fifties, sitting on a park bench under a large old oak tree, its branches spanning out over the boardwalk. The lights are strategically placed around it to make it look like a masterpiece of nature.

"I have a feeling he has a wicked sense of humor that we only get to see a part of."

"True." Flynn laughing, we fall into step next to each other as we come level with the oak tree.

The movement of the man standing as we approach doesn't startle me as much as the name that comes out of his mouth.

"Richard?" His very broad English accent makes Flynn glance sideways but not enough to stop him from walking. It was just a voice that sounded like home to him.

But to me, it makes my blood pump and a shiver run down my spine. I haven't heard that name in years, and in a broad English drawl. I freeze.

"Pardon?" My brain is too slow. I should have just kept walking and ignored him, but it's too late now.

"It's you, isn't it? You're Richard Nicholas Weston, Sally Weston's son."

My world stops spinning, and the ten missed phone calls from Mum suddenly make sense.

My hands ball into fists on instinct, because the words are screaming inside my head.

Are you my fucking father?

ENGLAND

4 Years Later

VICTORIA

"Why can't I ever get out of bed early, or on time even," I mumble, cursing myself as I run through the train station, hearing over the loudspeaker that the train I need to be on is about to depart.

There's no more air left in my lungs to be talking out loud to myself, as I'm madly waving at the guard not to blow that whistle, to wait for me to run that last ten steps and lunge for the doors that are about to close on me.

The smirk on his face tells me he feels sorry for me and holds his whistle out of his mouth for just the few seconds more I needed. Both feet planting on the floor inside the train carriage, the shrill sound of that whistle outside tells me I can finally breathe.

First day on the job, being late would not be the best start. Smoothing down my gray skirt, I straighten my matching tailored jacket and slip my black stilettoes out of the bag I have over my shoulder. Bending down all so gracefully, I pop my feet into them while I scoop up my black flats that are made for those late dashes for the train. They have a rubber sole and extra grip to give me more speed.

Standing up straight, I take a big deep breath in and then try not to laugh at myself. After all the craziness of what just occurred and how I must have looked to everyone that I almost bowled over as I ran past, I still managed not to spill a drop of my tea in my travel mug. Now that's talent, if I do say so myself.

This train commute will be a good thirty minutes into the city, so after standing here for all of five minutes, I know I need to find somewhere to sit. I can see everything in here is already taken, so I head down the carriage, ever so carefully on my heels in a moving train. I don't want to end up on my ass in front of all these people, after I managed to make it on the train in one piece and still look dignified. Looking forward, I spot a seat near the window about halfway down the carriage on the lefthand side. The gentleman in the aisle seat seems to be too interested in his phone to even notice me approaching, his legs spread out toward the window and his briefcase lying on the spare spot next to him. His body is angled away from me, and he is still transfixed on whatever is on his screen in front of him.

His body language tells me he doesn't want to be disturbed, but I couldn't give a shit. I need to sit, and so he needs to move.

"Excuse me, sir, is this seat taken?" He doesn't even raise his head or turn toward me after I speak.

I'm getting impatient waiting for his reaction, and not another person on the train even acknowledges that I'm standing in the middle of the aisle looking like a total idiot.

That's it, I'm not standing here the whole trip. Who does he think he is?

Tapping his shoulder startles him far more than I was expecting.

"Shit," he lets slip and then straightens himself in the seat, and only then do I see the earbuds for his phone as he pulls one out to speak to me.

Oh, my freaking God!

There must be some mistake in this morning's plan. How am I supposed to sit next to this man and concentrate on trying to get my head together for this momentous first day I'm planning on having. I can hardly breathe, let alone put a proper thought together.

His piercing blue eyes leave nothing to the imagination of what his thoughts are—pure irritation at me. But I'm still too busy admiring the chiseled jaw and lips that are drawn in a straight line. He might have shaven this morning, but already I can see the start of the faintest stubble. Oh, imagine what that would feel like on my...

"Can I help you, madam?" That gravelly tone is enough to make me want to answer all types of wrong things to that question. And that Australian accent, fuck, that's hot! Damn, pull yourself together and act like a proper English lady. Oh, who am I kidding, this is as close as it gets to me looking the part, but I'm as far from being proper as you can get. Well, not exactly, but I'm trying. Today is my one big chance to find a step up in the world from my life that I have grown up in.

Right, speak now, silly.

"Sorry, I didn't mean to disturb you, but is this seat taken?" Obviously, it is, by his bag, but no matter how drop-dead handsome he is and the gravelly voice that could lure any woman into his lair, if he refuses to give up this seat, I'm going to make such a scene... or not. Because I'm not so brave, really. I mean, in my head I am, but when it comes to saying my piece to a man who is hotter than the sun, sitting in front of me, well, all that bravery flies straight out the window.

Not saying a word, he turns back to his briefcase, releasing a small huff, and then stands to move so I can take the window seat.

Holy hell!

If I thought he was imposing the way he looked up at me from his seat before, the way he is now, looking down at me from his full height, I'm melting in a wet puddle from the things he is making my body do. Stop staring, you look stupid.

"Please, take the window seat. I can't fit my size in that small gap." That voice makes me think things I shouldn't. *Oh, I bet your size has trouble fitting into anyone's gap, sir.*

"Thank you," is all I can manage as I slide past him with my back to him. Totally forgetting my bag on my shoulder that, as I swing my body into the seat, bangs into him. Hearing the thud that is simultaneous with the whoosh of air leaving his chest, I don't even want to stop and look. The bag has thrown me off balance, and I'm already dropping toward my seat, praying it looks like I'm falling with style.

"Sorry," I manage to get out as I look at him rubbing his chest as he carefully places his briefcase on the ground in the aisle beside his seat and gracefully lowers himself on a slight angle away from me. About to put a strike against him for being a rude twat, it's then that I realize his legs are so long he can't fit them in behind the seat if he sits straight on. Then my mind drifts again to thoughts that a proper English lady wouldn't ever have. Maybe this being-sophisticated thing is overrated.

Trying to settle into the rest of the trip and not disturb him, I take my phone out of my bag and madly start messaging Elouise, my best friend, who will get the biggest laugh out of my morning's escapade, considering she is the more eloquent one between us.

> Tori: Today was supposed to be the start of something big. I almost missed the train, and now I'm sitting next to the most gorgeous man I've ever seen, constantly wondering how long his cock is and what it would be like to climb his body. Fuck my life!

When the dots pop up to show she's replying straight away, I know she's laughing at me from afar.

Finally taking a big sip of my tea, I pop my own earbuds in which will help me calm down. When I get a notification of her voice message, I hit play, but then I hear nothing, no voice in my ears, and I check the volume. I look down at my phone and notice there is no picture in the top corner of my phone showing my earbuds are even connected. And then I hear her voice, muffled by the earbuds in my ears.

> Elouise: Wait! You're sitting next to a guy with a big cock, hot enough to fuck, and you think you are having a bad start to the day? Tell me more!

Shit, it's playing out loud! At the same time, I feel movement beside me as he swings to look straight at me.

No, no, no, no, no, no. Please God, don't let him have heard what just came out of the speaker.

But the look on his face as I'm finally game enough to raise my head tells me the answer.

Worst day ever! And it's not even nine am yet!

"Oh yes, tell us more." His deep voice startles me, and the mouthful of tea I never got around to swallowing sprays from my gaping mouth all over his suit jacket.

Kill me now!

"Are you freaking serious! What is wrong with you!"

"Sorry, oh Lord, I'm so sorry, let me clean you up." I'm madly trying to reach for my bag to find tissues or something, forgetting my mug is in my hand, which is now nearly upside down in my panic. It might be a travel mug, but there is only so much it can withstand.

"Don't bother." His annoyed growl is such a deep voice that it vibrates through me as I look up from my bag I've been scrounging through to no avail.

Taking the handkerchief from the inside pocket of his coat, he starts trying to dab the material and soak up the mixture of English breakfast tea and my spit, with a scowl on his face.

And as if my day couldn't get any worse, while I'm still rummaging in my bag for another tissue, I must have bumped the play button on my phone again as Elouise, being her usually impatient self, already sent another message, and I hear the words start again.

> Elouise: Don't leave me hanging here, bitch!
> Get that sneaky picture so I can rate him too.

"Would you like me to pose with or without the tea stain I'm now wearing. Will it affect my rating?" For a split second, I can see the fury in his eyes is spreading across his face. Then it's gone as quickly as it came, and his composure returns to the stoic businessman he is.

I'm so mortified. How do I even answer that?

This day is doomed, I can just tell.

Chapter Two

NICHOLAS

There is something relaxing about spending a night out at the farm, or country estate as they call it here in England. Of course, it sounds more upmarket if you call it an estate, but to me it's just some land, a big house, and lots of animals. All of which I knew nothing about how to look after when I arrived here, but apparently, that's what I pay my manager Henry for. He started as my manager but has become a good friend and someone I can sit and drink a cold beer with at the end of a long day, talking about anything and nothing. He doesn't live in the high-flying world, and that's the way he likes it. Some days I just want to be Henry.

The first day I arrived at the estate, being told it was all mine, was daunting. But it also gave me a sense of peace I hadn't felt since this whole crazy debacle began. The moment I walked into the kitchen, it felt like home to me. It's the size of a commercial kitchen, with all the best appliances. This is what I needed. Everything around me was such a big upheaval that I just needed a place to be me. On my own and with no one asking me questions, wanting to know my intentions, and pointing a finger and staring, wondering who the hell I was and where I came from.

Thankfully, that finally settled down, and my life as the new heir to the Darby empire for the last four years has been more than I could have ever dreamed.

Life certainly is different when I went from being a man whose job it is to serve people, to now, having numerous servants around me, who want nothing more than to serve and please me. Like my personal driver who right now is dying of embarrassment at the fact the car we are traveling in today has broken down on the side of the road. He was worried there was something wrong, so he pulled off the motorway and into a town so he could check it out, and now it won't start again.

I'm not mad at him, but this is a problem I don't need this morning. I have an important day ahead, with some big changes on the horizon. I have given the board enough time to accept the fact that I have full control, and I'm about to put my own stamp on the Darby Hotel chain. Time to shake it up a bit and bring it to the modern age and a place of the present type of luxury expected from a chain as big as ours.

"I'm sorry, sir, I can't work out what is wrong with the car. I will ring to arrange a town car to come and get you." Wallace, my driver, tells me while I'm still sitting in the Bentley.

On the inside I'm about to explode. I hate public transport with a passion in England. Trying to keep my voice calm, I reply to the older man standing next to me, "No time, Wallace. I have a meeting in an hour that I can't miss. I can't wait for the car to get here. I have already checked the train timetable. There is one leaving in fifteen minutes at the station just around the corner. I'll leave you with it, old chap." Grabbing my briefcase off the seat and standing up out of the car, I slap Wallace on the shoulder.

"Right you are, sir," he says, starting to chuckle at me. He loves when I try to act like an Englishman and hide my Aussie mannerisms that continue to ooze from me, even though I have been living here for over three years now. "My apologies. I will get the car sorted and be back in London to pick you up at the end of the day. I will have Miles meet you at the station to get you to the meeting." His voice gets softer, as I'm already darting across the road and around the corner to the station for the train.

My long legs are a bonus at times like this, with my strides getting me places in a hurry. Arriving on the platform, the train is already in the station waiting. Getting here with only ten minutes to spare, all the seats are taken in some of the carriages, so it looks like I'm heading down the train to find a seat. There are a few single ones available at either end of the carriage, but with my large frame, I need a double seat if possible. That's why I hate trains, no fucking room!

Moving up the aisle to almost the middle of the carriage, I take the seat facing forward. Spreading my legs out and placing my briefcase on the seat to deter people, I try to look like I'm busy working.

When I was back home in Australia, I loved catching public transport, but ever since I moved here to the UK, I have hardly been on a train or bus. Having Wallace drive me everywhere is something I must admit I got used to very quickly. Especially in a country where I had no idea where I was going. It has become my favorite form of transport in my new home. Mind you, back in Sydney, the ferry was my favorite, and it's not like there is much call for that in the center of this country.

I've forgotten how small and cramped they make these seats for tall people. There are still a few spare seats around me, so I'll just spread out for the time being and hope that I can stay this way for the whole trip. I'll just wear my usual arrogant smirk and scare people away like I do to my staff most days. Gone are the days of having time to be nice. Too many people depend on me, and no one is successful in a business this size by being sweet.

There are many reports I should be reviewing for the meeting this morning, but it's Friday. Which for an Aussie a long way from home means it's Friday night in Sydney, and the rugby league has just kicked off the start of the game between my team, the Roosters, against the Rabbitohs. Loading it on my phone and putting my earbuds in, I'm in heaven. The commentators' voices are enough to make me feel like

I'm home. I grew up watching this game with my pop who is a diehard Roosters' supporter, which is why I kind of didn't have a choice. That's how it happens with sports. You either inherit the team your family already follows, or as a kid, you pick a team for some ridiculous reason, like their colors or the mascot, because you are way too young to understand anything about the game.

Hearing the crowd going crazy over a very poor refereeing decision, I'm picturing my pop in his lounge chair, yelling at the television. My nan would be at his side in her recliner, engrossed in a book and just making him feel like he has company, when really, she has no idea what's going on in the game.

I try to call my pop each week after the game if I've been able to watch it. Or even if I haven't, I quickly watch the highlights reel and then we chat about the game, and he thinks I've seen the whole thing.

I don't think he really understands the life I live now. I wanted them to come over to visit me, but he keeps telling me he's too old to be getting on a human cattle train and put up in the air, only for it to fall out again over the water somewhere. I said this to Wallace one day in the car after I hung up a call talking to Nan and Pop. Then I had to explain that what he meant was, he's past getting on a plane as he has never flown before, and it comes from a fear of the plane falling out of the sky. Wallace couldn't stop laughing at the way Pop had described it.

Yes, we have some weird sayings in Australia. Luckily, after working for so many years with people from all around the world, I don't come out with too many, but occasionally, Flynn looks at me with confusion and I know I need to translate.

The game is getting intense right from the kick-off. We are attacking the opposition's line and have almost scored a try twice already. *It's now or never, boys, come on, break over that try line.*

The feeling of a tap on my shoulder nearly makes me jump out of my seat, being so engrossed in the game.

"Shit." It just slips out of my mouth, without even seeing who it is that's touched me.

Looking up suddenly, as I pull one of the earbuds out, I have no idea how long this exquisite woman has been standing next to me.

"Can I help you, madam?" I'm not really thinking, it's the first thing that comes out.

"Sorry, I didn't mean to disturb you, but is this seat taken?" Her voice has that slightly frustrated sound to it.

Of course, she's after the seat I was hoping would stay free, but I can't be an ass and say no. My mum would kill me if I made a woman stand on a train. Damn it!

Pushing my body up out of the seat quickly is not an easy task. Reaching for my briefcase, I wave my hand for her to enter past me.

"Please, take the window seat. I can't fit my size in that small gap."

I don't know what is going through her head, but the look I just got tells me it's more than thinking what a gentleman this guy is. There's mischief behind those eyes. Maybe it's the red hair that gives her the look of a fiery spirit. Floating my eyes down her body, she is dressed to take on the day and make an impression. And it's an interesting impression she's currently making on me.

Turning her back to me to take her seat, her bag swings around and lands with a thump into my chest. Feeling the air rush from my lungs, I hold in the swear I want to say out loud. Even though I want to say, *what the ever-loving fuck, woman!* I somehow manage to keep it in my head while she is busy trying to apologize. I just need to sit down so I can catch my breath. I don't know what she has in that bag, but it's a lethal weapon. Not able to sit in the seat properly, I turn with my back to her and stretch my legs into the aisle.

Perhaps it's time to do some work instead of watching the game. I can catch up on emails and look over my notes for the meeting. The whole time I'm aware of the movement of her body, wriggling to get herself settled for the remainder of the trip. I thought I missed traveling on public transport, but now I'm not so sure. Perhaps I have been spoiled more than I realized since I arrived here.

My focus now on my emails, the sound of the recorded voice from a phone is speaking behind me.

"Wait! You're sitting next to a guy with a big cock, hot enough to fuck, and you think you are having a bad start to the day? Tell me more!"

Well, well, well, we now know the mischief in her mind when she was looking at me earlier.

The proper English gentleman in me would ignore this, but I'm far from being all English or that gentleman.

"Oh yes, tell us more," I sarcastically reply to her about her text message that has come out on her voice commands. Wanting to hold in my laughter is short-lived because it's instantly changed to anger as all beauty I saw in her a moment ago is replaced with the spray of liquid that comes from her mouth as she showers my suit jacket.

"Are you freaking serious! What is wrong with you!"

For fuck's sake, this is all I need this morning. To look like I'm wearing half my breakfast or something else all over me as I walk into my meeting which is focusing on our new image.

"Sorry, oh Lord, I'm so sorry, let me clean you up."

I can see the mortification as she tries to find something to mop up her mess.

"Don't bother," I reply full of snark, trying not to lose my temper at her again.

The sheer panic in her eyes now makes me realize how young she actually is. Before, when she was holding herself with all the confidence she could muster, I didn't notice. But right at this moment, when she is completely flustered and trying to fix her mistake, I see her vulnerability showing in her flushed cheeks. And something deep inside me likes this look on her... more than I should. Wanting to somehow calm her and take the embarrassment away from her is a strange feeling for me.

Why am I even thinking about this woman like this?

Get over yourself and worry about her bodily fluids that are now all over you.

Dabbing my handkerchief on myself, I try to make sure whatever she was drinking doesn't stain my Armani suit, and of course, today I chose a white shirt! Scowling down at the splatter pattern on my chest, I think it's a lost cause right now. Although I don't think it's coffee because I can always smell that powerful caffeine smell from a distance. It is my weapon of choice to get through those long days. Not that it is quite the same here, being a tea-loving country, so my guess is that I'm wearing her morning cup of brewed leaves.

The voice from her phone cuts in again to make matters worse for her.

"Don't leave me hanging here, bitch! Get that sneaky picture so I can rate him too."

And that's the last straw that breaks my annoyance. Part of me feels sorry for her now. Nothing is going her way today, but still, it doesn't fix my dilemma of looking a mess. Her feelings aren't my problem.

"Would you like me to pose with or without the tea stain I'm now wearing. Will it affect my rating?" I don't know why, but all of a sudden, I try to soften the way I'm looking at her, but I'm not sure I'm too successful or that I'm even capable of it right now. My asshole demeanor has become my norm these days. I'm looking to extend an olive branch by trying to make some sort of joke, even though I've done nothing that should have me being the one offering, but something inside me wants to take the fear and panic from her eyes.

"I'm sorry, I'm... oh Lordy, I don't... I can't. Oh, I give up!" Slumping back into her seat, I can see the defeat she is feeling by looking like an idiot. "Today was supposed to be the start of something amazing, and so far, it has become the day from hell and nothing I do seems to be helping." The sigh of defeat coming from her tells me there is a lot riding on this day for her.

Trying to turn my body to look at her more closely is a mission in itself, trying not to let out a groan as I almost bend myself in half. My knees come up nearly under my chin—well, not quite, but it feels like it. And I'm sure the guy in front of me is not appreciating the knees in his back or the jostling of the seat as I maneuver myself. By the glare over his shoulder, I'm spot on the money.

"That sort of defeatist attitude is not going to do anything to change things, is it." I can hear my mother's words come straight out my mouth. She would be proud, well, maybe of that sentence but not of any of the times I have opened my mouth to this woman before these few gentler words. "If you believe in all that rubbish about the universe and how it will put you on the right path, then that means you are right where you are supposed to be."

What the fuck am I even saying? This is the mumbo jumbo my mum would always tell me, and I never believed a word of it. Yet here I am spouting it to a complete stranger. I sound ridiculous.

And by the look on her face, she's thinking the exact same thing.

But instead of it calming her, I can see the exact opposite happening before my eyes.

"My attitude? What the hell do you know about my attitude? You don't even know me." Sitting up straighter in her seat, I can see the fire igniting inside her. She has fight in her and is not afraid to use it. A bit of a passionate spark, and I like it.

"Well, let's fix that then, shall we? I'm Nic, pleased to meet you." As I hold out my hand to her, she's reluctant, but her manners won't ignore the gesture.

"Tori," is all I get from her as she places her little hand in mine. Yet it's not a dainty handshake at all. She is determined to show me how strong she is, even if she isn't feeling it herself.

"Well, Tori, what is so monumental about today? New job, promotion, interview? Or perhaps not work-related, a new man, perhaps?"

"Why do I think you are trying to be nice, yet you sound so condescending? Maybe I'm off to quit a job because my boss is a guy in his forties, dresses in fancy suits just like yours, and is an utter twat. Hmm, sound familiar? Anyway, he looks down on people all the time, and it's time somebody told him that. But then that would just make me a woman with a bad attitude, wouldn't it. So perhaps that's what you meant, instead of being someone who has worked so hard to better herself and is trying hard to ignore every boulder that keeps getting in her way." She huffs, sitting up taller and looking straight in front of her to avoid eye contact with me.

"Right then, so the universe has done you wrong this morning. So, look out world, here you come. That's certainly going to make an impression wherever you are off to today." I get the impression she isn't in the mood to talk to me. I shouldn't have bitten back, but she is infuriating, and all I can think of is, God help the man, whoever he may be, whose balls she is out to rip off today.

She might be young, but man, she means business.

"Absolutely, I'm out to make an impression today. It's the start of something big and moving on from something that needs to be left behind." Her body language tells me there is a story there, and not one she is happy about.

"I sense it has to do with a man?"

"Why does it always have to have something to do with a man? Seriously!" she snaps, rolling her eyes at me like I'm an alien.

What is it about this woman that frustrates me and turns me the fuck on all at once? Is it the fire in her eyes? The fact she is willing to take me on or the fact she has no idea who I am or what I'm worth? Not that I think she would give a flying fuck anyway.

All things that are appealing in my eyes, but not that it makes any difference. I have about another ten minutes in her presence and then she is gone forever. Just as it should be.

"It doesn't, but tell me I'm wrong here. Maybe not a boyfriend, but there sure as shit is some guy who has pissed you off." She might be full of snark, but her body language tells me more than the words coming out her mouth.

"Fine." Even her huffing is sexy. "An ex-boss who took more than he should have from me." Her voice gets a little softer, and my body reacts with a rage I have no right to be feeling.

I'm almost not game to ask, but I need to know.

"Did he hurt you?" It came out gruffer than it should've. I don't know this girl from a bar of soap and already I want to kill her ex-boss with my bare hands if she answers yes.

"No, no, no, no. Sorry, no, not like you're thinking. He just stole from me, but nothing like that. Shit, sorry, not that." Her cheeks are flushed, and she looks slightly flustered.

"Okay." It's all I can muster, trying to pull back on my unnecessary rage.

Both of us sit in silence for a few moments too long which has now made this awkward. I try to change tack, but I'm too late.

"Anyway, I'm sure you were busy working," she says. "I don't want to interrupt you. Sorry about the stain. I'm sure it will dry okay. Enjoy the rest of your journey." Without waiting for a reply, she places her earphones back in and looks out the window at the surroundings that are whizzing past.

I think I have been dismissed, which makes me chuckle a little. Normally it's me doing the dismissing. But today, I'll take it.

"Yes, you too, Tori." As much as I would like to keep talking and find out more of what she means, my legs are thanking me for an excuse to turn my back to her and stretch them out into the aisle space.

I don't want to go back to the game I was watching. I'm irritated and don't even know why. Instead, I pull up emails again, that are just a never-ending part of my job. A job I never asked for, yet here we are. Living a thousand miles from home in a place that feels foreign yet in a way also familiar.

Noticing there are three emails on the top of my inbox from Flynn, one marked urgent, I can already tell that my day is not going to run to plan either.

Maybe it's Tori's fault. She spat the bad vibes onto me along with her cup of tea.

Looking at my watch, I see I have about seven minutes, so I shoot off a quick text message to Flynn and tell him to meet me in the boardroom before the meeting. Then I send Lucy, my personal assistant, a message to make sure she has my spare suit, shirt, and tie in my office bathroom ready to go, so I can change for the meeting. My phone buzzes in my hand with the replies, along with a message from Miles that he is outside the station waiting for me. At least I won't be late for my meeting.

Well, of course, unless we hit a traffic jam. Shit, now that I said it, I've probably jinxed myself. Feeling the train starting to slow, coming into Paddington Station, people are starting to move and collect their things, ready to hop off and change to the tube if needed. I could have done that, but no need with my driver waiting outside.

I need to stand before others do, so neither my bag nor my legs are in the way. I stand and hold onto the edge of the seat as the aisle fills with people and the train comes to a stop. Tori is up and standing so close I can smell her perfume. It's not all flowery and soft. Instead, it's powerful and slightly intoxicating. One that awakens the senses.

Everyone is in a hurry today, but I just want one more moment to take it in.

Hearing the guy behind me clear his throat, I want to spin and glare at him but decide better of it.

"After you." I motion for Tori to enter the aisle so I can keep the push and shove from the people behind me away from her, hoping this one small thing might improve her morning somewhat. She seems to have the clumsy gene, and I mean, Lord knows the shoving from the crowd behind might be the catalyst for her falling and creating a domino effect in here.

Once again, as she swings into the aisle, I dodge her bag that is like a lethal weapon. Shuffling along, we start down the stairs and out the door, along with hundreds of people all on their way to work. It's every man, woman, and child for themselves in this morning rush.

As fast as she came into my world, all I can see is the back of Tori's vibrant red hair as she moves away.

"Tori," I yell.

She quickly turns with a look of a little frustration because she doesn't have time to stop.

I might be a complete jerk most days, but something makes me want to reassure her that the rest of the day will get better. Call it a sensation of my mother screaming in my head to be nice, as if she can sense that I need to hear it. It hasn't happened very often lately.

"Hope your day is the start of whatever amazing thing you want to happen."

Finally, I get a smile, and fuck if it doesn't light up her face. She should try that more often. If she were mine, I'd make sure it was a permanent fixture.

Not able to stop as the crowd keeps surging forward, she just waves at me, and then turning, she is again swept away in the sea of people.

There is something tugging at me about her, but I'm not stupid enough to entertain any more than that thought. The last thing I need is a woman in my life. I have enough sharks circling me every time I step foot out of the safety of my office.

Besides, I have more to worry about than a young redhead with fire in her eyes that sets my body vibrating. I mean, who wants to spend time thinking about the energy she brings to other parts of her life. She has chaos written all over her.

A bang into my shoulder by a man running past brings me back to reality.

I don't have time to waste. Stalking toward the exit, I see Miles standing to the side and the car in the pick-up lane with the black cabs.

"Can I take your bag, sir?" he asks as I get closer.

"No, I'm fine, thanks. Let's get going so I make this meeting on time." As he holds the door open, I slide in and am back in the world of fast pace with no time to think except about what the next meeting is and what I need to know.

"How's the traffic, Miles?" I ask, pulling out my phone again to check more emails.

"Not too bad this morning, sir. We should be there with plenty of time."

"Thanks." I try to read my email from Jocelyn, our functions manager, who is also my second cousin. Her grandfather Lenny was my grandfather's brother. Although, being related is a curse when we can't stand each other. Blood doesn't necessarily make you a big happy family.

I can't be bothered to reply to her right now, because I don't have time to put up with the twenty minutes of emails bouncing back and forth when she doesn't agree with any of the answers I give her.

Instead, I choose to take a few moments to just get my thoughts together. They got turned upside down for a while this morning by a certain attractive whirlwind. I can't decide what part of her was the most appealing. Her stunning looks or the spirit that she obviously has deep inside her that infuriated me and had fire erupting in me, wanting to bite back at everything she said. Either way, it doesn't matter, because I'll likely never see her again. But she sure made an interesting start to my Friday.

The car now pulling up in the front of our corporate head office right in Central London has me sighing with relief that I am here in plenty of time. I hate to be late anywhere. I look out the car window at my office building that is part of my property portfolio. It is easier to run a global chain of hotels from an independent location rather than from one of the actual hotels. You are taking up valuable floor-space that could be used for rooms and visitors to keep the income flowing. And that is all that the board cares about. Besides, there are things that get done in the corporate offices that don't need to be shared in the establishments until we are ready for them to know.

Today is the perfect example. I've been wanting to reveal this to the board for some time, but I had to wait for them to learn to trust in me and my abilities. Judgment's been high, and they thought they could wear me down to become a yes man, or worse still, to walk away.

Their mistake!

With Flynn standing beside me as my right-hand man, not once have I backed down in what I believe in. Not sure they knew what hit them when I arrived off the plane unexpectedly.

Walking through the foyer on my way to the elevator, it's always a string of constant good-mornings. My mother told me that manners are free, so use them widely. She would kill me if I didn't reply to every single person who greets me. Although some mornings it's little more than a grunt they get, but at least they get one.

Standing in the elevator with the doors closing, at the last moment I see a flash of red hair that disappears. It's too late, the doors lock together, and we are heading up to my office. I shake my head. Surely it wasn't her. I mean, I assume she was taking the subway like most commuters on that train were, so she wouldn't have made it here this quickly. Besides, how many red-haired, pale-complexioned women live in the UK? I'm sure it's thousands, so there's no way it was her.

As my rational head kicks back in and the elevator reaches the top floor, I realize one important thing, though.

My heart started thumping and my cock gave a twinge when I caught the slightest glimpse of someone I thought may have been her.

Something about her captivated me, and I just can't seem to shake it.

"Good morning, Nicholas. You have five minutes to change suits. The vultures are assembling." Lucy holds her hands out for my briefcase as she follows behind me into my office.

"Morning, Lucy. Thank you." I slip into the bathroom straight away. When I started here, I tried to get her to stop calling me Mr. Weston and start calling me Nic. She refused, but we finally settled on Nicholas. It's what I call my semi-stuffy name. It's very rare I use Nicholas because it sounds too formal, but the British are all about formality I learned very early on.

Reentering my office, I collect my laptop and files from my brief-case. It's time to face the board. I don't understand if I own this company why I need them, but it's just how it is, and I can't change the whole British way of doing business and its history—well, not today, anyway.

Striding down the corridor, I see Flynn standing to the side of the boardroom door. Spotting me, he gives me that smile that says, *yeah, good luck.*

"How are the moods today for the English gentlemen and the lady who is not so much a lady?" I ask, reaching my hand out to shake his.

"As per usual, she walked in there like she has a stick up her ass and a face like a fish, with those Botox lips. Then she threw her nose in the air like I'm not worth her attention. As for the men, they look like they all need to just take a sip of whiskey and chill the fuck out." Flynn rolls his eyes at me.

"Ah, so a normal monthly board meeting then." We both start laughing, and I motion to the door.

"Shall we enter the lion's den and see if we can avoid being today's meal?"

Following him through the door, the murmurs in the room go silent and all eyes are on me.

I see they got the memo. Change is in the air, and not one of them is happy about that thought.

At the end of the day, though, this is my business and I'll do what I damn well please.

"Shall we begin?"

Chapter Three

VICTORIA

Normally I hate the push and shove of the train in the mornings. No one is happy to be here, and everyone just wants to get from A to B and get on with their day.

Today I don't even notice the crazy around me.

Because I'm trying to work out what the hell just happened!

I have no idea who he was, but he exasperated me and at the same time made me feel off balance. That's never happened before. I mean, don't get me wrong, there are plenty of people who annoy me with what comes out of their mouth, speaking before they think. But this guy was different. Part of me has a feeling he thought about what he was saying, knowing it would make me react. And that Australian accent just seemed to make the confidence and cockiness ooze from him. I've never been attracted to an older man before, but I kind of liked it, and I'm still not sure why.

Standing hanging onto the pole on the train, the fresh smell of aftershave and perfumes in the morning can get a bit suffocating in such a confined space. But I must admit, it's better than the afternoon trip home where the whole carriage air is thick with sweaty armpits and breaths that are a mixture of all the lunches eaten. Some days it's hard to breathe. As we pull into the station, I'm glad to get out and find some fresh air and personal space, which is hard, working in such a busy city. There is never much time where you are on your own in the hustle and bustle. Although, the majority of the time I love it.

The high-paced environment is great for my creative brain, and that is what drives me.

Finally, I'm standing outside the door to the offices of York and Webb Design and Marketing.

Looking up at the old stone building, it's a bit of a juxtaposition. The outside is years of history in this city, yet the work that happens inside these four walls is all about a change in the look and perception of something. That's my job, to launch a new brand or change the way the world sees an old company, which is a much harder task.

But that's what I love, to be challenged.

No time to be standing here staring up at the old girl. I don't want to add any more drama to my day by being late. I must admit, I'm usually skidding in the front door just in time most mornings.

"Good morning, madam," the receptionist greets me with a smile that looks totally fake. She's obviously trying not to show how much she's really over this week and can't wait for Friday to just be finished. For once I feel the opposite. It's a weird day to be starting a new job, but my manager starts her leave on Monday, so she wants to show me the ropes before she goes.

"Good morning, my name is Victoria Packer, and I'm here to start my new position today under Gwenda Francis of York and Webb Design and Marketing." I've got my shoulders back, standing up as straight as I can, portraying all the confidence I can muster.

"Ah yes. Hello and welcome. I have your security pass here. Miss Francis is expecting you. The security pass needs to be worn at all times, and it will need to be swiped in the lift to take you to level three. Good luck."

"Thank you," I say, smiling as I turn to head to the elevator. I always feel a little nervous when someone says good luck at a time like this. Does it mean I'm going to need luck in this job or is it merely polite to say that on my first day?

I don't really have much time to ponder the thought, as the doors start to close and a male voice calls to hold the elevator. Hitting the door-open button a few times, finally they start retracting, and a hand grabs them as his body lunges into the elevator with me.

"Oh, ta. Didn't want to be late again. My boss is a real cow, and I don't feel in the mood for the dressing down this morning," he says, leaning against the back wall of the elevator and taking a few deep breaths as the doors are again closing.

"Happy to be of assistance." As I straighten my jacket for the tenth time since I arrived in the building, I can feel the nerves starting to get the better of me.

"You're new, aren't you. I've not seen you before," he says, holding out his hand to greet me. Not sure I want to shake it, but it's polite. His hands are like I imagined, sweaty like his face, from rushing, I guess. "Hi, I'm Theodore Cheston, but everyone calls me Theo."

"Yes, it's my first day. Victoria Packer, pleased to meet you." The ding of the elevator ends this greeting before it begins as he steps out.

"Have to run. See you around." With that he is out and down the hallway toward the door I'm heading to. I try not to laugh to myself. Today couldn't get any stranger if it tried, and it's not even time for morning tea yet.

Opening the door, I get an adrenaline rush. I'm hoping this will become my new home away from home. The place I will make a name for myself and be respected and appreciated for my hard work. Let the adventure begin.

"Welcome, Victoria. I'll show you to your desk and then to Gwenda's office, after which you can get settled in. I'm Suzi, in case you forgot my name." Finally, a little bit of normalcy and a reassuring smile. I remember her from my interview appointment, although it was a fleeting moment that I spoke to her.

"That would be great, thanks, Suzi. I'm really looking forward to this job and can't wait to get started." I follow her down the corridor and into an area with six desks spread out in the open-plan office, each with backs on them to create a little privacy for your own desk but not enough to box everyone in. They're all pale wood finish with brown leather chairs. The room has six vertical windows set into the old stone walls that have been rendered on the inside, painted a very pale cream to give the sense of extra space and to lighten the room. The décor matches the room perfectly, in my opinion. It gives a good vibe of softness and where modern meets old world.

Over her shoulder, Suzi looks back at me with a welcoming smile and keeps talking while we're walking.

"Some of us all go for drinks after work on Friday. You should come and get to know everyone. There's not much time during the day, and especially with all the bosses watching." I think I'm going to like Suzi, she seems like my kind of girl.

"That sounds fantastic." Just as I'm about to place my bag down on the desk she shows me to, the same voice from the elevator comes up beside me.

"Well, would you look at that. We are going to desk neighbors, Victoria."

"Theo, be nice to Victoria and give her at least ten minutes to breathe before she must put up with your morning personality. She will at least need a strong tea to tolerate you." Suzi pushes him in the shoulder as he stands with his hand over his heart, faking his hurt.

"So harsh, Suzi. We are already the best of friends, aren't we, Victoria. Wait, is that what we have to call you? It reminds me of an old lady sitting with her cup of tea and her pearls, or you know, a stuffy old queen. Can I call you Vic instead?" Already I'm feeling more comfortable by the minute. These guys seem like fun.

"Sure, best friends. That's what usually happens after a thirty-second meeting in a lift. And no, it's Tori, well, that's if you expect me to answer. You are right, Victoria is my grandmother's name, and I can assure you I am nothing like her." My shoulder feels better after finally placing my bag on the desk. I really need to carry less crap in my bag, otherwise I'm going to be walking lopsided perma-nently for the rest of my life.

"Oh, this one has a sense of humor. That'll make a nice change from the last woman who sat at this desk. Anyway, welcome, Tori. I'm your desk buddy, I have the one directly in front of you closer to the front door, so let me know if there is anything I can do to help you settle in." Theo's still standing there just looking at me.

"Theo, tea, remember? You were getting one for Tori?" Suzi snaps at him to make him move.

"Right, yes. Tea, milk or sugar?"

"Thank you, make it a strong one with milk and one sugar." To be honest, with the morning I've had, I could really use a pick-me-up of caffeine. I don't always drink strong tea, preferring a mild milky cup, but this morning calls for the strong stuff.

Watching him disappear, I hear Suzi let out a sigh next to me. "He's hard work, some days. Actually, to be honest, most days." We just look at each other and giggle.

"I'm sure I'm about to find that out. But can I ask you some-thing quickly?" I feel like I can trust her already.

"Sure," she says, raising her eyebrows in wonder at my question.

"In the elevator he mentioned that his boss was a real cow, so I'm just wondering what I've got myself into." Waiting for an answer, Suzi starts laughing and not just a little laugh but a real belly laugh.

Once she comes up for air, she says, "He is such an idiot. The only reason he says that is because he is constantly late and never stops talking. Some days she has to tell him she is going to tape his mouth shut just to get the work out of him that she needs. A skill you will need to master, with him reporting to you from now on, from what I understand. Anyway, you will like her. Don't panic, sweetie pie." Suzi smiles at me, and for the first time today, I actually take a deep breath and think maybe, just maybe, the tide is turning, and all is not lost, after the morning from hell.

"Fabulous. Then I can't wait to get to work for her." I know she seemed lovely in the interview, but nobody shows their true self in those meetings, do they. I'm still not entirely sure she is the glowing boss that Suzi describes, but time will tell.

I hear him before I see him again. "Of course, Gwenda, I have been here in the building for a solid thirty minutes." He looks at us as he waltzes across the room, rolling his eyes with a childish smirk.

"You know I have access to the security check-in times, don't you, Theo?" I recognize the voice coming down the corridor as my new boss.

"Like you don't spy on me every day anyway. Control freak who thinks I'm hot," he mumbles, while handing me my cup of tea.

"Not even close. You won't have to worry about that now." Gwenda's voice comes from behind him as she walks toward us.

"Crap," Theo whispers, and I'm trying not to laugh as I can see the sheer wickedness in her eyes. She's baiting him, and it's working.

"Good morning, Victoria, and welcome," Gwenda says, greeting me properly. "I see you have already met your co-worker, who has a habit of being late most mornings and makes terrible tea, which I'm sure you are about to find out." Suzi can't hold back anymore and lets out a giggle. "Come now, we have a lot to go over before the day's end. You can leave your bag there. I have your new laptop and work phone in my office and all your login passwords." She continues toward the office that is to the side of the open-plan room.

I don't want to keep her waiting. Mouthing thanks to Theo and Suzi for the tea and help, I scurry off behind Gwenda. I sure as hell don't want to be a target of harsh words from a new boss.

"Close the door behind you, Victoria, and take a seat." My hands are now sweaty as I turn the doorknob and slide into my chair across the desk from Gwenda. I can feel my heart pounding, and I'm not sure if it's from nerves or excitement, maybe a bit of both.

"Thank you for starting today. I know it's weird to be starting on a Friday, but I need to be able to pass on everything I need worked on while I'm away. It was such a last-minute decision to take leave, I haven't even mentioned it to anyone yet. So, let us get started and then you can ask any questions that you may have as you work through the files I hand over. That way, by the time I return in a week's time, you should be well underway. Does that sound like a plan?" Gwenda's already typing away on her computer. "Grab your laptop off the desk. Here is your password to get in and the other passwords you need for the system," she says, reaching for a folder from her drawer and passing it across. "I suggest you record them somewhere safe and then shred that list, please."

"Of course." My fingers are fumbling on the keyboard as I try to type in the random letters and numbers. I know it's for security, but why can't they have passwords that are easy to remember?

You know like... *hotsexybum1* or *makemescreamyourname69*. Oh, I've got the best one yet... *aussieguyiwanttofuck*.

Shit, what the hell am I thinking? Concentrate on the job and stop letting wicked thoughts creep into my head. Not now. No matter how much I want to keep picturing the arrogant asshole and committing him to memory for later. The image of him in his suit, with his broad shoulders and clean-shaven chiseled jawline that screams dominance every day of the week. The sandy blond hair that is styled but you can tell is trying to break free from whatever product he uses. His tall stature towering over me, slightly intimidating but in a such good way. Mix in the deep Australian accent, and I think I have what I need to enjoy my time in bed tonight... even if it's on my own, sadly.

"As you can see there is quite a bit to be done." Gwenda's voice pulls me from my hot moment. Shit, what have I missed her saying?

"Yes," is all I reply, trying to look at my screen and hoping something will pop out at me and help me. Five minutes into the job and already I'm behind because I was too busy zoning out about some guy I will never see again.

Smart, Tori, real smart.

"You look a little blank there, Victoria. Can you get the workflow document open?" Gwenda's voice doesn't sound quite as friendly as when we started, a little frustrated at my floundering.

Workflow, right, this looks like it might be it. I click on the icon and pray for some divine intervention.

Bingo, okay, game on.

"Sorry, got it now, just trying to get used to your system. Please continue, which file do you want open?" That's it, try the sweet voice, it usually works.

Quickly any thoughts of the guy from the train are long forgotten, and soon enough, I look at my watch to see it is already eleven o'clock and we are just finishing up running through the jobs I'm taking over from the last person.

"I have a meeting with a client shortly out of the office, so spend the rest of the day familiarizing yourself with everything we just went through, and I will be back in the office later to catch up with you and answer any questions." With that, I know I am dismissed and it's time to get out of her office.

The day has gotten away from me while I've been head down in my files, wanting to try to make a good impression on Gwenda before she leaves today and make sure she feels like she has left the clients in safe hands. Theo kept offering to help, but I managed to shut that down early in the day. Plus, I know from experience that you need to concentrate on your own work and not share too much of your ideas with your co-workers. Sure, help them, but don't give them your golden ticket of knowledge.

That part of me I will be keeping close to my chest.

So far, I have looked at three of the files. The first job involves a chain of dance schools that has been in business for twenty years. The second file is a new app that is about to launch and they want help with designing their branding and marketing strategy. These are the jobs I love, where your creative mind can run wild. And the file I've just finished reviewing is a restaurant that opened three years ago, and things haven't gone quite as planned. They are looking for a new chef and are about to change the type of food they serve. So once that is finalized, we will help with the new design of the restaurant and how to market the new concept.

It's one of the great things about having a dual degree in design and marketing, that we can combine it all and offer an overall solution. My tuition fee loan balance may argue that a dual degree was not a great idea at the time, but I have the rest of my life to pay that back, right? It was either that or I spend the rest of my life like my parents, never pushing myself to live a better life than I am now. They have both worked a lot of jobs and earn enough to live comfortably but with not much extra for luxuries. They are happy and content, but I want more, and I'm not ashamed to admit that.

For a long time, my dreams have been to work hard and gain as much experience as I can, save some money, and then start to travel the world. I want my passport to tell a story. I want to meet new people from different countries and be able to sit back and feel proud that I made it happen all on my own. I don't ever want to be a kept woman, doing as I'm told or agreeing on the direction of my life just so it blends in with someone else.

I mean, I'm not saying as I get older that I won't meet a man who changes all that, but right now, when I'm only twenty-six, there is no tying me down.

Independent and powerful in my own space, happy without effort, those are my priorities right now. And that's all I need to concentrate on.

The day has gone by so quickly, and after sitting here with Gwenda just clarifying my last few questions, a sense of achievement sits on my shoulders. After the way the morning started, I have managed to turn things around and end on a positive note.

My life needed a change after my last job. I tried telling myself I could bounce back and keep moving, but I wasn't as convincing as I thought I had been. When you build yourself up that today is a new beginning and nothing is ever going to be the same again, then you sit down and spit tea all over a handsome stranger on the train, you start doubting yourself.

Thankfully, I pulled my big-girl panties up and got on with it, and I'm now looking at Gwenda smiling at everything I have achieved today.

"Great start, Victoria. I love some of the ideas you have and the little tweaks you have made on some of the projects that were already underway. I think we'll work well together," she says, closing the file and pushing it back toward me.

"Thank you, I appreciate the feedback. I'll have everything ready for you when you return, and please, call me Tori. Victoria makes me feel so old," I tell her, picking up my paperwork. "I also have all the notes you sent over on your meeting from today. It sounds interesting, and I'll start collating some ideas for your return."

"Wait, sorry, did I not add that the client wants the prelim report by Wednesday? I hate doing this, and I'm taking a big risk with a new client, but I need to trust you can come up with something to keep them interested until I return. Don't disappoint me. He also doesn't know I will be on leave, so he may be a bit shocked. I sort of wanted to keep my leave private from everyone." Gwenda might be soft most of the time, but I can see that if you cross her, then you'll get a completely different side of her.

My gut drops of the pressure she has just landed on top of me. It's bad enough filling in for the boss after the first day, but trying to land a new client? That is huge.

"I won't. I'll do my best and make you proud. You just worry about having a lovely holiday," I say, standing and trying to sound way more confident than I am. I've just left a job where I was critiqued at every corner, to this job where I've been given the keys to the kingdom and told to run with it but don't let it burn down while she's away.

Not terrifying at all.

"Sure, no problem, but I wish it was going to be a holiday, where I would be lying on a deck chair around a pool in the sunshine. But that's not the case. Just some personal business I need to take care of. And while I'm away, do not let them corrupt you out there. They are all great at their jobs, well, most of them, and they each have their own little quirks and devious habits that they think I don't know about. Especially Theodore, but I think you have already worked that out for yourself. Watch him, Tori, he's not quite what he seems." And on that ominous note, she stands too.

"I have agreed to drinks tonight, which I'm not sure was a smart move with him. But I guess I'm about to find out." As I walk toward the door, she says one last thing before I open it.

"My only advice is to avoid doing rounds of shots with Theo. It never ends well. Take that from my experience that I will live to regret, unfortunately." The look on her face tells me that she has been on the losing end of that game.

"Duly noted, and thank you for giving me the opportunity. I'm truly grateful and excited to see where this job leads me."

"Keep up that attitude and you will go far. See you in a week and good luck tonight." The slightly serious look on her face tells me I need to be on guard tonight. I don't want to be trying to get home at some weird-ass time in the morning by myself and drunk off my face.

That would be just stupid. Leaving yourself vulnerable in a big city, alone, is not a good start.

Repeat after me, Tori. *I will not drink too much tonight, and I will not get drunk.* Now one more time for the dummies. *I will not drink too much tonight, and I will not get drunk!*

Famous last words…

―――――――

Walking side by side with Suzi and Theo, I'm totally regretting bringing my work bag with me. I should have left it in the office and collected it on the way home, but I wasn't sure about the whole security process of getting back into the building later at night.

My shoulder is aching a little and, still in my high heels, walking any great distance won't be much fun.

The bar they convinced me was the go-to place is somewhere I've never been. And the closer we get, I understand why. This is not where the regular Friday-night work crowd would congregate.

To have security on the door already at seven pm gives an indication that it's a popular place to be. There is a small line outside, and when I join the queue, Theo takes my arm and pulls me toward the doorway.

"Hey, Jimmy, place warming up inside yet?" he asks, slipping the man on the door something into his hand on his way past, that I'm guessing is money for letting us skip the line.

"Still early, but the crowd is building. Have a good one," Jimmy replies as Theo drags both Suzi and me in with him.

Like any bar, its lights are a little dim but still bright enough at this time of night that you can see what is happening around you.

Pulling me toward one of the free tables, we all dump our bags at our feet, and before I even have time to get a good look around, Theo throws his hands in the air and yells above the music, "Shots!"

Oh, I just know I'm in trouble. I should have eaten something before we got here, because shots on an empty stomach is never a good idea. To be honest, shots for me are generally not a smart thing. Elouise warned me, when I messaged to tell her I was going for work drinks, to behave, that I'm trying to make a good first impression.

"Not for me," I tell Theo. "I'll just get a gin and tonic to start with."

"Boo! That's boring, but whatever. Friday nights are for partying." With that he's gone, and I'm left with Suzi and a few of the others from the office who are chatting amongst themselves.

Looking around, I can now take in the design of the bar.

There are two floors, and the downstairs area is filled with tables, and to the side there is a dance floor that is empty at the moment. I'm guessing the night is young and plenty of time for that to start up.

Next to the bar where I can see Theo ordering drinks, there is a grand-looking staircase that heads up to a mezzanine level. It's empty of people, and the stairs are roped off. I'm guessing they open that later as the bar starts to fill up.

The music is pumping, and I can't help but start to move with it. I love dancing, although I'm sure I look like a baby giraffe out on the dance floor. I've never had much co-ordination.

"Right, bottoms up, people," Theo declares as he places the tray of shots on the table, along with my G&T. "Oh, and drink up slowly to our boring new work friend over there." He waves his hand at me and everyone else laughs. Already I can tell Theo is the head of the crowd in the office. He tends to lead them and always tries to be the comic relief and center of attention.

Although I need to be careful, I also want to fit in at the new job. I already know that I should never listen to peer pressure, but despite that, I know I'll be joining them on the next round of shots.

Little do I know the shots never stop! And I don't know how to say no after the first one.

Chapter Four

NICHOLAS

"That went well... not," Flynn mumbles under his breath as we head down the hallway from the conference room.

"I don't give a fuck what they think. It's happening anyway." The annoying feeling of having to answer to them keeps my shoulders rigid and my pulse rate up. Flynn struggles to keep up with me as I stomp toward my office. When I'm in a mood like I am now, his shorter legs are no competition for mine when I'm in full stride.

Lucy knows not to even ask as we pass by her desk, and I hear Flynn closing the door behind him.

"They do know that I don't really have to ask their permission. I have the majority of the shares and own the company. They are just token board members. Overpaid and overopinionated figureheads that think they're important," I rant, pacing my office with built-up frustration I have no idea what to do with.

"Calm yourself down. They might not get a say, but they can make life difficult for you if you piss them off, so how about we just smile like we always do, tell them what a great suggestion they had, and we will take it on board. Then as usual, we do what we damn well please anyway." Flynn drops onto the brown leather couch that I'm sure has a permanent impression of his ass in it. He never likes to sit at my desk with me, proclaiming he doesn't want to be known as one of those stuffy businessmen. Not sure how the difference between the couch and a chair changes that, but I gave up arguing with his weirdness years ago.

"When my grandfather was alive, I understand that he needed help from them to run this place, but he's been gone now for three years. I have not only maintained the company but improved sales and profitability in a tough market and with a product that was old and tired. How much more do I have to do to prove myself to them, that I've fucking got this and to trust me?"

The door opens and Flynn's brother Forrest, who is my Chief Financial Officer, walks in, and knowing I'm in full rant mode, he just slides into the chair next to my desk. Having been in the board meeting too, he knows how pissed off I am.

"Well, if they didn't know how you felt, they surely will now. I'm certain they could hear you loud and clear as they were exiting the boardroom. So shut your trap and sit down. Let's get on with the day and make this happen. Then tonight we are going out for a drink or two, and you need to get laid. Burn off some of that tension you are carrying around like a monkey on your back."

Ugghhh, I know he's right, but it's the last thing I feel like doing tonight. My facial expression gives me away.

"Don't you even think about coming up with an excuse," Flynn says. "I know what's in your diary. Lucy already confirmed you are free. What about you, my boring brother? You up for a pint or two, or probably something stronger?" he asks Forrest. He looks very proud of himself as I finally feel settled enough to sit down in my chair.

Forrest nods. "Firstly, when will you stop calling me your boring brother? You know how much it pisses me off. But your awful vocabulary aside, the answer to your question is, fuck yes, I'm in. Something to wash away the words from those twat mouths." I can't imagine growing up in a house with these two, who are constantly at each other. Shaking my head at both of them, I pity their mother and father… a lot.

"By the way, I'm sure Lucy is my assistant, and not yours," I say, pushing my mouse on my desk to bring my computer to life for the start of the day.

"Amazing what the old British charm will do when it needs to," Flynn says, brushing his knuckles against his chest.

"You do remember she is married to another fine British man who works out at the gym to be twice the size of you. Not sure how happy he would be to find some forty-year-old man flirting with his wife." I'm flicking my pen up and down in my fingers which has become a habit of mine when I have a lot to think about.

"Thirty-nine, thank you very much. There is only one of us in this room that has a four in his age, and it's not me." Laying his arms on the back of the couch and relaxing, it looks like he is settling in for a while.

Forrest leans over and thumps his brother on the arm. Being forty-two years old, he is the senior of the group, which we never let him forget.

"Make that thirty-nine years and ten months," I remind Flynn. "In case you aren't aware, that means in two months' time, you are turning forty, my friend. So, you two will both be sporting an age that puts you in the decade above me. Better try to hang on to the thought that you are young, for the very short time you have left."

All he can do is give me the middle finger.

"Very grown up of you, Flynn. Showing your immaturity again." At least it makes me start laughing. No matter his age on paper, I'm not sure Flynn will ever grow up.

"Fuck off. You are only six months younger than I am. By this time next year, we will all be over forty, well, except Remington. Don't they say life begins at forty? Bring it on!" Flynn now laughs to himself.

"You have been squeezing every single bit of life out of your forty years, Flynn. What makes you think that will change?" Forrest rolls his eyes at him.

"Okay, enough of this, let's get started on the rest of today's agenda. Are you still meeting with Jocelyn later today to go over the budget for the food in the function rooms?" My fingers tap away on the keyboard as I sign into the system. I look up at Flynn, waiting for his answer, and his face says it all. "She's not that bad. I mean, she wants to rip both of our balls off most days, but besides that, she is good at her job. Anyway, you can always blame Forrest, he sets the budget, you just need to make sure she implements it."

"She likes me because I pay her wage, hence the man that controls the money will always get the girls." Forrest smirks at us.

"Ughhh, please," I groan, "you might manage the pot with the money in it, but I'm the one who fills up your pot, idiot." Giving him the bomb-drop action with my hand has Flynn laughing out loud and then looking straight at me.

"You have to be nice to her, she's related by blood." He gives me a look of pity of someone who has been dealt the worst hand in a card game by having her as a distant cousin. "Me, I can tell you now, I don't have to smile and be polite to her because she is not even close to my distinguished bloodline. She gets on my nerves and is a right royal bitch to everyone she speaks to. So, to answer you, yes, I'm still meeting her today. Why do you think I told you we are going out drinking tonight? I need something to get me through the meeting with the dragon on steroids. When are we shipping her out to be based at one of the other hotels again, you know, the one is Siberia we need to buy?"

"She's not that bad," Forrest adds, already typing on his laptop. I look back at my screen as the emails just keep rolling up in front of me.

"Whatever," Flynn complains, throwing a cushion across the room at Forrest that he dodges as it hits the wall behind him, trying to get my attention and annoy Forrest at the same time.

"Real mature," I grumble. "Don't you have a job to do, you know, the one I pay you for?"

"I just thought that was because you are such a good friend that a large—but of course, it could always be larger—sum of money arrives in my bank account each month." He finally pushes to his feet and stands up again. "Anyway, my job here is done. I have calmed the growly boss man and locked him in for a big Friday night out, after what is going to be the day from hell. All in a day's work, and it's not even lunchtime. He's all yours, Brother. Try to keep him from scaring the staff too much for the rest of the day, will you."

"Flynn?" I call, looking him straight in the eyes, while Forrest looks like he wants to kill him.

"Yes?"

"Fuck off and go do some work, will you."

His smirk and chuckle sum up our relationship.

"Yes, sir, Mr. Weston." He knows that pisses me off, closing my door on his way out.

"I'll leave you to it too. I have a little brother to go pull into line or put in a head lock before he does something stupid to alienate Jocelyn, more than she already is complaining about. She thinks we all pick on her and never give her any support in her job. Not sure what gives her that idea." Slapping his laptop closed, Forrest is up and out the door too.

He is far more intuitive than his brother has ever been; thank goodness someone can read the room. He obviously knows that I need to be on my own with my thoughts, before I rip someone apart.

I shouldn't let the board get to me, but I do.

This company should have been my father's, but that wasn't meant to be. For all those years the hatred I felt toward him has now turned to anger at the hand he was dealt. To be honest, I had no idea any of this existed until that pivotal night back in Sydney, almost four years ago, when Broderick, my grandfather's private investigator, approached me.

Nothing was ever the same again.

Leaning back in my chair, I glance at the photo of Mum and me, the day before I left Australia. We're standing on the edge of the harbor, the opera house in the background, the water blue and shimmering. The sun is shining and there's an iconic Sydney ferry in the backdrop, heading into Circular Quay. That was my life and all I had ever known. I was happy in my life, but that was because I didn't know what else was out there. The memories are now taking over my mind and squashing any thoughts of boardroom clashes.

"It's you, isn't it? You're Richard Nicholas Weston, Sally Weston's son." Broderick's voice echoes in my head as clear as if I were back there that night.

"Who are you?" I ask, not confirming or denying who I am. I stare sideways at this man, not turning fully around to acknowledge him. I can see him well enough that it's now hard to believe he could be my father. We look nothing alike, and he's not as old as I thought at first glance.

Still, my body is on high alert and my mind is in meltdown. Hardly anyone except my mother and grandparents know my full name. I never use Richard and have always been called Nicholas. But Mum never gave up the love she had for my father, so she named me after him. I have hated it every day since I was old enough to understand he left us. To the world, I'm Nicholas or Nic, but this man is stepping into a place I never want to be... ever!

"My name is Broderick Jones. I'm a private investigator working for Charles Darby, who is your paternal grandfather. Is there somewhere more private we can go to talk so I can explain everything?" His broad English accent worries me that he might actually be telling the truth.

"No, not interested." Turning forward again and putting one foot in front of the other is the only thing my brain can manage. I feel like I want to hit something and throw up at the same time.

"Wait, please, Richard. Give me a chance to explain," he calls, chasing behind me. Flynn is also mumbling words that I have no idea what he is saying. My panic is shutting everything down, trying to push it all away.

"I wasn't expecting to see you tonight, but when you walked toward me, I knew without a doubt it was you." His feet thumping the pavement behind me, I know he isn't giving up.

I hear Flynn's voice beside me loud and clear. "I don't think he wants to speak to you. Now fuck off!" He has no idea what is going on, but just like I would expect, he has my back.

"But it's vitally important I speak to him." The guy is now getting frustrated.

"Don't care." I can feel the anger in me building like a volcano.

The thought of who he is goes over and over in my head, screaming at me. The eruption is starting, and there is nothing I can do to hold it back.

Feeling myself snap, I turn so fast I almost lose my balance. I'm in his face quicker than he can do anything about it.

"Why isn't my father looking for me? Or is he still the weak, gutted excuse for a man he always was?" My teeth are grinding and my fingernails digging into the palms of my hands from clenching my fists so tightly. Flynn grabs at my shoulder, trying to pull me back, but he's got no chance. Between my size and the adrenaline pumping through my veins, as I am in full flight-or-fight mode, there is no way he can compete with that.

"Because he died thirty-six years ago." The pity in his voice has me stumbling backwards. The noise of the city is long gone, I can't hear anything else except those words over and over again inside my head on repeat.

He's dead… he's dead… so long ago… he died.

Instead of Flynn trying to pull me off this man, I know he's the only reason I'm still standing.

On a breath no more than a whisper, my whole life comes together with one sentence.

"He died before I was born…"

Just trying to breathe, Flynn slowly lowers me onto the concrete steps next to the water. I can't seem to focus on any rational thought.

The man standing in front of me doesn't say a word, letting me take in what he just said to me.

"What… how… why…" I can't even seem to get out what I want to ask.

What happened to my father?

How did you find me?

Why now, what made my grandfather wait all this time?

Does my mother know any of this?

"Shit, Mum! The phone calls. Does she know? Is she okay? I need to get to her." I try to stand, but both Flynn and Broderick's hands force me back down as I stagger a little on my feet.

"Steady on there, son. You mother is fine."

I feel my ass hit the step again. "You've spoken to her?" I know her heart must be breaking into pieces. I think she always believed she would see him again someday. That he would come back for her. And as crazy as I always thought that was, right now, I wish that dream of hers could come true more than anything. But now I know, that's never going to be possible.

"Yes, this afternoon, I finally managed to find her. We have been looking for a while. We sat for a long time over a cup of tea, and she knows everything. But the plan was for her to talk to you and then we would arrange to meet. The universe obviously had other plans by putting you right in front of me tonight."

"That doesn't mean she's okay. She is good at putting on a brave face, and you don't even know her. So, I'll be the judge of whether she is all right or not!"

She might annoy me some days, but my mother would never hurt a fly. Every bone in her body is gentle and full of love and kindness for everyone she touches. I often wondered where I fit with her. I'm totally different to her in that way. I have no patience, I can be a snarky, arrogant asshole most days, and besides my mum, nan, and pop, I've never loved another human being. Love just causes hurt, and it's not fucking worth it.

"I think we need to find a bar for you to sit and talk and drink a strong whiskey or two." Flynn's voice startles me a little, as I'm so in my head, I'd forgotten he was still beside me.

"Good idea," Broderick agrees at the same time I'm yelling.

"No. I don't want to be in some claustrophobic room, having every nosy person listening in about a life I'm hearing about for the first time. We talk right here!"

"Nic, settle down and stop being an ass. I know you are in shock, but this guy sounds like he holds a lot of answers to questions you have had all your life." I know he is trying to help, but right now, I want to shove Flynn and tell him I can be the biggest ass in the world if I want to be. This is my fucked-up life!

"It's okay, here is fine. Can I sit down?" The man, who has all the information that I'm not sure I will cope with finally finding out, points beside me on the steps that go for yards along the side of the wharf.

I nod a little. "Start talking," I spit out in my gruff grumble, looking out to the water. I can't look directly at him, because I know he is about to say things that are going to hurt more than I have ever experienced. Flynn takes a spot on the other side of me.

"Where do you want me to start?" the man asks quietly, trying to soften the moment.

Where I want him to start is a very hard question to answer. All I can think to say is probably the most logical.

"How did you know it was me?"

"I knew the moment I saw you that you were Richard's son. You look just like him. Just a little older, of course."

My heart sinks. Did he know him, my father? Or just from photos? Where the hell do I even go with my questions? I don't know what to ask first or if I will even make any sense.

"Start at the beginning and don't leave anything out. You've got one chance of talking to me, and then from tonight on… I decide if you get to speak to me or my mother again." I know my mother will tell me I can't speak for her, but anyone who is here to hurt her must get through me first. End of story!

"I will tell you as much as I know, which I'm sure is going to fill in the initial blanks you have right now. But after that, you will need to talk to your grandfather. He will be the one to tell you who your father really was. He knew him the best."

I beg to differ on that. I'm starting to think my mother may have known the real him, even though I had doubted that for so many years, but I'm holding my judgment on that until I hear more from this guy.

"Mhmm," is all I can answer, and before Broderick starts again, Flynn speaks up.

"I think I should leave you two to talk. This sounds like it's private and something you need to do on your own." As he starts to stand, I grab his forearm and reef him back down on the step next to me.

"Stay," I growl at him. I hope he understands the gruffness is not directed at him and more at how much I need him here right now. He is like a brother to me, the only person I trust in this world to hold me together tonight.

He reaches for my shoulder and gives it a slight squeeze, letting me know he's got me, and that's all I need.

"You mother told me that you know about your father and that he was going home to the UK, with plans to return quickly to her side." My blood is already racing at the words that have fueled my anger all my life. *"But sadly, he never made it back."*

My heart feels like there is a vice squeezing it tighter and tighter with every word he speaks.

"Richard arrived in London on a miserable rainy day, with no one knowing he was coming. So instead of his parents arranging to pick him up, he caught a cab to head home, and there was a car accident on the way. He bore the brunt of

a lorry hitting the side of his cab that had lost control and was sliding sideways in the water, across into the path of the lorry. Both Richard and the cab driver were killed on impact, in what was a very sad and terrible tragedy."

The tears are building in my eyes for a man I never knew, yet for the first time in my entire life, I wish I could have had that chance.

"Did he suffer?" I suddenly feel desperate to know if the man who gave me life felt any pain.

"All reports to your grandparents at the time said it was instantaneous, and he wouldn't have felt anything." He reached out to put his hand on my knee to comfort me. I don't want him to touch me, but I don't have the energy to push him away. He understands the message, though, when I flinch, so he slowly removes it again. I've never been a man to show emotion, so I'm so far off kilter at the moment, and luckily, he sees that.

"He was an only child, so you can understand how devastated your grandparents were. So, to find out that he had a son has given your grandfather the greatest joy."

"But how did he find me, and why now? Why after all these years?" There are so many questions now rushing into my head.

"You need to remember that the internet and social media didn't exist then, like it does now. Your grandfather never knew about your mother because he didn't get to speak to Richard at all about his travels in Australia."

"You keep saying grandfather. What about my grandmother?" Seeing the look on his face, I know the answer.

"Sadly, Aileen passed away five years ago, and that was when Charles found a letter in her treasure box from Richard, that he had posted to them both before he left Australia. She had opened it all those years ago but never shared it, and Charles didn't even know it existed. I'm guessing it was too painful for your grandmother to read his words, and she wanted to spare Charles. But I guess we will never really know why she kept it a secret."

"What did it say? He wouldn't have said anything about me, he didn't even know I existed. Mum didn't find out until he was gone." My head hangs low as the words I just said sink in. My father never knew he had a child. That pain in my chest is getting harder to bear.

"No, you're right, but your father did talk a lot about your mother and how much he loved her. He had every intention of going back to live in Australia and marry her."

"Fuck!" I can't stay sitting any longer, and I stand abruptly and storm toward the water's edge. Everything I had doubted for all these years was just as she told me it was. They had fallen in love in such a short time frame, but their happily ever after that they both were dreaming of was never meant to be.

I don't know how long I stand staring out at the ripples of the harbor water catching the city lights on it. Broderick and Flynn just leave me to take all the time I need to digest the bomb that has just been dropped on me.

I take a big deep breath to try to get some oxygen into my lungs because I feel like I currently have an elephant sitting on my chest, then I turn back to my best friend and the man who just blew up my world.

"But he didn't know her surname, so how did you find her? There must be thousands and thousands of women named Sally living in Australia." Slowly walking back to my seat, some of the anger from earlier is overtaken by such sadness.

Sadness for my mother and father, who lost their one true love. To my grandparents, who lost their only child. And something I never expected to feel, deep down in my soul. The pure, heart-wrenching sadness for myself, for losing my father.

"That's true, we only knew her as Sally, but that's the greatest twist in all of this. It was actually the actions of your mother that found us, not the other way around." Just when I don't think tonight can get any more intense, the next wave of confusion hits me like a brick wall.

"Wait, what the hell? What has my mother got to do with you finding us?" I sit up a little straighter, with energy I didn't know I had left.

"She listed your DNA on one of those ancestry websites, where you track down long-lost relatives, a few years ago," he says, looking at me and knowing I'm so confused.

"What the fuck, how did she do that? Like, what the ever-loving fuck! I don't understand."

"No, hang on," Flynn says. "Remember a few years ago, when she said the doctor thought you might have some genetic thing, like your pop, and she gave you a DNA kit to do two samples so the doctor could check. I remember it, because I joked with her about what sexually transmitted diseases would show up. It was right before you landed head chef at work." This would have to be longest Flynn has ever stayed silent, so when he speaks, I nearly jump off the step. But as soon as he mentions it, I remember that, and she came back a few weeks later and said everything was clear.

"Shit!" I don't know what to say. I'm so confused.

"I think that might be a conversation you need to have with Sally, but no matter how it got onto that site, the absolute positivity of this is us finding both of you." He rests his hand again on my forearm, and this time I have to admit it feels nice. Like he cares.

"Why did you go to my mother first?" I ask, trying to piece things together.

"Because she was easier to find. Still being old school, she has a house phone that is listed in the telephone directory that gave us her address. You, on the other hand, don't have your full name listed many places so were harder to find."

I had been telling Mum for years to get rid of that phone on the wall. The only people who call it are the telemarketing companies, or charities, or the oh, so exciting automated surveys for the government. But the real thing that worries me is that she is too kind, and the scammers that now target those phones would trick her into giving them money. Never in any wild irrational dream did I think a stupid old landline phone would bring us to this.

"Good to know, never get a landline if I don't want all my past girlfriends to track me down," Flynn blurts out to break the tension a little.

"Got a list of them, huh?" Broderick asks with a grin.

"Sadly, yes," I say. "He can't seem to hang on to them. But I'm not sure how many would ever want to find him again." I can't help but throw the smallest amount of humor at him.

"Now that's my Nic. Always has the smart-ass answer. You back with us?" Flynn's shoulders sag a little, like he finds some relief in seeing me not looking like I'm about to pass out anymore.

"Far from it. Just breathing is an achievement right now." Running my hand through my hair, I realize how wet my scalp feels from the sweat of my panic.

"Do you want me to keep going or leave it at that for tonight until you talk to your Mum, and we can all meet tomorrow?"

"Christ, how much more is there to share? I'm not sure I can take any more surprises tonight."

"I totally understand that. It's not more surprises, just filling in the gaps. But one thing I do want you to know is that once I let your grandfather know I've found you, he'll want to be on the first plane to Australia."

"Not sure I'm ready for that," I whisper under my breath.

I don't know if he heard me or not, but his next statement puts me at ease and worries me all at the same time.

"He might want that all he likes, however he is an old man and can't fly anymore. So, he will want you and your mother on a plane to the UK as soon as humanly possible. It's been thirty-six years since he has hugged his son, and you are the next best thing. I'm sure this is all very overwhelming, so I think we are best to get together tomorrow to continue talking. You need rest, and like your friend said, a stiff whiskey or two."

Standing slowly, Broderick pulls out a business card and hands it to me. "This has all my contact details on it."

Taking it from him, I stare at it like it has the answer to my life on it.

"Don't be scared. Only good things will come from all of this," he says, placing his hand on my shoulder. "Try to get some rest and we will talk tomorrow." Nodding at Flynn, he starts to walk away when I ask one last thing.

"What if I say no?" Because to be honest, I don't know what the hell just hit me.

Not even turning back to look at me, he answers while continuing to walk away. "You won't."

And that was the first time I learned Broderick is usually right.

I know in my gut that a door has been opened tonight that can never be closed.

So, the only thing left is for me to work out how to walk forward through it . . .

The knock on my office door brings me out of my memories.

I sit up in my chair and try to get my head around what I was supposed to be doing so I don't look like an idiot.

"Yes," I call out.

"Nicholas, I just need to remind you that your appointment with the design consultant has been pushed forward to midday, and here is the file you asked me to prepare for you," Lucy says, stepping into my office, and I'm back in the thick of another busy day.

"Thanks, Lucy. Can you make sure Flynn has the change of

time too? I want him at this meeting. And that doesn't mean sharing my whole calendar with him," I call after her as she leaves the room.

"You need to relax once in a while, it won't hurt you. The only person you trust to let your hair down with is Flynn and the boys. Just go." Her giggle makes me smirk. How Lucy puts up with my grumpy demeanor, I have no idea. But what I do know is I pay her handsomely to do it.

Like I trust Flynn, anyway. All he does is lead me astray.

I should be afraid when he says we are going drinking. Not afraid like it will cost me a fortune in expensive whiskey. No, that I can cope with. But I should definitely be afraid that tomorrow, I'm about to feel like shit!

My phone lights up with my mother's name, making my stomach fall.

Nothing has changed since I left Australia. She never calls me at work unless it's urgent, which is hard to manage with the time zone differences.

"Mum, what's wrong?" I can't help the worry from dripping from my words.

Chapter Five

NICHOLAS

The big sigh before she speaks tells me all I need to know. She's stressed.

"Hi, Nic, sorry to bother you, but I wanted to make sure you heard it from me before any of those silly reporters plaster it on social media." She sounds tired, but I can't gauge her voice and guess what she is about to say. Little does she realize, I don't pay attention to social media. That stopped the moment I became newsworthy.

"You are never a bother," I tell her. That's not exactly true, though I would never tell her that. "What's wrong?"

"I had a car accident today. Well, that's not entirely true, the car had an accident without me today." Her giggle makes me relax a little, as she sounds fine.

"You're okay, not hurt?" I'm annoyed she didn't lead with that information, which is the most important.

"No, silly. I would have had to be in the car to get hurt."

"What the hell are you talking about, Mum? You aren't making any sense. Start at the beginning." My frustration of the morning now comes out in the tone of my voice with my mother.

"I had a bad headache, so I drove instead of walking to the shops today. I parked on a street near the shopping center and forgot to put the handbrake on. The car got a little excited and decided to roll off down the road and into a tree. Well, it would have been more than rolling, because they tell me it's not repairable. I'm so sorry, Nic, I wrecked the car you bought me." Now her happy laugh is replaced by a little sniffle. She's crying.

"Mum, I don't give a fuck about the car. As long as you and everybody else around you weren't hurt, that's all that matters." Standing and pacing in front of the windows in my office, I wonder what else the world can throw at me today.

"More importantly, how did you forget to put the handbrake on?" Thinking about her being on the other side of the world, I should have been there to sort this all out for her.

"I really don't know. I've never done anything like that before. I'm so stupid." I can hear in her voice it scared her.

"We all make mistakes, Mum, don't worry about it. I'm sure it won't happen again." But part of me is worried at the uncertainty in her voice. I have a feeling there is more to this that she isn't telling me. Now is not the time to push her, though.

"Yes, you're right. Anyway, I won't need to worry about that on the bus and train."

"Mum, you don't have to rely on public transport. Go and rent a car tomorrow, I'll pay for it. Just until we can organize you a new car."

"No, Nicholas. I'm a grown-ass woman, I can pay for it myself." I didn't know my dad, but it's pretty obvious at times I have my mother's stubbornness to stand on my own two feet. It's what got her through raising me on my own, so I can't say it's a bad trait. Except when she is firing it back at me.

"And in case you haven't noticed, I am a grown-ass man who is worth more money than I can ever spend in my lifetime. So, suck it up and let me look after you, the same way you always looked after me. I will get Lucy to deposit the money in your account whether you like it or not." This time there is no hiding my frustration in my voice. Placing my hand on the window and leaning my forehead on it, I try to control my temper so I don't let everything from this morning come out in this conversation with Mum.

"I don't have a choice, do I? You are just like your father." I don't know that she knew him long enough to be able to make that claim, but what would I know. Part of me hopes she is right. To know I'm like him would be comforting at times, when my back is against the wall in this business.

"You know the answer to that. Now go and have a good night's sleep and we will talk in the morning," I say, looking out at the gloomy sky outside. London can be a depressing place some days. I miss the sun and surf at home. The beaches just aren't the same here.

"Okay, and I'm sorry, Nic. I don't want to become your burden as I get older." Hearing the sadness in her voice, I know I need to lighten the conversation.

"What is this getting older nonsense? Aren't you already there?" I laugh into the phone as she reacts just like I pictured.

"Richard Nicholas Weston, don't you dare call me old. I'm still, what do they call them, a yummy mummy."

"Oh my God, you did not just call yourself that. I can't even… I'm hanging up now. I have visions in my head that you should never have of your mother."

She's giggling to herself now. "Or did I get it wrong, am I a MILF?"

"What the fuck, Mum, where are you getting all this from? What stupid television show are you binge watching now?"

"Never you mind. But I can't be a GILF yet because you haven't found yourself a girl to give me some grandbabies."

"That's it, I'm going. I can't deal with this." I'm shaking my head, but at least now with a small grin on it. "Love you, Mum, and make sure you get that car sorted first thing in the morning. No arguments."

"Thanks, Nicky." She knows exactly what she is doing by calling me that. It drove me nuts as a kid and annoys me even more now.

"Bye, Mum. Behave." I hang up the call as she is telling me she loves me.

The guilt of being so far away when she needs me rises the moment the call ends.

"Fuck!" I shout, kicking the cushion across the room that was still on the floor from Flynn this morning.

"Lucy!" I can hear her moving at her desk.

Not even knocking, she comes rushing through the door.

"Are you okay?" She can tell something isn't right.

"No! Find a private jet company that can get me to Australia at limited notice. Put them on standby that I might need to fly in the next few days. And if not, then book them to fly me home next Friday, I don't care what it costs. Mum needs me. I'm going home for a short visit. Start clearing my schedule. Only leave the urgent things."

"On it. Are you flying on your own?"

"Yes." I need Flynn and Forrest here to keep their fingers on the pulse and watch for the knives being sharpened behind my back, because they are always there. And Remington will need to put out the spot fires as they begin simmering, like they constantly do. I couldn't do this without these men.

"Plus, get me the details for the BMW dealership in North Sydney. I need a new car for Mum waiting for me when I land. I'll let you know the model I want." I could just order it from here, but I need to see Mum for myself. Something seems off, and I want to know what.

Without another word, Lucy's gone, and I know before I even get through this next meeting everything will be in place. She's that good at her job.

"Thank you, Miss Francis. I'll look for the initial report by close of business on Wednesday." I close my door behind her, knowing that Lucy will show her out.

I know the director of York and Webb wasn't impressed at my fast track of the project, but I need this moving. Can't give the board time to form too much of an opinion. Plus, with the possibility of being away to Australia, I wanted it started pronto.

I have hours of work to get done before I can even think about going out with the guys tonight. Messaging them to give them the heads up that I want to cancel is just futile. It will waste more of the time I don't have, because Flynn will start blowing up my phone for trying to ditch them this early. And if I don't respond, then he will end up in my office, which is worse.

Instead, I shoot a message off to Lucy that I'm not to be disturbed and ask if she can organize me some lunch to eat while I'm working. Opening the next email I need to respond to, I block everything out. It's the only way I'll get anything done. I learned very quickly after meeting my grandfather that he was a hard-ass, but it's what got him to this level of success. He trusted me to continue his legacy the way my father never could. I'll be damned if I let him down. Instead, I'm determined to make it the greatest privately owned hotel chain in Europe. Something my father would have been proud of me for. Because that's the closest I can ever get to making him proud of the son he never knew.

My body is now fueled with food and a strong coffee that Lucy has learned how to make for me just the way I like it. I had to teach her purely because the British have absolutely no idea how to make a good coffee. Now I'm powering through my workload. The hours pass, with me finally getting a lot of the work sorted, and I feel like I'm back on top of everything. Even if the day has been so draining.

I start as my door is thrust open. "She is fucking infuriating!" The door slamming behind him, Flynn comes into my office whether I like it or not. Poor Lucy never stood a chance at holding him back. He doesn't think any of the rules apply to him.

"I'm busy, Flynn, go complain to Forrest." I don't even bother to look up at him. It's the same old story after every meeting he has with Jocelyn. To be honest, I don't have the patience for it today.

"Well, I doubt you're too busy to hear the bomb she just happened to drop about you." I know Flynn can be dramatic but not usually like this. Something has ruffled his feathers, and it involves me.

I throw my hands in the air. "Seriously! Like today can't get any more painful. What now?"

VICTORIA

"I can't believe you are ditching us. The night is young, we have other bars to hit," Theo screams over top of the music. What was supposed to be a few quiet after-work drinks has escalated into a Friday night of partying. Gwenda warned me!

"You can have a dance for me then. I'm tapping out. I still have a long trip home." No way I can be dancing now. The room's already swimming a lot and I feel a little weird. I didn't think I'd had enough to be this drunk, but I know I'm past my limit of safe drinking to get on a train by myself, but here we are. Story of my life, trying to fit in with the crowd.

"Stay at my place," he says, putting his arm around me, and we sway together. I'm not sure if he is trying to make me dance or if we are just both far tipsier than I realized and can't stand up straight.

"I don't even know you." My best friend Elouise would kill me if I went home with a stranger. Plus, I don't want to screw this job up. Don't cross the line with co-workers, that's my rule.

Theo must have seen the worry on my face.

"Not like that, you'd be sleeping on the couch. I don't fuck on first dates." He smirks at me as I push him away.

"What the hell, you're an absolute tosser. We work together, this isn't a date." Suzi, hearing my raised voice, turns and smacks Theo around the back of the head.

"Don't be a dick and scare her away on the first day. Just ignore him. You can stay with me if you like, but there's no pressure from any of us to stay here drinking with these crazy people. Plenty more nights out to get pissed with this lunatic," she says, pointing at Theo who is currently well on his way to drunk city. "Theo practically lives in this bar. How else do you think we got in to such a swanky place. Money talks, girl." I'm not sure what that is supposed to mean, and I'm so confused. But the only thing I'm sure of is that I need to get on the subway to go home.

Starting to look around me and gaining my bearings on where the exit is, I start noticing that the clientele has changed somewhat since we got here.

The after-work dress on the women has been swapped out for the short, fitted dresses that if a guy ran his hand down over her ass, it would end up in her underwear, or lack thereof. Or the tightest pants with the see-through sequin tops or a crop top that shows off her best assets. I wouldn't be game to bend over in pants that tight; I'd rip them clean open, from my pussy to my asshole.

Now the men, mmm, holy freaking cow! I could get lost running my hands over the verrrrrry expensive suits, checking out every single thread, and don't even get me started on the tight shirts with the rolled-up sleeves. The men in here are flashing some very hot arm porn in every corner of the room. My sudden hot flush has probably got more to do with what I'm picturing is hiding under those suits, because fuck me every day of the week, this is a meat market for hotness in here. I guess it's true what they say, money can buy you happiness, because if I was riding one of these rich hotties in here, I'd be more than happy—I'd be fucktastic.

Oh dear, drunk-potty-mouth Tori is in the house. Now I just need to keep these thoughts in my head, before I totally wreck the nice, sophisticated Tori image I built in the office today. I check the faces of everyone from work that is still around me, and thankfully, no one is looking at me shocked. Yay to scoring a point for my inside voice tonight.

Ughh, where is Elouise when I need her. She keeps me under control, well, most nights anyway. I shouldn't be allowed out drinking without her. Note for future sober Tori, invite her to Friday-night work drinks. Just the thought of her and Theo in the same room has me giggling. It would be like a stand-off of pushiness. That would be entertaining without any drinking.

Looking at my phone, I see it's later than I realized. Shit, I need to get out of here. But having a quick visit to the toilet is a must before I leave the bar. No way I can cross my legs all the way home, and this morning's train trip was already embarrassing enough. I'll try to keep my bodily fluids inside my body this time. Although it wasn't a complete waste of a trip. I did have a scrumptious view. I should have offered to lick him clean of the tea I spat all over him.

Pointing toward the ladies' room to Suzi, she nods at me as I start making my way through the crowd. That's the problem when you're drunk. Finding the gaps in the crowd becomes a little more of a challenge as you stagger. And the closer I get to the edge of the dance floor full of people, the more my bladder has decided it's time to explode.

Lord, please let there be no line up.

Yeah, sure. The odds of that are like winning the lottery. None!

Damn it, if this line doesn't hurry up, I'm going to wee my pants.

The side shuffle along the wall of the bar is moving but still slowly. Trying to distract myself, I look up into what I have now worked out to be the VIP area on the mezzanine. It's like I have conjured up my hottie from this morning.

Surely not!

I can only see this tall blond guy from behind, but what a glorious behind it is.

I must be seeing things, or I'm drunker than I thought, which is pretty drunk. His arm is hooked around a little silvery disco ball. Well, that's what she looks like to me, with all the flashing lights hitting her shiny dress. Just like I said, his hand is almost slipping into the land of pleasure as he slides it down past the hem of the dress.

No, it can't be him. He didn't seem like this would be his scene. I picture him home in front of the fire at a big old wooden desk, still working on his computer. Men like him never sleep. Plus, he was on my train. He's probably long out of the city by now if he had any sense. Not still here like me and almost flooding the floor trying to stop my bladder from bursting.

Finally, it's my turn to step in through the door, and the urgency of being so close to the toilet, the relief overtakes any need to care if it is him or not. It's not like I even know him or that he would remember me. Well, maybe spitting tea on someone makes you memorable, but let's just say I'm not keen to find that out.

Standing at the sink and washing my hands, I can't help but listen to all the gossip around me.

Women can deny it all we like, but we love to gossip and talk about other people. The three women beside me are all puckering up in front of the mirror, touching up their lipstick and checking themselves out. Making sure the hair is still perfect and the dress is sitting just right. And I just know there will be a bathroom selfie taken as soon as they are done.

I've never been to this bar before, and I had no idea how swanky it is. I am way out of my league for a Friday night out. Listening to the talk from these women, the bar Indulge is the playground of the rich and famous suits in the city. And of course, all the high-flying society girls who are either trying to snag themselves a man or playing the field before they settle down with the man they are "supposed" to marry, according to their family. I'm glad I don't have to worry about that kind of pressure. I'm in charge of my own destiny, and no one gets to make choices for me.

Just as I'm drying my hands and walking out, they start setting their pose for the selfie I knew would be happening. So predictable.

It's like I have released some of the alcohol from my body because I feel a little bit more in control. It's marginal, but I'll take any little bit of sobriety I can get to help get me home.

Glancing up to the mezzanine, the blond god has gone, and as I predicted, I was imagining him.

Making my way back across the dance floor again, I run straight into Evan my ex-boyfriend from a few years ago. Well, I wouldn't say a boyfriend really, he was just multiple one-night stands, and we knew it wasn't going to work. We both wanted different things. He wanted to settle down, I wanted more out of life.

"Tori, what are you doing here?" I was actually thinking the same thing about him. This place is full of money, which neither of us had when we were together.

"Oh my God, Evan, how are you?" I say, trying to act less drunk than I am. We embrace each other like long-lost friends, which we aren't. I haven't spoken to or messaged him since the day we walked away from each other.

"I'm great. You look good." He pulls back from me to look me up and down. Ugh, I probably look like trash. "Really... good." The way he draws out his words, I have a feeling he has had plenty to drink too.

"I'm here with work friends, what about you?" I say, trying to steer the conversation back off him looking at me, taking a little step backwards out of his grasp.

"Same actually, I've got a job in the city now, and this is a regular Friday-night hangout." Oh great. Just what I need, running into an ex-boyfriend every Friday night. Hopefully they change it up each week where they go for drinks. Maybe I can suggest that. Yeah, that will work. "Dance with me," he says, stepping closer and wrapping his hands around my ass, dirty dancing with me.

"No, no, I need to go. I'm heading home now, nice seeing you, though." I push off his chest with both my hands and almost fall over. I know I have to keep moving backwards, though, even if I'm feeling unsteady on my feet.

"I'll come with you. I should probably head home too." Shit! Now what do I do?

"Oh, I'm not going to my place, I'm staying with a work friend in the city."

Finally, I manage to get out of his grasp. "See you around, Evan." Turning sideways to slide between some more people, I hear him calling out to me that we should catch up again, and that's a big no from my drunken brain. Quickly he is swallowed back up into crowd on the dance floor, and I know I need to get out of here now. It's not that I have any problems with Evan, I'm just too drunk and will probably do something stupid that I'll regret later.

Saying my goodbyes to Theo and Suzi and their friends, I finally hit the fresh air outside. It's the end of September where the nights have the coolness of Autumn but are still gentle enough that it is actually a bit refreshing at times. And boy, do I need the freshen-up feeling. The exhaustion of my first day on the job, all the responsibility that has been placed in my lap, and of course, a few too many drinks tonight are all catching up with me. And then the blast from the past, that shook me a little. I'm so tired. I think I might need to set the alarm on my phone once I'm on the train to make sure I don't miss my stop.

I pull my jacket a little tighter around me, while I think about which is the quickest way to a train station. My handbag is slipping off my shoulder, probably because there is too much weight in it. But it gives me a brain wave that I should change into my flat shoes again. The last thing I need is to roll my ankle. That would really finish off the day of clumsiness for me.

Balancing on one high-heel shoe while trying to change my other shoe, however, is not as easy as I was picturing. I don't want to put my bare foot down on the dirty pavement, so in my head, the one-foot shuffle is the smartest move. It looked a lot more gracious in my head, but in reality, I look like one of those blow-up inflatable men they use at festivals and sales to attract attention. The arms and body flapping all around with no control. Of course, all the wobbling has now made my stomach feel like I've been on a boat for a few days. I just need to get home to bed.

With both shoes on, I'm just trying to take a few deep breaths. In my head, I keep telling myself I will not vomit. My stomach may not be on the same page, but I'm fighting it. My head still spinning, I lean forward, placing my hands on my thighs just trying to gain my steady place.

Concentrating on holding it together, I don't hear the footsteps behind me until he speaks in that deep accent.

"Tori, are you all right?"

I squeal and fall flat on my ass from fright. So much for not touching the dirty ground.

"Shit, sorry, I didn't mean to frighten you. Let me help you." He is quickly in front of me, holding out his hands to help me up.

Looking up into those deep blue eyes again, I can't help but let my embarrassment fuel my stubbornness. "No! I'm fine." Well, that answers that question whether he would remember who I am.

I get awkwardly to my feet, a little wobbly, but I'm up. Shit, my right ankle hurts, I must have twisted it as I fell, not so graciously. But I'm way too close to him now to bend down and take a look. His cologne wraps around me, and as much as I know I should step back, I'm not game to move and fall again.

"Clearly you aren't." Why does his accent make me shiver each time he speaks to me as if I have annoyed him? "You've been drinking."

"So have you!" Wow, great comeback, Tori.

"Great, now we have established we have both been drinking. Some more than others, obviously, so I'll organize for my driver to take you home." Wait, what did he just say?

"I'm no damsel in distress like your little floozy disco ball inside." Crap, that's when I notice her standing next to him, and if looks could kill, I'd be dead right now. I'm guessing I'm not what she was expecting when she walked out of the bar on his arm.

"I don't need a man to step in. I'll take the train home like I do every other day. Thank you anyway." I start to move away from his side because I know I need to get away from the man before I do something stupid, like fall on him. Pain shoots through my ankle, but I try not to show any pain on my face.

"Not happening. You will go with my driver. It's safer." The dominant stare pins me to the spot, and I can't seem to move my feet, but it doesn't stop my mouth from working.

"Yeah, right. So much safer to get into a car with a strange man I don't know and let him drive me to God knows where. Are you for real? How stupid do you think I am! I might be drunk but not dumb!" Oh, I'm all class now.

"Flynn, call your own car. I'm staying the night at the farm," he yells across the road to another man standing with a blonde hanging off his arm next to a dark navy Range Rover with heavily tinted windows. "And take Simona home too." Disco ball girl's mouth now pouts at the disappointment that she isn't getting laid by the golden dick tonight.

"Do I even want to ask why the fuck you are heading out there this late at night and sending your lady friend home with me?" His friend laughs loudly at him and closes the car door he had open for the woman to slide into the back seat. The blonde bombshell looks confused as she is pulled back from the car.

"No! And I said take her home, but not with you!" Nic grumbles and then turns back to me. "Let's go, so we can get this painful trip over with. I have things to do tonight."

"I'm not going anywhere with you. I'm going home on my own!" I'm not taking any more of this high-handedness from him.

"Wrong, you aren't catching the train by yourself in this state. Now move it." He motions with his arm to the car across the road and for me to step forward.

"I'm not catching the train with you!" I snap, making my point with the most dramatic placing of the hand on my hip that I can manage. I turn and start down the street, only to stumble on my ankle that hurts more than I want to admit. I thought when you were drunk, the alcohol is supposed to numb things.

Before I even have a chance to straighten back up properly, hands sweep under my legs, and I'm up off my feet being carried toward the car.

The sparkly girl calls his name as we keep going, and he doesn't even look back or bother to answer her.

I should be screaming that a man is carrying me to a car and is about to drive away with me, but I'm too busy taking in the feel of being this close to Nic. The chest I'm leaning against is solid as a rock. He isn't even puffing trying to carry me. Man, this guy must be fit. Probably does those crazy weight workouts in the gym every morning while normal people like me are still fast asleep. And his cologne, oh my Lord, it is having the same effect it had this morning, making me feel tingly in all my girly parts.

The moment he places me back down on the ground next to the car, it's like his super stud spell he cast on me is broken.

"I'm not getting in this car with you. You could be an axe murderer or something!"

"I'm something all right, but if you don't get in this car, you are going to turn me into a very grumpy man." Glaring at me, he runs his hand through the loose blond waves on the top of his head. Oh, I'd like to run my fingers through those locks.

Shit, focus, woman.

"So, this isn't grumpy then?" It's like I push his buttons without even trying. I can see he is about to lose his patience with me. His jaw is ticking, and he is trying to work out what to say next.

"Tori, you are drunk and now have an injured ankle. It's not safe to be on a train this late at night by yourself. Let my driver take you home." His words are spoken through his gritted teeth.

"That's the word isn't it, safe," I can't help throwing back at him.

"For fuck's sake, what will make you get in the car and feel safe?" Not giving up, he has thrown the ball back in my hands.

I'm trying to think quick on my feet, which is not easy when my head is spinning, stomach still rolling like I'm about to empty the contents, and my ankle hurts like a motherfucker. To be honest, to be driven home to my door sounds like heaven. Think, Tori, what can you do?

"I know, I want a picture of you and your license so I can send it to my best friend. Then the police will know who to arrest when I disappear." Deep down, I don't feel one bit scared of him, but I know I should. Sober me probably would be.

"Ughhh, fine, but I don't have my wallet with me. I don't need it in this bar. So, you can take a photo of me and then my driver Wallace and his license. Is that enough? Because I would really like to get home sometime tonight. It's been a long fucking day!" He motions for me to take the picture and nods at Wallace to get his ID out too. I can't very well say no now that he has done as I asked.

"Fine. Smile for the nice policeman that will see these." God, I'm being a real bitch here. To be honest, this guy is trying to be nice, and I'm just cutting him down at every turn.

There is no way he is smiling for me. I can hear the growl under his breath from here.

I hear from the front of the bar someone calling my name. Looking up, I see Evan waving at me, trying to get my attention. Shit, I don't want to go with him. I'm mentally berating myself for choosing the stranger over my ex, but weirdly, Nic feels like a safer bet tonight.

"Get in the car, Tori." Another forceful demand, but this time, I'm too tired to argue.

Ooh, nice warm leather seats. This car is posh.

"Seatbelt," Nic demands, sitting next to me.

"So freaking bossy."

"Yes, now just do it." I have a feeling if I don't do it, he will be leaning across me in a minute and doing it for me. And being that close is a big no-no.

The driver pulls out onto the road and asks me my address. Yeah, nice one, boys. I'm not that silly. Giving them Elouise's address will at least stop them from coming back to find me. Oh, shit, but then they will find her. Crap, I'm so freaking dumb.

> Tori: If I disappear tonight, it's the train tea disaster guy from this morning.

> Elouise: OMG are you okay or just being dramatic?

> Tori: Thanks for caring if I'm dead or not!

> Elouise: Sorry, forgot the unalive have access to their phones to message friends.

> Tori: Seriously, bitch, listen. I'm in a car on the way home, with the Aussie god, and I need someone to care.

> Elouise: What the fuck! Why?

Tori: Never let me go out drinking alone again!

Elouise: Where are you and why is he with you? You were just going for a few work drinks.

Tori: Famous last words.

Elouise: And I still don't have a picture. I need one now, for safety reasons, of course.

Tori: Yes, shit, I took these. Him and his driver. Not bad mug shots for the media when I go missing.

Elouise: Holy fucking shit, he's an off-the-charts hot stud. He can kidnap me anytime. At least you'll die with a smile on your face.

Tori: Thanks for caring. And no, you can't have him, I saw him first.

Elouise: Why would you want a man you think is going to kill you? Why did you even get in the car with him?

Tori: He's super bossy and trying to be all protective and shit. Wouldn't let me travel on my own.

Elouise: You don't even know him.

Tori: Right! But he wouldn't let me get on the train when I was drunk. Wanted his driver to take me home.

Elouise: What did you do this morning, spit some attraction potion on him or something?

Elouise: Wait, he has a driver! What the hell was he on the train for?

Elouise: Driver means money – who the fuck is he????

Tori: If I knew, do you think I would be texting you?

Elouise: How do you get into these messes, seriously!

Tori: Pure talent.

Elouise: Where is he sitting? Next to you????

Tori: Yes. Looking extremely pissed at me.

Tori: Shit, have to go, typing in the car makes me want to vomit more.

The way he has been glaring at me, I can tell the mood he's in. I made it obvious when we got in how frustrated I am with him. I'm not taking any of this alpha asshole shit from him.

He takes a bottle out of the side door and hands it to me. "Drink it! You'll thank me in the morning." That came out as an order, and I don't do orders.

"You must be talking to someone else. I will not be drinking anything while I'm alone with you," I say, sitting up straighter in my seat.

"Are you always this stubborn?" He glares at me as he places the water in my lap anyway.

"This is a slow day. You should see me when I dial it up to a ten on the stubbornness scale. What, are you used to everyone obeying your commands?"

"Yes!" Turning away from me and glancing out the window, I

see Wallace's face in the rear-view mirror. The smirk on it tells me I hit the nail on the head.

Putting my head back on the seat, I know it's a bad idea as my eyes are trying to close, but it feels nice to just sit in the quiet for a minute and not be sparring with the jerk next to me.

This man infuriates me.

He told me this morning he wished today would bring me what I was looking for. Well, my wish list didn't include a controlling cocky prick!

Thanks, universe. You totally misfired once again.

Chapter Six

NICHOLAS

I should have just walked straight past her outside the bar.

Then I would have been close to heading home to my city apartment by now, enjoying a long hot shower after releasing my day's frustration with Simona in one of my hotel rooms. Not here sitting once again next to this woman who is getting under my skin, and I'm not sure it's in a good way. Flynn is going to get great mileage out of this tomorrow when he starts pumping me for details.

This verbal sparring match isn't over yet, I'm sure. I know without a doubt when we get to her home, she will have something sarcastic to say, and I doubt it will be followed up with a thank-you. Why can't she just take the gesture of me trying to be nice and make sure she gets home safe as just being that and nothing else? I don't do this sort of shit normally, so I expect a bit of gratitude at least. But so far, every conversation has been a battle, and it's driving me insane. I should be the one who is running a mile away from her. This morning she spit tea on me, and tonight, I'm more worried it will be vomit, on either me or in my car.

Looking at her, I can see she how fired up she is. The alcohol has her pale skin flushed, or maybe it's from her temper. Hard to know at this stage. She has been messaging her friend ferociously since we got in the car and looking sideways at me to make sure I wasn't reading whatever was on the screen. To be honest, I couldn't give a shit what she is telling her friend. I just want to make sure she gets home safely and then I'm done. If I don't see this woman again, it will be too soon. The next sixty minutes in the car will be torturous enough.

And who was that idiot screaming her name from the front of the bar? What was he hoping, she would go back inside with him? Maybe it's her boyfriend. Surely not, no sane man would let another man take his drunk woman away in a car with him. No matter who the dickhead was, he wasn't keeping her safe, and that makes me even more angry.

We are hardly out of the city and on the motorway when I hear the first snore. It's not a delicate little one either. Head back, mouth open, a full drunken snore coming from such a tiny woman has me wanting to laugh for the first time in the last hour. If truth be known, it's the first time today I've truly smiled at something so innocent.

Reaching under the driver's seat, I pull out the throw that Wallace keeps there. He always had it for my grandfather as he aged, but it still gets pulled out occasionally on those nights where the snow is falling, and the temperature is so low that this southern hemisphere blood is frozen to the core. I do miss the Australian climate.

I take her phone from her hand and place it in her handbag. Once the bag is on the floor, I gently drape the blanket over her and find myself really taking her in for the first time. Not while she is busy arguing with me, but while the peace of sleep has taken over her.

I've never really been taken by a woman with red hair, but Tori has a beauty that suddenly catches me by surprise at how attracted to her I am. Even with the small trail of drool coming from the corner of her little pouty lips that are wide open at the moment. I'm sure she would be horrified if she could see herself. But to me, she looks perfectly messy.

Ever since I moved to London, I've been surrounded by flawlessly beautiful women who don't have one single thing out of place. They know how to hold themselves, what to say and when, and they're always looking for a man with an arm to hang off. Don't get me wrong, I have taken plenty of my fill of the women who are virtually throwing themselves at me. But it's just sex, a need to get off. Much to my mother's dismay, there hasn't been one of these women that I would even consider a second date with. I decided so long ago that relationships weren't my thing, and I'm happy with my life that way.

As I lift the blanket up high to cover Tori's shoulders and make sure she is comfortable, her head drops to the right slightly as I'm removing my hand. My fingers gently swipe across her cheek. The tingle shocks me, and I pull my hand away quickly before she wakes. I don't want her thinking I was touching her. Sitting back in my seat, focusing out the window, I collect my thoughts. I haven't realized how I'm stroking my fingers that touched her cheek with my other hand. What was that sensation? Not something I'm used to, and my brain is overthinking it.

Wallace's soft voice snaps me out of my thoughts. "This one's a firecracker, sir," he says, smiling at me in the rear-view mirror.

"That's an understatement. Let's get her home before she fully explodes." I chuckle quietly to myself because that could be taken two ways, and I know I would prefer it being the explosion of words rather than of vomit.

Like she knows we are talking about her, Tori lets out a sigh and then continues to fall farther to the right until she is now leaning against my shoulder. I should move her, but part of me likes this soft side of her.

"Smells sexy too…" she mumbles, making me smile, surprisingly pleased that she might be thinking about me too.

The trust she has that I won't hurt her must be buried there somewhere in her subconscious, even though when she's awake, it's a different story. Settling in for the drive, I take in the quiet that is surrounding us. Her snoring is now gone, and I can hear a sweet little breath every so often over the sound of the engine as we speed down the motorway.

Her silence is golden.

Pulling up to the address she gave me, it's just like I pictured. A small home in a row that are all joined, mirror images of each other, just different colors and with a mixture of yards, from the gardens that people treasure, to the opposite, with concrete on every square inch.

A small porch light is on above the door. Did she leave it on or has it on a timer, or worse, does she live with someone who is about to attack me for forcing her to get in the car with me? Contemplating waking Tori up, I decide against it. To be honest, I'm too tired for any more drama tonight.

"Wallace, please go and see if someone can open the door for me to carry her inside. I don't want to wake this little sleeping Tasmanian devil." Wallace looks at me, a little confused, but he steps out of the car, doing as I asked.

Waiting for someone to answer, I see the door open to a bleary-eyed woman around the same age as Tori, dressed in her pajamas and a dressing gown wrapped tightly around her. She looks confused but pushes her door wide open, ready for me.

Propping Tori up straight, her little snuffle only lasts a second as she falls back into her slumber. There is nothing like a drunken sleep. It's equivalent to being in a semi coma. She is out of it by now, which surprises me, because I didn't think she was that far gone when I found her outside the club.

Walking around to her side of the car, I open the door and take my last look at this young woman who has piqued my interest more than it has been in a very long time. Shaking my head, I decide it's a good thing I won't see her again, as she is far too young for me and completely wrong to fit into my world. Today is going to end the way it started. With me walking away from my little redheaded firecracker.

Lifting her off the seat and into my arms with ease, I back away from the car so Wallace can grab her bag and close the door.

Not expecting her to nuzzle into my neck and sigh with content, I feel my cock hardening at the feel of her against my body. Down, boy, this one's not for us. She is just a moment of beauty that will keep moving forward in her own direction, which won't be ours.

Walking through the little wire gate and up the pathway, I imagine this to be the sort of house my grandparents grew up in. The year I spent with my grandfather, I would sit for hours and listen to his life stories. I will be forever grateful for that time, however short it was.

"Oh my, it's you… the Aussie god," the young lady at the door exclaims as her hand covers her mouth, trying not to let anything else out that she didn't mean to say.

Wallace laughs from behind me.

"Where shall I take her?" I'm guessing this is the friend Tori was talking to this morning and sending her proof-of-life pictures to tonight as we got into the car.

"Oh, um yes, straight down the hall to the spare bedroom at the back," she says, scurrying down the house in front of me.

Spare room—this isn't her home. Oh, well played, Tori. You were keeping yourself safe, and the protective bones in my body are very happy with that.

Placing her gently on the bed, still wrapped in the blanket from the car, she snuggles down into the pillow and pulls it up, stroking her face with the softness of it.

Taking one last look at her, I wish I could see her eyes one last time but know I'm better off not to. This vision is the one I want to photograph in my mind and take home with me. The quiet beauty.

"Make sure she drinks plenty of water, and she will need paracetamol as soon as she wakes. Ice on that ankle, and she needs to keep off it for a few days. Take care of her. Good night." I turn and walk out of the house and straight into my waiting car. Wallace closes my door and jumps in, starting the engine. As we pull away from the curb, I see her friend standing at the door, looking like she has been hit with a stun gun. I bet the conversation in that house will be interesting in the morning.

Looking at the time, it's now officially the weekend. Almost two am, and I just need to crash. It might be Saturday, but that means nothing in my work week. There is very rarely a day that passes that I don't need to do some work.

I take the opportunity to message Mum, knowing it's ten in the morning there. I want to make sure she is feeling okay and has organized the rental car. She looks after my nan and pop too, so must be able to get to them in a hurry if they need her.

Watching as the dots dance on the screen as she's replying, it finally hits me how tired I am. Luckily, all my years of being a chef have taught my body to survive with limited sleep.

The appearance of her reply on the screen has my bad mood returning quickly.

"Seriously!" I can't help but let my frustration out.

"You okay, sir?" Wallace has become more than my driver. At times, he has been my confidant, and I know I can trust him that what is said in this car stays in this car. He has worked for my family for a very long time, and his loyalty is treasured. We have developed a friendship built on trust. We might not socialize, but we spend more time together than I do with most people.

"My damn mother. She wrote off her car, so I told her to hire one until I can replace it. And she fucking hired a car the size of a jellybean to save me money. Those things are like a speed hump for a truck in the city. What was she thinking? I could buy her a whole car dealership, yet she sticks to a budget car. For crying out loud!" My finger hovers over the call button, but I know I'm too frustrated to speak to her.

"You need to remember, son, she didn't grow up with money. It is hard for her to change. She will never want to mooch off you, no matter how much you have." His voice is always so calming.

"But my father would have wanted me to look after her with his money. Something I'm sure he would have done all his life if he were able to." Thoughts of a man that I only know through stories and pictures consume my mind like they often do when I'm alone at the estate and walking the grounds. To me it is like walking the beach back home. The sound of the waves crashing, the wind on your face, the smell of the ocean. My calming place. The estate has become a close substitute. The sound of the birds in the trees, the different animals calling out, and the rustle of the leaves in the English breeze. The smell of freshly cut grass in the fields and hay in the feeders has become home. But more importantly, I know I'm stepping across the same fields both my father and grandfather have walked, and that is the most comforting thing of all.

"True, sir, but he would also want you to give her space to live her life as she chooses." His words resonate in my head, and as much as I know that is true too, I can't have her struggling while I'm here living a life of luxury.

Silence now falling over the car, I need to just finish out the day, and hopefully tomorrow—well, later today, to be accurate—is a little less eventful.

I'm sure every member of my management team has ended up in my office today. All except Jocelyn who avoids me most days, and I'm okay with that. I haven't seen her since Friday's board meeting, and with it being the end of Tuesday's workday, she has successfully managed to get through another day of not seeing me. Pity she is about to get an email from Lucy asking her to meet with me and Flynn tomorrow morning at nine am. I need to reiterate to her that this is my company and that is not going to change, ever.

Her words to Flynn on Friday were that if I didn't watch myself and my high-handedness, the board will have no choice but to push a vote of no confidence in me as the CEO. She must think I'm stupid not to have all my bases covered, but I can never trust her. She is always working behind the scenes to undermine me. My grandfather did warn me about her but insisted she is family and that she always have a place in this business. I want to honor his request, but if she keeps stepping on my toes or sharpening knives behind my back, I will squash her!

My desk phone rings, and I pick it up. "Yes, Lucy?" I'm hoping that this afternoon is not about to blow up in my face with some drama I don't need right now.

"Marco is on line one for you. Says it's urgent." Her voice trails off as she hangs up to put the call through, knowing I will never decline a call from one of my hotel managers when they say it's urgent. I employ these people to handle things, and they only call pronouncing urgency if there is a serious problem.

"Marco, are you about to ruin my Tuesday?" I ask, trying to lighten the mood before he deals me the bad news.

"Nic, you know I would never do it on purpose." His Italian accent is thick, but his English is excellent. He's a valuable asset to our Italian hotel in Rome. He also manages our other locations in Italy, Milan, Portofino, and Capri. My recent trip to Tuscany was to check out a few other potential places. I was on holidays, but we all know that means work for me. The only time I truly switch off is in Australia because I'm so far away, and with the time difference, my staff have usually sorted any major problems before I have woken up for the day.

"Can we just pretend you are calling me to tell me about the rave reviews from the customers on this month's surveys?" Sitting back in my chair, I brace myself for the true reason for the call.

"*Si*, they are excellent, but that's not why I am calling." Taking a breath, he starts, and although his English is good, when he talks at speed, I struggle to understand anything.

"Okay, slow down and tell me again," I ask.

"*Si*, sorry, Nic. The water pipes, they are old. They burst on the first floor, which collapse the ceiling in the reception area and kitchen." I can tell he is waiting for the explosion from me, and I'm trying so hard not to prove him right, but I'm failing.

"Fucking hell! Was anyone hurt? How bad is the damage, are we able to stay open?" Knowing our bookings are strong there, to close down now would be detrimental to our chain's reputation. Especially when I'm looking to expand there.

"No injuries, no. I am setting up a temporary reception area in the ballroom as we speak, and so far, the builders think the first floor is safe, so no rooms affected with flooding. We have shut off the water until we can get some temporary pipes laid to get water to those rooms affected. A big mess, but I am handling it." The confidence in his voice tells me that he is. "Do I need to do anything for insurance?"

"No, *grazie*, my office will handle it. I will send our building supervisor, Laurence Wetherington, as soon as I can to help. He will take over from you so you can concentrate on the hotel operations. Timing could have been better, but at least we are over the summer peak season."

"*Si*, Nic. I will handle it." He yells something in Italian to the side of the phone. I can imagine the chaos that is happening there.

"Go, Marco, and just keep me up to date with what is happening. I appreciate your help."

"*Arrivederci*, Nic. Talk soon."

As soon as the call is over, I want throw something across the room. What is happening here? In the last week, there has been more drama than in the last six months. I'm not superstitious, but I keep thinking back if I have walked under a ladder, or a black cat crossed my path. Or maybe it was a certain fiery redhead!

Shaking my head at the ridiculousness of my thoughts, I know what I need.

With no hesitation, I punch a message into our group chat.

Nic: Beers at 6. Meet at the usual.

Flynn: I could go a pint.

Forrest: Make that 3.

Flynn: 3 pints? Steady on there, brother.

Forrest: 3 people, you twat! Why do I always have to explain everything to you?

Flynn: Because you love me.

Forrest: Barely.

Nic: Settle down, children, can we just concentrate on the beer? I need a cold one, it's been a day.

Remington: What did I miss?

Nic: Beers at 6pm, be there! Cold ones, not those warm-as-piss ones you drink.

Remington: That's because we don't live in a country that's hotter than hell.

Flynn: Wait, you are back in the country, and I wasn't told?

Forrest: Are you his boss?

Flynn: No, his work husband, I need to know these things.

Remington: Fuck off, Flynn. But just to shut you up, I landed an hour ago.

Flynn: No respect in this group.

Nic: Just shut up and be at the pub at 6. Your turn to shout the round for being annoying.

Flynn: WTF?

Forrest: I second that.

Remington: Third and deciding vote. Majority rules.

Flynn: You are all cocks, you know that?

Remington: Oh, did you miss me, work hubby?

Nic: Fuck, you two have started, so I'm out. See you at 6.

Flynn: You never had a chance of getting in. Shit, I'm funny.

Forrest: I swear we can't be related. Switched at birth, I say!

Remington: Hard to argue when you look so alike.

Flynn: No way he is as good-looking as me.

Flynn: What, no comments??

Flynn: Where did you all go?

Flynn: Fuckers!

I might have more work to do now than I was counting on, but I know beers with the boys is better than therapy and much cheaper. I don't need to sit and have some doctor tell me how fucked up I am. I know that for myself.

"So let me get this right. You took her home, carried her to bed, and walked away, without taking it further?" Remington lifts his beer up to me. "That takes restraint, my friend."

"I'm not going to hit on a girl who's drunk and way too young for me. Besides, all we did the whole time she was awake was argue. She drives me fucking crazy." I'm not admitting to them that part of me sparked at every snarky comment she threw at me.

"She was hot, a fiery redhead. I'd do her," Flynn chimes in with his take on Tori.

"You fucking touch her and I will end you." The guys all fall quiet in front of me. Shit, where did that come from?

Flynn bursts out laughing. "Ooh, way too touchy for someone who is trying to tell us he's not interested."

"Flynn," I growl at him, not that he ever seems to get the message.

"What? Just stating the obvious here."

"You're wrong. Conversation finished." I glare at him to let him know I meant it.

"So, what's the plan about Rome, boss man?" Remington understands the message and changes the subject.

"It's fucked up my trip home to see Mum. I'll need to head over there to make sure everything gets sorted out. Laurence is on his way over tonight to get things moving, but I want to be in front of any negative publicity before it happens. Social media can escalate things so damn quickly." I'm already thinking ahead at what I need to get cleared here before I can leave.

"Hey, this is a work-free zone! Rem, how was the holiday?" Forrest is usually the quiet one in our group, but tonight he seems to be more vocal than usual.

When you work in the hotel business, it's actually hard to take a holiday and not be thinking of work. But Rem takes it to a new level of distraction.

"Oh man, diving with the sharks was insane. I almost crapped myself at one point when the great white swam straight at me and took the cage in his mouth. I thought his jaw was going to snap the metal. Fuck, it was so intense and the best adrenaline rush ever." The look of pure excitement on his face tells us that he lives for this shit.

"What, better than climbing Mount Kilimanjaro or heli skiing at the peak in the Swiss Alps, in the snow that is the most unstable and could have taken you down in an avalanche any minute? What the fuck is wrong with you?" Flynn asks, shaking his head at him as he lifts his beer to his mouth.

"You only live once. No point holding back." And Rem means it without hesitation. He has an unofficial death wish, I'm sure. It's why we let him go and get it out of his system on his own a few times a year, while we all sit in the safety of our cozy life here.

"True that, but it doesn't mean you should invite death any quicker than you need to, you crazy bastard. You can have that shark shit all on your own. When I swim, I want it in the calm waters of the Mediterranean." Forrest signals to the server that we need another round.

"Nothing beats surfing a wave off the coast of Australia," I say wistfully. "You don't even know what real waves are here, or a proper summer for that matter. Fuck, now I am really pissed I'm not heading home." The weather would be starting to heat up there, and maybe I could have found time to sneak in a few mornings of surfing.

"He's lying. Their water is bloody cold, and what he calls waves are the washing machine from hell. They have these weird-as-shit things called blue bottles that wrap themselves around you, stinging you worse than anything you have felt in your life. Plus, there are sharks in the water! At least Rem was in a cage." Flynn taps his card on the machine to pay the waitress for the beers she places in front of us.

"You're such a drama queen. How many times did you actually get in the water in Sydney in all the years you lived there?" I watch him squirm at having to admit he's scared of the ocean.

"Enough to know it is a disaster waiting to happen. Give me a beautiful pool in a resort any day of the week. Plus, the bikini beauties scattered around said pools are like a candy shop with so much to choose from." He spreads his arms out like he's the king of the ladies.

"You have no class. Women aren't there for you to ogle at," Forrest says, giving his brother the same glare I often see between the two of them. They might look similar, but their personalities couldn't be any further apart.

"I'm not twenty anymore. Don't make me sound like a dirtbag. But you can't tell me those women don't enjoy the sexy flirting as much as I do. Like Rem said, you only live once, so I'm going to enjoy every opportunity that appears before me." Grinning at us, we all know he is not short of playing the field. Nothing has changed since I met Flynn all those years ago. I'm not sure he will ever settle down with just one woman. I have my reasons to avoid commitment, but I'm not sure he has any, and I'm certainly not asking him. To each their own, I say.

Getting to the bottom of this last beer, I know it's time for me to head home. It's taken the edge off the frustration enough that I can go and get a bit more work done before bed, and then tomorrow will be another day.

"I'm off. See you all in the office in the morning. Flynn, don't forget the meeting with Gwenda Francis about the new branding concepts they have come up with. In my office instead of the board-room. Don't want Jocelyn getting wind of anything until I'm ready to reveal the final specs." Standing with my hand on his shoulder, he gives me a nod.

We might rib each other when we're together, but when it comes to work, the four of us are a tight unit and friends I couldn't do this without. They have my back and are pivotal in the success of the Darby Hotel chain. It might be my name on the door, but these guys are the driving force that are helping me bring it into the twenty-first century. With or without the board's help.

Flynn is sitting across from me at my desk in my office, much to his disgust, fidgeting while waiting for Ms. Francis to turn up.

"Not a good look when she is late for the first meeting," I groan at him. "I don't have time for incompetence."

"It's only two minutes past three, give her a break. You know London traffic." Flynn is far more laid back than me in these situations.

"Two minutes is twelve minutes late as far as I'm concerned," I say, typing more notes in a file I was working on before Flynn arrived.

The knock on the door signals her arrival, and Lucy brings her in.

The door opening, Lucy steps in as I stand from behind my desk, buttoning my jacket and walking around to greet her. Flynn rises at the same time.

"Nic, your appointment is here. Ms. Francis has been called away for personal reasons, so she has sent her second-in-charge for the meeting."

That pisses me off. Why didn't she tell me on Friday she would be on leave? Ugh, she is filling in for the boss and can't even be bothered getting here early to make a good impression.

Lucy steps to the side as she announces the substitute brand designer. "This is Victoria Packer of York and Webb Design and Marketing to see you."

My back is already up, and I'm ready to give her the cold shoulder for making me wait, until I see that vibrant red hair, the tantalizing lips covered in red lipstick, which I always consider a power color, and dressed in a navy business suit. Her shoulders are back, ready to make her impression walking into my office.

Until the moment her eyes meet mine and the shock knocks every bit of confidence from her face and all I see is despair and panic.

"Well, well, well. We meet again, Tori."

Flynn, standing beside me with his hands in his pockets, can't help himself. "Oh, this is just perfect." His snigger pisses me off. I'm trying to keep my own emotions in check, I don't need him making it worse.

"Not sure perfect is the word I'd use," Tori mutters under her breath.

Collecting herself, she steps toward me, hand forward. "Nice to see you, Mr. Darby, and we are sorry about the late change of plans. Ms. Francis sends her apologies and will be back in the office next week." I'm still getting used to hearing people call me Mr. Darby now. I made a promise to my grandfather I would carry on his name and that of my father.

"Oh, we are playing that game, are we. Okay, yes, please come in, Ms. Packer, and take a seat."

I point to the one next to Flynn's, and she sits down on the edge of it, back ramrod straight and sliding her laptop and portfolio out of her bag.

There's this determination radiating off her to show me she is not the woman I met on Friday. I'm going to look forward to this.

As she looks at me waiting for my cue to start, I leave the silence hanging that little bit longer while I take her in. While the messy argumentative Tori of Friday triggered all my senses, this power businesswoman has me intrigued and pushes buttons I didn't know I had.

Fuck, I'm in trouble here.

"The floor is yours, Ms. Packer, time to unwrap your best pieces." I know I'm being an asshole, but watching that slight flush on her cheeks, her legs pressing together that little bit tighter, gives me the rush of testosterone that I've been holding back.

But what makes my cock awaken is the fight that is twitching in her eyes.

Oh, bring it on, Tori, I love a good challenge.

Chapter Seven

VICTORIA

Every morning this week, I've been getting on the train feeling nervous I might run into him. Why he was on the train I'll never understand, considering he has his own personal driver. If I had a driver, there is no damn way I'd be doing this commute with every other unhappy person heading into London for the daily grind.

I can't get out of my head what happened on the weekend. My ankle still being a little tender is a good reminder of my stupidity.

Although it wasn't the first thing I noticed hurting when I woke on Saturday morning, in Elouise's spare bedroom.

Ugh, who invited the jackhammers into my head to take up residence. The throbbing isn't pleasant, and it won't even disappear if I keep my eyes closed. I knew I shouldn't have started drinking with Theo last night. Gwenda did warn me.

I roll to my side and reach for my phone on the charger, wondering what time it is, but all I can feel is empty space. No bedside cabinet that is usually there.

My brain starts racing. I'm almost scared to open my eyes because it is obvious I'm not in my own bed.

Very slowly opening just one eye, I breathe a sigh of relief at seeing the curtains of Elouise's spare room, a place where I have crashed many a night in the past when we have had girls' nights in. Opening both eyes, I stretch my arms above my head and my legs straight out. My arms don't move that easily because I still have on a business jacket. Crap, last night must have been messy, and how the hell did I end up here?

I need to find Lou to fill in the blanks for me. As I pull back the soft blanket that I'm wrapped nicely in, the smell wafting around me is familiar, but right now, I just need to get to the bathroom and then maybe I can think straighter. Standing and taking the first step, pain shoots up my leg. Great, what have I done? Limping down the hallway toward the bathroom, my head is still pounding from a killer hangover, and my mouth is as furry as it gets after a big night. I feel like rubbish as I enter the bathroom, and oh my, looking in the mirror, I look like it too.

I finish up in the bathroom after using my spare toothbrush Lou keeps here for me. Trying to tame the rat's nest on my head, I'm in search of my friend to find out how fabulously I made a mess of myself last night.

"And she has risen from the dead." Lou laughs as I pull out the stool at the kitchen counter, resting my head on the countertop. That's exactly what I feel like, death. I don't remember being that drunk at the bar, but hell, this morning it feels like I drank a bottle of tequila last night.

"What the hell happened?" I ask, lifting my head to see her placing a bottle of water in front of me and two painkillers.

"Take those so I don't get in to trouble." She giggles as she turns back to the stovetop.

"What?"

"Never mind." Her laughing continues, and I'm so confused. "I'm frying you up some breakfast, the fat will help with the hangover." I'm not totally convinced of that, but who am I to complain when she is looking after me.

"Spill the beans, Elouise, how the hell did I end up here?" I ask, swallowing down the pills and hoping to God they work quickly.

"Do you remember going out for drinks after work?"

I nod once but discover that doesn't make my head feel great. "Yeah, with Theo and Suzi and some of the other staff. I can't remember their names."

"Right, well, I wasn't there for that obviously, but perhaps next time I should be. Anyway, that's for another discussion. But all I know is you started messaging me after midnight, that you were in a car with a stranger and getting driven home."

"What the actual fuck, why would I do something so stupid like go somewhere with a complete stranger? Why didn't you stop me!" My head is spinning trying to remember any slither of information.

"Well, technically, he wasn't a complete stranger. You had met him before." Lou grins at me like she is enjoying my pain and panic.

"Come on, woman, no riddles, spill it!" I snap, getting frustrated.

She lifts the frying pan off the flames so she can concentrate on our conversation.

"All I know is you turn up in some luxury SUV and get carried into my house by the incredibly hot Australian god that you met on the train yesterday morning. You told me in the message he wouldn't let you catch the train, as it wasn't safe. He went all alpha caveman on you, and the next thing I know, you turn up on my doorstep fast asleep in his arms, with his personal driver carrying in your bag."

"Oh, for crying out loud, he must think I'm absolute trash," I groan, dropping my head into my hands. Lou starts to read out our texting exchange, and flashes of memories flood back into my head.

I can remember some of the exchange before the car trip, but that's it. Whatever happened in the car, I'm drawing a complete blank.

"And then he was all gruff with me, demanding I look after you, with instructions on what to do with your injured ankle—which I have no idea how that happened, so don't bother asking. Seriously, Tori, when you do something crazy, you go all in, don't you."

"I'm glad you think this is funny. I'm freaking mortified. And the only thing that is saving me from burying myself in some deep dark hole right now is that I'll never see him again, and he doesn't even know my name." This whole thing is so weird. "Thank God I didn't give him my real address either."

Lou reaches out and smacks my hand that's on the counter. "No, but he knows where I live, so he better not be a stalker. Then again, if he wants to visit me and talk dirty in that controlling voice from last night, I'll happily open the front door at one in the morning again."

"No, you goddamn won't. We dodged a bullet with the weirdo. Do not even entertain that idea. He could be some kind of sex pervert or something. Or one of those, you know, doms, who frequent clubs and pick up women to take back to his dirty dungeon." Lou is back cooking again, and all I can think is that all the words that came out of my mouth were crap. My gut tells me Nic is a good guy, but my head gives me all the preconceptions of what society believes all men are capable of. No one trusts anyone these days.

"Well, your drama queen exaggeration is dialed up to a ten this morning, isn't it. Maybe he was just being a gentleman and looking after a damsel in distress," she says, turning and looking at me, and we both burst out laughing.

"Nah, he's definitely a bad boy between the sheets. He just has that look about him. One I probably would have agreed to seeing for myself if it was offered. Thank God I didn't waste the chance, though, and then not remembered it in the morning. What a waste of a good roll in the sack that would have been." I daydream of his big hands roaming over my body. My hands running through his hair and his lips on my skin. "Ughh, a missed opportunity there," I grumble, taking a sip of the strong cup of tea that Lou places in front of me.

The plate of food that follows the cup of tea taunts my stomach. I'm hungry but not sure I can eat anything and keep it down.

"So, I'm guessing today is a TV binge day on the couch. Do you want some comfy clothes to change into?" Lou is now showing the sympathy that a true friend will give you in a hungover state.

"A hot shower and change of clothes sound perfect. Thanks for this." I look down at my plate that I haven't managed to touch yet.

"You can thank me once you have eaten it. Now get started, I'll find you those clothes." Watching her walk away, my mind drifts back, trying to remember more of last night's interaction with Nic. Why does a man who rubs me the wrong way keep taking up space in my mind? I need to move on and forget about the whole weird-ass day that was Friday. Wait, it wasn't the thirteenth, was it? That would explain so much if it was.

Glancing down at my watch tells me it's not even close. Instead, it was just one fucked-up Friday.

Arriving in the office each morning this week, I've been trying to avoid Theo, getting in earlier than him so I can get work done. I'm not sure what he actually does here except talk and distract everyone. How he keeps his job is a mystery. But that's not my problem to worry about. Even though I'm more experienced and have higher qualifications than him, he isn't reporting to me yet, so I'm just concentrating on my workload this week.

My nerves are racing about the presentation I have this afternoon. Gwenda said she would be in contact, and I have emailed her my thoughts, but she's been radio silent since she left. Nothing like being thrown in the deep end and hoping like hell you can swim. This is the chance I need to show the hierarchy what I can do and put my name to it without someone else making a claim over my ideas. It just would have been nice to get some guidance from her since she did the initial meeting. Plus, it's a new client, and from what I can get from the meeting notes, they are potentially going to be a big one going forward. Rebranding a whole hotel chain is not easy. When it's a very well-established business that has been around for over sixty years and nothing has changed, the pressure is intense.

But I feel the timing is right for a new way forward. I'm ready to help bring Darby Hotels into the modern era.

"You sure you don't want help for your meeting? I could come with you if you need me to," Theo asks again, popping his head over the cubicle wall, making me jump a little. My mind was buried in triple-checking my notes and making sure that I have everything printed for my portfolio.

"Thanks, but I'm okay." I hope he takes the hint that I'm busy freaking out and I don't need his nose in my face at the moment.

"It's a bit much, expecting someone so new to run such a big campaign. I could have taken it on with you and shared the workload. I'll tell Suzi that I'm heading with you to help out this afternoon. I'm sure it will look better with a united front. Plus, if they are old-school men, then they will expect a man in the meeting."

The hair on the back of my neck immediately stands up. My hands on my desk, I push myself to my feet. "You did not just say that as a woman I can't handle this on my own, right? What the actual fuck is wrong with you, Theodore! What century are you living in?" Everyone in the office is now looking at us, and I couldn't care less.

"That's not what I meant. Of course you can handle this project, but you know what these toffee-nose businessmen can be like. Calm yourself, Tori, otherwise you will explode before you make your meeting."

Breathe, Tori, big deep breaths before you take his head off. Try not to get fired in the first week for punching a fellow employee for being an absolute twat.

I need to talk to Gwenda when she returns about moving desks to another spot on my own as far from Theo as possible. Otherwise, I'll kill him before the month is out.

"You can tell Suzi that I have left for *my* meeting with Mr. Darby, and I won't be back this afternoon." Shoving my laptop into my bag, rougher than I probably should and collecting my portfolio folder off my desk, I stalk toward the elevator.

"You took it all wrong!" he yells from behind me, but I couldn't care what he is saying. I just need to find a café and get a cup of tea to calm myself before I arrive at the Darby Hotels head office. I don't have a lot of time, but I don't want to arrive there all wound up, looking unprofessional.

In hindsight, the cup of tea was a stupid idea, because now I'm rushing to be there on time. Why do I always do this to myself? It wasn't until I was in the bathroom fixing my lipstick that I looked at the time. I'm such a mess. Seriously, how do I even function to get through a day?

Coming through the entrance to the building, I've got two minutes to be upstairs so I'm not late. But I wasn't counting on having to explain to security the whole change in who was having the meeting with Mr. Darby. Luckily, I had my work ID, so they could see I was from York and Webb and let me through anyway. The security is necessary, I'm sure, but the guy behind the counter was in no hurry. So now I'm late, and it's not the best first impression I wanted to make. Thankfully it's only two minutes, which is nothing. Fingers crossed he is still held up in another meeting.

Standing in the foyer, I learn that he is ready and waiting for me, and it has my nerves on high alert. It's okay, Tori, you've got this. Trust in your instincts and ability. He is going to love your proposals.

Being introduced and stepping into the room, there is this moment where my heart feels like it stops dead.

Holy mother of Hell, it's him.

He looks as perfect as that first morning I saw him. Completely put together with not a hair out of place and a suit that fits him perfectly to accentuate all his greatest assets. Broad shoulders, with firm arms that fill out his jacket nicely. That jawline that shows all power and strength and a mouth that looks like it would be a nice kind of rough on my skin.

Christ, Tori, stop thinking of him like a piece of meat in the butcher shop window. Business meeting, remember?

With his friend standing beside him laughing at the two of us sizing each other up, I step forward with all the confidence I can muster and continue as if we haven't met before. Which, technically, we haven't met in this sort of environment, so I need to continue along those lines. All businesslike and without a hint of weakness the whole time I'm here.

"The floor is yours, Ms. Packer, time to unwrap your best pieces."

You'd like that, wouldn't you, Nic, to unwrap me. Well, not happening, no matter how much I might have fantasized about it. I'm so done with these male chauvinist pigs today. You might have served the first ball, Mr. Darby, but I plan on winning this, game, set, and match. Just watch this.

He sits back in his chair like he is the damn King of England, I find his stillness unnerving. I'm partway through what our process would be with a complete rebrand and how we would handle every step of the process for them. His associate, Mr. Taylor, asks a few questions, but Nic is just sitting there with the blank face, like a canvas that doesn't have one spot of paint on it yet. No story to tell and not giving away a thing.

Keep pushing through, believe in yourself.

"I think you will agree that the name Darby Hotels is old, outdated, and it's a bit boring in today's world. What worked in the

1960s is not going to take you into the current world of tourism. So, we have come up with a concept of modernizing the name of the chain, along the lines of the way everything is shortened with social media and the younger generations loving acronyms. To do this, we need to take away your family name, as it no longer brings you value in your branding. We want it to be known world-wide and something that stands out aside from the family name but is still associated with it in some small way." The anticipation in the room is like we are waiting to hear the meaning of life. To be honest, I wish I'd had more time to work on my ideas, but with such a short turnaround, I had to go with the idea that seemed the strongest by the end of Sunday to give me time to pull it all together before today's meeting.

"Please remember that this is the very early stages of our thoughts and proposals. There will be a lot of refining and design work to be done before anything is finalized. But this is a concept that we firmly believe has some merit and a strong direction to go forward with erasing the old."

Taking a breath, I start my final pitch and hope to God I have done enough to get this new account over the line.

"The new name will be a simple one that will roll off people's tongues," I say, placing the concept board on the desk in front of them both. "Welcome to *'The D'* formerly known as The Darby Hotel." Holding my breath, the silence in the room is not a good start.

The waiting is killing me as Nic looks at his colleague, with a storm raging in his eyes.

He stands and walks around his desk so he is close enough I could almost touch him. My skin is tingling as he leans down so his face is level with mine. His alluring scent is tantalizing me, while giving me that same comfort I've been sleeping with the last few nights, from his smell that was on the blanket he left me warmly wrapped in.

But as the words start leaving his mouth and slashing the air in the room like a sword, the comfort is ripped from me as quickly as it came.

"If you think I'm paying your company a hundred thousand pounds to rename my hotel The Big D, you are out of your mind. What the hell were you thinking about while developing this?" Anger is now creeping into his voice, his body radiating annoyance as he strides away from me. "Can you imagine the ridicule I would get? 'Where are you staying when you travel? Oh, I'm staying at the Big D.' That might be the first letter in my surname, but it is also a letter that carries so much more weight. I'm surprised you didn't also come up with calling it The G. The jokes that would roll off people's tongue when they ask for directions to find the spot where The G is." His rant is totally out of control. What is wrong with him?

I don't know if I'm about to burst into tears at him tearing my proposal to shreds or if the rage that is also building is about to let loose.

It doesn't take long for the tears to be pushed aside, and I let him have it.

"The G, something I'm sure you are frequently being questioned by women about. Doubt you know where to find it or what to do with it, if you got to that point. As for your absolutely disgusting critique, what the hell is wrong with you, Mr. Darby! Is that all you had on your mind the whole time I was talking, your dick? Really! In a professional business meeting and you stoop to this. I could have had that conversation with you on Friday night, and you probably would have got a laugh from me. But here, in your office, I expected so much more respect and a working discussion on your likes and dislikes." I'm also up out of my chair and find myself going toe to toe with him.

"Likes? There is nothing to like. The disrespect to my father and grandfather's name is enough for me to tell you to get out and take your childish ideas with you. Is this the best you have, Ms. Packer? I pictured you having more to give me."

"Oh, I'll give you plenty, Mr. Darby. You have no idea the pressure I have been under to get you a whole proposal in four days, including one of those days which I couldn't work even if I tried, because I was so confused and freaked by how I got home from a night out or what the strange man did with me in the hours I don't remember. I started this job on Friday, got this dumped in my lap, and wasn't here for the brief of what you wanted. My new boss is unreachable, and I'm just supposed to read the mind of a client I had no idea was you. I don't know your hotels well, and of course, being as high-handed and demanding as you are, you demanded this brief in an unrealistic timeframe, just because you can. And against all my better judgment, I'm about to tell you to stick this contract where the sun doesn't shine, but I can't afford to lose this job, so I won't. Unlike you, sitting up here and having all your little minions running around at your beck and call across Europe, I have to work for a living, and the way you just reacted, it looks like I'll be searching the job ads again because I have just lost a major contract in my first week. So, to be honest, I don't have anything more to give you, because you have just managed to strip any confidence I had left after the last asshole I battled in the workplace. And to be honest, for the last three days I've been secretly hoping to see you again, a thought I totally regret now. The mystery man is no longer someone I want to find out more about. He's about to become nothing more than a bad memory."

All of a sudden, it's like a switch has been flipped in my head, and I slap my hand over my mouth to stop another word from escaping. I can't believe what I have done. What kind of hold does this man have over me? Every time I am near him, all I seem to do is yell at him for being a dick to me.

I can see the steam almost pouring off his head. His eyebrow has this twitch thing happening which scares me that he is about to unleash on me more than he already has, and truth be told, I probably deserve it. Mr. Taylor is just sitting there with his eyes flitting between us, probably unsure what to even say. Because not one part of this meeting has been professional since the moment I uttered the words, "name it The D."

"Lucy!" Nic screams out while I'm still glaring at him in shock.

His fists are clenched at his sides and his mouth is in a rigid straight line. With his feet slightly apart, he is standing in such a defensive pose. I feel like I'm about to be removed from the office and quickly escorted from the building.

The door opens quickly, and his rather-worried-looking secretary comes in, ready for her instructions.

Before he says the words, I move and start packing away my information that is on his desk. I'd rather keep my dignity and walk out on my terms than be thrown out by security for being a raving lunatic.

"The private jet that is on standby for Australia, change it and have it ready to fly to Rome tomorrow, then we will need it for the next week. Ms. Packer here will be accompanying me on the trip. That will be all."

Sliding my laptop into my bag, all of a sudden in my head, I compute what he just said.

"Wait, what? What do you mean I will be going with you? I'm not getting in another car with you, let alone a fucking private jet!"

"This just became a non-negotiable part of the contract. You claim you don't know my hotels. Well, now you will. My driver will pick you up at eight am tomorrow morning. I suggest you give Lucy your correct address on the way out because we both know that the bed I carried you to was not your own. I will give you a week to re-present this proposal to me, and then we will forget today ever happened. I will clear it with your company that you will be traveling with me as part of the contract negotiations, and you will be compensated well for your time. See you tomorrow and don't be late!"

"Do I need to come to be the referee for the week?" His friend's voice breaks the quiet of the intense stare-off we are having, with a bit of comedy. Instead, it just brings more yelling.

"No!" we both look at him and scream at the same time.

"Flynn, please see Ms. Packer out and have her details passed on to Lucy. Good day, Ms. Packer, I look forward to our week together. I'm sure it's going to be a joy for the both of us." Then he stalks straight past me and out the door, slamming it on his way out. I'm left standing in his office with Mr. Taylor, absolutely gobsmacked.

I don't know whether to scream in anger or sit down and let the tears fall. Why do I always seem to find the bastards in this world. And the guy that just stormed out of here I think takes the top of the list of bastards I've ever met. All the craziness is racing around my head, but the loudest thought that pushes to the front is that I'm so freaking confused.

"What the hell just happened?" The whisper finally leaves my lips.

"Well, my guess is… Nic just gave away more about himself than you will understand." Mr. Taylor walks to me and places his hand gently on my arm as a sign of kindness after a moment of sheer hostility. "Come with me and I'll get you a stiff drink in the boardroom. I have a feeling we could both use one." As he motions toward the door, I don't even know how to move my feet.

"Mr. Taylor…"

"Please, call me Flynn. I have a feeling we are about to become firm friends," he says, his eyes softening.

"Flynn, am I in danger with him?" I know it's a stupid question to ask his friend because he is not the most objective to give me the truth, but I can't help but panic slightly.

"Oh, Tori, the answer is, yes, absolutely. But not in the terrible way you are picturing. Trust me, he is worth the risk of finding out." Flynn opens the door in front of me. I'm still totally confused, and I know the last thing I need is alcohol. That is what got me into all this trouble.

"I think I'll skip the drink, Flynn. I need to leave now," I say, walking toward Lucy who gives me a soft compassionate look of feeling sorry for me.

"I understand. Let's just give Lucy what she needs, and then I'll take you downstairs and arrange a car to take you home. It's the least we can do."

Just wanting to get out of this office, I tell Lucy everything she asks. The ride down in the elevator is deathly quiet. I'm not sure Flynn knows what to say to me, so it's easier to say nothing.

Exiting the building, I see the familiar navy-colored Range Rover SUV from Friday night, and there's a man waiting at the passenger door for me.

"Thank you, Wallace. Please get Ms. Packer home safely."

Feeling so numb, I just want to escape this mess and work out how I can disappear before tomorrow morning.

"Tori." Flynn once again places his hand softly on my arm. Turning to look over my shoulder, I see a genuine man who wants to help me in the only way he can.

"Give him a chance to show you the real man he is. What you just saw upstairs is thirty-nine years of pain breaking free. No one has ever scratched the surface of his tough outer shell, but you, little lady, just made the first crack in it. It's something I never thought would be possible."

"I don't understand." And to be honest, I'm too mentally exhausted to think about it.

"No, but if you get on that plane tomorrow, I have a feeling by the end of the week, you will."

"I don't know... I just don't know." Sliding into the car, the driver closes the door, and I burst into tears.

Chapter Eight

VICTORIA

"What's the worst that could happen?" Elouise is laughing at me from the other end of the couch.

"Ummm, I don't know. I get on some private jet, fly to fuck knows where, never to be seen again," I huff, throwing my hands in the air with frustration at the absolute mess my brain feels right now.

She's typing away on her laptop, where she has been googling Nicholas Darby for the last thirty minutes since she arrived at my house from work, because I sent her an SOS message. Girl code for I'm freaking the fuck out over a guy, so get your ass here right now!

"Or better still, you could join the mile-high club in a private jet, with some billionaire hottie who owns a hotel chain spread all over Europe. Sounds really freaking terrible to me too. I mean, he is the talk of social media and all over the internet. It's not like he would do something that stupid, like kidnap a woman and take her to his lair."

"Why do I get the sense you are enjoying this? If you were really my friend, you would be telling me it's the stupidest idea ever on this planet and I should lock myself in my house tomorrow, claiming I have the plague or something drastic!" I can't help thinking back to Friday when all I wanted was for it to be a new start of something fantastic. For my life to change for the better. Then Nic appears out of nowhere and everything turns upside down in a heartbeat. There is no way he is the new something-better I was praying for. He drives me insane!

"Have you even searched this man? His story is pretty interesting." She looks across at me, her head still stuck in the computer.

"Like I even had time to do anything in the limited days I had. If you remember Saturday, I was a hungover mess, and then Sunday all I could think about was the man that drove me home to keep me safe, yet I was missing part of the night. Don't tell me that wouldn't freak you out too!" I'm not sure she is even listening to me, obviously engrossed in what she is reading. While she is busy stalking Nic, I need to message Suzi and Theo before they arrive at the office tomorrow and wonder what the hell is going on.

> Tori: I won't be in the office for the rest of the week. Have to travel for work.

> Suzi: What? I didn't have that in your diary.

> Theo: WTF you've been here 4 days and are getting to travel. I've never travelled for a job.

> Suzi: Shut up, Theo, and let the girl explain. Where are you going?

I'm not someone who likes to lie to anybody, but in this case, I'm too embarrassed to answer the truth.

> Tori: Mr. Darby wanted me to get a better understanding of the hotels to help with the rebranding. So, we are visiting some of them.

Suzi: What? As in you and Mr. Darby are travelling together. OMG he's a total babe!

Tori: No, he's a total asshole!

Theo: That's what they all say when they are pretending not to like the boss.

Tori: It's a business, Theo, what part of that did you miss?

Theo: I missed the trip, that's what. If you had taken me with you, I would be travelling with you tomorrow. This sucks big time!

Suzi: Stop complaining, Theo. Maybe if you worked harder, you'd be given bigger accounts.

Oh, that was harsh, although I totally agree. Theo is a nice enough guy, just not good at his job. I don't have the mental capacity to listen to his childish complaining right now.

Tori: Got to run, I have a lot of work to do before tomorrow. See you next week.

Theo: Does that mean you will miss Friday drinks?

Suzi: Obviously, stupid. Have fun, Tori, call me if you need anything.

Tori: Thanks, Suzi. Theo, there will be another Friday.

Putting my phone down, Lou starts up again with whatever she has found out.

"Did you know he was raised in Australia by his single mum and his father died before he was born? His grandfather found him a few years ago and brought him to London to inherit his empire. Like, what the actual fuck? One day you are poor, then the next thing you are a billionaire and living a life of luxury." Lou spins her laptop around for me to see what she's reading.

"It doesn't give him the right to be such an asshole, though," I say, before taking the computer from her and reading through the article myself.

"Oh yeah, a real asshole. He hated your idea you pitched him, but instead of kicking you to the curb, he is flying you all over Europe to check out his hotels with him. On a private jet, all expenses paid, and then giving you a second chance to come up with a totally new proposal. Yeah, he is such a dick." When I look up at her, she is rolling her eyes at me, but I know she has a point.

"There sure are a lot of different women hanging off his arm every time he is photographed out in public. I suppose that's what money buys you then, pretty arm candy."

There is something bugging me about all these pictures. He is never smiling. Why is that? Don't any of these women make him happy? Maybe he should be reexamining his attitude and that may change how the women perceive him. Although, I'm sure by these photos, how they look at him is as a man who has lots of money and is sexy as sin. To me, that is not enough to fall in love with a man. I want more than that in whoever I finally fall for. And I don't plan for that to be for many years yet. I have a career to build… on my own without the help of a man.

"That's it! Give it back, little miss negativity. I'm taking your place on this trip. Tell him you're sick and your assistant will take your place. I'll start googling now how to be a designer and marketing guru. It can't be that hard. Pick a name better than The Big Dick Hotel, draw a logo, and pick out some fancy colors to decorate the inside with. That's what you do, isn't it?" Lou is trying to keep a straight face, although not very well.

I can't help laughing out loud. The more I laugh, the more the tension leaves my body.

"You… do… my… job." I can't even string a sentence together. "You teach five-year-olds and spend all day tying up their shoes and wiping snotty noses," I say, trying to get myself under control, even though Lou is laughing along with me now.

"Hey, I spend a good part of my day working with colors and trying to make things sound way more exciting than they are. I think I'm perfectly qualified."

"Well, I better watch my back, otherwise you will be taking both my job and my man."

Shit, why did I just say that!

Nic's not my man, nor would I want him to be. Well, maybe just a smidgen, but we aren't going there. Or even for a moment in time, just to taste him and see if the saying is true, about if a man with big feet has a big dick. But who am I kidding, there is no way, no how, I'm even in this man's league, and after the way this morning went, I doubt I want to be either.

Seeing the smirk on Elouise's face at what just fell out of my mouth, I point my finger at her. "Don't you even say a word, not one!"

Giving me the most dramatic "who, me?" action, she pretends to zip her lips, but I know that is never going to happen. Neither of us can keep our mouths shut when it comes to guys.

I resign myself to the fact that I knew from the moment he opened his arrogant mouth I was always going to take the flight tomorrow, and my head is screaming the biggest red alert in my brain.

"Oh crap, what the hell will I wear?" Both of us jump off the couch and run toward my bedroom, giggling like schoolgirls, knowing the next few hours will be fashion parades of outfits, trying to dress like I can fit into his world. Well, just for a few days, anyway.

NICHOLAS

I have no idea why I did what I did this afternoon.

After storming out of the office, I came home and threw myself into work because I thought the stupidity of my actions would unravel themselves in my brain to make sense. But instead, all it's done is make me ponder how I'm going to manage a week with a woman who pushes my buttons like no one has ever done before. Yet I can't stop thinking about having her underneath me in all sorts of sensual ways.

Knowing that can never happen doesn't stop my cock from reacting to the thoughts anyway.

She infuriated me so much in the meeting, talking about my family name with such disrespect. Doesn't she know how important it is to me and the reputation of the business? Did she even bother to research me? Fuck, my whole life is broadcast across the internet. Most of it is bullshit, yet people will believe it anyway. That's what they do. I don't care what they say about me, because all I care about is what my mother thinks of me. It's my motto in my life and business decisions. If it's not something my mother would be proud of, then it's not the right decision. At times, it's questionable whether I have stayed true to that. Sadly, today is one of those days.

Running for an hour on the treadmill with a mixture of old-school Aussie rock, AC/DC, Cold Chisel, and Jimmy Barnes screaming in my ears didn't even help. All I could think of when the song "Thunderstruck" came on was her. The red whirlwind of fire that stood in my office and challenged me like no one ever has. She struck me, all right, and not in a good way. I lost my mind. To the point I'm now spending the next seven days with her. I can't seem to spend more than five minutes around her before something goes wrong. How will either of us survive a week in close confines? Maybe I can shut it down early, make up some emergency that I need to come back to London for. Or get one of the boys to take my place.

Wait, no, that's a terrible idea. I wouldn't trust Flynn or Rem anywhere near Tori. The only one I might contemplate is Forrest, but then they always say you should watch out for the quiet ones. And to be honest, Tori would eat Forrest alive. That would just be cruel to make him suffer through that.

Don't get me wrong, these three men are the best friends and business associates that I could ask for, and I would trust them with the security code to my safe. But deep down in my gut, I know that I'm not letting any one of them near Tori.

That thought alone sends dangerous alarms off in my head.

Rolling to the side in my bed and looking out the window, I wish I could see the stars, but yet again, it was another gray day in London, with plenty of depressing cloud cover. The clock beside my bed shows one twenty-five am, and I'm still overthinking it all. I need to get some sleep to find the calm in my body. If I turn up at the airport tomorrow wound up this tight, then it's just going to start the trip off badly.

Closing my eyes, the voice in my head finds the rational spot. This is a business trip. Treat it like one. You are not with a woman you want to fuck. She is here to get a job done. And that job isn't me. Treat her like Jocelyn, a necessary part of the job that you tolerate but will never get close to. That's it, the key to getting through this week.

It's like my brain found the answer, and sleep finally finds me. In my head, I just keep repeating the mantra for the week.

Business, not pleasure, and do not fucking touch her.

As I drift off to sleep, the more mixed up the mantra gets, until it becomes, *"pleasure of fucking her,"* and the dream that will also end up being my nightmare begins.

I could have taken the car with Wallace to pick Tori up, but that would be giving her the wrong impression. Plus, I need to put distance between us in place from the beginning of the trip, for my own sanity.

Sitting on the plane waiting for her, I wonder if she did as I asked and made sure she was ready on time. If she thinks I'll put up with disorganization, then she's mistaken. Hearing a car door outside the jet, I look at my watch. I'm a little surprised that she's early. I'm settled already in my seat, waiting for her to enter, feeling apprehensive with the anticipation of how this is all going to go.

The steward escorts her into the cabin, and stepping to the side, I finally see her. And to be honest, I think for the first time I am actually seeing Tori's vulnerable side. The confidence she had marching into my office yesterday morning is long gone.

Wanting to put her at ease a little, I stand and extend my hand to her. Tentatively, she reaches out, and as we shake, there is that persistent niggle in my body from her touch. One I push down and choose to ignore.

"Good morning, Ms. Packer, please make yourself comfortable in whichever seat suits you," I say, motioning around the cabin which has eight single seats available, minus the one I have already claimed which is at the back of the plane, letting me see everything in front of me. More importantly, seeing Tori.

"Good morning, Mr. Darby. Thank you for this opportunity." She slides into a seat that is the farthest one from where I am already set up. I understand why she's choosing to avoid me after our encounter yesterday.

"You're welcome, and can we drop the formalities? It's going to be a long week otherwise." Although I love being referred to as Mr. Darby, and the memories it holds, I just want to try to relax her a little. The tension in her body is evidence of the way she is feeling. Her shoulders are hunched, and the constant fidgeting of her hands are tell-tale signs she's nervous.

"Okay, should I call you Nicholas?" Her sassiness is starting to raise its head again.

"Only if you want me to call you Victoria." Which I do like on her. It suits her, and the vision of her asleep on my shoulder creeps back into my mind; that is how I see her as Victoria. Her quiet beauty radiating from her in her stillness. Usually, she is so unaware of how others see her because she is too busy trying to tackle the world.

"Fine, Nicholas it is then." Ughh, I can see the antagonistic Tori has now decided to join us. Like I said, we can't last five minutes without irritating each other.

"Can I organize a drink for you, Victoria?" I ask, emphasizing her name, trying to piss her off enough she will drop it, but instead, I see her confidence picking up as she sits a little taller in the seat, rolling her shoulders back.

"I don't think that's a good idea, do you?" she says, placing the belt over her lap. "We both have a lot of work to do." She's already reaching into her bag to pull out her laptop and phone. "Considering you aren't the only portfolio I have to work on this week. I do have other clients who are important, although not so demanding."

And there it is. The first barb thrown for the day.

"Not as important as me. You are now on my time, and you will concentrate on me and my proposal and only that. Nothing else." The harshness of my words takes us both aback a bit. Why does she manage to draw it out in me?

"Yeah, right, and who is going to tell my boss that when she returns?" Her eyes are now challenging me.

Taking my phone from my jacket pocket, I scroll through the contacts and press call on the one I need. I push the loudspeaker button so Tori can hear every word. Apparently, that's how she uses her phone, anyway.

"Doug, Nic Darby here, how has your morning been already?" I say, smiling at Tori like I hold all the candy and she can't have any of it.

"Nic, going grand so far, but it's early yet. What can I do for you, did Ms. Packer arrive for the trip with you?" His voice is a smooth one, but I can tell he is distracted with something else while we're talking. Something I can admit to doing when I'm in the office too.

"Yes, yes. She is here now with me. If you could just inform her that she doesn't need to worry about any other projects this week. She seems to be under the impression she must still complete all her other work while she is on my time." I stare straight at her with sheer delight at the cringing she is doing while I talk to the CEO of York and Webb, which is her ultimate boss. One she probably hasn't even had time to meet face to face yet.

"Oh, certainly not. Ms. Packer, please just give Mr. Darby all your attention for the next week. Learn his business and help him to come up with the best rebranding project that we possibly can. I will make sure your other projects are handled. Is that understood?" The stunned look that she initially had has been wiped clean off her face and replaced with fury. Through gritted teeth, she replies to

Doug in a super-sweet and polite voice, "Of course, Mr. York. I'm sorry the brief that was relayed to me overnight may not have been complete with all your instructions. I will email management the other projects that need dealing with straight away." Flicking the top of her laptop open roughly, she sends daggers at me at the same time.

"Wonderful. Have a productive trip, Nic, and I will talk as soon as you return."

"Thanks, Doug, talk soon," I say, hanging up the call and smiling at her with great satisfaction.

"Well, that's settled then. Sit back and relax while we fly to Rome," I say, taking my seat. I watch her typing like a demon, trying to get her email sent before we need to shut off our devices for take-off.

"Settled? The only thing that is settled is that you are in fact the asshole I told Elouise you were," she mumbles under her breath. I want to answer her, but I figure there will be plenty of time for our first full screaming match. No need to rush things.

As Tori slams down the lid of her computer, I can't help but smile. Let's see if she is talking to me again by lunchtime. The bets are on the answer being no, but the Australian charm has been known to sway plenty of women.

The flight gives me time to catch up on my emails so that when we arrive in the hotel, I can devote my time to assessing the damage with Marco and see how everything is functioning through the interruption to business. I'm sure Laurence and Marco have it all under control, but I want to see it for myself.

Landing in Rome after a smooth flight, it doesn't take long for the hotel's chauffeur to whisk us through the packed Italian streets toward the hotel. Today has already become a normal workday. I was consumed with emails in the air and now phone calls as soon as we touched down. Tori and I haven't spoken a word to each other since the plane, and I can feel the tension coming off her of how uncomfortable she feels around me. I should be making an effort with her, but the calls just keep coming. I don't think she is still as annoyed as she was on the plane with me, but I can't say we are friends yet.

"Thanks, Lucy, I'll sign off on it as soon as I have read the report. Let Flynn and Rem know I want to see their thoughts on the second report by five pm today. Can you also tell Forrest I want the numbers on that new location by tomorrow. Talk soon." Lucy is used to just listening as I talk at her, it's how we work. We don't waste time with idle chitchat.

As I push the end button on the phone, Victoria shifts slightly on the seat, reminding me that she's beside me. I do get caught up in work, and once I'm in that zone, my surroundings sometimes get blurred. I can't say I forgot she was there because her perfume is wrapped around me like a lustful blanket that I can't get away from. It's just that I wasn't giving her the time of day. I should be reading the report on my computer that Lucy just sent me, but my conscience pokes at me that maybe I'm proving Tori right and I am an asshole.

"Sorry, Victoria, my phone won't stop and nor will work. You will just need to shadow me for a few days and take in what you can from the hotels and what is around us. I'm sure you weren't expecting a sight-seeing holiday with me—or were you?" I look across to find her watching the world speeding past her from the car.

"Pfft. Furthest thing from my thoughts. I imagine you are an all-work, no-play kind of man anyway. Of course, except for your nights out with the disco ball woman." Her contempt for me is welcoming and will help us to keep this a professional work trip. I don't care how much she doesn't like me really, as long as she gets the job done, that's all I care about.

But I can't help but laugh at her description of Simona that I was out with last Friday night. She's not a regular fling but someone who is always pleasurable. And if it wasn't for Tori's interruption, then Simona would have ended up at home in my bed with me, enjoying such pleasure. Looking back, I'm glad that didn't happen. Although blowing off some steam that night might have helped me get through the frustration of the next week.

"Disco ball woman, really, Victoria, how old are you?" It was a rhetorical question but one I'm quite curious to hear.

"Old enough to be able to pick a money muncher when I see one." Turning to look sideways at me, I can see her disgust at someone she knows nothing about. Simona is not someone I would marry, but she's nice enough and has never done anything bad to me.

"What the fuck is a money muncher? Or do I really want to know." Why does nothing that comes out of Tori's mouth ever surprise me. I have only known her a few days but already nothing shocks me.

"Someone who will sink her teeth into anyone who looks like money. Nibbling away until she can taste the main meal and claiming him by the end of dessert." She looks quite satisfied with herself for being able to educate me in the language of the weird and wonderful world of Victoria.

Deep belly laughs in the middle of a workday are not what I'm used to, but there is nothing stopping the laughter from escaping me right now. I can imagine what Flynn would make of Tori's description, and he would probably add a few colorful words to it.

"Why is it so funny?" Tori demands to know.

"If only you knew how close to the truth you probably are. Did you make that saying up?" I ask, trying to control myself to get the conversation back on track.

"Of course I did. Oh, and I know I am describing them perfectly. Just because I don't have money or some high social status like you all do, doesn't mean I don't see through people to their real motives. And every woman in that bar on Friday night was eyeing you as a piece of prize-worthy food. Surely you aren't dumb enough to think they are all in there looking for love," she says, rolling her eyes like I'm stupid if it hasn't yet occurred to me.

Her words about her social status piss me off, though. I have never looked down on a person in my life, over the size of their paycheck or where they live. She is again making assumptions but this time about me. I want to set her straight, but that would be giving away too much of myself which I vowed not to do this morning before I even left my apartment. The words *business trip* again spring into my mind, but it doesn't stop me from instead wanting to know more about Tori's personal life. Pushing her to open up and reveal more of herself, no matter if it's a one-sided information trade.

"And what makes you the expert on the dating scene, Victoria?" It occurs to me that I don't even know if she has a boyfriend, or a husband for that matter. Only that mystery guy from Friday night which I've been thinking about. But the answer to my question could also be the answer to my prayers. She will be so far off limits then that my dick will finally shrink back to a normal state— somewhat disappointed, of course, but still, it will be the best outcome.

"Didn't say I was." Getting defensive, she takes her hands and rubs them on her skirt to wipe the sweat off them. Paying attention to her delicate hands, I don't notice a ring, so marriage is off the table, but now I need to know more.

"What does your boyfriend say about you being so opinionated on your fellow women?"

Her cheeks flush slightly as her chin drops. "I don't have one and wouldn't care what he thought if I did." She pushes her shoulders back and sits up that little bit straighter as she finishes the sentence. "And it's just the way I want it."

Those words are like the challenge I didn't want to hear. I'm already fighting an unwanted attraction to a woman too young for me and a business associate. But my ridiculous manhood loves to think I could break her. Have her begging to be mine before she has time to breathe a word of complaint.

Trying to snap myself out of the image of her on her knees, I fire my answer back without even thinking. "Good to know. Nothing wrong with living a single life. I've done it all my adult life, and I can't see it changing anytime soon." And for the first time in my life, that truth tasted like vinegar rolling off my tongue. Why is that?

"Doesn't surprise me, but okay, I'll ask the question. Why are you still single?" Her voice is softer now, and she looks like she is genuinely curious.

I debate in my head what to say, but in the end the truth is the easiest.

"I don't believe in love." For the first time, hesitation creeps into my thoughts at that statement, because lately, I'm not entirely sure it's true. But what I do know is what I decided early on in my life—love is not for me, and that hasn't changed.

"Then your life must be a very sad and lonely place to be."

Looking into her eyes that are full of pity for me, and the worst thing is, I think she might be right.

Not that I will ever admit that to her or to anyone else.

Luckily, we are pulling up in front of the hotel which saves me from a reply. The conversation is over, and I'm ever so thankful for that.

Am I any different to my mother who lived her whole life on her own?

But I already know the answer to that. She loved and lost.

I've just never loved, yet feel lost anyway.

Chapter Nine

VICTORIA

Who doesn't believe in love?

I might not be looking for it right now, but I know it's out there for when I'm ready. Otherwise, what's the point of life?

I suppose it explains Nic to some degree. His hardness that he tries to portray, and what Flynn told me yesterday about him never letting anyone in. What happened to this man to make him so cynical? Someone obviously broke his heart, and she must have done a damn good job of it. He claims he has never had a relationship, but something happened to make him so distant. It shouldn't interest me, but the truth is, I desperately want to know now. Like, I'm making it my mission this week, with a sort of desperation for knowing him and to get behind that wall. I want to find out who the real Nicholas Darby is.

Just as the driver opens my door and I get out of the car, Nic's phone rings again. He wasn't kidding when he said it never stops.

"Flynn, is it important?" His demanding voice is back after the one tender moment we had in the car.

Standing next to the car waiting, I watch his expression get harder. Whatever Flynn is saying, Nic is not happy about it. By the way he's running his hand through his hair, I would say he's frustrated and trying to think hard.

"Are you kidding me!? She is so close to being shown the door no matter what my grandfather said." When he turns away from me to continue talking, I get to check out the view. And not just of his firm shoulders and tight ass that his trousers frame nicely. But the street around the hotel.

I didn't tell Nic that I have never left the UK and that my first flight was on his fancy private jet. Nothing like starting at the top. No flight will ever measure up to this one, that's for sure. Luckily, I had already applied for a passport a few years ago, for my future travels. So, with this being my virgin trip, to be standing in Rome right now is surreal. It's the first tick on my bucket list of destinations that I want to travel to. Pity I won't really get to see much of it, by the way he was talking, but hey, I can say I have walked on Italian soil.

Everything is just like I imagined—old. The street in front of the hotel is cobbled stone, and everything around us was probably built hundreds of years ago. The history here is something that I need to know more about. The thought pops into my head that I need to get a journal and start documenting everywhere I visit and what I see. So, one day, when I'm old and gray, I can look back and read through the memories of what I saw on my travels. Or to be able to read it to my children or grandchildren would be a treasure. Especially when all that family time is going to be so far in the future that I will have enough to write a whole book or two on my adventures.

If I can get some time on my own, I want to see the Trevi Fountain. I already know what I will be wishing for — that the fountain is the first of many tourist attractions I'll visit all around the world. When I was growing up, I watched a *Lizzie Maguire* movie over and over again, where she traveled to Rome. I used to dream that someday I would stand where she did in front of the fountain, flip the coin over my shoulder, and find my man, you know, the love-of-your-life kind. But now that just makes me laugh because I'm not that young dreaming girl anymore. Instead, my dreams are far bigger now and don't involve a man to make them happen.

"I'm going to need more than luck. You might want to say a few Hail Marys that I'm still in one piece when I tell her. Later." Nic's voice brings me back out of my memory, only to see him turning toward me, and his body language tells me he's pissed. Seems to be a regular occurrence for him.

Walking toward me, he grasps my hand and whispers in my ear in a deep voice that sends shivers up and down my body. "Don't make a scene, I'll explain everything when we get to the room. I need you to pretend to be my girlfriend. Please, just trust me." He pulls back, looking down at me with piercing eyes.

My stupid brain is trying to make sense of what he just said. I try to pull my hand from his, but his grasp just gets tighter.

"What the hell are..." My voice increases in volume as I start to lose my shit.

"Tori." His deep growl stops me mid-sentence. It's the kind of voice that I can't ignore as much as I want to, I just can't.

"Please." Although his word comes out of him in such a forceful way, it's almost a plea from a man who has never had to rely on anyone for anything in his life. The constant personality changes in this man just confuse me, until I can't even think straight. Which leads me to shut my mouth and just nod yes to him.

His grip on my hand releases slightly so he is no longer cutting off the circulation in my fingers as he tries to stop me from escaping his grasp.

"Thank you," he grumbles. As we start toward the doors of the hotel, Nic is greeted by the doorman, and his reply I'll say is less than civil, but at least he still replies.

Stepping around the mess of the foyer, I can tell it's stressing Nic more than he was five seconds ago, and I didn't think that was possible. One of the staff is talking to him and points him toward the boardroom where they seem to have made a makeshift check-in desk, where a woman stands, ready to assist guests. I don't know what happened, but there is a problem, and I'm guessing that's why we're here.

"*Ciao*, Mr. Darby. Nice to see you. Do you want me to call Signor Rossi?" Her hand is already on the phone, and I can tell she's nervous. Who wouldn't be if the big boss of the company is standing in front of you and looking like he wants to smash something.

"No, *grazie*. Please tell him my girlfriend and I will have lunch in our room, then when I'm ready, I'll speak to him." I can tell he is trying to show some politeness but is not doing very well at it. "Is my usual room ready?" he asks, holding his free hand out for the key. I hope like Christ that it is, because I pity this girl if she has to say no.

"*Si*, Mr. Darby. I hope you have a pleasant stay with us. Please let us know if we can help in any way. Your bags are already being placed in your room as we speak." Must be nice never to have to worry about anything in your life, having people wait on you every minute of the day.

Nic takes the key cards, with what I would say is almost a snatch, but he manages to pull back the aggression at the last minute.

"*Grazie*."

Looking at her name badge so I can acknowledge her personally, I try to smile as big as I can so she doesn't feel like it's her fault that my supposed boyfriend is being such a prick to her.

"Thank you, Francesca. I'm sure the stay will be lovely." But my words are drifting behind me, as I'm already being dragged to the elevator.

"Nic!" I curse under my breath.

"Don't," he says. As we wait for the elevator doors to open, he looks straight ahead.

What the fuck is wrong with this man?

Finally, the doors open, and we enter an empty car. As soon as the doors are closed, I try to pull my hand free, but again, I'm being chastised like a child.

"Not here," is all he says and keeps looking straight forward, not even making eye contact with me.

"Fine, but you better start talking soon!" My patience is now shattered, and I'm not prepared to be used like a puppet for much longer without a very long explanation of what the hell just happened after Flynn's phone call.

Reaching our room, which of course is on the top floor and looks like there is only one other room up on this floor, the bell boy is just coming out of the room from placing our few bags inside. It's not like I had many clothes to pack, and Nic must pack light because his bag was smaller than mine, but he of course had the accompanying suit bag.

"*Grazie,*" Nic mumbles as we push past him into the room and close the door behind us.

I'm so angry and immediately pull my hand free from his. But as soon as I look up, I stop dead in my tracks.

The man I'm about to tear strips off is standing in front of me, starting to apologize before I even have a chance to open my mouth.

"Christ, I'm so sorry about that, Tori. Please let me explain before you explode in front of my eyes. Because I can see you are about to let loose on me." He places his hands on my shoulders, trying to calm me, but instead, it just lights the fire.

Stepping back and stomping farther into the room, I spin back around and let loose just like he knew I would.

"Explode? Gee, what makes you think I would do that? What the ever-loving fuck just happened! I'm not here as your personal slave to do as I'm told when you growl at me. Too right you better start talking, before I take my bag and walk back out that door, hopping on the first plane back to London." With both my hands on my hips, I give him the biggest staredown I can muster.

"See? Like I said, exploding. I told Flynn I'd be lucky to make it out alive, and he laughed. But he's not the one here and about to have his nuts kicked in." Rolling his eyes, Nic walks straight to the drinks cart set up in the corner, pouring himself a whiskey and pointing the bottle at me to ask if I want one. I could drink it like a shot right now, but the angel on my shoulder who looks a lot like Elouise in my vision shakes her finger at me, signaling what a bad idea that would be.

"Less drinking, more talking, asshole!" I watch him take a long sip and close his eyes for a moment as he lets it slide down his throat.

I shouldn't be enjoying the vision of his Adam's apple bobbing as much as I am.

"Take a seat, Tori," he says, motioning toward a couch to my right.

"No! And it's Victoria, remember?" I'm too angry, confused, and weirdly turned on to be able to sit still. What is wrong with me?

"Seriously." He rolls his eyes at me and unbuttons his jacket when I don't respond. He takes a seat himself even though I refused his offer. "Fine, if that's the way you want it, Victoria." Taking another sip of his whiskey, he takes his time because he knows it's annoying me even more than I already am.

It's like he is waiting me out before he'll start.

"Fine!" I drop onto the couch opposite him, but only just on the edge of it. I'm still so agitated that my back is ramrod straight and my hands are clasped together in my lap so tightly I can clearly see the whites of my knuckles.

"Fine." He starts to laugh a little.

"Yes, so you said, now get on with it." Stringing this out is bringing him pleasure, I can see it written all over his face. His anger from downstairs is gone, and it's like he enjoys provoking me.

Leaning back on the couch and placing his arm along the top of it, he looks like a GQ model in a photoshoot, advertising some high-priced whiskey label.

Hell, just looking at this man, like he's sex personified, would make me buy whatever he's selling.

The strong jawline that has just the right amount of stubble and the glisten on his lips from the whiskey take my mind off why I was angry. Watching him slowly raise the glass to his lips again, the veins in his hand are popping, and I can't imagine what his arms look like under that jacket and shirt. Would he be one of those guys that's strong enough to lift me and pin me against a wall while he slowly fucks me? Or throw me onto the bed, pushing my legs apart over his shoulders and feasting on me until I can't do anything but explode all over his face.

Explode. The word bringing me back from my fantasy. Shit, how long have I been staring at him?

"Enjoying the view, Victoria?" His words are so smooth, like cream rolling off his tongue. The view is more than enjoyable, but I can't admit that to him. I'm supposed to be angry.

"Not really." Lies, all lies.

The asshole is laughing at me! He knows what he's doing to me, but I won't let him take advantage of my stupid lusting for him.

"For God's sake, can you just get on with it?" I blurt, feeling flustered now.

"Of course," he says, placing his glass on the table next to him and sitting forward a little so we are closer. Laying his hands on his thighs, he finally looks more serious as he starts talking.

"I know we don't really know each other very well, and this is asking you to do something that will be completely out of your comfort zone."

"Playing a fake girlfriend to a man who virtually gave me no choice but to get on a jet with him and spend seven days somewhere I have never been before. With no idea what is happening, and at the same time work my ass off to please him with some amazing portfolio, otherwise I will probably lose my job. Oh, and that is after he put me drunk in his car with him, a total stranger. Umm, let me see, where even is the line for the comfort zone? Because I think we jumped straight over that yesterday in your office." Dammit, Tori, you need to learn to shut up with the word vomit. I can't seem to keep my thoughts inside my brain today. I'm losing the game this morning. My inside voice has the upper hand in this match.

"What is it with you, woman? You want me to explain, but then you talk before I can finish. Although, I will say you make a fair point. I've thrown a lot at you in the last few days, haven't I."

"You think! Carry on." I try to shut down my thoughts before I start on another rant.

"It's a long story that maybe we could talk over tonight, but the short version is that I own this company and I want to rebrand it. Which should be the end of the story, but sadly, it's not. I have a distant cousin who works for me and is on the board, and she is trying to undermine me at every opportunity. I have told the board my plans, but I don't want them to know any more than that, until we have all the final specs that I want to run with. The reason being I can't afford for her to get the chance to poison their minds and make the whole thing a shitshow." I can tell this is difficult for him to tell me, and I doubt he is a person who shares much with anyone.

Taking a breath and relaxing back into my couch, I ask the obvious question. "So, what does that have to do with me? It's not like I'm telling her anything. I don't know her, and to be honest, I don't even have a clue on where I'm going with the portfolio yet." I feel my face blush at admitting that I feel like a failure already.

"Tori, I trust you with this job, so let's clear that up right now. I was a dick yesterday, and again, I'll explain why one day. But for two reasons we need you to pretend you are here as my girlfriend. The first one is that we don't know who she has as allies within the company and who will be sending her any little piece of gossip they can get. The second is that if she believes you are my girlfriend and that Ms. Francis is working the job, then she will leave you alone. I don't want her targeting you. She is ruthless, and I want to protect you and your name in this industry. Honestly, she will do anything to take me down and won't care who she hurts in the process. So, as ridiculous as it sounds, I'm partly doing this for you. We will both benefit if we can make it believable. And don't worry, I'm not expecting you to be all over me all week."

I can't help but giggle like a schoolgirl at his comment. That lusty woman deep down inside me is yelling loudly about how much she wouldn't mind that. The look on his face tells me he might be thinking the same thing too.

Gulping, he continues. "Maybe holding hands or the occasional kiss on the cheek." He looks at me, waiting for my answer, but I don't really know what to say. "Please know you can say no, and it will make no difference to your job with me, and I will treat you the same as I would have before Flynn's phone call."

"What, so you will remain the biggest arrogant asshole there is?" I want to slap my forehead for the second time today for the inside thought that slipped out.

But I don't quite get the reaction I was expecting. Instead of him defending himself, Nic starts laughing.

"Yes, touché. I'll try harder to be less of a jerk. And can I just say, it's one of the things I find so attractive about you, your complete honesty and how you aren't afraid to tell me your inner thoughts. It's refreshing in my world." He reaches forward with his hand, palm up and the most genuine look on his face I have seen since I met him.

"What do you say, think you can do me this favor? I mean, who knows, we might even become friends after the week together."

How can I say no to a man who is virtually begging for my help without getting on his knees to do it. And I have a feeling he might be pulling down his walls to show a bit of vulnerability, more than I think he ever has before.

To cover the embarrassment and tingling at hearing him say he finds me attractive, of course I can't help but reply with sarcasm. "Let's not get too ahead of ourselves. Friends sounds like a big leap for two people who yell at each other for fun." Reaching forward, I place my hand in his, and it's the most affectionate clasp I have ever felt from a man.

His thumb rubs the top of my hand as he quietly says the simple words, "Thank you, Victoria." The way my name leaves his lips has me tingling.

And I feel a little crack in the layer that I had firmly wrapped around my heart to protect it from doing anything stupid.

God, what the hell have I agreed to. I knew this week would be hard as hell, but not like this.

Taking a deep breath, I start telling myself I can do this. Surely I'm dramatic enough in day-to-day life that I can play this part like it's a role in a movie.

Yes, I can do that. Pretend I'm not the real me. Because I've got a life plan, and it does not involve falling for him!

"Excuse me a moment, I need to use the bathroom," I say, standing and trying to put distance between me and the man who is making me all confused.

"Certainly, it's down that small hallway and the first door on the right." Nic also stands and points me in the right direction.

I walk quickly, and it's not because I actually need to use the bathroom; it's because I need to pull myself together. My breathing is more rapid than normal, and my heart is racing. It's what his touch has done to me.

Stepping into a bathroom that's big enough to be a bedroom, I close the door and lean against it, closing my eyes. I just concentrate on breathing, which sounds crazy because we breathe without thinking about it, but right now, I need to focus on something, and breathing seems like the perfect thing.

Why did I say yes to that? How am I going to keep myself from saying all the stupid things that fall from my mouth on a regular basis? That's what people my age do! We aren't expected to be all sophisticated and look like we have our life together, because I'm so far from that.

Like anyone is going to believe that I am even girlfriend material for this super-wealthy, sexy-as-sin man. He is always dressed impeccably, knows all the right things to do and say, and probably fucks like a sex god. Oh man, seriously, Tori, pull yourself together. Nic didn't offer up his cock for the week, so stop thinking about having sex with him. There is no question that sex with him would be out of this world. I mean, just look at him. But all he's asking from you is to go out there, smile, hold his hand, and suffer a few kisses on the cheek. Now, if that's what suffering is, then I'm all for it.

I'm not sure how long I have been standing here for, but I need to get back out to Nic. He'll think I've fallen in. I'm sure he already thinks I'm a ditz, I don't need to prove he's right. I flush the toilet and run the tap so he doesn't think I have been hiding out in here, which I totally have, but he doesn't need to know that. Standing at the sink, I finally register this bathroom I'm standing in.

Holy shit!

This is obviously what people with money expect. So much gold, it's everywhere. Taps, towel rack, lights, everything is just dripping with money. It's all heavy cream Italian marble that oozes high class. The shower is a walk-in and big enough you could have a party in there. Which is totally not my thing, but hey, for some it is. I walk into it and run my hand along the glass wall. If this is his regular room, then he has stood here naked before. My mind is already drifting off to being pinned to this glass wall while his mouth devours my neck and his hands roam all over my wet body.

"Fuck. You need to get out of here, Tori." Straightening myself in the mirror, I open the door as I hear him hanging up the phone in the room.

"Hey, I have ordered us some lunch. I hope you don't have any allergies."

My head is spinning from the change of thoughts. "Umm, no," I manage to say and sound half intelligent.

"Great, I ordered a mixture of things, so at least there will be something you like. Antipasto, bruschetta, pizza, and of course, some tiramisu and cannoli for dessert." I look at him with confusion about how much food he has ordered. We aren't feeding a football team.

"Of course, you can order something else if you don't want any of that."

"No, sorry, I love Italian food—well, food in general. I was just surprised at how much you ordered." Walking over to the window, I look out onto a stunning courtyard. It looks like the hotel is a square shape and the courtyard is the center beauty. Metal tables and chairs are scattered around, and there are vines growing all over the various trellises to give ambience.

"I wanted to make sure you had choices, and I like to test a variety of dishes while I'm in my hotel to make sure everything is still up to my standard." I feel him close behind me.

"Which is high, I bet," I say, smirking while I'm still facing away from him.

"The highest. I won't accept anything less than the most alluring beauty and flavor." His voice is close enough now that I can feel the air on my neck, his chest touching my back ever so faintly. "I won't take second best."

"You can afford to be picky," I say, trying to keep my voice from quavering.

"It's been worth it." The air from his breath is tingling my ear, and I know his lips aren't far from touching me. I don't know what his cologne is, but it makes me weak at the knees. It's strong and masculine, with just the tiniest hint of sweetness to it. It's been imprinted on me for days, ever since he wrapped me in his blanket to sleep in on Friday night. It calms me and heats me up at the same time. A potent combination.

Just as my brain starts to misfire and I know I'm about to do something I'll regret, like leaning back into his touch, there is a loud knock at the door, and Nic is gone. Which leaves me panting at the window, knowing that there is no way I will be able to survive this week without buying more underwear. Because I have a feeling mine will be continually wet while I'm around him.

Needing a few more moments, I just keep taking in the view until I hear the door close, then I turn and see the waiter has left a beautiful spread of food on the table. It's almost like my nose leads me to the table with the aroma of the dishes smelling so enticing.

"Nicholas, we are never going to be able to eat all this," I scold. His laughter as he pours us both a glass of water is infectious. I start to laugh with him.

"You sound like my mother. She uses my full name when I'm in trouble." He might be a hard-ass, but you can tell he loves his mother by the way he smiles when talking about her.

"What makes you think you aren't in trouble now?" I ask, taking an olive off the platter, popping it into my mouth.

"Oh, I know I am." He digs his finger into some of the cream in the cannoli and then lifts it to his mouth, his lips wrapping around it and sucking it ever so slowly. This man has gone from zero to one hundred on the flirting scale, and I'm down for it. Nothing to say I can't enjoy some flirting, if we are both strong enough not to take it any further.

"And yet you are starting with dessert. You really are a naughty boy, aren't you." I take a seat where he has placed my plate and watch him nearly choke on his finger.

Yes, Nic, two can play this game, and I'm not very good at losing.

"Who made up the rules for what order things need to be consumed? Wine?" he asks, holding the bottle out for me to look at what he ordered. Not that I would know a rosé from a Shiraz. Wine is not my thing. It might have to do with the quality of what I've tried, and I'm not sure the wine that comes in a shiny silver bag is ever going to be the prestigious flavor Nic would enjoy.

I decide to push that little bit further. "Okay, well, I'll let you choose the order in which we eat our meal, shall I? I'm sure it will be an interesting time."

I nod at him for the wine because I don't want to insult him. Who knows, maybe it will surprise me.

"Any time with you, Victoria, is always guaranteed to be interesting, among other things. Now eat, please. We have much to do this afternoon." He takes his first sip of the wine, testing it, and then continues to pour our glasses.

"I want to show you my hotel and let you discover what a special place Darby Hotels can be. My grandparents built a beautiful legacy, and I intend to carry it on in the best way I can." Both of us take a selection off the antipasto platter and a piece of bruschetta, and already my stomach is growling at the sight of it. I didn't realize how all the craziness of the morning had made me so hungry.

Lifting his glass toward me, I raise mine too, and all I can think is, *"Don't hit his too hard and smash it."* The glass is probably worth a day's wage for me.

"Cheers, or as they say here, *salute* to a good week." The look in his eyes tells me his words have a double meaning.

"Keep feeding me like this and let me stay in such beautiful rooms, and you'll keep me happy. Then everything will turn out perfectly."

We clink our classes and put them to our lips. The first sip is far smoother than I expected.

"I can assure you a Darby man knows how to please. I promise not to disappoint."

And with that, I manage to spray my mouthful of wine all over my food and clothes.

"What is wrong with you?" Nic barks at me as he pushes back from the table, and I'm starting to wonder the same thing.

"Well, stop oozing sex and we will both stay dry."

From the look on Nic's face, I know instantly that it should have been another inside thought.

And not because he looks angry.

Because he looks like he wants to devour me right here, right now.

Chapter Ten

NICHOLAS

I'm going to kill Flynn! This must be the stupidest thing I've done.

A fake girlfriend is one thing, but trying to play happy couple with Tori is like trying to lie to your mother. There is nothing fake about how much I want to strip her bare, swiping this table clean and laying her out as my lunch.

There is no point trying to hide the attraction I have for her. My ramrod cock straining every thread of cotton on my trousers gives it away anyway.

All I can do is sit and drink the wine that's in my glass.

Don't talk, just get her a clean plate, and watch her flounder over her mess. Seeing her flustered is not helping me to calm my thoughts. The pink on her cheeks, the sheen of sweat on her brow, and her red hair that she had tied off her face now falling in strands that highlight her complexion. If I were less of an asshole, as she likes to call me, I would be assisting her, but instead, I'm enjoying the show.

Why do I love this look on her?

"Sit, Victoria," I say, almost strong enough to be an order but not quite.

"What?" She's not even looking at me, as she is still trying to clean up her mess.

I slide the chair out next to mine. "It's just wine, better than the hot tea from last time. Now, sit here, Victoria. Ignore that." She looks up at me, embarrassed and not sure what she should answer.

I start placing food on a clean plate and set the clean cutlery next to me, taking the choice from her. The moment I see her succumb to my instruction just makes me harder than I already was and leaves her red flush on her cheeks now creeping up her neck too. I would give anything to see where else she flushes like that.

Watching her sit and trying to smooth her clothes, I know there is no going back from this woman.

I will have her the moment she gives me signal that she is finished fighting the intense pull we have to each other. Never have I wanted a woman like I want Victoria, and in such a short time after meeting her.

I know the moment we connect, it will be the type of intensity like no other. And then I just hope like hell we both survive the fallout.

This is not what this trip was supposed to be about. I don't mix work and pleasure. Ever!

But within the first few hours, this woman has me wanting to break all the rules. I don't know what she is doing to me, but whatever spell she is casting every time we argue, it's working.

People always say makeup sex is the best, but how does that work when you have never had each other before? We're not like two lovers trying to calm the anger toward each other by fucking it out.

Instead, the fighting and the turmoil is the biggest turn-on for both of us. It lights both our flames, and I can see it in her eyes that she loves the fire as much as I do.

No matter how much I want her, now isn't the right moment.

But when it is, nothing will hold me back from claiming her. Even if it's just for one night and that's all I get. It'll be worth every second she gives me, because that's what it will be. Victoria giving herself to me.

I don't want to take what I want from her, but instead, give her the highest pleasure like she deserves.

First, I need to get through this meal and the rest of today, which will be even harder than I imagined the moment she walked onto the jet this morning.

"Eat, Victoria." My words are stern and gain her attention.

Her embarrassment is gone, and the fire is back. "Why are you so high-handed?" Her glare tells me I need to be careful being this physically close to her. She is fighting the same problem I am.

"Because I can," I say, taking a piece of cheese and salami into my mouth and waiting for her to do the same.

Before she can reply, her phone starts ringing from across the room and startles us both.

Jumping up from her seat, she tries to put it on silent to stop the shrill noise. She has one of those annoying ringtones that is so high-pitched it almost hurts your ears.

"Sorry, sorry, sorry," she mumbles in a hurried voice as it finally stops ringing. "I didn't know I had bumped the silence button." This woman is a walking disaster, and I don't know why it doesn't bother me like it should.

"Do you need to call them back?" It's none of my business who was calling her, but it doesn't stop me from wanting to know who it was.

"No," is all I get as she places it back in her handbag.

"Okay, then let's eat, we have work to do." I try to clear my mind of all these lustful thoughts and concentrate back on work for the afternoon. This alone shocks me because I never put women before my business. Yet Victoria is taking up more space in my thoughts than I know what to do with.

I'm in real trouble here, but I'm finding it harder and harder to care.

———

"Thank you, Marco. You and Laurence have this under control, I hope. When are we going to be fully operational again?" I'm trying to be polite in the way I speak to my hotel manager, and Laurence, my chief of buildings. Apparently, I have been too much of an asshole lately, and although I want to chastise both these men for not flagging this risk before it happened, I can't. With Victoria standing right beside me, I know it will come back to me later when we have our next war of words. There is no point denying that it will happen, because we can't seem to go more than an hour in each other's company without a heated discussion. It's inevitable.

"We think it will take a week. We are having trouble sourcing local contractors that are able to start the work, so we are flying in our London team. Marco will help them negotiate the language barrier with supplies." Laurence is quite sheepish with me and keeps looking more at Tori than I do. He is treading on thin ground right now.

I can feel my temperature rising, and I'm not sure how much longer I can maintain being the nice guy.

"Then who will be running the hotel if Marco isn't! Find someone else to help them. You are the fucking manager, not a translator. I want a full brief in my emails by the morning." I take Tori's hand and glare daggers at Laurence. "My girlfriend and I will be out for the afternoon." It takes all my strength to walk calmly with her and not storm away like I want to. I make sure I remind them that she is mine, even if it's only temporarily.

Passing through the front doors of the hotel, Tori is just walking with me and thankfully has not opened her mouth. She's learning.

The chauffeur opens the car door as we approach but I shake my head at him, and we keep walking down the road and past the other hotels that are close by.

Thinking we must be far enough away, finally Tori starts talking. "Is that how you treat all your staff? No wonder this evil cousin of yours wants to give you the boot from the company."

And just like that she lights my wick with her fire.

I push her into a small alley between the buildings we are passing. I know I should stop, but I can't.

Crowding her against the old stone of the wall, my hands land on either side of her head on the wall and I press my body firmly against hers. Looking down at her, all I can think is how it would feel to ravage her.

"That smart mouth of yours needs to be silenced," I growl, dropping my head and dragging my nose up the side of her throat, taking in that scent that drives me crazy every time she walks into a room. The voice in my head is telling me to back off, but the horse has bolted, and I can't rein it in now.

My face level with hers again, I look for any resistance or fear, but instead, I see her pure sexual want that mirrors mine.

"Then silence it." And that's all the permission I need.

I take her lips with such urgency. I won't risk her changing her mind before I can show her what she's doing to me. Her taste is addictive on my lips, and there is no innocence or patience in the way we devour each other. Tori is in this kiss as much as I am, with all the pent-up tension that has been building between us. She grabs at my arms like she is hanging on for dear life.

I drop my hands down to her shoulders and pull her off the wall and into my arms. I need her as close as I can get her. Sliding a hand onto her luscious hair, I pull her head in exactly the angle I want it. Our lips are still taking each other like it's the last time they will ever meet. And maybe it is, if I had any sense.

Suddenly, it feels like I'm being watched. I pull back quicker than I should. It's become an awful sense I have inherited in the last few years, as soon as I became newsworthy. Every bastard has a camera these days and wants to be the next big star breaking the gossip on a trashy media site. The British media are the top of the tree when it comes to ruthless gutter journalism. The way they treat the British royal family here is disgusting, but sadly, it's not limited to them. Anyone that will bring in money is their target too.

Looking around, I can't see anyone, but it doesn't mean they aren't there. Maybe I was lucky this time.

Tori's looking at me, totally confused. One minute I'm all over her, and then I'm pulling away.

"Sorry, I shouldn't have done that," I say, stepping back to put a bit more distance between us.

"Why?" Her voice is so soft.

"Because you deserve better than that," I tell her, straightening my jacket, just to give me something to do with my hands.

"Do I?" She also takes another step away from me now, but to the side because she is still so close to the wall that she has nowhere else to go. "Actually, I do." She stands up that little straighter, and the dreamy look that I put on her face is gone and replaced with the strength I see in her every day. She smooths her hands over her hair and her clothes, until we are both now standing here staring at each other, not knowing what just happened.

As expected, it doesn't take long for Tori to be back to her feisty best. "Now what are you going to do?" she asks, challenging me to fix what I just started.

"Walk, for as long as it takes." Holding my hand out to take hers, I hope I haven't just completely wrecked our agreement.

"Why do you want to walk?" she asks, but I suspect she already knows the answer; she just likes poking the bear.

"To calm us both down." I glance down at her hand, giving her the hint that I want it and not to choose now to be as stubborn as I know she can be.

"Good luck with that, big boy." Stepping closer to me again, she runs her hand up my cock that's hard as a rock.

I grit my teeth, trying not to give her the satisfaction of letting out the hiss that I so desperately want to. She is pushing me past the limit of restraint for my poor penis, which I didn't think could get any harder, but somehow, she just managed to make it. Walking is the last thing I want to do, but it's the only way I can keep my hands off her.

Putting her hand in mine, it is her dragging me out of the alley this time.

A few steps down the road, the first thought of guilt creeps in. "Do we need to talk about that?" I reluctantly ask, but knowing I should.

"Nope." I can't judge a thing from her tone that has no expression in it.

"O… kay."

"I enjoyed it, didn't you?" She is still looking straight ahead, not giving me anything to work with.

"You felt how much I enjoyed it." And finally, she turns to look at me, and we both burst out laughing at the same time. Something that feels so natural to do with her.

As we finally get the laughter under control, I need to check. "Are we okay?" I ask, nervous for her answer.

"Of course, nothing has changed. Now show me some of the sights." And just like that, the Tori who lights up my life with her smile is back. But she is wrong about one thing.

Everything has changed!

I'm not sure how I can come back from that, even if I wanted to try.

And I know deep down, I don't.

"I wasn't exactly dressed for walking in these shoes, so I think I deserve a foot massage when we get back to the room." Her smile is infectious. She knows what she's doing, and I'm not opposed to having my hands on her again, even if it is her feet.

"Only after they are washed and perfumed. I draw the line at touching smelly feet."

Her mock gasp makes me chuckle slightly. "Are you saying my feet smell? That is not very gentlemanly."

"I think we established a long time ago that being a gentleman is not my strong suit." No matter how much I want to say I can change for her, I know I can't. This is who I am and have been for a long time.

"Oh, I don't know, I think you certainly rock a suit," she purrs, her gaze running down my torso.

"Not helping me here, Victoria," I scold, waving my hand above my crotch that is hidden under the table. And her smile tells me she knows exactly what she is doing to my body.

We're sitting at a little outside table at one of my favorite restaurants near the hotel. I might not get to cook much these days, but that doesn't mean I will eat just anything. I'm picky, and it's not always the big-name restaurants that are the best. Especially when you travel, finding little family-owned and run restaurants, where the food is made with love, is like finding a hidden jewel.

Pepe's place is certainly a diamond in the rough. Pepe and Angelina have been cooking here together for thirty years, and now their kids are running the restaurant with them. No matter how busy they are, they always find a table for me when I'm here. Once it was even in the kitchen, and we talked all things food and cooking while they kept working and I ate my freshly made seafood linguini pasta. I couldn't help it, though. They were so busy, as soon as I was finished, I grabbed an apron and started helping. It was one of the most enjoyable nights I have had since I left Australia. It reminded me of being back in the kitchen with my grandparents.

"I don't think I can eat another bite, Nicholas. I have eaten more today than I do in a week at home." That makes me a little uneasy, because in my eyes, we haven't eaten more than average today. It makes me wonder if there is more to that statement.

"Do you want them to package up your leftovers and you can snack on it later?" I ask, nodding to Giulia that I'm ready for the bill.

"Oh God, no. A girl has to watch what she eats. Too much pasta and these curves just get curvier." And there it is, she is self-conscious about her body, giving me a little insight into the Tori insecurity she hides from the world. Hence the eating comment before. I want to tell her how beautiful she is and that women should have curves and that can mean in any shape or form. But that is just putting me in a bigger hole than I am already trying to dig myself out of after this afternoon's kiss.

Instead, I take my last sip of wine from my glass and then tap my card on the machine that Giulia brought to the table. I let her know that, as always, the food was amazing and to say hello to her parents. As I leave a sizable tip as usual, Victoria now stands and joins in complimenting the food and apologizes that she couldn't finish it, not wanting to insult the chefs.

Giulia hugs us both, then I take Victoria's hand which feels like the normal thing to do now. We say our goodbyes and start the short walk back to the hotel. Everyone eats later in Europe, so the streets are still busy and noisy. Italy is never a quiet place. They love to eat and socialize, which is why I love the culture here.

We don't talk on the way back, instead just enjoying the silence between us for once. And the unusual thing is we are never silent unless one of us is mad at the other. But this afternoon has been different.

Seeing the joy on Victoria's face as she stood in front of the Trevi Fountain with her eyes closed for a moment before throwing the coin over her shoulder to make her wish was so mesmerizing. I didn't realize how much I have lost touch with reality and the simple things in life. When she told me of her childhood dream, I had to make it happen.

The photos on my phone that she asked me to take for her remind me of my mother in a way, believing in the power of the universe to bring her what she wished for. In the moment when she was saying her wish in her head, eyes closed, a real calmness came over her face, and I couldn't help but capture that beauty. That is not the photos she asked for, that one was for me.

I can tell her feet must be getting sore like she mentioned, as her pace is slowing the closer we get to the hotel.

I should have called for the car, but walking hand in hand today is something I have never enjoyed so much with a woman. No plans, just wandering and taking in the view around us. We hopped on and off the tourist bus a couple of times when the distance was a little long but always sat upstairs in the sunshine and took in the view. By this stage, we have both taken off our jackets and I'm carrying them. Next time we go sightseeing, I need to plan it so we can dress a little more casually. I don't really enjoy being around all the people, and crowds are not my thing, but the look of joy on her face made it worth the suffering.

"Would you like me to carry you?" I don't know where that came from, but I can't have her in pain.

"Oh, don't be silly. Sure, my feet hurt, but not that bad." Her voice is a little quieter than before. I can tell she is hesitating in saying something. Stopping her isn't an option because I don't want to delay getting her to the room where she can put her feet up.

Squeezing her hand gently, I ask, "Then why are we walking slowly?"

"Because I don't want today to end," she whispers, looking down at her feet rather than at me.

I don't want to embarrass her so just give her hand another little squeeze. "I understand," is all I reply, because the truth is, I feel the same.

We continue in our silence until we make it back to the room, both in our own heads with our thoughts.

We stop just outside the room. Before I tap the keypad, I want to say something to her, but I know I must stay strong.

Finally opening the door, it's funny how it feels instead like it's the closing of the day. Both of us just stand there, not knowing what to say or do. I don't have much more restraint left.

"I think I'll take a shower," Tori quietly mumbles, turning and walking toward the bathroom without looking at me.

"Take a long hot bath, it will help soothe your body," I call after her, which makes her groan, and I try not to laugh. Because I know what she is thinking, and neither a shower nor a bath is going to soothe the ache we both have.

Hearing the door close and the bath water start, I know I'm safe from the temptation for a short while. As long as I don't think about her in there naked, surrounded by bubbles.

Fuck, that wasn't smart to start thinking about. I need to occupy myself.

Kicking off my shoes and socks and unbuttoning my shirt and dropping onto the couch, I decide to send a quick message to the guys before I take a shower in the ensuite which is far smaller than the bathroom that Tori is in.

Nic: If Flynn ever tells you he has a good plan. Don't fucking listen!

Forrest: Could have told you that.

Remington: I feel like I'm missing something again. Details?

Flynn: Hahahahahahahahahaha

Nic: Such a dick.

Flynn: I always have the best plans.

Nic: Bullshit.

Forrest: Lies.

Remington: Again, details! What the fuck have I missed!

Flynn: Boss man is playing happy fake boyfriend with Tori for the next week.

Forrest: Wait WTF why?

Remington: You beat me to it.

Nic: Because your idiot brother thought it would be a good idea to keep Jocelyn off my back and in the dark about everything.

Flynn: Wait, that's not all my fault. You started this by taking Tori on a little fuckfest

Forrest: FLYNN!!!!!!

Remington: He's got a point, Nic.

Nic: You can all fuck off now.

Remington: Not denying it????

Flynn: Christ, he didn't even last 24 hours. You fiend. Should I have had her sign an NDA before you left?

Nic: What for?

Flynn: That she wouldn't tell everyone how bad you are in bed.

Nic: I give up with you.

Remington: Again, still hasn't denied anything.

Forrest: Rem's right.

Nic: I can't go there, she works for us.

Flynn: Then keep it in your pants, Romeo.

Nic: Easier said than done.

Shit, I shouldn't have said that. There is no way they will have missed what my comment means.

Flynn: Holy shit.

Remington: Does that mean what I think it does?

Forrest: I think it might.

Nic: You are all bastards. Go fuck yourselves.

Flynn: Perhaps you should do the same!

Forrest: Be careful, Nic.

Remington: Bullshit, he should go for it. No woman has made him second-guess himself. EVER!

Nic: Whatever, don't you all have work to do?

Flynn: Yes, boss man, we are holding down the fort while you are away holidaying.

Forrest: Ignore him, I always have. Talk tomorrow.

Remington: Flynn, meet me at the club. We will be *cough* working *cough*

Nic: Later.

I'm done with the ridiculousness that is my friends. The shower is calling me, and maybe Flynn has a point. I need to take the edge off. Then I might be able to get through the rest of the night without being so uncomfortable.

I didn't exactly think when I was packing. I sleep naked. I don't have any track pants or pajamas with me. The only thing I have is a pair of running shorts, which may come in handy when I need to run off some pent-up frustration.

I drop my trousers to the floor beside the bed, unbutton my shirt, and I'm about to walk into the ensuite, when I hear the most bloodcurdling scream coming from Tori.

"Fuck." Not even thinking, I race through the penthouse and burst through the bathroom door, wearing only my shirt that is open and a pair of boxer briefs.

I come to a screeching halt with Tori standing in front of me completely naked and dripping wet. She has one arm across her voluptuous breasts and the other covering her sex with a face cloth, neither doing it very successfully.

I can hardly speak, and all that comes out is a growl of her name. "Victoria." Oh fuck, woman, there is only so much a man can withstand.

Her eyes are as wide as a possum's and move quickly between me and the bath. There are tears in the corner of her eyes and her lip is trembling.

"A… spi… der." But her fear has her not thinking clearly, and she moves her arm from her breasts to point to where it is, and all I can see is her on full display, and I can't take any more.

As I step toward her, she panics and takes the hand off her sex to help cover the breasts she just flashed to me, and then leaves herself exposed there.

I'm done!

"Fuck the spider, you should be more scared of me," I growl as I pick her up in my arms. She is panicking again, realizing that she has just shown me everything she owns, but it hasn't occurred to her that her naked ass is now also in my hands.

I can see her brain racing, but she can't seem to speak, which is a first.

I carry her from the bathroom, coming to a stop in the main bedroom at the end of the king-sized bed that is calling us.

Lowering her feet to the ground, I drop my shirt that is now all wet to the floor.

Then she does the bravest thing and moves her hands to my waist and starts pushing my briefs down herself.

It's like she is making the choice, so she can look back and know that she didn't get pushed to make the leap. I've never been so grateful for the strength in a woman to challenge me.

My cock is so hard that as soon as the briefs have fallen to the carpet, it is standing solid and at attention. The ache of lust is almost killing me.

I want to take her straight away, but I'm using every tiny shred of restraint left to hold back and let her have control.

Her hands on my chest, still a little damp, are running over every inch of my pecs and abs, sending shivers through my skin, and my nipples are so fucking tight. When her fingers touch them, I feel myself leaking from the tip of my cock that's about to explode. It just feels unbelievable.

Her soft voice breaks me from the trance I have been in just watching her take what she wants.

"What are we doing, Nicholas?" I've never liked my full name, but hearing it fall off her lips like this, I can't get enough of it.

"Relaxing," I say, my hands now on her hips and slowly making my way up her sides.

"How?"

The only way we are going to be able to. "By fucking this sexual frustration so hard out of us that we won't come up for air tonight." Her skin is so soft and supple as I take her breasts in my hands, slowly squeezing them and listening to the moan it brings from her.

"You don't care that I'm not like your other women I've seen pictures of?" Oh, but you are so much better, Victoria. Why can't you see that?

"No!" I lick her throat as I whisper in her ear, "It's the very reason I can't walk away from you, Victoria." Her body shudders with electricity as I pinch her nipples and release them as I pull my hands away.

"This won't change... anything between us." Her hands slide around me to my back just above my ass. It's almost like she is too frightened to go any farther south.

"No," I say, my voice strong and husky from trying to settle her fear.

"But you are my boss."

I grab her ass cheeks in my hands and tightly grasp them, kneading them, kissing her on different parts of her face as I answer. "Technically... you are... my consultant. So, no... I'm not your boss." I finish with a quick a kiss on her lips and pull back as she tries to lengthen the kiss.

"You can't fire me," she says.

I'm now attacking the other side of her neck as I push my body into hers. I can feel how wet she is as she is starting to ride against me.

"No," I grit out. My patience is about to shatter. "You are off the clock now, Victoria, and I'm not your boss, remember?"

"Then who are you?" She slides her fingers that little bit farther and takes my ass in her hands. There is not a gap left between us anywhere.

There are so many ways I could answer that question, but my honesty just rolls off my tongue. I stop us from grinding against each other, our breathing rapid, and I feel like there is no air left in the room as I look straight into her eyes. "I'm a man who doesn't know how to resist you."

And then I see the fear in her eyes leave with the fire I crave now back, and her whisper tells me her truth.

"Then don't…"

Chapter Eleven

VICTORIA

I feel like I can't breathe.

This man is more than I was ever made to handle. And I'm not just talking about his size.

It's everything. The whole package that is Nicholas.

I'm not in his league. He dates glamorous women who are shaped like catwalk models, who have money and all the style.

Yet he tells me it doesn't matter. I'm not sure it's true, but I'm too far gone over him that there is no turning back now.

My body craves him like nothing I have ever felt before. And there is no way I'm denying myself when he is standing here fully naked in front of me, offering me a night of what I know will be, without a doubt, the best sex I will ever have.

Giving myself over to him was so easy, the moment I decided deep down that it is okay to fully let go.

It's my choice, and there will be no regrets when he walks away from me.

And he will, that I'm certain of.

He slides his hand down to my sex and through my folds that are already dripping wet—and it's not from the bath. I have been like this since he kissed me senseless in the alley.

Lordy, this man can kiss like nothing I have had touch my lips before. His lips are like a weapon that disarms anything they touch.

Oh, fuck, I'm about to come, and he just started touching me. The moans I can't keep inside are making him smile at me, but not all sweet and innocent. This is the look of a man determined to string every emotion out of me, and I'm all for it.

"Victoria." The growl of my name off his lips while I'm riding his fingers has me on the precipice of the most powerful orgasm that is about to be let free.

"Why do you call me that?" I have no control of my mouth or my body. He has it all.

"You told me to. And now I love it on my lips." His reply, at the same time his thumb presses down firmly on my clit and his fingers are inside me, makes me erupt, and all I can do is scream.

"Nicholas!" And in one movement, he has me on the bed and is between my legs, lavishing me with his tongue and enjoying what he has done to me. Not caring how sensitive I now am, he continues to work my body to a high I never knew I could reach. No man has made me orgasm twice in such quick succession, to the point that I feel like I'm about to have my soul ripped from my body.

"Taste… amazing… just like… I knew you would." Lifting his mouth from my body, he kneels above me on the bed, and his cock is long and thick and almost looks painful at the tightness of it. The veins are protruding, and the tip is turning purple from being so turned on. I've never wanted to do this before, but grabbing his hips, I pull his cock toward my mouth. But his resistance is too strong.

"You put your luscious lips on me, and it will be all over. When I come, it's going to be when I'm pounding my fucking cock so hard inside you that you won't want me to stop." Oh, I can take his dirty talk all night long and let it live in all my future dreams.

I don't know if there is much energy left in my body, as I'm lying slightly limp under him, but my hand is still going toward his cock just to get a single touch. He moves off the bed and leaves me confused. Until I see him pulling his wallet from his pants pocket, a shiny gold packet being ripped open in his mouth, and already my legs are quivering.

He wasn't joking when he said he was going to fuck every bit of frustration I've had completely out of my body tonight.

"You are going to take this hard and fast like the little fiery girl you are. You are mine tonight, and I'm going to punish you for every time you have had me wanting to spank you and fuck you all at the same time. You drive me fucking crazy, Victoria!" Kneeling between my legs, he holds his sheathed cock at my entrance that's begging for him to enter me.

Before I can say a word, he fills me to my core. Hard and with no hesitation. There is no holding him back now.

"Oooohhhhh yessssss," I hiss from the intense pain but even greater pleasure as he starts to pound me into the bed like he promised. There is no working up to it. I'm being shown the way he wants me, and I can't stop myself from crying out with words that don't even make sense.

"This is what you do to me." His gaze is so intense. My hands are on his biceps, and my nails dig into his skin while I try to survive the ride.

"You are so fucking stubborn that I can't help but want you naked in my office, standing in front of me telling me exactly how you feel. The more you hate me, the harder I want to fuck you." How can he even breathe enough to talk to me? I'm about to pass out from lack of blood flowing to anywhere except my pussy, as she gets all his frustration with me taken out on her.

Hearing his words like this tells me why I push his buttons so much. And if this is what it makes him do, I'll be ramming every button so fucking hard every day and all day.

I'm so close, and I don't think I can take any more.

"Oh, Victoria, that's it. Clench that tight little pussy around my cock. Drain every drop from me. Fucking come for me like the filthy little bitch you are. You will come now!"

I can't stop myself from doing exactly as he ordered, screaming like a feral animal at the release of everything that has been building up in me for days.

"Fuckkkkkk, Victoria!" he roars as I feel him pulsing inside me as he continues to pump a little slower a few more times. My eyes closing lightly, I'm just trying to regain some balance in my head. The stars that were shooting across my vision subside, and all I can feel is his breath on my face as he's still holding himself above me. I want him to drop and smother me, but instead, he leans down as I open my eyes again, and he starts to kiss me with his killer lips. Nothing like this morning. This is full of passion and feelings that I'm not quite sure what to do with.

This wasn't supposed to happen.

I can't fall for Nicholas because it will hurt like hell when he lets me go.

And he will let me go.

I try to remind myself that this is all just pretend, because Lord knows my libido didn't get that memo.

His lips softly dust mine as he starts falling to the side of me on the bed. Both of us just lie staring at the ceiling, and the sounds of our breathing fill the room. The smell of sweat and sex are strong, and there is no denying what has happened in here.

After a few minutes, Nic turns to me.

"I will get a warm cloth to clean you up, or better still, can I take you to the shower and we can both clean up together?" In my head, I'm screaming, "*Option two, option two!*" but I manage to sound a little more civilized.

"A shower sounds perfect." And it does, but I'm just not sure how I'm going to be able to walk there. I think Nic has wrecked me, in more ways than one.

"Give me a moment to get it ready." With that, he is up off the bed, and all I can see is his perfect tight ass walking away from me. I knew it would be hot as fuck, and he has not disappointed me, that's for sure.

Lying here, my mind is racing at the ramifications of what I've just done, and all I can think of is the phone call with Elouise that will follow this. After she finishes telling me what a tremendously stupid idea sleeping with him was, then she will want every single detail. But I'm not sure I'm ready to share any of it. There is something inside me grasping at all the tingling feelings that I can't seem to stop, that knows how special the last day has been. I'm afraid if I tell anyone, then it will all disappear, like it never happened. People will be too busy telling me all the negative things, and I'm just not ready to hear it.

I hate secrets, but so far today, I seem to be the queen of them.

Instead, I'm fantasizing about the rear view of Nic, with his tight ass and back muscles. Now I understand how he carried me with ease. He appears in the doorway, and oh, the full-frontal nude is mouth-watering. Yeah, I'm not sharing details on this delightful specimen with anyone, but I will be dreaming night after night about it. That is a given.

I thought that the shower would be another earth-shattering round of sex, but I was so wrong.

The tenderness of being washed clean by a man is like nothing I could have ever imagined. His fingers are so soft, and the way he massaged my scalp is better than any hairdresser I've been to. I mean, I could have come all over again just from his touch, only I don't think there was anything left in me. Wrapping me in the softest, biggest cream bath towel so large it could have almost gone around me three times, Nic worked to make sure every part of me was dry.

Who is this man?

From the demanding, domineering man that he is to me and everybody else in the outside world, the Nicholas in this bathroom is someone I'm not sure he has ever let anyone see before.

Why me, why now?

He's treating me like his princess after he fucked me like his whore.

What even was that? I mean, it was so fucking hot, but I'm still wondering who that man was.

He carried me to my bed because the sheets are clean, and he didn't want me to have to sleep in the mess we just made of his bed. Who even thinks about that after sex? I'd be happy to have his scent imprinted on my skin for a bit longer, but who am I to argue when the sex god is carrying me and placing me so tenderly on the bed. At first, I thought he had fulfilled his urge and was done with me, but he assures me he will be back in a moment. In the meantime, I'm trying to find the position on the bed that will make me look a little more attractive than I feel. If I lie flat, will he see that my stomach isn't toned? If I lie on my side, will he notice my waist is not tiny like other women? Even better, crawling in under the sheets hides everything.

I barely hear his footsteps on the lush carpet as he enters the bedroom. I'm not sure how to navigate our relationship now.

"I wouldn't have been surprised if you were asleep." He has two bottles of water in his hand, a bag of chips, and what looks like a small box of chocolates.

"How can you be hungry? We ate enough to last me a week." My stomach still feels so full of pasta.

"Because I worked up an appetite." That smile of satisfaction does something to me that I wasn't expecting—softening me to the man who I only thought knew how to be a jerk to everyone around him. I think the word I'm looking for is that he has a caring side I never expected.

In what alternate universe am I lying in a bed in a five-star hotel in Rome, with the most delectable man in front of me, stark naked holding water for me?

Maybe I'm still in my drunken sleep from Friday night, and this is all some weird-ass dream.

Even stranger is that he is smiling at me and climbing back into bed, under the covers so his skin touches mine and makes me feel all the sizzle from earlier.

I lean up on my elbow but make sure the sheet is caught under my armpits on either side to keep me covered. I take a drink of water, not realizing how thirsty I am. I'm laughing on the inside at how the thirst has come from losing so much body fluid in the last few hours. The laughter now makes my throat do that stupid thing it does where it starts to constrict. I can feel myself starting to panic that I'm going to choke again and spit water all over him. I think that might be the final straw. Twice has been ridiculous, but a third would be the end of the line, I'm sure.

Managing to calm my throat, I settle back on the pillow. I look up at Nic who is propped up against the headboard, munching away on his chips. He offers me one by holding it to my lips, as his mouth is full. I want to say no because I'm truly still full, but there is something about him wanting to feed me that makes me open my mouth and take the chip anyway. After he feeds me a few more times, the bag is empty, and he settles down next to me.

"Tell me about yourself. I don't know much except what you do for work and where your friend lives." He smiles sarcastically at me, but he's lying; he knows much more than that.

"You know all the wrong things about me," I say, laughing at him because it's the God's honest truth. "Like that I have a tendency to say things out loud when I probably shouldn't, I won't back down when I'm passionate about something. Determination and stubbornness can be great assets, but the way it comes out in me, maybe not so much…"

"Stop, Victoria. I didn't ask for all the things you think are negatives, because personally, I love that determination and stubbornness. It's what you need to survive in the business world, but more importantly, life." He reaches out and pushes my hair behind my ear. "Now tell me about the real Victoria and what makes her happy." His hand now settles on my waist so we are still connected by touch, even though there is a layer of sheet between us.

I don't know if I can answer that fully, because I don't know who I am yet. Let's just say I'm a work-in-progress. Instead, I say, "That's a very good question. She's a complicated woman." I laugh at myself because I don't know how else to react when I feel uncomfortable.

"Okay, then let me ask some questions. How old are you?"

"That's an easy start. I'm twenty-six years old. My birthday is in October, and I'm a Scorpio, if you believe in all that."

He rolls his eyes, and just when I think it's my comment about my star sign, he starts mumbling under his breath, "Fuck me dead, twenty-six, what was I thinking?"

"What are you talking about?" I ask, confused at his words.

"I'm about to turn forty soon. I'm an old man compared to you," he says, chastising himself for no reason.

"That man who just made me lose my mind and doesn't have one muscle out of place on his sexy-as-fuck body cannot be worrying about being old." Again, I'm sharing more than I should have.

"Thanks for the compliment, but still, I'm too old for you." He looks like someone just kicked his dog.

"Who cares how old I am? Is there some rule you follow? Oh God, don't tell me you are one of those obnoxious men who has a checklist for women. Let me guess…" I hold my index finger to my chin, really dramatizing my answer. "She needs to be beautiful, tall, thin, with blonde or brown hair. A wealthy socialite who can fit into all the popular circles you move in. She doesn't talk back, she's polite, and she never spits any fluid from her mouth onto you!" As I was running through the list, I could see him getting angry at me for making fun of him, until I got to the last part, which has the desired effect of making him laugh.

"You don't take yourself too seriously, do you?" he asks, relaxing a little more into how he is lying next to me, his foot now playing with mine.

"No, not really. There are many things I am serious about, but you have to let go of the things you can't change. Like this," I say, waving my hand between us. "No matter what we thought, from that moment you growled at me on the train, we were bound to end up here. You can't deny there was a crazy amount of chemistry buzzing between us." I can see him thinking, but he is not about to deny it.

"As much as I want to disagree, you're probably right. Because believe me, as much as I tried to resist you, you kept pushing me. I might be a good guy, but no mortal man could resist you naked and wet," he says, winking at me, and I know he didn't mean just wet from the bath, the dirty bastard.

I want to ask him why he was resisting me, but I know. I don't fit his mold, but something I didn't know was one of the things in his list was age, and obviously, I'm not in his range of acceptance. I can't change that, so no point fixating on it.

"Okay, my turn. Tell me one thing about you, not your age because I don't care about that," I add to put him back in his place a bit.

"Noted. I'm not sure what to tell you because most of my life has been well-documented on the internet now, and if you were smart or at least cared about your own safety, you would have googled me before you got on the plane." There is a sadness about how much his life is public knowledge.

"Elouise made sure I did, but to be honest, it was because she was yelling at me for not doing it before my presentation."

"Your friend sounds like a smart woman."

"Does that mean you think I'm not?" I ask, pretending to be upset at the revelation.

"Tori, I don't have the energy to fight now, so don't even think about starting to scream at me."

"I'm offended you think I would do that." His hand on my waist squeezes a little tighter, making me giggle from my ticklish spot there. "Anyway, come on, it's still your turn. Tell me something about Nicholas Darby that is not on the internet."

"He's recently discovered he likes redheads," he says, leaning over and kissing me on the top of the head, which is kind of sweet.

"I think I already know that one, so it doesn't count. Try again." His smirk tells me how little he likes to share things about himself.

"Hmmm, okay. I hate the color purple."

"Random, but okay, I'll ask the question, why?"

"I don't really know, I just don't. You will never see me wearing a purple shirt or tie, and there is never any purple decor in my hotels." His face is beginning to relax a little more.

"And you don't think that would have been a smart thing to include in your rebranding brief? Far out, some clients are so annoying." I roll my eyes at him which has him laughing at me. He might be right, we might even get to the end of this week as friends… or maybe a little more.

"What else?" I ask, wanting to keep him talking.

"Nope, it's your turn." Ughh, I hate talking about myself as much as he does.

"I have a fear of spiders." My skin crawls even saying it out loud.

Laughter bursts from Nic. "Nice try, I think I know that about you now. Something else." He pulls me closer, seeing the discomfort the whole talk of spiders is making me. As I lift my head and lay it on his shoulder, he brings his arm around me tightly across my back, our bodies wrapped together again.

I wonder if I should tell him something, but I figure I have nothing to lose. "I didn't quite tell you everything when I told you I had never been to Rome or Italy. The truth is, I have never traveled anywhere out of Britain. Never been on a plane and certainly never stayed in a five-star hotel like this one, and probably won't again."

"Wow, so the first plane you step onto is a private jet. That's going to be hard to come back down to normal travel." His hand is rubbing up and down my back ever so gently. It's so soothing that the exhaustion of the day suddenly starts to hit me.

"You think? But that's okay, I'm sure I'll cope. It's my dream to travel the world. See every place on my bucket list."

"That's quite an expensive dream." His hand stills on my back.

"I know, but I will work along the way and just keep moving to another country." I think of all the places that are on my list.

"Who will you travel with?" he asks, his voice a little more forceful than it has been since earlier today.

"No one. I don't need someone to hold my hand. I'll do it on my own. I don't have anything holding me here." Of course, I have my family and Elouise, but no one else important.

The silence in the room is not what I was expecting and is a little off-putting. Just as I'm about to lift my head up to look at him, his hand moves from my back to my head and holds it on his chest tightly. Almost like he is making sure I can't move on purpose.

Clearing his throat slightly, he says, "So, you intend to leave England and not come back?" What a strange thing to ask.

"I'll come back at some point. I just want to experience life. I'm still young, and there is so much to see out there." I know he doesn't understand what it would be like.

He has probably been to every country in the world by now, owns a hotel or two in most of them, and I'm sure shagged plenty of women there too.

Again with the silence. It's creeping me out.

"I'm tired. Best we get some sleep," he mumbles.

That's why he is quiet, idiot. He's falling asleep. Poor old man can't handle the young filly.

Luckily, that statement stayed as an inside thought this time.

"Yes, I agree. Good night."

"Good night, Victoria." His voice is not one of a man who has been sated by sex and wrapped around a woman for the night. But hey, I've given up trying to figure out this man, and to be honest, I'm exhausted.

Closing my eyes and listening to his breathing is enough to send me off to dreamland.

Only tonight's dreams will be a whole lot more real.

"Victoria, wake up, please."

Mhmm, I could get used to waking up to that voice, all gruff and sexy.

My cheek is touching a pillowcase that has a higher thread count than I know how to count.

I reach out to find the body I had fallen asleep on is gone, and there is nothing there but the feeling of cold sheets. My eyes slowly blink open to my name again.

"Victoria." He sounds more impatient and certainly not the same tone I heard in my head all last night.

"Come back to b…" I don't quite get the words out when I see him standing in the doorway, fully dressed in a dark navy suit, white shirt, and a navy tie that has a white pattern on it that my bleary eyes can't quite make out what it is. He is such a stylish man. But then again, I'm definitely a sucker for a man in a suit. And if yesterday is any indication, it's also my weakness, along with a man with strong hands. You know the type, with the veins that run across the top of them and have that bit of ruggedness to them too.

Snap out of it, idiot. That look on his face is serious and not happy I'm too busy ogling him rather than paying attention to him talking.

"Sorry, what did you say?" I knew he was talking, I just wasn't listening. My brain is only just waking up and trying to function.

"Christ, pay attention, Victoria. You need to pack and eat breakfast; I've had it already brought to the room. Plans have changed. We are flying back to London in one and a half hours. Please be ready." Turning on his heel, he is gone from the room before I can even utter a word to ask what happened.

Instead, all I hear is the front door of the suite banging loudly as he leaves me alone.

"What. The fuck. Just happened." My voice echoes in the empty room.

How heavy did I sleep to enable him to leave the bed and I didn't even notice?

Throwing the bedding back and jumping up, the cold air on my skin reminds me I'm still completely naked. Shit, where are my clothes? Thank God my bag is in this room.

Rummaging through it, I find my fluffy robe and quickly wrap it around me.

I don't want to give him the luxury of seeing this body that he devoured again after the way he just spoke to me.

My thoughts are spiraling down in panic about what I've done. I need to find my phone. I jump up and run into the bathroom, where I left it last night, as I was in the bath before that thing that we won't discuss crawled up beside me on the wall.

Thank goodness I have Wi-Fi in this room. Pushing the Face-Time button, she better goddamn answer to talk me off the ledge I feel like I'm standing on. No wonder this man is still flying solo in life. Because he is one hard person to work out what he is thinking.

Elouise's face fills my screen.

"Morning." Her scratchy voice tells me I've woken her up.

"Shit, what time is it? I didn't even look." All the curtains are still closed, and I have no idea what it's like outside. Is the sun even up?

"Stupid o'clock. I don't know, all I know is my alarm hasn't gone off yet."

I glance at the clock in the top of the screen. "I'm so sorry, Lou, it's only seven here, which means it's six am there."

"Ughhhh, why are you doing this to me? If this is to tell me what an awesome time you are having, surely it could have waited until later," she grumbles, pushing her hair off her face and trying to sit up more in her bed, obviously waking more each minute.

"No, I'm coming home today."

"Wait, what?" And now she is fully awake and pulling her phone closer to her face. "What the hell did you do?"

"Why do you assume it was me! This fucking bastard is playing table tennis with me. I can't keep up. One minute he is being the normal asshole I know. Until I'm pretending to be his girlfriend and he is kissing me like a man on a mission. We spent a magical day in Rome that finished with him fucking me senseless."

She slaps her forehead and groans at me. "Really! The first night and you already jumped his bones. I want to tell you how stupid that was, but... was it good? Is he the Aussie sex god we drooled about?"

"I can't even tell you... like the kind of sex I think has ruined me forever. Holy shitballs, it was so fucking epic." The warm feeling spreads through my body at just the thought of last night.

"So why are you coming home? Ride that stallion all week long, baby! And why were you pretending to be his girlfriend?" We are both giggling a little, and then reality smacks me in the back of the head, reminding me what is happening.

"The girlfriend thing doesn't matter now. And don't worry, I planned on taming the stallion, but he just marched into my bedroom, telling me to get up and pack because we are going back to London. No explanation and certainly no charm. What the hell happened? Like, does he have split personalities or is it just a one-and-done thing?" Now it's me smacking my hand onto the bed I'm sitting on.

"That's it, isn't it? Now I understand his change in plans. He got what he wanted. Made me fall for his sex appeal, fucked me the way he wanted to, and now I have no use. He's scratched his itch." I'm up and walking around the room now, my anger overtaking any panic I felt earlier.

"Tori, whoa, slow down. You don't know that. Maybe something has happened, and he needs to deal with that." She always sees the good in people, that's why I love Elouise.

"Nope, he would have said. The way he spoke to me was like I was just another random he was getting ready to kick out of his bed."

"Tori…"

"No, I'm not taking that shit! He wants to treat me like a hooker, where he is paying me to be here and fuck him… well, he better be ready to deal with the backlash. I'm nobody's floozy. I have more self-respect than that. Asshole! No man gets to push me around."

I pull an outfit of the bag to wear today, like a woman on a mission.

"Tori, stop and listen to me, bitch! You still work for him. DO NOT BURN YOUR BRIDGES!" Even her screaming at me does not stop me from my train of thoughts.

"Yes, right. I'll behave. Have to shower. See you tonight."

"Don't you hang up on—" Her face and voice are gone as I march into the bathroom, ending the call.

"You want to play games, Nicholas Darby, then I'm all in, baby."

Taking a look at myself in the mirror, I see the small red scratches that are still evident on my neck from his rough stubble.

"Well, at least the universe made me see the real you," I snarl, dropping the robe to the floor. "Just why did I have to fall for the Nicholas I met last night? Ughhh. No, he doesn't exist." My heart locks itself back up again. "Time to give him what he wants from me. Absolutely nothing."

Except rage. Oh yeah, he is going to get that in spades.

What a prick!

Chapter Twelve

NICHOLAS

"I don't care what it costs, just get it fixed, today!" I yelled across the room before stomping back through the hotel to the elevator.

I've been inspecting every part of the hotel that I could, to give myself the distraction from her that I need. The poor kitchen staff have just found out what a bad mood I'm in.

This whole week has been the biggest clusterfuck, and I can't seem to break the cycle. Every time I turn around there is another disaster. The biggest one is the one I left upstairs, with her soft, flowing red hair spread all over the pillow where I had been lying with her all night.

I couldn't stay in the room with her while she dressed and ate. Victoria naked? There would be no way I could ignore her like I need to.

She'd have too many questions, and every time she opens those lips that I want wrapped around my cock, with another sarcastic comment, I can't help biting back. She is the only person I can't manage to tame with my words. Every time, she just bites back even harder.

Fuck, stop thinking about her biting me back, leaving teeth marks on my skin like her trophy. I can't exactly walk back into the room with a raging hard-on.

Why is it that my cock responds to her fire, and not her supple softness? That needs to stop right now.

Last night was a big mistake. Well, big isn't even the right word. I'd say a fucking *huge* mistake! One I don't know how to fix except to push her away. And that push needs to be harder than I have ever pushed before. If she thinks I was an asshole before, then she hasn't seen anything yet.

Standing at the door to the suite, I take a deep breath before I walk into the dragon's lair. And that's what it is, with Tori inside. The angrier she gets with me, the greater my pull is toward her. It's like she pumps the sexual attraction into the air and my body just wants to quench its thirst for her. The problem being, now that I've had her, I know what I'm missing—perfection!

Something I know I won't get again.

"Grow some balls and get in there. You have a plane to catch." Swiping my card, I put my game face on.

I find her sitting at the table, sipping her cup of tea that I made sure I ordered for her with breakfast this morning. For me, being in Italy means good coffee. The British people have no idea what they are missing.

Out the corner of my eye, I see her bag sitting next to mine, ready to be taken down to the car.

She hasn't even acknowledged me standing in the room looking at her. The silence is deafening.

"I will call the porter," is all I say, raising the phone on the hall stand to my ear.

"Mhm," she murmurs in acknowledgment, looking toward the windows that overlook the gardens. She brings her cup back to her mouth and slowly takes another mouthful, in no rush to stand or move from her spot.

Oh yeah, she is pissed at me.

But this reaction is not what I was expecting from her. I had been bracing myself to walk into a wall of words being sprayed at me for being so rude this morning. Or badgering me, asking what is wrong with me and what the catastrophe is back in London that we need to rush back for.

Little does she know the catastrophe is what is happening in this room. Me burning every rope that she has unknowingly wrapped around me and is pulling me toward her.

I can't just stand here while she is ignoring me because it gives her the power, and that's not how this works. I'm driving the narrative today!

I need a distraction. Walking away down the hallway, I do what my mum used to call the "idiot check" in my room, checking that I haven't left anything, even though I had hardly unpacked last night before we got distracted. The idiot check was the last thing we would do when we were leaving some accommodation, but not that any of those rooms ever looked like this. Most of the time it was actually just a caravan.

As expected, there is nothing here, only the memories of my night with Victoria and a hint of that damn scent she wears. It hypnotizes my sensibility.

Hearing the porter in the suite, I know it's time to go.

Entering the main room, I find the porter is already gone, and still Victoria is sitting there calmly drinking her tea.

"Time to leave, Victoria," I say, using my stern voice that I usually reserve for Jocelyn. I have to learn to hate Victoria like I despise Jocelyn. It will help.

Glancing at the watch on her wrist, she looks at me for the first time since I returned. "I'll be down when I'm ready."

I feel the hair on the back of my neck stand up and steam building in my body. She did not just dismiss me, did she?!

"Pardon?" I ask, trying not to react the way she wants me to.

"Sorry, are you a little deaf this morning? I said, I'll be down when I'm ready." She's a little huffier this time.

"You are ready now!" I snap, holding the door open and glaring at her, letting her know I'm not taking her crap.

"Oh, another order I must obey. Hmm, well, according to my watch, I have ten minutes left from the time frame given in the last order. So, I will be down in the foyer at eight twenty-nine am on the dot and not a minute earlier." Placing her cup on the saucer, she stands and walks down the hall into the bathroom, slamming the door behind her.

"For fuck's sake!" I knew it, I just fucking knew it. No way she could just do as I asked.

What's the point of arguing with her? It's not like I can march into the bathroom, put her over my shoulder, and carry her to the car while she's screaming at me. Although, it's not totally out of the equation if she continues like this.

Leaving the suite is the only option I have, before I explode.

Pacing in the foyer is out of the question. The owner of the hotel does not pace in his own establishment, in front of his staff and patrons.

The truth is, I need to be pounding on the treadmill like I did for two hours straight this morning while the rest of the hotel slept. I couldn't stay in bed with her. Her soft little foot moving up and down my leg, her breath whispering in the hair on my chest. Even the small little dribble of drool that pooled on my chest where her open mouth was lying on me. The longer I touched her, the harder it was going to be to leave. Instead, I got up and took the hotel Maserati out for a spin around the city as it slept.

One of the things I have implemented since I took over the business is a luxury car to be at each hotel for the use of our high-end clients who want all the bells and whistles when they stay with us. Plus, it gives me a car to use when I'm in town.

My life is so different from what I pictured. Never did I imagine driving a Maserati! But I love the feel of speed and being thrown back into the racing-designed seat with the G-forces every time I plant the accelerator flat to the floor, like I did many times last night. The whole time I was picturing Victoria in the passenger seat, hair down, spilling all over her bare shoulders in a strapless evening gown, showing off her body for me to ogle at. A nice split up the side has her closest leg to me on display, and I smooth my hand up and down the inside of her thigh, getting closer to her pussy every time.

Trying to get the thoughts of her and what I wanted to do to her in that car from my head, I ended up, as ridiculous as it sounds, stopping and visiting the Trevi Fountain again, making my own wish this time. I wished for Tori to hand in a spectacular presentation on the rebranding, securing herself a great reputation in her job, and then most importantly, move on far away from me!

The whole time I was thinking of her at the fountain, I could still feel the sense of panic that woke me from my sleep. Sweat pouring off me like I had run a marathon. Last night as we lay talking, her telling me her dreams of traveling, my heart constricted, and it was like all the breath in my lungs left me. All I could think of was my father traveling to London with the promise of returning, but he never did. His sense of travel only brought pain to us all, losing him. I know I won't survive the pain of having someone leave me in the same way. What if she never came home again? It would kill me. That's why I panicked and jumped out of bed. I just can't afford to get caught up with a woman who is so much younger than me and at a totally different stage of life. She is still finding herself, and I found myself years ago—and I wasn't the man I thought I knew.

Returning to the hotel in the early hours of the morning, adrenaline still pumping from my drive, was when I went to the gym and tried to sweat Victoria, the red goddess, out of my system, only leaving room for Tori the designer and twenty-six-year-old walking whirlwind most days.

When I was done, I hit the shower in my room, surprised that Tori hadn't woken at all. She sleeps like she is in hibernation, unaware of anything moving around her, while she has that cute little snore happening.

Stop it!

Don't think about her being cute. It'll just make it harder. I just need to get her back to London and keep my distance.

I check my Rolex that was my father's, something that means

more to me than the hotel I'm standing in. Enough is enough. I'm done waiting.

"Call the car," I tell the doorman.

If her ass is not on the seat next to me by eight-thirty exactly, I'm leaving without her, and she can find her own flight back to London.

With the door opened for me, I hear the click-clack of shoes behind me. Glancing down at my watch discreetly, I see it is eight twenty-nine, exactly like she told me.

All the way walking around to her side, she is so pleasant to everyone and thanking them for the lovely stay. If she gets in this car and continues the sweet chatter, I'm going to lose my mind.

With the door closing behind her, she is perfectly seated next to me, and everything falls completely quiet.

The driver pulls away from the hotel and into traffic. I know I can't look at her, even though I want to, because the moment I do, the war of words will erupt, and nobody needs that.

The whole trip on the plane, no more than one or two words are spoken to each other. I catch numerous looks from Victoria that speak volumes, but for once she has managed to stay quiet, and that worries me more.

While we're on the plane, I have been drafting an email to Victoria to set out what I want from her. In the moments we spent talking yesterday, I learned why this job means so much to her. After working on a major project with her co-worker for months, he took the project to the client a week earlier than planned, in a meeting without her, plastering his name all over her ideas. He secured the lead designer job on the project. When she protested that it was her ideas that he used and nothing of his own, management—who were all men—dismissed her. I might be a jerk, but I would never treat a woman any differently to a man in my organization. I don't treat Jocelyn badly because of her gender. It's purely because she is a bitch.

I save the email into my drafts so I can send it when it's time. The plane landing, we make our way down the stairs to two cars on the tarmac. Both Wallace and Miles are putting our bags into the separate cars. As I stop at the bottom of the stairs to thank the pilot, Miles is already ushering Victoria into the Bentley, and I walk over to the door before he closes it. I need to speak to her before we part.

Miles nods at me and walks away.

"I have sent you an email with my instructions for the project," I tell her, then hesitate, seeing her eyes getting wider by the minute. I'm sure she thought my reaction this morning meant everything was over.

Gripping the door and doing the exact opposite to what I should, I lean in and softly kiss her cheek. Her breath hitches, and I'm frozen in time, inhaling that scent that makes my body crave hers. The feeling that races through my body being so close to her again shocks me into pulling away quickly, knocking the back of my head on the car as I escape backwards from her sexual pull she wraps me in every time.

"Fuck," I hiss, rubbing the back of my head and standing up straight.

Victoria still looks confused at my kiss. I need to leave before she speaks.

"Thank you, Victoria, I had a good time." Closing the door, I turn and walk away as I hear her screaming at me.

"You asshole! Is that all I was, a good fucking time…?"

I wince, as both my drivers can hear her rant.

"Get her home safely, Miles, and perhaps pop in some ear plugs," I tell him before climbing into the back of the Range Rover and pulling out my phone.

Pressing send on the email, I then shut my phone down and drop it on the seat next to me for the rest of the ride to my estate. I should be in the office, but I can't today. I need space from every- thing, and the only place I get that is in my home that no one can touch. I don't bring people out here, except occasionally the guys.

My heavy sigh must have given away my anguish.

"Short trip, sir." Wallace knows I wasn't due back for a week, but the call he received to come to the airport this morning has him checking in that I'm okay. Others might think it's being nosy, but Wallace is someone I trust, and I know he genuinely cares.

"Yes." It's all I can manage right now. My mind is off thinking about Victoria reading my email.

From: Nicholas Darby
To: Victoria Packer

Dear Victoria,

I wish to apologize for our work trip being cut short and not quite as either of us had planned.

My plans changed quickly, and I needed to return to London.

Please continue this week with your rebranding project, and I will have Lucy schedule a meeting with you for us to review your next proposal.

Any information you may need help with, please contact Flynn Taylor, who I'm sure will be more than helpful. He has been working with me since the day I took over the business. I will organize for him to take you on a tour of our London hotel for you to get a feel of what a Darby Hotel has to offer. I'm not sure your stay in Rome gave you the right impression.

I trust you with this job. I have a feeling you are far more talented than you give yourself credit for. The situation with your previous job will not happen here, and I will make sure we continue to work together on a professional level. Trust your gut and don't take the safe option. Show me what you can do.

Thank you,
Mr. Nicholas Darby
CEO/Owner of Darby Hotel Chain

I know it was the gutless thing to do, but I just couldn't face the fight. At some stage I will need to explain to Flynn that I have just dumped Tori in his lap, and if he touches her, he will die.

What the fuck is wrong with me?!

Watching out the window as the world whizzes past me in a blur, I can't think clearly. My brain keeps going back to my core belief. Is this something you would be happy to tell your mother, knowing she would be proud of you? And the answer is a big fat no! I stepped over so many boundaries with Tori. All against my better judgment, yet I couldn't stop.

I crave her on a level I have never experienced before.

Did I do the right thing sleeping with her? Probably not, but do I regret it? Not a chance. Her peachy skin in my hands last night was something I'll never forget and won't get again. I've sworn off Tori for good. The two of us together would never work. We are too volatile when we are around each other, and the other problem is that it just makes me want to fuck her harder. Such a bad combination of lust and hate. I take the blame for my part, being controlling, yet I can't hold myself back with her.

As we reach the entrance of the estate, the old square stone pillars and iron gate are the sign I'm home. My apartment in London is where I stay, but this is truly home for me.

The crunching of gravel under the tires makes me take that deep breath I need. The breath that allows me to finally breathe, strip off the literal suit I wear when others see me, and let myself unwind to just be me. Nic, the chef who is living another life that he inherited and is determined to succeed in. But that doesn't mean that every so often I can't be the guy who surfed and ran every morning. Who cleared his head with the saltwater running over my skin and the sun heating his blood, not a care in the world.

But here I am, everyone's property. I need to be at the top of my game to make sure that every person I employ, and in turn then every family I support, are happy and paid well. My family's reputation is still held up high, and the legacy of my grandparents and father will continue for many years to come. I don't want to disappoint them or my mother, who is so proud I followed in my father's footsteps.

A high expectation to maintain, yet I'm managing.

Well, I *was,* until a certain woman walked into my life, and since then, the world seems different. Chaotic, yes, but there's also something else I can't put my finger on, and it's driving me crazy.

Walking through my back door into the kitchen, I know what I need to do. I need to cook!

The kitchen is my happy place, cooking the one thing that gives me true joy and no stress. Because I'm not cooking for anyone else but myself, and even though I'm my own worst critic, I can handle that.

Normally I would want to cook something extravagant and a full three-course meal, but now, I just want comfort food. Homemade macaroni cheese, with my own little twist of roasted pumpkin, zucchini, and spring onions.

Yes, that's what I need to do. Take the memory of the taste of Victoria off my tongue and replace it with good food.

Deep down, I know it won't work, but I'm willing to try anyway.

I thought not being around her would soothe me, but instead, all I can think of is her anger at my actions and email. And even though she is miles away, my cock is still hard as hell, thinking about the fire in her eyes that I just put there.

There is something wrong with me.

Who gets turned on from pissing off the woman in his dreams?

Chapter Thirteen

VICTORIA

I still can't believe the way he dismissed me, and that email was just the icing on the cake.

After arriving home from Rome, crawling into bed and feeling sorry for myself was all I could manage yesterday. I keep wondering how we could switch from having such intense chemistry between us that resulted in the off-the-charts sex, to a man who just orders me around and grunts at me when he speaks.

I would call him Jekyll and Hyde, but he has more than two sides to his personality. When he has his business personality on, he is polite, yet arrogant, confident, and makes things happen. A dominant man! But the man who took me to bed exerts such sexual control. It's a power that has every cell in my body tingling just from his voice, and then his touch only fuels my fire. Yet the man who cleaned me and took care of me afterwards is nothing like the other two. He was soft and gentle, the man I can see behind the walls he has built and someone who truly cares. That's the man I want to get to know more.

But the man who walked away from me at the airport is Captain Asshole. Kick me from your bed, don't talk to me, and then kiss me as you leave, telling me I was a good time. He was the most confusing of them all.

Although, he is all those things rolled into one. I can't help but want to know more. Call me crazy, but something is pulling me to him, no matter how much I want to run the opposite way. I mean, how can he get under my skin after one night?

I didn't call work to tell them I was back yesterday, but I know I need to show up at the office on Monday and explain why I'm back. Not that management will care, but it will be Theo and Suzi who are over me. Thank goodness I have the weekend to get over the rollercoaster that was my week. Plus, I need to start trying to get my head around another completely different angle for the rebranding of fuckhead's hotels.

What even is my life right now?

"You know the old saying, the best way to get over someone is to get under someone else?" Lou says as she scoops another spoonful of banoffee pie into her mouth, cream left on the corners of her mouth.

It's our go-to dessert when one of us has had a shitty day, or in my case, week. We have the best little bakery around the corner from Elouise's house. I'm not sure it's great for my waistline, but it's perfect for my mental health. Sugar fixes everything. Well, maybe not everything, but it feels good for a while, and that's enough for me.

"Ughh, men suck! I wasn't looking for anything, and now he has my body craving sex again. Him and his super cock!" I snap, shoving another mouthful of pie into my mouth.

We are sitting on the grass in a small park down the road from the bakery. There is a pond where the wild ducks nest in the reeds and the swans spend time cruising the water. There isn't much of the warm weather and sunshine left, so we are soaking up what we can. A few families are out with their kids and dogs. It's the perfect setting for a sweet picture, yet most times we're here, Lou and I are too busy bitching about something.

Today is Mr. Darby's turn.

"Be thankful you got some dick. I'm in a drought over here." Lou looks at me, and we both burst out laughing.

"Oh, because we are such good catches. Look at us, with cream all over our faces while stuffing ourselves full of pie. I can't imagine why the studs aren't all lining up at the door." Picking up my phone, I take a selfie of both of us with evidence of the dessert around our mouths and the piece of pie on the plate half demolished.

"Shut up." Lou bumps her shoulder into mine, and I almost drop my pie.

"Watch it. Don't mess with a woman and her pie!" Our giggles continue until all the pie is gone and we are lying on our backs on the blanket.

"Is there something wrong with me?" I ask out loud, when really it was just a thought in my head, but now it's out there. I'm still so confused on what went wrong yesterday that Nicholas has rocked my confidence in myself. Maybe the sex wasn't as good for him as it was for me.

"No, not at all. Don't you dare think that. He's the jerk here."

"Agreed," I say, looking up at the clouds floating past us.

"I wish I believed you," she says beside me. "I don't know what he did to you, but that is some spell he cast over you."

I allow the break in conversation and just listen to the sounds of nature around us, falling over us. I know she's right, but I just can't seem to shake that part of the night where he was so tender and thoughtful. And the day spent in Rome was so romantic, even though there was no intention for that to happen. He just treated me like I was special and he was trying to make a good impression. It's just not something that I would expect from a man who is so bossy and rude at times.

"I'm glad I don't have to work closely with him again. I'll talk to my boss when she returns on Monday and get taken off the portfolio."

Sitting bolt upright next to me, Elouise points her finger at me forcefully. "No, you won't! Don't back down from him. You go in there and give him the best freaking rebranding you can and show him what he is missing out on. These old pricks think they can take what they want. Well, this one picked the wrong woman to go to war with. She's tough and will fight back. Won't you?" Man, Elouise might be a schoolteacher that needs to be refined and calm all day, but don't mess with her. She can come out swinging if she needs to.

"I can't even think about where to take this project. I spent more time checking out the CEO than the hotel itself." Sighing, I sit up and remember the words in the email. Talk to Flynn and trust my gut. As mixed up as my gut is, it's telling me not to let go of this opportunity for my career.

"You're right," I say at last.

"Always," Lou replies with confidence.

"Fuck him. I'm going to go in there and blow him away." Not quite sure how, but I'll work it out.

"We need to go out tonight. Girls' night!" Elouise stands and offers her hand to me to pull me up.

"Hell yes, we do! Let's go get wasted," I shout, and the family at the duck pond turns with scowls on their faces. Okay, perhaps with a little less volume next time.

"Um, let's not get too carried away," Lou says, putting her arm around my shoulders. We look at each other and laugh.

Yeah, that's not going to happen.

NICHOLAS

Working from the estate on Friday is not normal for me, but I just needed space to breathe.

I'm still worried about my mother and the whole crashing the car. Something is not right there, and she won't tell me much. I'm trying to work out if I should take on this new location in France that I have been eyeing off for a while in secret. I don't tell the board anything until I know what direction I am going with something. Flynn is driving me crazy after I ignored him most of Friday. And of course, I can't get Victoria out of my head. That woman has done something to me, and I can't shake it. She haunts my thoughts day and night. I just wanted to get away from her and push the memories away, but it's impossible.

When I spoke to my mum last night, she could tell something wasn't right with me, but I didn't want to share anything with her. Not until I know she is okay. Instead, today I have been walking the fields with Sid, my black-and-white border collie. He was just a puppy when I got him from the neighbor next door whose dog had a litter. He reminded me of home in Australia where these dogs are common. So, I named him Sid, short for Sydney.

Coming over the crest of the hill in the field closest to the house, I chuckle to myself, seeing the Porsche, Audi, and BMW parked near the house.

"Looks like we have visitors, Sid. Go give them the Darby welcome." As I motion for him to go, he takes off down toward Rem who bends down, waiting for him. Sid loves when he visits, although it's not that often. Flynn and Forrest lean on the front of Rem's black Porsche while Rem is being welcomed in the only way Sid knows how, by almost licking him to death.

"What are all doing here? Can't a man be left in peace for a few days?" I ask, walking past Rem and Sid still playing. I stop and lean on Flynn's Audi, waiting for a response.

"Not when he leaves the country with a woman for a week and is back twenty-four hours later, then avoids the office. So, if you won't come to us, we will come to you. What the fuck happened?" Flynn knows me too well. He has been beside me through some of the toughest times of my life and still hangs around.

"They didn't need me in Rome, so I came back. No point wasting time over there. Now, who is up for a beer?" Pushing off the car, I walk toward the back door, ignoring Flynn's reply.

"That's the biggest load of bullshit, and you know it." Forrest laughs at Flynn yelling at me while they follow behind me.

"Jesus, Flynn, back off, we aren't here for some freaking intervention or some shit. Beer sounds great," Forrest replies, heading inside with the rest of them. Rem finally drags himself away from Sid.

Flynn rolls his eyes. "Christ, that's not what I'm doing. I just want to know the details of why he came back early. You guys weren't there when he went all nuclear at Ms. Packer in his office. There was some chemical meltdown of his brain," he says, accepting the beer from my hand and taking a seat on one of the kitchen stools.

"Do tell." Rem perches on the stool beside him, taking his first drink of his beer.

"Yes, Flynn," I seethe, "please tell me why you then came up with your amazing idea of her being my fake girlfriend." I glare at him as the memories of my time with Victoria start pouring through my head.

"No, don't deflect from the question," Flynn fires back at me.

"Fine, you want to know? I took Victoria to Rome, trying my hardest to stay away from her. Then you came up with this bright idea that we play happy couple. Oh, we played happy couple, all right. And I knew as soon as we did, I needed to stop that from happening again."

"Oh my God, you fucked our consultant on the first night." Forrest shakes his head at me, always the conservative one in the bunch.

"Yes, and it's Flynn's fault," I snap, taking another large mouthful of beer to quench my thirst and settle my thoughts.

"It's not my fault you can't keep it in your pants." Flynn laughs at me.

"Twenty-six! She's only twenty-six years old and is just beginning her life. She's not a jaded old man like me." I push myself up to sit on the kitchen counter beside my sink and the large window overlooking the back yard.

"Oh no, you like her, don't you," Rem pipes up with a big smile.

"I can't like her. She is too young, ready to start her life adventure, and works for me. End of story," I say, turning my head to the side and glancing out at the two horses in the field closest to the house. Occasionally I will ride one, but it's not a hobby of mine. They were here when I took over the estate, and Henry, my manager, rides them and keeps them happy.

"Please tell me you left on good terms, so we don't get our asses sued off for you taking advantage of her," Forrest cautions me.

"I wouldn't say good, but we definitely left on some sort of terms," I say slowly, alluding to what happened.

"Great! So, in other words, you left her seething at you from your usual happy demeanor. We are screwed then." Forrest is always the one who worries about the things that can go wrong.

"That's why I asked her to deal with Flynn from next week, until the final meeting with her new proposal."

"Like I've got time to babysit your fuck-up on top of everything else." Flynn walks around the island counter and thumps me in the arm as he sits beside me.

"Victoria is not a fuck-up!" I stress to him. "And if you make her feel that way, you will have me to deal with!" My anger is simmering, and I'm trying to keep it under control so they can't see what I really feel about her.

"Oh, boss man is a little touchy." Rem sniggers.

"Can we just end this? I'm sure you didn't come all the way out here to talk work." Jumping down from the counter, I change the subject. "Who's coming to the soccer match next weekend?"

"You mean football?" Rem laughs.

"Same thing." The difference is that in Australia, we play three different codes of football, and soccer is the fourth. It gets confusing.

"I'm in. I mean, if I have any spare time left, after Mr. Darby here has filled up my schedule," Flynn says, pointing his thumb at me.

Both Forrest and Rem are keen to come as well, to the corporate box we have at Old Trafford. I must admit, I do love the atmosphere at the historic site. My grandfather and father were Man U supporters, so it only made sense to carry it on.

After the first beer has gone down, we grab another round and head back outside onto the outdoor deck to enjoy them. This is one of my favorite spots on the estate, where I can just sit and be me. Take in the sunset over the fields and green for as far as the eye can see.

The conversation started flowing about other things thankfully, and the afternoon that ran into the night is just what I needed. I always have plenty of meat in the freezer, and my vegetable garden is full of fresh produce thanks to Henry. So, between Flynn and I, we whipped up dinner and continued to drink into the night.

The guys stay over in the guest rooms, because everyone has had too much to drink to allow them to drive home.

The next morning, while having breakfast with them, I hear the crunching sound of wheels on the driveway. Who else could be here? It's not like this is a place that people just drop in.

The weather a bit warmer today, I'm just in a pair of jeans and white t-shirt, feet bare as I head to the door to greet whoever it is.

Opening the big front door, to my surprise, there are two police officers standing there looking at me.

"Good morning, sir, we are looking for Mr. Richard Darby," one asks, with no emotion or indication of what they are doing here.

"You found him. What can I do for you?" I ask, standing a little taller now, straightening my shoulders and holding my breath. Part of me is panicking that something has happened to Mum.

"I'm Sergeant Collins, and this is Constable Smith. May we come in to talk for a moment?" The straight poker face they are both wearing is starting to concern me.

"Of course, come through. Just having breakfast with some friends, so I'll take you into the lounge room."

I can hear the guys still carrying on in the kitchen, oblivious to who is in the house.

My heart is racing slightly as to what this is about. "Please, take a seat," I offer, pointing to the couch behind them.

The older one shakes his head. "No, we'll stand, thank you."

Okay, it's one of those conversations then, one that is not a friendly one.

"What can I do for you then?" I stand with my arms crossed, more defensive now.

"Mr. Darby, are you the owner of a Maserati, registration plate DH 0012 stored in The Darby Hotel in Rome?" the younger less-aggressive cop, Smith, starts.

"Yes, I do, is there a problem?" Part of me breathes a sigh of relief that it's not anything to do with Mum.

"Were you at the hotel last Thursday night?" he continues.

"Yes, what is going on?" I ask, getting frustrated very quickly at his slowness at getting to the point.

"Were you driving the car that night?" Grumpy Collins asks.

"Yes, I was. Now what is all this about? Just spit it out, for God's sake." I'm about ready to lose my temper with them. Don't come into my house talking in riddles. I hear the chairs moving on the tile floor in the kitchen, the guys obviously hearing my voice raising.

Just as they walk into the room behind me, words I never thought I'd hear are directed at me. "Mr. Darby, we will need you to accompany us to the station in London for questioning."

"What the hell for!" There is no holding back now.

"Distribution of drugs." Sergeant Collins holds handcuffs in front of him.

"You have to be fucking joking." What the actual fuck is going on?!

"You have the wrong person." Flynn is beside me and saying what I should be saying, but I'm still in shock.

"I'm calling our lawyer, this is bullshit." Forrest disappears out of the room with his phone to his ear.

"More will be explained at the station in London. If you will just come with us now, sir, please," Constable Smith asks.

Taking a deep breath, my brain clicks back into rational thought. "I'll come with you, but not in those," I say, pointing to the handcuffs in his hand. "I'm no threat and I'm not resisting, so put them away. I have nothing to do with drugs, but if there is something going on in my hotel, I want to know about it." Turning to

Flynn and Rem, I say, "Meet me at the station, because I'll need a lift home once this is sorted out. I'll just get some shoes and my phone." I walk toward the doorway of the room.

"Sorry, sir, but one of us will need to accompany you."

Standing still to allow them to follow me, I mumble under my breath how ridiculous all of this is.

Having everything I need, Forrest lets me know Phillip Beck, our lawyer, is already on his way to the station to sort this shit out.

I can imagine the look on Mum's face if she knew I was in the back of a police car being taken in for questioning. Or my nan and pop. Pop would be demanding answers and not from me—he'd be taking on the police.

The whole ride I'm trying to work out what is going on. I just want answers, and Dumb and Dumber in the front seat aren't about to give them to me.

Is someone running drugs through the hotel? Did one of my staff use the car without permission? Both of those are incomprehensible. I'm glad my grandfather is not alive to see this. To have his family name tarnished by some lowlife would have devastated him. I need to get to the bottom of this before the media gets a hold of it.

Just when I thought the week couldn't get any worse...

VICTORIA

I'm standing at the bar at the Chester Arms Hotel, ordering another gin and tonic for Lou and me, when I feel someone slide up beside me, making me step to the side slightly.

"Always running away from me." Evan's voice grabs my attention.

"Oh, it's you again." I tap my card on the machine being held toward me, our drinks being put on the bar in front of me.

"Wow, what a way to say hello," he says, laughing at me as he orders his beer.

"Sorry, you just caught me off guard." To say the least. I'm out to drown my sorrows over one man; I don't need another one lurking around.

"We keep running into each other. Let's say we catch up a bit over this drink," he suggests, lifting his beer in the air.

I want to say no, but it's a bit hard. I don't want to be rude.

"I'm here with Elouise, just over there. Sure, join us." I want to kick myself for giving in, but he is a nice guy and is maybe just looking for a friend to hang out with for the night.

Placing the drinks on the table, I can see the surprise on Lou's face when Evan stands beside me, waiting for me to sit.

"You remember Evan, don't you, Elouise?" I know she does by the way she looks at me, but her acting is perfect.

"The face is familiar. Where do I know you from?" she asks, looking so innocent but really is playing a game with him.

"Tori and I dated a few times before we realized that we weren't compatible, except just as friends." I feel a bit of relief at his statement, knowing that he isn't looking for anything.

"Oh, that's right. What are you up to these days, Evan?" She is good! She's trying to get all the intel she needs on this guy for me, without me asking the questions and appearing interested in any way.

"I'm working in London for a big architectural firm. Finally landed the job I have been wanting for a long time. I'm actually living in the city now, just home for the weekend for Dad's birthday tomorrow. I just came down to the pub to take a breather from my mother fussing over me." He rolls his eyes like we all do when talking about our parents not understanding that we are grown adults who don't need them for everything anymore.

"Good for you," I reply.

"What about you, Tori, what are you doing these days? Still working for that dick you were when we were dating?" he asks, making himself comfortable in his seat. Shit, I think he is settling in for a long catchup.

I want to say "*no, but I'm working for an even bigger dick this time,*" but instead, I just reply with the basics.

"No, thank goodness, I have a new job I just started a week ago. It's being a big change." And that's an understatement, looking back at what my first week on the job has been like.

"Well, while you two are slumming it with the big wigs in the city, I'm still learning my ABC's and numbers, getting plastered with paint and glue on a daily basis, and I love it. You can have your stressful jobs. Give me little-people problems any day of the week." Lou is making sure she is still in the conversation and stops it being just directed at me. We all start laughing, and then topics become much lighter, like what is the best type of beer in the pub.

Laughing at the last thing Evan said, I realize that we actually do make better friends, when the pressure of sex is off the table. The night has gotten away from us, as the bartender announced last call.

Although Nicholas has been in my head most of the night, the more I drank, the more determined I am to show him he messed with the wrong woman. I don't have to put up with his shit. If he thinks he can just push me to the side and not have to deal with me on this job, well, he's mistaken. I'm going to give him the best freaking proposal on his rebranding, and he won't be able to ignore me.

"I don't think I should have another drink. I'm on the edge of falling over the cliff of waking up with a hangover, and I don't think I want that two weekends in a row." Evan and Lou laugh at me, both having seen me at some stage of the disaster that was my drunken Friday night last week.

"Fair enough, and I have to cope with my mother bounding into my room at some ridiculous time in the morning for birthday break-fast for Dad. Ugh, I'm already regretting drinking so much and staying late. I blame you two," Evan says, pointing his fingers at me and Lou as we giggle.

"We didn't force you to drink. In fact, you kept buying, so it's all self-inflicted, mister." Lou stands, and Evan leans in as he puts his arm around her shoulders and gives her a squeeze. Then he walks around and hugs me, which surprisingly feels so different to when we were trying to date.

"True, but I'll be blaming you when I explain to my mum in the morning why I'm a bit slow getting out of bed." Evan starts laughing as we make our way to the door. "Let me walk you both home, you know, be the gentleman."

A week ago, I would have said no, but after spending a fun night together, why not.

"Sure, protect us from the midnight gremlins," I say, smiling to myself, knowing that I'd be far scarier than any gremlin if they tried to get near us. Drunk Tori has no filter.

Pushing between the two of us, Evan puts his arms out for us and links us all together as we walk down the road laughing, which turned into a really bad karaoke version of *Follow the Yellow Brick Road* at the top of our voices, while we skip down the road. I'm sure the neighbors will love it.

I think Evan turned up for a reason tonight, reminding me what I don't want in a relationship. He is a sweet guy, but he's not strong enough for me.

It's becoming apparent, I only fall for assholes!

NICHOLAS

The last few hours have been a blur.

I'm furious, and I need to burn off the anger somewhere. I know what I really want, but I can't even be thinking about her right now.

Instead, I just want to get home to my apartment and into my gym, to punch the shit out of a punching bag until I can't hold my arms up any longer. Because I can't imagine sleep is going to come easy tonight, if at all.

Flynn drives me home from the police station, still talking about how pissed off he is at today's events that have stretched into tonight. I can't talk, otherwise I will explode. I haven't been charged yet but have been told not to leave the country. How fucking dare they! I don't know what they think they have to prove it was me, when I know it damn well wasn't, but it can't be enough to press charges. They are getting all their information from the Italian police at this stage, and that is part of the problem, I think. Who knows what is happening over there.

I can't decide what will upset me more. If someone is running drugs through my hotel or if they find I'm being set up. But I'm not waiting around for these idiots to work it out. I have already messaged Broderick, and he is on the case. If this man can find Mum, which would have been like finding a needle in a haystack, then I trust him to get to the bottom of this too. We have remained good friends, and he has always had my back ever since I met him. Grandfather told me that I could trust him with my life, and it looks like that's exactly what I'll be doing.

"Are you listening to me?" Flynn whacks me on the arm to gain my attention.

"No," I growl.

"At least you are honest. Want to talk about it?" he asks, offering to be the shoulder he thinks I need.

"No." I echo my first growl with just as much emphasis.

"That's not healthy." The concern in his voice tells me he is as worried as I am.

What if they can make this stick? I can't go to jail for something I didn't do. It would be a catastrophe for the hotels, and who would look after Mum and my grandparents? So much is rushing through my head now.

"Probably not," is all I can say.

"All right, silence it is then. But just know that we have your back on this. There is no way we are letting this happen. Forrest and the lawyer are on the case, Rem is flying to Rome tonight to see what he can find out from the staff and start reviewing security tapes, and we all know Broderick treats you like a long-lost son. There is no way he will let this rest until he finds out the truth."

We pull into the garage of my apartment. I know everything he is saying is the truth, but I just can't discuss it.

Opening the door of the car, all I can manage to say is, "I know. Thanks, Flynn, talk tomorrow." Closing the door before he has time to try again to get me to talk, I walk to my private elevator.

The ride up to my penthouse apartment seems to take forever tonight. My brain is racing with thoughts, but the main one is, what if I can't fix this?

And then as the doors to my apartment open, a stab to my heart stops me in my tracks, staring out the window at the view. What will Victoria think of me if this gets out?

It should be the least of my problems, but I know deep down it's the most important problem to me.

Chapter Fourteen

VICTORIA

I knew this morning would be painful, arriving in the office to the thousand questions of why I'm back already. Not a great way to start a Monday morning.

"He had some business he needed to get back to London for. It's not like he has to tell me what it is. We are no more than business associates," I say defensively, standing at my desk, trying to fend off Suzi and Theo.

"Sure, you aren't more than associates. Why else would he take you to Rome?" Theo's jealous streak is out again.

"Theo, seriously," I snap, trying not to give anything away with my answer.

"So, are you still working on the proposal?" Suzi looks at me, a little disbelieving of my response. They don't really know me yet, so they are still trying to work me out.

"Of course, I'm heading over to the offices today to have a meeting with him and his offsider, Mr. Taylor, so we can go over a few things we didn't get time to in Rome. Mainly about the London hotels." I should win an Oscar for my Academy-Award-winning performance and bold confidence this morning.

I haven't even set up a meeting yet, but maybe that's the trick. I just turn up at his office and ask to see him. Surely, he won't be stupid enough to ignore me. I mean, I could make a big scene in his office about him being such a douchebag. Not that I ever would, but the way we left it, he could get scared that I might.

Even if I can't see him, I'll try to see Flynn and find out what the hell is going on.

I try to change the subject so the heat is off me. "Is Gwenda in yet?" I ask, hoping that she doesn't take me off this project. I have a whole explanation for what has happened in the last week, praying that she doesn't want to take back the reins on this job.

"Oh shit, I forgot to tell you." Suzi slaps her forehead. "There is an email from the big boss, you will it see when you log on. It says she is on leave and no confirmed date of return yet."

Well, that solves that problem, but I'm also a little worried about her. She said it wasn't a holiday.

"Don't you think that is a bit strange?" I ask both of them.

"Absolutely. She didn't say anything to you before she left?" Suzi looks at me for answers, and Theo is unusually quiet.

"No, but she hardly knows me, so why would she talk to me?" I look at Theo, trying to provoke him to answer. "She spent more time telling me not to drink with Theo."

His head whips up. "What?" He looks a little shocked, and I don't know why.

"And she was right. That little Friday-night drinks session after work was lethal. Next time, no shots for me," I say, trying to make light of how drunk I was.

"Famous last words, Tori. No Friday night with Theo goes shot-free." Suzi is now giggling and starts to walk away as the clock is ticking closer to nine am and we should be working.

"You had fun, that's all you need to worry about." Theo starts to snap out of his strange mood. "Now, let's talk about this job. Do you need my help now that Gwenda is not here?" What is it with Theo?

He constantly wants to get involved in this job. It's not like he was that excited about the other files I was handed on that first day.

"No, I'm fine, thank you. Were you given my other jobs?" His face tells me he was, and he isn't happy about it.

"Yep, I got the shit ones, nothing like what you got, golden girl."

Time to back away, Tori. Theo is not a happy boy this morning. Obviously got out of bed on the wrong side. I've learned not to take on anyone else's problems, just stick with your own—and I have plenty of them this morning.

Opening my emails, I see that Mr. York, the head boss that Nicholas called on the plane the other day, has emailed me directly, explaining that Gwenda will be away and that I am to step into her role temporarily. My main portfolio is the Darby Hotel file and to supervise Theo in all the other files he has.

Oh, wow, no wonder Theo is pissed at me. I've walked in and straight away been promoted above him. That must hurt for someone who has a belief that men are needed in high places. A bit of his ego must be crushed, but I don't give a damn.

After working on the file all morning and doing my research, my brain is fried, and I could use some food to fuel it. Evan surprisingly messaged me this morning asking if we could meet for lunch at a café nearby. It turns out that our offices aren't that far from each other. And his office is close to the Darby Hotels' headquarters. So, I'll meet up with him and then head to the office and see if I can get in to see the jerk face himself. The element of surprise will hopefully get me a meeting. If I tried to schedule one, I'm sure he would be busy from now until Christmas.

"Hey, you." Evan stands up from the table that he already grabbed for us when he got here before me. It looks like this is a popular place and is currently in the throes of the lunchtime rush.

"Hi, Evan, sorry I'm a bit late," I say, giving him a hug, which is what friends do, and since we are now firmly in the friend zone, it seems appropriate.

"Nothing new. You were late to every date we had," he sasses.

I laugh with him because he is right. Being punctual has never been my strong point.

Conversation flows easily like it did the other night, and I wonder why we didn't discover this back when we were together. I've never really had a male friend before, and although on the first day of this new job I thought Theo might be one, he's turned out to be a whining co-worker who just wants what I have.

Finishing up my salad, I know we will need to wrap it up shortly so he can get back to his office and I can try my luck with Mr. Darby.

"This was fun, we should do it again," I surprise myself by asking for another lunch date with Evan.

"I agree. I'll message when I have a free lunch time again. But I can go one better. I actually have a big favor to ask you." He hesitates for a moment and then continues, "I have this charity event on Saturday night that I need a plus-one for. Would you be free, by…" His eyes almost pop out of his head before he can finish the sentence.

Before he even says a word, I know Nicholas is behind me. That alluring aftershave he wears is already swirling around me, making my heart race.

"She'll be with me," his deep raspy voice booms from behind me. My body responds to him like I have no control over it, but this time, I'm not taking his bullshit.

"Victoria." His eyes are burning through me as he steps into my view. He says my name in such a deep dominate tone. He turns me to mush, and I don't know how to resist him, but I have to try.

"Nicholas, good afternoon," I say, not giving anything away and trying to hold my voice strong. I had my whole speech rehearsed for when we met in his office, but this is not the place for our verbal foreplay, which is what it has become.

Feeling a kick under the table, I remember Evan.

"Nicholas Darby, this is Evan Ratten." I should have said a friend of mine, but I want to keep him wondering, making him feel irritated, like he makes me on a regular basis.

No hand is extended to shake, and Nicholas's eyes have moved to stare down Evan. If he could incinerate him, he would. He is pissed, and I can't help but feel satisfied at his obvious jealousy. And at least it confirms that our night of passion wasn't one-sided like he made me feel it was.

So, what the fuck is wrong with him?

"Time to leave, we need to discuss your proposal," he says, not even looking at me, his attention still on poor Evan who looks like he is about to shrink into his chair.

"Wait, what meeting? I hadn't even scheduled one." That he knows of, anyway. Surely, he can't read my mind.

"I'm scheduling it now." He pulls me up out of the chair. Although gently enough he doesn't hurt me, it's very controlling. This man really needs to pull himself together.

Only because I need to see him and thrash this out do I relinquish and lean down to grab my bag. It has nothing to do with my body being on fire from his possessiveness because he thinks I'm on a date.

My memory kicks in that pushing his buttons brings all sorts of fun, so I decide I'll play with him a little more.

Leaning down and hugging Evan, I hear Nicholas growling from behind me. "Thanks for lunch, Evan, it was fun. Sorry I need to go."

Nicholas throws money on the table. "Lunch is on me."

"Seriously!" I snap, looking him straight in the eye, letting him know I get what he is doing. He doesn't want Evan to have the joy of claiming he paid for me.

"Yes," he snarls at me.

Before I can step away from the table, Evan stands and pulls my arm toward him. He whispers into my ear, "You do know who he is, don't you?" I'm guessing he is a little starstruck by the rich guy and the awful way he is speaking.

"Yes, unfortunately," I say, looking back at Nicholas who is about to explode at Evan being so close to me.

"Haven't you seen the news today? He just got taken in for drug distribution in Italy." He tries to whisper it, but at the same time, the room goes quiet, and it was loud enough that I know Nicholas heard him too.

Spinning straight around, I find myself standing toe to toe with Nicholas, which we seem to make a habit of doing.

"What the actual fuck!" I yelp, never one to keep my voice at an appropriate volume. "Is this true?" I ask, watching him flinch and dip his head a little.

"No," he says forcefully but not as strong as when he arrived here. "We are leaving now!" That was definitely an order, and there is no question as to whether I am choosing to accompany him or not.

I'm so confused and trying to process what Evan just said, but when Nicholas speaks like that, I know he needs me to do as he asks, and the explanation will come later. Just like when we arrived in Rome. What fucking alternate universe did I fall into that first morning on the train?

Is he telling the truth or am I just some pawn in this whole game?

After reassuring Evan I am fine, we start walking out of the café, with Nicholas holding my hand in that same death grip like when we walked away from the hotel. If I don't end up with broken fingers from being around him, it will be a miracle.

The faster he walks, I notice he is looking around him constantly. Like he is watching out for someone. I never manage to have the right shoes on when he insists on dragging me along footpaths at such a rapid pace. When I dressed this morning, I had him in mind, but not like this. I put on my most flattering suit, with a straight black skirt that is a little shorter than work appropriate, paired with a blouse that is a bit lower cut than I would normally wear to work, but I wanted to remind him of what he threw away. Nice high shoes show off my legs and give me more height next to this giant. When you are vertically challenged like I am, you need every advantage you can get.

As I see the Darby offices come into view, my head is like a hamster wheel going flat out. What the hell is going on? The Nicholas I spent the day and night in Rome with is not someone I would ever suspect of being into drugs, but how am I to know? Do I really know him, or just who he wanted me to believe is the real Nicholas Darby?

Marching me across the reception area and straight to the elevator, still holding my hand, he uses his other hand to push the button several times, clearly frustrated it is taking so long. He still hasn't said a word to me, but I'm used to that. The doors finally open, and as we step into the elevator and turn to face the front, a man is about to enter as well, but the look Nicholas gives him has him backing away and offering to take the next car. *Good choice*, I think to myself. I wouldn't want to be in here either if I had the option; the air is so thick with tension it's hard to breathe.

I have so many questions I want to ask, and he has a lot of explaining to do. Firstly, what the hell was that caveman spectacle in the café? And secondly, what the fuck was Evan talking about?

The look on Lucy's face as we approach says it all. She is worried, and seeing Nicholas storming toward her just makes her stress more.

"No interruptions!" he barks at her as we pass, and she and I share a look of holy shit. We both know he is close to bursting.

The door slams behind us as we enter his office, and in a flash, he has me pushed up against it and is kissing me. It's not a happy-to-see-you kiss, or an I-want-you-naked-now one. This is pure claiming. He is making sure I understand what he wants.

Pulling back, he looks at me like he wants to eat me.

"You're mine, understand?" His lips are on me again, and I can't resist him. His body is pressing into mine with such force that I can feel every muscle of his, including his cock, that just reaffirms his words and actions. My Nicholas has a jealous streak that is strong enough it drives him crazy—or crazier than normal.

Wait, stop! I'm not his, and he isn't mine. That was made very clear the moment I woke up in his bed, alone and being ordered back to London.

No matter how much I wish it was true, there is so much shit that needs to be sorted out first. Like drug charges!

I shove him off me with every bit of strength I can muster,

which is more than I knew I had. His raging body stumbles back-wards, and the shock on his face tells me he wasn't expecting that from me.

Gasping for oxygen to help me think clearly, I say, "Your lips might be mesmerizing, but they don't make me forget everything that has happened. Get over there, far away from me, don't touch me, and start talking. Otherwise, the only action that dick you were so happily grinding on me will get will be my knee far into it, and your balls too."

Catching my breath, I walk toward the window to distance myself from him as he goes to his desk, throwing his phone down on it and taking a drink of water. Bending down, he opens a cabinet and stands with another bottle of water, throwing it at me. I desperately need it, too. I know if he touches me, I will melt into the sensation, so the only way I'll get some answers is with distance.

"Such a gentleman." I crack the top of the bottle off and take a long mouthful of cold water.

"I'm not allowed near you, remember?" He walks around to the front of his desk and tries to stand still, but I can see that the electricity buzzing through him is making that impossible.

"I'm waiting," I snap, glaring at him to start talking. I have a feeling it's rare anyone ever orders Nicholas around, and he isn't quite sure how to handle it from me.

"None of it is true, I promise you on my mother's life," he says, pulling his jacket off and rolling up his shirt sleeves. He runs his hands through his hair and holds onto the back of his head. I can finally see the vulnerability in him. I know how much his mother means to him, and he would never throw her name into this unless he truly means it.

I soften my voice slightly, hoping he will continue to talk. "None of what, Nicholas? I have no idea what is going on." Walking from the window, I sit down on the couch in front of him. "Explain it to me."

It wasn't until now that I could see how tired he looks.

"You haven't seen the media reports?" he asks skeptically, dropping his hands and placing them on the edge of his desk, hanging on like his life depends on it.

"No, I've been busy working for some cantankerous client," I say snidely, giving him a small smile to try to calm the situation a little.

"Then you should get rid of him. Sounds like an asshole." His words are still strained, but he is trying to calm himself down, knowing I'm prepared to listen to him.

"Funnily, I call him that on many an occasion. And he usually deserves it." I take another drink of water from the bottle and then place it on the table.

No matter what he is about to tell me, I don't feel scared to be in his presence. It's the same feeling of getting into the car with him, or the plane off to another country. Not once have I ever felt unsafe with him.

"Victoria, I'm so sorry to drag you into all of this. I was taken in for questioning on Saturday about some drugs that were found in my car at the hotel in Rome after we were there on Thursday night. I can assure you they aren't mine, but I need to prove it." He taps his fingers on the table from his nervous energy.

"That's easy to prove. You were with me." Why didn't he just tell them that? It's so obvious.

He sighs like he is about to tell me that he ate the last cannoli. "The problem is that I wasn't with you all night." He drops his head so he doesn't have to look at me. "After you fell asleep, I needed some air to sort through some things. So, I went for a drive in the Maserati to clear my head and then went to the gym downstairs for a few hours to work out."

Wrapping my arms around myself, I feel a cold shiver run over me. "You weren't in bed with me all night? But I would have felt you leave, wouldn't I?" In my heart, I believe he is innocent, but something in the back of my mind is still scared he is playing me.

Looking up, he gives me the smallest of smirks. "I wore you out. You were snoring and in a deep sleep. You didn't even flinch when I got up." He looks slightly proud of himself.

"Ah yes, multiple orgasms will do that to a girl." I squeeze my legs together, remembering every single one of them that had me screaming his name in ecstasy.

He must see the tiniest doubt in my face. "But I promise you, that's all I did. I would never put you in danger by involving you in something like that. I might be an asshole like you tell me on a regular basis, but I'm not a bad person." Deep down, I know it's true.

"Then why did you leave me? I don't understand. I thought that night was incredible, and then you totally shattered me that morning. What did I do wrong?" I can feel tears welling in my eyes, that I have probably been holding back since that morning. I told myself that I was too tough to let it affect me, but I was wrong. It hurt... a lot.

In seconds he is across the room and sitting on the coffee table in front of me. His long legs are on either side of mine, and he takes my hands from around my body and holds them in his, gently stroking his thumbs over the tops of my hands with such emotion.

"Oh, beautiful, it wasn't you. My demons make me do stupid things, and I fucked up epically that night by leaving you. I can't explain it, but just please trust me, it had nothing to do with you and how amazing you were." He drops one of my hands into my lap and takes my cheek in his large masculine hand. I can feel his sincerity in the way he's stroking my face with all the emotion he has been holding inside too.

I lean forward, needing to feel close to him. I want his lips on mine again. But just as we are about to touch, the door flies open and in storms Flynn and two other men I don't know.

"Out!" Nicholas screams at them.

"No can do. Trouble is brewing, and you are needed in the boardroom," Flynn announces while one of the other men walks to his chair where he threw his suit jacket. "Good, you're here, Victoria, you might be helpful." The creases in Flynn's brow let me know this is serious.

Nicholas jumps up and stands in front of him. "Leave her out of this!" he demands.

"No choice now, Nic, Jocelyn has rallied the board, and they are arriving now to pass a motion of no confidence in you to run this company. So, anyone who can save your ass needs to be in the room. Like your girlfriend that was with you in Rome." Flynn is not taking any prisoners with Nicholas. "The lawyer is on his way, but you two need to have your stories straight."

My heart is beating so hard it feels like it's about to jump out of my chest. I might be strong, but this is next level.

I blurt out, "I won't lie for you." My hands are starting to tremble, the shakes now moving through my body.

"You don't need to, sweetheart, they know he left the hotel. It's on the security tapes. But can you at least keep with the girlfriend story?" one of the other men asks me, a look of hope in his eyes.

"Who are you?" I ask. I feel a little overwhelmed with all the men around me.

"Sorry, I'm Remington Elders, and this is Forrest Taylor. We are this idiot's friends who are trying to keep his ass out of jail and at the head of his own company."

I look at Flynn and then Forrest, seeing the similarities their last name implies.

Forrest steps forward with his hand extended. "Yes, we're brothers, unfortunately, and I'm sorry this is happening now, but we don't have a lot of time." Shaking my hand, he then steps away quickly as Nicholas glares at him.

Nicholas takes my hand and pulls me toward a door I hadn't paid attention to, until we end up in the bathroom. Closing the door, he places his hands on my shoulders.

"Tori." Why do I hate him calling me that now? Victoria sounds so beautiful rolling off his lips. "You don't need to do this. You can walk away right now, and I would totally understand. This is my mess to solve, not yours. I'm used to my life being turned upside down. I got through it four years ago, and I can do it again now. I don't want you hurt in any way." The hurt and sorrow in his voice makes my heart stutter for him. He is talking about when his grandfather found him in Australia. He mentioned it briefly in Rome, but the details were vague. I know there's more to the story, and I decide right now that I want the chance to find out everything about this man. What happened to him back then and everything in between.

Taking a deep breath, I stand taller. "I said I won't lie for you. But if you tell me I'm your girlfriend, right here, right now, then I won't be making it up, will I." Shrugging my shoulders at him in the most stressful moment since we met, we both start laughing uncontrollably.

"You want me to ask you out, like behind the school toilets in primary school?" Leaning down, he kisses me on the forehead.

"Yes," I say, pretending to demand that he does it.

"Victoria Packer, will you please be my girlfriend and let me hold your hand? And tomorrow, I promise to share my sandwich with you at the lunch table," he says, kissing my cheek as the smile creeps up my face.

"Depends, what's on the sandwich?" I whisper as his lips are now hovering just off mine.

"Whatever you want, beautiful." His breath on my lips seals my fate.

"Okay then," I agree, leaning just that fraction more so we are again kissing like the world is about to explode. It's hot and passionate, expressing everything we can't seem to say to each other right now.

Bashing on the door makes us jump.

"I'll kill him," Nicholas growls as he takes me in his arms, almost squashing me in a hug that tells me how grateful he is for what I'm agreeing to. Little does he know I would have done it even if he hadn't agreed to my request.

My little giggle escapes as we pull apart. "Shall we go slay this bitch?" I ask as I take his hand and open the door.

"Fuck yes, we will!" Flynn says when I open the door. "I knew we would be good friends." He grins at both of us as we straighten our clothes, and Nicholas puts his jacket back on, placing his phone in his pocket before taking my hand again.

We start our walk down the corridor toward the boardroom, and to anyone else we would look like an epic scene from a movie when the characters are walking together in formation.

Don't mess with these men, and they are about to find out that I'm more frightening than all these guys put together.

Just push me, Jocelyn, and see what I mean.

You'd think walking into the boardroom would make me feel nervous, but I'm far from it. If there is anything I hate, it's a bully, and that's what this woman sounds like.

Not that I don't think Nicholas can handle her all on his own, because it sounds like he has been doing that for the last four years. But sometimes, you need another woman to think like her opponent.

If she wants to play games, then bring it on.

"What is she doing here?" the only woman in the room screeches from the other end of the table.

"Thought I would bring my girlfriend to watch me explain to one of my employees how this company is run. Especially since I own it and control it," Nicholas conveys to her in a very firm but controlled voice.

"Not for long," she replies with the most fake smile on her face, pretending to be so sweet. "My great-uncle, the founder of this company and your precious grandfather, would be rolling over in his grave at what has been revealed today."

Feeling his body tense, I squeeze his hand to pull him back into the moment. She is baiting him, and I'll be fucked if I'm going to let her get away with it.

With the sweetest voice I can muster, I put her back in her place, as only a woman protecting her man can. "Oh, you must be Jocelyn, the cousin. It was so kind of Nicholas's grandfather to give you this job, seeing as he knew he could never trust you to be in charge of any part of this great company. I would have thought you got over being passed over by now, but obviously, you are still holding the childish grudge that Nicholas inherited what was rightfully his father's, and of course, then his."

She sucks in a breath as she is about to start her ranting.

"Sit down, Jocelyn," I say. "Shall we get on with this trivial meeting then? Nicholas and I have some plans this afternoon, and you are interrupting them."

Take that, bitch.

This time, Nicholas is almost breaking my hand with his squeeze, but I know it is to say thank you.

You're welcome, my asshole.

The boys might have your back, but I'm right beside them.

Chapter Fifteen

NICHOLAS

This woman!

I just want to clear the room and worship Victoria on the boardroom table.

Everything about her has me panicking to stay away, yet I just can't. Every time I turn around, she is doing something that makes me want to take hold of her with my two hands and never let her go, even though that scares the hell out of me.

It doesn't matter that it has been such a short time since we met, because this woman gets me in every way possible. She ignites me and calms me all at the same time. Her challenging me is my biggest turn-on, but watching her stand her ground and put Jocelyn in her place has my cock so fucking desperate to be inside her.

Now is not the time to let my sex drive take over my brain, but damn, it's hard to hold it back.

Pulling a chair out for Victoria to sit next to Flynn, I take my rightful seat at the head of the table.

"Let's get this sorted, shall we?" I say, trying to remain calm and not show my anger at Jocelyn. Professionalism is a tool that you need when you run such a big business. Regardless of what you are thinking or feeling.

Jocelyn is still standing and looking at me. "I would like to table a motion of no confidence in Richard Nicholas Weston Darby as the CEO of Darby Hotels." Her shoulders back and the bitch face she wears most days show that she means business.

"On what grounds do you bring this motion to the board?" I ask, almost grinding my teeth, as I know I need to go through the proper steps if I have any chance of shutting her down.

Opening her tablet that is in front of her on the desk, she makes sure she doesn't miss anything she has prepared.

"The media reports that were released this morning of your questioning over drug-related matters when you were in Rome, in a Darby Hotel. Are these allegations true?" Oh, Jocelyn, what an open-ended question. You need to do better than that.

"If you are referring to being questioned about drugs found in the Rome hotel on Friday, then yes, that is correct. However, there have been no charges laid as there is insufficient evidence to prove it had anything to do with me. And I can stand before you all and deny having any involvement with any drugs, whether it be in Rome or anywhere in the world. To me it is of bigger concern how the drugs got into the hotel if it wasn't me, don't you agree?" I look around the room at every other board member, making eye contact and not shying away from them.

Scoffing at my words, she continues, "You just expect that we will all pat you on the back and say we believe you and sweep it all under the carpet? These allegations are tarnishing the family name and this whole business. Not to mention the paparazzi photos also released this morning of you and that woman acting in a sexually inappropriate manner in an alley down the street from the hotel."

I can't help but laugh at her now. "Jocelyn, have you ever been in the public eye? Not just at some charity event where you make sure you are photographed for the tabloids, but really in the public eye? The chance of having your privacy invaded at any moment without you knowing it?" I wait for her to answer, but she just stares me down, unable to give me the answer she wants to. Because she doesn't live a life like I do. "I didn't think so. Well, let me explain what that photo will be, not that I have seen it.

"There are certain things in your life you don't want to share with the whole world." Taking a breath, I shift my focus to Victoria. "Like kissing your girlfriend with passion to show her what she means to you, and contrary to what you prefer in your life, Jocelyn, Victoria is not looking for her spot in the limelight. I wanted to protect her from having her face splashed across the tabloids. But once again, that decision was taken out of my hands by people who are making money from my private life. So, unless you have something against a man and a woman showing affection to each other with a kiss, because that's all it was, then I suggest that is a moot point here."

The strained smile on Victoria's face gives me the strength to bury this once and for all. "Take a seat, Jocelyn, and rescind your motion so we can get on with the more pressing matter of security breaches and how the public relations team is going to handle this mess today, until we can find out who is responsible for the drugs."

Her mouth falls open, and I can see the red fury creeping up her neck. "You don't get to tell me what to do!" Her voice is elevating, and she is about to crack and show how irrational she is when put under pressure. "You are using our hotels for bad things and behaving disgusting in public. *I* should be running this business! You were never good enough to step into your grandfather's shoes. You weren't brought up to understand the way the business works like I was. You just turned up out of nowhere and assume you can take the role from under me." She is getting worked up to the same old rant I've heard many times from her but not usually in front of the whole board. And to be honest, I've had enough of her shit.

Standing with my hands on the table, I lean toward where she is standing so she gets the full brunt of these words. "Wrong! These are MY hotels, not ours! I own them all, and you work for me because I promised my grandfather I would keep you employed. But this is your last warning, continue this witch hunt to try to destroy me and you will regret it, finding yourself unemployed and in no way associated with my business. Do I make myself clear!" Standing up straight again, I look around the room slowly.

"Now, if there is anyone here who would like to second the motion put forward by Ms. Darby, please raise your hand." I wait to see if any of these old farts have the balls to take me on, but of course, they all just want their cushy job on the board to be safe.

With no one raising their hand, she finally explodes. "Gutless! You are all so gutless! We have a drug lord as our CEO and none of you care. I'm getting legal advice, and we will be revisiting this, I guarantee!" Her words are bouncing off the walls she is yelling so loud.

"Then I suggest when you talk to a lawyer, you ask what the ramifications of defamation of character are. Because I promise you, if I hear the words drug lord in relation to me come out of that toxic mouth of yours again, you're going to need that lawyer!" I need to get out of this room before I lose it at her and say more than is a good idea right now.

"Now, if we are done here, I have work to get done and wrongful allegations to get to the bottom of. For the rest of you, we will report back once we know something, but rest assured we have all our manpower on this and want it solved just as quickly as you do. I apologize for the waste of your time this morning and hope we are clear where everything stands. Any further questions?" I don't think anyone is game to open their mouth, and Jocelyn is too busy still huffing over no one backing her.

"Excellent, and Jocelyn, I'll let HR know that you are on leave from now until this matter is settled. I think we can all agree we don't need the negative energy or toxic behavior here. So you can collect your things, and I will make sure that your second-in-charge is informed that she is in charge until further notice." As I push my chair back and start to walk toward Victoria, Jocelyn steps in front of me.

"You can't do that," she hisses, her eyes looking crazy, placing her hand on my chest to stop me moving.

Looking down at her hand and back at her with death in my eyes, she gets the hint to remove it before I remove it for her.

"I just did. Be thankful I didn't terminate you on the spot. Take it as a small win. Good day, lady and gentlemen." Stepping around her, I take Victoria's hand and exit the boardroom, taking a small breath before I pass out from anger that was building the whole time I was in there.

The guys will stay there and talk to the other board members, smoothing everything out, and I know Rem will shadow Jocelyn to exit the building without her laptop or security pass. He flew back in from Rome early this morning, knowing that today he might be needed if there was any trouble. I was hoping we could keep it from the media a little longer, but that was just a fairy tale. Rem will already be messaging his security team to put her logins on hold for the time being. I have enough drama, I don't need her undermining me or the business at the same time.

Walking through my office, I don't feel relieved at all. Jocelyn isn't wrong in what she was saying. This will hurt our name, and if the gossip rags really want to build it up, they can. I can only hope someone else does something stupid today that will hit social media and my story will quickly slip away.

Feeling Victoria's hand in mine is calming, and even though we haven't said a word since we left the room, I can tell she is under control too. Her hand is soft and feels natural where it is.

We pass Lucy at her desk. "Lucy, can you clear my calendar for the rest of the week? I will be contactable when you need me, and Flynn will field all calls for me unless they are urgent. If the media are after a statement, refer them to the PR team, please." I can't be here right now. I need to get out of London, otherwise it will be like living under a magnifying glass.

"Understood." And that is why I pay her the big money. I know I can trust her to handle it all, and she knows when it's time to disturb me.

Entering my office, I close the door a little softer than the last time I walked in here with Victoria.

"Nicholas." Her gentle voice next to me is a surprise. I imagined she would already be rambling about what just happened, but instead, she is taken aback as much as I am.

Turning toward her, I take her face in my hands. This woman is nothing like I imagined that first morning we met.

"You are incredible," is all I can manage to say to her, kissing her forehead and pulling her to me. I need to hold her tight and just breathe. I think we both do.

Standing in the silence is what I need to clear my rage. I don't want that to touch Victoria over something that is not her doing. Slowly releasing her and giving her some space, she is confused as to why I didn't kiss her like before. But the next time I kiss her, I want her to be totally on board before I take control. Whenever she is close to me, I find it hard to restrain myself, but we met under the strangest circumstances, and I think we need time to take that all in.

"Tori…"

"Victoria." She looks at me with determination.

"But I thought you didn't like when people call you that." I'm confused by her smile.

"Until I heard it off your lips." And before I have time to say another word, she pulls me down toward her and tells me what she wants. All my plans for restraint are now thrown out the window. She is struggling just as much as I am to stay apart. Her soft lips take mine with all the pent-up frustration of the last hour, and maybe the last few days too.

Her scent is intoxicating, and I can't hold back even when my brain is telling me to. I slide my hand into her hair, pulling it tight enough to bring out a moan as she opens her lips for me. My tongue traces every part of her mouth, and the hotter the kiss gets, the harder our bodies press together. I'm not in this alone.

I want to fuck her! Desperately!

"You are coming away with me for a few days," I gasp as we separate our mouths.

"Oh, another order."

I won't deny it. But by the look on her face, she loves it.

"Yes." I'm about to devour her again, but she pulls back from me. Damn woman, why does she always want to use words when actions can seal the deal so much quicker.

"Nicholas, I can't keep disappearing from work. I'm not like you." She moves to her bottle of water that was left on the table.

"I'll fix that," I say.

She rolls her eyes at my words as she takes a drink. "Money doesn't fix everything. I have a job to do." Little does she understand that as soon as they work out who she is, the paparazzi will be stalking her after she was outed with me.

"True, but it helps. Plus, you *will* be working... on me." I step toward her again, wanting my hands on her. I wink at her, hoping she gets the gist of what I'm saying.

"Nope, stay there, keep your hands off me, big boy, otherwise you know I will agree to anything." Her words are saying one thing, but her body is telling me something different. The sparkle in her eyes, the blush on her cheeks she gets when she is aroused, and her breathing is now quicker than it was when we walked into the room.

"That's the idea. Now, I'm making the phone call to your boss again, this time explaining that we are going to work on your ideas for the next few days so we can make some excellent progress."

"My work ideas..."

"Among others. Plus, I have some suggestions of my own..." Ignoring her words, I take her arm and pull her toward me, while a small giggle comes from her.

"Please, come with me, not an order but an invitation."

She lays her head on my chest above my heart and finally gives in.

"Okay... but we are working." She lifts her head with the most devilish look, like she already knows the moment we leave here, work is going out the window. "Where are we flying to this time?"

"Oh, I see, you just want me for the private jet," I tease, though I've never gotten the impression it is about money for Victoria.

"Absolutely, and of course your big... assets." That's it, we are getting out of here. I'm not going to be responsible for what happens in here if we keep flirting like this.

"All I'm telling you is that we aren't flying anywhere. Now let's go. We have a lot of research to do on a Darby..."

"Hotel," she says, always quick with her comeback.

"That too." Grabbing my bag and tucking her under my arm, we walk from my office. I know I'm inviting a whole lot of trouble getting involved with a woman who is so much younger than me and still wanting to discover the world. But right now, I can't stay away from her, and she seems to have the same problem.

One day at a time, they say.

While Victoria packed a bag, I waited outside her home in the car, calling her boss Doug and explaining the situation. I told him everything. I don't want him to have the wrong impression of Victoria. I need to protect her from the frenzy that will swarm around me now. He was very professional and asked me to keep him up to date as the week progresses. I promised him we would be working on the account, because what better way for Victoria to come up with ideas than to get to know the real me?

I know she was expecting me to have a car waiting for us outside the office when we left, but I had messaged Wallace to bring my Maserati from my apartment. The way her eyes nearly popped out of her head made me smile. Everything is new and sparkly to her; she's not concerned about how she appears to others. Her words of *"holy shit, this is a bit fancy"* had me laughing as I helped her in.

The guys have been updating me since we left, and Jocelyn, as expected, is making noise, but thankfully, the board members have all said they are on team Nicholas. I'm sure they are concerned, probably even more than when I arrived and took over, but hopefully, I have gained enough trust since then.

I hear Victoria coming out the front door before I even see her. "Sorry I took so long. Had to message Elouise, and of course, she rang me straight back. Even left her classroom when she is not allowed. Oops."

I laugh at her bumbling explanation.

"Does she need proof-of-life pictures again?" I ask, taking her bag from her which is smaller than I was expecting.

"Oh, good idea." She grabs her phone out of her handbag that

KAREN DEEN

she placed on the front seat. "Smile for the policemen," she says before rethinking her words. Watching her face drop is priceless. "Sorry, not so funny this time."

"Come here, beautiful." With my hands on her waist, I spin and place her on the hood of the car next to me. Taking her phone from her, I pull her into my side. "Now, let's smile for Jocelyn who wishes this was her car." It has the desired effect with the most natural laugh falling from her as I click the picture.

"I can't believe you let me sit on your car. Do you have a thing for Maseratis or was it cheaper to buy by the dozen?"

As I lift her down again, my brain is commenting that I now have a thing for her on the hood of my Maserati. It's a thought to tuck away for another time.

"Why drive an old man's Volvo when you can have a car like this?" I say, holding open her door and helping her into her seat. "Besides, I'm told women like things that are powerful and with the perfect amount of thrust."

"True, but I've also been told vintage cars fail to perform due to age." She pulls the door from my hands to close it as she laughs to herself at getting the last say.

Just you wait, my little fireball. I'll show you that age and experience will far outweigh youth any day of the week. Lack of stamina is not in my vocabulary.

Pulling up to the entrance of the estate and waiting for the gates to open, I can see the wonder in her expression.

The sign on the front stone pillar gives it away.

"Welcome to Darby Estate, the place I call home," I say, driving slowly through the entrance while she is taking it all in. That iconic sound of the tires on the gravel is like the trigger point for me to finally breathe. While I'm within the boundaries of the estate, I feel like I can be me. No one to see me or judge what I'm doing, wearing, or saying.

I don't think Victoria has any idea of the gravity of me bringing her here. The only woman who I have brought here is my mother, and besides that, the guys are the only other people who I let into my personal space.

If she could have seen the comments in the group message with them when I told them where I was taking her. They know what it means. The problem is that I do too, and that's what scares me.

"Nicholas…" It's barely more than a whisper from Victoria, and it makes me smile as we pull up to the house. It's everything you would imagine of an old country estate. It was the first thing my grandfather purchased for my grandmother when he made his first million.

It's a two-story house that is much bigger than I need, with six bedrooms and bathrooms. But to me, it's home and somewhere I know that my father spent time as he grew up, riding horses and learning to hunt. Neither of those things interest me, but I feel him here when I come home. It's a comfort I had longed for all my life and didn't realize until I stepped foot on the grounds.

The driveway circles a large fountain in front of the house, with gardens all around the edge. The traditional box hedge borders the driveway and two shaped pine trees in large concrete pots sit on either side of the solid front door. It's not a door I use often, preferring to go in the back door after parking in the garage. It doesn't feel as ostentatious as the big grand entrance at the front. I didn't grow up in this life, so falling into it like I did took some adjustments.

"What, this old place?" I pull around the side of the house to park where Victoria can see all the back garden area. My grandmother loved to spend her time back here, and now Henry gets a gardener in to maintain it at its best. It's the least I can do for a woman I never had the honor of meeting.

"Old seems to be the flavor of the day. You can't just shrug this off. It's absolutely gorgeous and not what I would have picked for you. A flashy London apartment is more your style." Undoing her seatbelt, she turns toward me and sees the smirk on my face. "Of course, you have one of those too, don't you." I don't want to correct her that I own a whole building of them, because it's not important to me, and I hope it's not important to her either.

"Come on, I'll show you inside." As we get out of the car, I realize I should have warned her about Sid. Before I have time to call him off, he jumps up on her with both front paws, looking for some loving.

"Oh, hello there, puppy, who are you?" she greets him, not caring that he is getting hair all over her black suit as she pats him, making his tail wag like crazy.

"Sid, down." I use the tone of voice he understands. He turns his head and gives me the disappointed look but reluctantly drops his paws back onto the ground. Yeah, I know, buddy. I like having my hands on her too.

"He is adorable, Nicholas." Crouching down to love him up again, I can see she is a softie at heart. The way people respond to animals says a lot about their soul, in my opinion.

"When he wants to be, but he can also be a pain in the ass." I slap my leg, signaling him to come to me, and he does as he is told straight away. "Good boy, Sid. Have you been looking after the place since I was home?"

Wagging his tail at me, he darts off to find his dirty, slobbery tennis ball, dropping it at my feet. "Not now, Sid, we have a guest that I need to get settled. We can play later. Go annoy the sheep like you love to do." Taking off up the back field, he forgets about Victoria while he is in the search of something to chase.

Taking her hand, we walk through the back door and into the kitchen, stopping at the sink so we can both wash our hands from the dog smell that Sid inflicted on us.

"I've never seen a kitchen this big. Is it wasted on you, or do you have a personal chef?" she asks, laughing as I lean against the island counter.

"That is very presumptuous of you, Miss Packer. I do in fact have a personal chef—me." I point to my chest, and she smirks.

"Right, so what is your signature dish, eggs on toast?" she teases, running her hand along the counter across from me, feeling the solid white marble with flecks of silver and black through it that makes the kitchen look as good as it does.

"Actually, for starters, it's a mixture of homemade breads, served with my secret recipe herb butter and olive oil infused with garlic. Then, on to main with roast duck with a cooled plum sauce, served on a bed of garlic sweet potato mash, broccolini, and garden-fresh carrots. Then I finish the meal off with a triple-chocolate tart, with King Island cream." I look at her, frozen in her spot.

"What's wrong, not to your liking?" I ask, waiting for her brain to kick in.

"You like to cook?" I'm walking toward her now as she asks the question that makes me laugh.

"Victoria, in my former life, I was a chef and a good one. You really need to do better research on your boyfriend."

Covering her face with her hands, she tries to hide her embarrassment. But to me, it speaks of so much comfort. She doesn't know the me that the world all thinks they know. Instead, she gets to meet me here in the relaxed environment of my home.

"I'm not one of those internet trolls," she says. "And to be honest, you haven't really given me much time to do anything. Every time I turn around you are whisking me off to some undisclosed location. Okay, so you're some super-duper chef. What other talents have you got?"

I try not to groan. She could not have made it any easier for me if she tried. But then again, maybe that's what she's planning on.

Taking her hand, I lead her to the stairs in the hallway.

"Many, and I think it's time I show you." Just as we reach the bottom of the staircase, I can't wait any longer. Pushing her against the wall, I lean over her just as we were in the alley in Rome.

"Feels familiar," she whimpers.

"Maybe so, but I can guarantee I won't be stopping at a kiss."

And doing exactly as I did that first day, I kiss her like my life depends on it, leaving us both panting.

I kiss up her neck and nibble on her ear. "You had me as hard as stone in that boardroom. Your fire is my aphrodisiac, and I can't control myself." I drop my hand to the front of her leg and pull her skirt up slowly so I can feel her thigh.

"Fuck..." I moan, biting down on her lip as my hand finds thigh-high stockings and a garter belt. "These better have been worn for me and not him," I growl, thinking back to finding her with another man earlier.

My possessiveness taking over, I pick her up in my arms. I don't want the answer, and there is no time to waste. I need to claim her once and for all in my bed. I take her to where she belongs.

"What if I said I was on my way to your office after lunch to try to seduce you after we had our usual discussion..." Now she is running her hands through my hair as I charge up the stairs and into my bedroom.

I place her down on the rug at the end of my bed in front of the floor-to-ceiling mirror. "Then I say, fucking seduce me, you horny minx. You have my full attention."

I begin unbuttoning my shirt as she stands there looking at me. "I'm waiting, Victoria, naked now!"

And my command is all she needs to fall into the spell.

Our lust is insatiable, and I intend to explore it fully to see if it can be more.

Against my better judgment and the fear of being hurt, today is the beginning of opening my heart to a woman I can't say no to.

I think I understand my father on a level I never knew until now.

Chapter Sixteen

VICTORIA

His eyes pierce my soul, breaking every hesitation I've been holding on to.

But it's his voice that almost brings me to my knees instantly. I didn't know how much I loved to give over my control until I met this man.

I've never felt as sexy as I do right now, with him standing before me, shirt open, and the button on his pants undone.

Wanting me.

Seduction like this hasn't been something I've ever done, but the way I feel with Nicholas brings a tingling confidence to try.

Sliding my jacket off and throwing it to the chair at the side of me, I know my nipples are rock hard, and his eyes fall to them through my white silk shirt. The pattern of my lace bra is now visible through my shirt, and I can see his hands itching to take hold of me. But his restraint is incredible as he stands and takes me all in, his eyes roaming slowly up and down my body.

Instead, I'm the one running my hands over my breasts, squeezing them for him, just like he wants to be doing. I run my fingers down the swell of my breasts that are visible at the shirt's neckline and take the first button, opening them one by one. More and more of my skin is exposed for him to rake his eyes over.

I shrug my shoulders as the blouse stars sliding down my arms, and it brings a deep groan from him the moment my breasts, nicely contained in lace, are visible. My nipples push through the holes in the bra, restrained and ready to be licked just the way I like it. Just thinking about his tongue on me sends electricity surging through me.

Wanting to even up the show, Nicholas drops his shirt to the floor, and that makes me want to hasten this strip tease up. The tightness of his abs and the bulge of his biceps has me salivating over him. It's like he just stepped out of the gym, all pumped up and toned. Now it's my hands that I wish I was sliding down that eight pack to the V that disappears into the top of his black pants. There is something about a man in a suit, but this is a hundred times better. His feet are now bare, his pants hanging low on his hips, and there's a hint of hair on his skin on the V just above his Calvin Klein boxers. Fuck, he just radiates high-level sexiness. With the button undone, that leaves his cock pressing firmly on the zipper that is struggling to contain it.

I start on the side zipper of my skirt that is fitted perfectly over my curvy hips. Consciously aware of what will send him over the edge, I turn my back to him so he can watch as my skirt slides over my bare ass and only the single thin piece of my G-string wedged between my cheeks. The garter belt ties are clipped to my stockings, adding the extra heat I know he loves. Bending over, I can hear his breathing increase, and I raise my head to watch his reaction in the mirror while my skirt slowly falls down my legs.

"Victoria… you filthy girl. I can see how wet you are for me." His words make my body tingle all over. I feel so exposed but in the best way possible. In the mirror, I see him unzip his pants and pull his cock out, taking it in his hand for a long slow stroke up to the top and running his finger through the leaking head, before spreading it over himself as he slides his hand back down.

Oh, I want his cock! Badly!

Starting to stand, his voice makes me freeze.

"Stop!" The way he commands me has me dripping more. Walking behind me, he flicks the elastic garter belt straps on my bare cheeks, giving me a little sting and I'm sure a nice red mark for him to admire.

"Perfect..." he purrs, drawing his word out as he undoes the clips on my stocking and now places both his hands on my ass cheeks. "...and edible." Leaning forward, he bites me hard enough to leave his mark.

"Fuck!" I scream, as he has me quivering uncontrollably. He slides his hands around my front and grabs my breast firmly while pulling me slowly up to standing, with my back to his bare chest. He's as turned on as I am, judging by the sweat I can feel on his skin.

My head falls back on his shoulder as he plays with my body just how he wants to, where he makes the rules and I'm happy to be his plaything.

"I'm taking that ass one day, just like that, with you bent in front of this mirror screaming my name as I own you, all of you." The rasp in his voice is enough to tell me how much he means it.

He places his middle finger in my mouth with one word, making me shiver. "Suck."

God, I wish it was his cock. But just as I'm dreaming of what it would feel like with my lips around that large throbbing cock, his finger disappears from my mouth.

His right hand moves down my body and around to my crack, between my cheeks, running his wet finger up over my puckered hole. I jump a little because I've never had anyone touch me so erotically before. I don't know if I will be willing to take the final step, but with Nicholas, he takes me to places where I lose all control and can't say no to him.

Maybe it's the forbidden nature of what he is doing, but I'm about to orgasm just from the thought of being so naughty.

"Ohhh... oh God..." I'm panting as he starts to slide his middle finger coated in my saliva inside my ass. I can't take much more, I'm hanging on the edge of exploding.

"You like that, don't you, my dirty girl," he says, pulling the finger back and continuing to circle my pucker. "Oh yessss, you will make a nice little naughty ass bitch for me, won't you. You want it bad, I can feel it in the way your body is responding. Look at yourself in the mirror, Victoria. Your skin is blushing, so alive. We will be exploring that, but not right now, you will wait until I choose to take you here." He pushes his finger back in as my mouth drops open from the sting and pleasure of what I never knew I wanted.

Until now.

He's taking great satisfaction of virtually fucking me with his words. They are enough to have every nerve in my body firing.

"Today, I'm going to fuck that wet little pussy until you are so exhausted that you don't think you can come again, but you will." My moans are getting louder at every promise he makes.

"You will do everything I demand and pleasure me just the way I want you to. My pleasure will then be to give you the most extreme highs and take you to a place that you've only ever fantasized about." His index finger is now pushing forward toward my sex, and I know if he hits my clit, it will be all over.

The hand still on my breast that has been squeezing me just the right amount, while pulling on my nipple between his fingers, moves to my throat and just holds me there, not tightening in any way. But just the thought of him about to choke me takes my breath away. I can't think with all the sensations that are firing together. Quickly, he pushes his finger up through my folds and hard against my clit as he now puts a little pressure on my throat, and the world explodes before me.

I scream his name like I've never screamed it before. It's not loud but has all the emotion of the most powerful orgasm I've felt run through my body. While I gasp for air, he licks up my neck beside his fingers, and it gives the tenderness of his touch against the roughness of his dominance. He doesn't need to take my ass to own me. There is no going back from how I feel in his arms, struggling to regulate myself enough to speak. He releases his hold, and I can hardly stand.

"That's just the beginning. I wanted you ready for me to eat."

Lifting me like I'm a doll, he carries me to the bed in the center of the room. Still in my underwear and my stiletto heels, the shimmer in his darkening eyes tells me he is going to enjoy stripping me further.

Sex like this with Nicholas is so intense, I don't know if I will survive today, but oh, what a way to die!

Being sent to dirty sex heaven.

NICHOLAS

With her body in my hands, it's like this is a power I've been hiding from other women.

The trust she has with me is enough to make me feel like I can conquer anything, including my fear of love. I'm not there yet, but for the first time in my life, I can picture it as a possibility that I want.

But only if it's with her!

It's like there is this indescribable heat burning through my body. I can't contain it, and all I want to do is release it on her.

"We are going to need a lot of pairs of these," I warn, kneeling above her on the bed, ripping both sides of her panties off and taking the scrap of lace to my nose and inhaling the intoxicating allure that is Victoria. Placing it in my pocket, I see the shock on her face.

My finger imprints still on her throat make me unashamedly proud of the pleasure she felt from it.

It looks like that orgasm has rendered her speechless which I never thought possible. Challenging me to make her moan or scream is a red flag to a bull for me. I want all her sounds of ecstasy ringing in my ears for the rest of the day.

Leaning over her, I take a pillow and place it under her ass, and it leaves her wet sex on the perfect angle where I can see it all plump and pink, with her clit engorged just waiting for me. I flick her shoes to the floor and roll the stockings down her legs, one at a time, nice and slowly, torturing her with my mouth and tongue the whole way down and back up again. I keep one arm across her perfectly shaved pussy to hold her still so she can't release any of the build-up sensations that I'm making her feel.

"Yes, that's right, I want you whimpering for me. Don't you dare come until I tell you." With both legs bare, I nip at the skin on her thighs so close to her sex. Knowing it's driving her crazy, I pin her down to intensify the burning on the inside.

"I can't…" she whispers from the lack of energy to speak.

"Oh, you can, and you will wait for my order, won't you, Victoria!" It's not a question, and she knows it. Nodding at me, she closes her eyes, breathing deeply to savor the sensation.

Pushing her legs a little farther apart, I look up at her as I begin to lick up the side of her landing strip of hair. Her head thrashes on the pillow and she bites her bottom lip, trying to hold on. Pondering if I should push her further, my inner demon wants her to feel so out of control that she flies to a place she has never been before.

"Breathe and take what I'm giving you," I say as I drag my tongue straight up her folds and over her clit with slowly tantalizing pressure that has her whole body shaking. "Mhmm, you taste superb." I lick every drop of moisture, and my tongue just brings me more from inside her.

Her hands hit the back of my head with force as she tries to hold off coming. Her desperation is making me leak, but I'm not ready to fuck her yet. There is so much of her mouthwatering body left for me to explore. And I know the moment I start pounding her into this bed, there will be no holding me back.

"That's it, let me feel your pain." Her fingers instantly pull on my hair to the point the pain has me starting to rut against the mattress.

Using her legs, she squeezes my head, trying to stop me, but she doesn't realize she doesn't want that to happen. Edging her is a whole other level of pain that she will learn is worse than if I stop now and then start again.

Looking up from my feasting on her, I see the odd tear running down from her closed eyes. Ah yes, she is at her peak, and I need to let her release before she can't hold on anymore, which she will regret later as a sense of failing me, and I don't want her feeling anything but proud of what she is enjoying with me. I move my hand from her thigh to her sex and position two fingers at her entrance. She is wet enough to take the pain that will be her euphoria.

My mouth hovers right above her clit where my tongue is flicking slowly to drive her insane.

"Come, Victoria," I bark as I bite down on her clit and push my two fingers inside her hard and fast and find the spot that has her flooding my mouth. Watching her throw her head back and mouth open like she wants to scream, but she's in a head space that nothing verbal is coming out. The shudders through her body are big, and there is no way I'm stopping until I have all she can give me in her intense moment of release. The pain I'm feeling in my cock is what gives me the greatest form of arousal. By holding off her orgasm, I'm holding off my own too, and it hurts so fucking good, like I'm sharing her pain.

Standing at the end of the bed, I drop my pants and boxers to the floor, and grabbing the condom from my wallet, I can't seem to get it on quick enough. I want her while she is still floating. I'm back kneeling between her legs, her body glistening with sweat, and the pheromones are oozing from every pore on her body. It's a scent I want lingering in my bedroom even after she's gone.

Watching her eyes flutter, I hook her legs around me and start dragging my engorged cock up and down her sex, waking her from her delirium. Lifting her hips up off the pillow, I wait for just the right moment when she starts to see me. I want her to know who is fucking her, and I'm desperate to see her looking into my eyes as she comes all over my cock buried deep inside her.

"Eyes stay open," I growl at her as she starts to close them.

As I thrust forward, her voice has returned with force. "Fuck, Nicholas... so... oh God... so... hard." Yeah, baby, and you made me this way. It's all you.

"You will take it as hard as I can give it," I demand, pounding harder and harder into her, knowing I won't last much longer. I need her to come again.

Her body is still so tender that as I lean down and take her nipple through the lace and bite down on it, her scream is deafening. Rising back up, her tight little pussy clenches me tightly, the ripples pleasuring me over and over again as her final orgasm races through her body. The fire I've seen all along in her eyes is burning so intensely that I'm done and can't hold back any longer.

"You're mine! Fucking mine, say it!" I shout, pumping through emptying myself inside her. I want her screaming it.

"Yours, all… yours." The exhaustion is written all over her face, along with a completely sated smile.

Slowly drawing out of her, I pull her luscious body up to sit on my thighs where I sink onto the mattress, wrapping her in my arms.

"What have you done to me, my beautiful Victoria," I whisper into the top of her head that is now lying on my shoulder, and the whisps of her red hair stick to the side of her face. I know we need to clean up, but I don't want to move. Everything that has happened since she lay in my arms in Rome is finally pushed away, and all I can feel is the calmness she's bringing to me.

It seems impossible that the whirlwind that is Victoria is the same woman lying so peacefully in my arms and just listening to my heartbeat. One thing I know for sure, make-up sex will be off the charts with her, and we are guaranteed to have plenty of that with the amount we argue.

"Same," is all she replies, and I can't help but laugh at her.

"I'm going to put you down so I can get rid of this condom." Kissing her lips so gently, I then lay her softly down. "Don't move."

A cute little giggle escapes from her as her words say it all. "As if I could."

Walking into my bathroom and disposing of my mess, I turn to the huge egg-shaped bath that I think I have only used maybe twice, but now I'm so glad I put it in when I renovated, purely for this moment. Turning on the water and getting the temperature just right, I wish I had some bath oil, but I'm a guy, and we don't think of those things. Nor did I ever really think I would be sharing the bath with anyone.

Stepping back into my room, Victoria is right where I left her, and I'm not even certain she is still awake. If only she was this quiet all the time. Then again, who am I kidding? I love her feistiness, it's what drew me to her. She is so real. What you see is what you get, and there are no airs or graces put on depending on who she's around. It's the most amazing thing about her—oh, and her rocking hot body!

"Beautiful, let's take a bath," I say, lifting her into my arms and carrying her through to where the steam is building above the hot water.

Placing her feet on the tiled floor, I reach around her to undo the bra that she still has on. Her voluptuous breasts fall free, and I can't help myself, bending to take one in my mouth and suck it.

"Nope, no way, back off, big boy. Let me recover first." Before she can push me away, I'm smiling to myself that she's back and the sassy mouth is starting up again, and I take the other one in my mouth next. I mean, they need to get even attention.

"Big boy, huh?" I laugh, holding her hand as she lifts one leg into the bath and then slowly lowers herself into the water. She sighs at the nice feeling of the warm water on the muscles that are screaming at her.

"Don't try to deny it. That thing is the weapon of mass orgasms. A warning label should be included," she says, waving her hand in front of my cock that hasn't completely deflated, mainly because she is still naked in front of me. But to be honest, I'm semi-hard whenever she is around me and opens her mouth.

"Seriously, where do you come up with these things? They think us Australians have weird-ass sayings." Motioning for her to shuffle forward, I lower myself in behind her and pull her back against my chest.

My dick is already getting excited with her so close. Down, boy, she needs time to rest.

"I don't know what you are talking about. They are just my Tori-isms. I'm sure Lou has sent half of them into the urban dictionary for inclusion."

"Why doesn't that surprise me," I say, laughing at her. Thank goodness I got the super large bath, as my legs are still bent slightly trying to fit in.

Just lying here with the water slowly creeping up to the point that it is lapping at her nipples, I lean over and shut off the tap. If I can't touch those breasts, I at least want to be able to see them.

Her hands now lying on my thighs and slowly rubbing up and down is not helping to keep my dick under control.

"We need to talk." Her voice so sweet in broaching the hard things we have both been avoiding.

"Ugh, can't we just stay in the moment?" I gripe, wrapping my arms just a little tighter around her waist. "Don't ruin the peacefulness."

"We can't avoid this forever." She turns her head up to look at me.

"I know, but let me take care of you first, then feed you. The hard words can come later." I'm almost pleading with her on the inside. I'm not ready to be serious.

"And they will be the only things coming later. You and your filthy mouth have wrecked me." Lifting herself and kissing my jaw, I can't help but burst out laughing.

"Oh, Victoria, you have no idea what I have in store for you."

"How can an old man have so much testosterone in him?" she says, baiting me for a reaction.

"Be careful, miss, otherwise I will show you just how much sex drive I have, on you, in this bath."

"Okay, point proven." Victoria settles back on to my chest, and I'm struggling with how good this feels.

Why is she different than any other woman I have slept with or dated? Is this why I have never wanted more than a few nights with them? They never challenged me or let me release my inner alpha. It's like sex with Victoria has opened a door I've been holding shut my whole life.

I'm not a dominant by any stretch of the imagination, but I crave to dominate her, with an intensity that I have never felt before.

I think that's why her standing up to me in the outside world triggers my immense burning need to fuck her. I want her on her knees for me and only me.

I don't know how to explain that to her without sounding like a man who is more than the asshole she already thinks I am. Resting my chin on the top of her head, I know the answer won't come to me easily. Nothing in my life ever does.

All I know is that I'm desperate to keep her for as long as I can. Because deep down, I know eventually she will want to fly and find herself, and it won't be with me.

VICTORIA

Every muscle in my body is reminding me of what just happened upstairs.

Who even am I?

I have never desired sex like that, but to be honest, I didn't know I would desire a man like Nicholas either. I never expected such a soft side to a man that all I could see from the outside was an absolute fucktard. Now I should rename him as the man who loves to fuck hard, and oh God, did I love it just like that.

Maybe he's right, I am a dirty little girl for him. I would have let him do anything to me in the moment, and although I shocked myself, he is helping me to discover a part of me that I didn't know existed.

The part deep down where I want to be his to control. Completely!

Lying on the daybed on the back porch, I can't wrap my head around what has happened today. One moment I was at work, preparing to face the growly bear and challenge him about why he fucked and dumped me. But instead, here I am relaxing after being completely worshiped, while my personal chef is preparing me a lush meal. I know he doesn't want to talk about anything, but I do. I can't just fall into this without my eyes wide open. Too many times in my life I have done that, and it has come back to bite me. Elouise is going to kill me for letting him back in so easily, but I can't seem to stop his charm from mesmerizing me. Even the constant banter we have has some magnetic pull that I can't seem to avoid.

The weather is balmy as the night starts, and I could easily fall asleep here—except for the stomach rumbling that keeps happening.

The man worked up my appetite to a point that he better be cooking me a five-course meal. He wanted me to relax, but I wish I was still in the kitchen watching him. The ease in the way he glides around his workspace and whirls the knife, chopping and preparing, is fascinating.

The tenderness he uses on me after sex is such a contradiction of what the world sees, but now I realize why he loves his home out here. Away from everyone, he can just be himself, and that's the person I really want to know. The asshole in him stokes my fire in the best way possible, but the softness of the man who bathed me upstairs and is now cooking for me is someone who needs to be loved. I can tell that from the small moments he has let himself free.

Am I that woman who can love this Jekyll-and-Hyde man?

My heart says yes, but my head is still saying we'll see.

"I brought you this to nibble on until dinner is ready. It's in the oven but will take about an hour." Nicholas's deep voice startles me from my thoughts. I'm sure he must walk on his toes to be that quiet.

He places down a platter of meats, cheeses, fruit, crackers, bread, and so much more. There is abundant choice in his selection, and of course, in his other hand is a bottle of wine and two glasses, ready to start the night off right. I'm not sure I should drink around him, but just one can't be too bad. If this is all one big mistake, then I've already made it, and it had nothing to do with alcohol.

"Thank you. Your presentation even looks impressive, oh master chef." I smile up at him as he hands me the glass of white wine he just poured. Taking the first sip, it's light and fruity. He probably has his own wine rack in the kitchen stocked with all the best wines. Who am I kidding, he probably has a freaking wine cellar, or better still, a damn vineyard.

"I aim to please, Victoria," he says, taking a seat beside me with the food platter between us. He stretches out his legs and leans back on the pillows.

This man is sex on a stick. Seriously!

I mean, how am I supposed to ignore his body when he is just wearing a pair of soft gray gym shorts that sit just perfectly on his hips. His full abs are on display, and oh my God, the arm porn. It's almost like he knows that I lose all rational thought when I see arms with bulging veins, which he has plenty of. And his large strong hands, I know what they can do, and that makes me blush at the thought.

"You okay over there? Your breathing just hitched, and you're flushed." The satisfaction in his voice shows he knows what he is doing to me.

"Don't be a jerk. I mean, seriously…" I scoff, waving my hand up and down his torso. "How many hours in the gym does that take?" My stomach decides now is the perfect time to growl loud enough I'm sure they heard it all the way back in London.

"Not much, I'm blessed with good genes." He feeds me a strawberry before I have time to reply. "Now eat, you will need your energy."

Savoring the taste of sweetness on my tongue, these strawberries must be freshly grown here in his gardens. There is no way they come from a shop tasting this good.

But his words are lingering in my head. I need to stand firm on what I want. Before our bodies touch again, we are talking this out whether he likes it or not.

Waiting for dinner to cook gives us the perfect opportunity.

"Yes, talking takes a lot of energy, I know." I laugh at him rolling his eyes at me. "There is no more putting it off."

I sit up and cross my legs so I'm looking directly at him, so he knows I mean business.

"All right. What do you want to know?" As he rolls on his side and looks up at me, I can tell there are so many answers inside this man, I just don't know what I want to ask first.

"Everything! What a stupid question." Taking into my mouth a piece of cheese on a cracker, I wait for him to start talking, but there is only silence between us. Maybe he doesn't even know where to start either.

"Okay, I'll go first. Walking into the café today, was it just fate? Because I have a feeling there is more to it." Starting with the small stuff seems easier than jumping right to the big one of why he walked away from me.

"I won't apologize for what I did today, because I just wanted to protect you." Scared what he is about to say, I drink my wine way too quickly, but my nerves are already racing.

"After I was told I could leave the police station, I had Rem instruct someone on my security team to watch over you." My heart starts to thump harder in my chest. "I didn't know what the fallout would be, but having you in Rome with me, I knew at some stage you would be linked to this shitshow. So as soon as it hit the media, thirty minutes before I was by your side, I knew I needed to get you out of London."

"So, you've been stalking me!" Thoughts of a man staring in my bedroom window race through my head.

"No, Victoria!" Sitting up, he places his hands on my cheeks, obviously scared how I'm about to react.

"I have been protecting you. I will always protect what is mine!" His lips on mine say what he doesn't understand that he is feeling. The kiss is so possessive that I can't do anything but completely understand him.

Pulling back from him, I ask, "What are you so afraid of?" I see fear in his eyes.

His answer is not much more than a whisper. "Losing you, like she lost him."

Chapter Seventeen

VICTORIA

The intensity of his words tells me there is past hurt buried deep inside him.

"Do you want to talk about that?" I don't want to push something that is so hard for him this early in our conversation. I think that would be like going from zero to a hundred with Nicholas, a man I have struggled to get anything from.

"Not really," he says, kissing me on the forehead and then sitting back to give distance to his emotions that are bubbling below the surface.

"Then can we talk about what happened in Rome?" It's my biggest question because I can't get past the fear that it will happen again. I know he needs me at the moment, but when it's all over, will he throw me to the side like last time?

"Somehow there were two hundred grams of methamphetamine found in the boot of the Maserati after I drove it that night." He says it so matter-of-factly, like it's just trivial information, but I can tell he is pissed about it, and rightly so.

"Yeah, yeah, I want to know about that part, but that's not what I meant, and you know it." I poke him in the chest with my finger, but before I can pull it away, his hand lands on top of mine and holds it to his chest, right above his heart. This man needs physical touch to connect emotionally which is so sweet, and I never thought I would be using the word sweet when it comes to describing him. Not in a million years.

"See, this is why I hate talking. You pick all the hard questions," he grumbles like a schoolboy over having to do his homework.

"Nicholas, you can't deny there is something pretty intense between us. That just now, upstairs, that's more than just fucking for fun."

"Oh, it was definitely fun. Did you not enjoy it?" He fakes horror that I was disappointed.

I laugh at him and use my free hand to slap him lightly on the arm. "Be serious," I say, chastising him in a joking way, but I'm not sure it'll make a difference. I know he will only tell me what he wants to share. I have no chance of pushing him past that point, so I may as well accept it.

"Okay, if I agree to do this talking thing, will it make us argue? Because I looovvveeee when we argue. The results are worth it."

"Oh my God, you are incorrigible. Is that why you keep being an asshole to me?" I try to pull my hand off his heart, but he has it in a firm hold.

"Nope, that's just me being me," he sasses, unapologetic for being himself.

I roll my eyes at him, because deep down, apparently, I like this asshole, who would have thought. "I see what you are doing, trying to change the topic. Not happening. I want the truth. What am I to you? Just a fling, a solution to a problem, someone you are now stuck with so you thought you might as well have some fun? Because I can cope with that, but I need to know, before I let my heart get involved." All lies. My heart is already swimming in the murky waters of whatever this is, and I'm not sure I can see any ladder to get back out before it's too late.

His body tenses slightly the more I talk. "You may think I'm a monster, but I would never treat you like that. Christ! I hope you see that I'm more than that!" By the scowl on his face and the roughness of his words, I know I've hit a tender spot. "If you were a fling as you call it, I would have told you before I ever touched you. Fuck, you must not think very highly of me." Releasing my hand, he stands and is now pacing the porch in front of me. I'm beginning to understand that's his thing. When he is stressed, he stands and paces.

I need to try and calm him down before this ends up escalating. "Nicholas…" I hold my hand out toward him, encouraging him to come back to me.

"I might not be very good at this, nor do I know what the hell is happening," he says, running his hand through his hair in frustration, "but you're someone different." I can see the turmoil in his eyes about how much he wants to reveal.

"Good different? Or crazy different?" I'm not sure what the answer will be, which makes my stomach sink.

"Both, and that's why I can't seem to walk away from you!" Storming toward me, he grasps me by the ankles and slides me down the daybed, pulling me up to sitting in front of him as he falls to his knees. His hands go straight to my head, quickly entwining his fingers in my hair. The pressure on my scalp has me already tingling at the sensation.

"I fucking crave you, Victoria!" He devours me in a kiss that leaves me gasping for air as he pulls back. "That's all you need to know!" He pulls me toward him again, but this time, it's me fighting to stop it.

"What if I want more?" And I do. I want to know everything behind his walls.

He scowls at me with frustration. "Then you will have to be patient."

"Not my strong point!"

"Why doesn't that surprise me." As he rises off his knees, I know I have missed my chance. "Don't push me, Victoria, you won't like the outcome." And I don't doubt it. Walking back toward the door to the kitchen, Nicholas calls over his shoulder, "Just checking the dinner, back in a minute.

I don't disbelieve he is, but it's also to give him space and time to gather his thoughts.

I won't let this rest. He might think he can push me away, but he can't fuck me like he does then claim he isn't interested in what we have going on.

I'll give him space through dinner, but then we will revisit this, whether he likes it or not.

After he returned from the kitchen, it was like the conversation never existed. We chatted about his estate and some of the things he wants me to see tomorrow, all while I'm reminding him that we are here to work among other reasons. For him it's to hide me away from the world, and although I know that isn't the answer to anything, I understand for now that it's the best option.

He pulls out the chair for me. I can't believe the food that is spread out in front of me, but I'm confused why there is only one large plate of everything. "I hope you are hungry." Nicholas takes the seat next to me and turns my seat on an angle so I'm looking at him.

"Ravenous," I purr, licking my lips, and I know he understands what I mean.

"I need to feed you first, you dirty girl, and if you eat all your dinner, I might let you wear your dessert."

I gulp as he trumps me with his words again. "I think you should wear the dessert, and I get to make the rules this time." My heart is racing at the thought of pushing his boundaries, even though it won't happen, and I'm not sad about that either.

Nicholas seduces me easily with his words, but it's his control over me that I crave more, and that is what has totally floored me.

My mother raised me to be an independent woman, but I'm quickly learning I can be all that and still be a sexual woman too. I have desires that have been untapped until now. Things I didn't even know I wanted, but fuck, now I'm desperate for more.

"You know that's not how you want it. Tell the truth, Victoria…" His hand is already sliding up the inside of my thigh, knowing full well I'll melt with his touch. "Your body tells me what you need by the way it reacts to me…" I want to be able to control my reactions, but I can't. He plays me just the way he likes, and I lap it up like someone who hasn't been fed for weeks. My mouth opens on a sigh as his finger so tenderly traces the edge of my panties. I knew wearing a short free-flowing dress would be perfect.

"The more you eat, the bigger the reward." His voice, oh my Lord!

With his free hand, he lifts an oyster shell to my mouth, his eyes burning through me as he watches me swallow it down whole, gaining me another swipe over my panties, slightly firmer and a little closer to my sex.

I'm panting already and I can't stop myself.

"Are you trying to seduce me with oysters?" My voice quivers a little as I try to speak. His Adam's apple bulges as his own oyster slides down his throat.

"I don't need any aphrodisiacs, Victoria. I know how to turn you on, don't you agree?" His hand is now rubbing so softly up and down the inside of my thigh again, and I want to squeeze my legs together to give more pressure, but I know he'll punish me for it. He is doing this to torture me, testing my patience that I have proclaimed I don't have.

"If I say no?"

He drops his head to my neck, just below my ear, and licks upward. His gravelly voice makes me shudder. "Then I stop…" His hand stills, and his lips hover just above my skin.

"You're cruel," I whisper, the words falling from my lips.

"Oh, I can be… and I assure you, you will love every moment of it." He sinks his teeth down on my earlobe.

I had no idea that pain could be so erotic!

My body is no longer my own, as he pushes my legs slightly wider so he has better access to what he wants.

"Now show me how good you are at swallowing again." He holds another oyster to my mouth, but before he gets close enough to tip it, his middle finger moves from the shell, starting to stroke along my lip… sliding it inside. "Suck." The moment my lips close around his finger, my tongue takes over, licking him too. "Yes, show me what you will do to my cock when you take it… all of it…right down that pretty throat of yours." And just as quickly as he told me to suck, his finger is gone, and the oyster is in my mouth. "Swallow." His demand makes my body do exactly that. "Good girl, just how you will swallow around my cock when I demand it."

This time, he lays his hand over my sex and places the firm pressure I'm desperately longing for.

"Nicholas…" My moan is more like a plea to take it further.

"I know, precious, you are learning how patient you need to be with me." Bastard is playing me.

"Asshole."

There's satisfaction on his face at how strung out I already am. "Hmmm, yes, and it won't be long, and I'll be taking that too."

Oh, my fucking God, I can't sit still, squirming on my chair. I didn't think after what we just shared earlier that I'd be back here so quickly, but my body is already screaming for release.

Placing his hand on the side of my throat, he runs his thumb up and down my windpipe.

"Breathe, Victoria." I'm trying, but you keep stealing my air every time you open your mouth with these words of yours. And he keeps encouraging the dirty girl inside me to come out to play, and she also wants you to take my breath away with your hand like before. He has total control of me!

I know this whole seduction with food is to distract me, and let me assure you, I have no idea what I wanted to say before this. All I can think about is his touch and the anticipation of what he is about to say and do next.

Missing his fingers on my throat, the first forkful of a beef tenderloin strip with a red wine sauce is being placed halfway into my mouth.

"Bite." His enjoyment of feeding me is turning him on as much as it is to push me to new heights. I can see it in his eyes as he takes the other half of the piece of steak into his mouth now.

"Mmmm. So good." The beef is so tender it almost melts in my mouth. Just as I'm voicing my appreciation for his cooking, he gives me my reward, his finger running straight up my sex and pushing down on my clit through my panties.

"Fuck!" I can't help but scream out.

"When I'm ready, but you aren't even close yet." Where the hell did this man come from? I mean, his idea of fucking is like what I imagine it would feel to be on crack. It's next level and in a world all its own.

The more he feeds me, the wetter I get, and my body is buzzing on the endorphins that are racing around inside me. Just like he promised, every mouthful brings me pleasure somewhere on my body. Slowly he opens his shirt buttons one at a time, but his demand not to touch him just makes me crave that contact. But I'm still completely clothed, and he is playing with me like his doll, taking what he wants, testing me in ways I never imagined. Nicholas, however, is now completely naked . I can only look at his body that is reacting to every whimper and moan I let escape.

Taking his finger and dipping it in the sauce still on the plate, he coats around the rim of his cock then places his finger on my lips.

"You want my cock in your mouth, don't you. Tell me how badly you want to suck me off."

He must be in so much pain, because I know the ache I'm experiencing is hell. With the tightness of his cock, it has to be excruciating. Yet he remains still and calm, in total control of his emotions.

"Fuck, you know I'm desperate. You have been teasing me to the point of pain. Let me suck you. Please, Nicholas, I'm hurting…" The whine in my voice is what he wants. He is looking to make me beg. He doesn't need to tell me, I know I'm not allowed to come until he tells me I can, and it's becoming almost impossible to hold myself back any longer. "I need… naked… fuck, even my clothes hurt." They are like a secret restraint he has on me when all I want is to be free of everything.

"You are the perfect pain minx. You respond so beautifully to everything that makes you ache. The pinking up of your skin tells me how close you are to your orgasm, and it's going to be so strong that it will give you the pain you desire. How lucky I am to find you," he says, placing his finger on my tongue.

"Lick and taste what you can't have yet. Wine and my cum mixed on your tongue. Imagine what it will taste like as I fuck your mouth with it."

"Yes, please, fuck my mouth." Licking the taste from his finger has me wanting everything he has promised.

"Stand and strip." Oh, thank fuck. Jumping to my feet, the little baby doll dress is over my head before he has time to change his mind. I didn't bother with a bra after our bath, but he knew that. Every time he dropped his hand to my breasts and pulled hard on my nipples, pinching me to the point I was crying out in pain and pleasure, and he would smile at the reaction he got.

My breasts bounce as I hurry to drop my panties to the floor. I can feel the moisture between my legs, coating my thighs, and I haven't even come yet.

"That was very naughty of you not to wear a bra, Victoria, but I will let you off this time with just a little punishment. On your knees now!" Not caring how hard the floor is below me, I'm on my knees for my man, mouth dripping with anticipation. "No hands, but you may run your nose around my cock. Remember that smell of want that you have put there."

Holy fuckity fuck, this man is over the top.

He's bad, so fucking bad in all the best ways.

"But you will not suck me yet. That is your punishment for tantalizing me with those beautiful full breasts that were begging to be played with. You will now lay your head there and wait while I finish my dessert." I look up at him through my misted eyes from almost crying in pain. He knows how far he can push me, and I want that. I need that! To go to my absolute limit because I know on the other side of that limit is pure, utter ecstasy.

The spoon of chocolate mousse he places in his mouth and almost makes love to it has me whimpering on his leg. I smell all the sex pheromones coating his skin. Then just as I think I can't hold on any longer he takes the second spoonful and grasps my hair hard, pulling my head back so I'm looking up into his eyes.

"Would you like your dessert now, Victoria?"

He told me in the beginning, the more I ate, the bigger the reward. And I'm aching for my reward.

"Yes. I'll be good, please, yes, dessert." Opening my mouth, I wait for the spoon, but he stops halfway to me and instead smears the chocolate mousse all the way down his cock that is so hard it looks like it's impossible to get any bigger. The veins are protruding, and the purple head is leaking profusely.

"Suck me clean. You will take it all and enjoy your dessert for being such an obedient girl." The hand in my hair tugs tighter against my scalp as he pulls me straight up onto my knees between his legs again. "I want to feel the back of your throat. Relax, my precious." He pushes my head down as I open my mouth and close it around his cock, and I sigh with relief of touching him. He's so big I don't know how I will take him all, but I need to try. It's what he is demanding, and I don't want to disappoint him.

"That's it, beautiful. Breathe through your nose and relax those tight throat muscles. Oh, you are perfect, just the perfect fucking little bitch. All mouth when you want to challenge me, but I knew that mouth would be worth the wait. You have no idea the view I have of those lips that tantalize me, wrapped around me and silenced in the best way possible."

My body is quivering, drool running from the corner of my mouth, and all I want to do is come and have him come down my throat, hard. I want it all. I'm moaning and rocking up and down over him. Using his hands, he desperately sets my rhythm. Again, he wants to control it all.

"You need to come don't you, Victoria?" I bob my head up and down, trying to signal to him without stopping. My hands are on the tops of his thighs, my nails digging into his skin so hard while I try to hold myself back.

Say the word, Nicholas, fuck, say the word already!

"Stop moving but don't pull your mouth off." I can feel the vibration in his body too. He is on the edge of exploding but isn't ready for it to be over.

"Touch yourself. Now! I want to feel you moaning on my cock

while you try to hold in that orgasm. Show me how you like to finger yourself and think of me."

The tears are falling from my eyes as I touch my sex and try not to let myself go. I can't do it. I can't hold back any longer.

My fingers move faster, rubbing my clit so hard. I'm screaming all around his cock in pain. He knows I've reached my limit, yet he is pushing me that little bit further. I can't hold still, my mouth now moving up and down. I'm back devouring him and screaming, my other hand now at the base of his cock squeezing him as hard as I can. I want him to feel it too.

As impossible as it seems, I can feel him swelling further in my mouth, to the point my lips are so tight around him.

He is grunting now like an animal, giving me the satisfaction that is racing through my body at making him lose his precious control. I can taste him in my mouth, and the salty precum is divine. His body tenses under me, and he finally screams his words into the room. "Come... fucking come... for me."

The buzz in my ears starts, my body shaking with pain as every muscle lets go in euphoria from my orgasm taking over. But it doesn't stop me. I'm so heightened, and I want him to explode in my mouth so desperately. I move my hand to his balls and pull them down and squeeze them so tightly. The roar of my name echoes off the ceiling as the ropes of cum hit the back of my throat. There is no relief as he keeps thrusting into my mouth with every squirt. There is so much of it, and I swallow everything I can, but I can feel it dribbling from the side of my mouth too.

I've never wanted to taste a man as desperately as I want Nicholas. Suddenly, though, I'm pulled off him, and he drags his cock toward my breasts, painting my skin with him.

I want to be marked by Nicholas Darby!

I don't know if I will get to keep him, but I will always be his. He has broken me for any other man. Deep down I know that, and I'm not sure I'll be able to walk away. I know I should, because I have a life planned, but his powerful pull over me is making my dreams slip through my fingers like sand. I promised myself I wouldn't let any man rule my life so he couldn't break me. So why am I so worried, it's already too late!

Nicholas reaches down under my arms and pulls me up onto his lap. His breathing is ragged, and his eyes are full of desire. Placing me straddling him, he uses his right hand to massage his cum into my skin. I'm not the only one who wants to make sure he claims my body. My soul is still so wrapped up in confusion, but he owns my body. There is no going back now.

Laying my head on his shoulder just trying to come back to earth, his chest is still rising under me. I'm not sure he was as in control of that as he thought he was. I feel like his head is racing as much as mine is.

We shouldn't fit together like this, yet we do. And neither of us understand it or wants to accept it. Because if we admit it, then it gives it wings, and I doubt either of us is ready for that.

"We need to get dressed." The moment he starts to speak, his body tenses up again. It's like he has this switch that brings the armor back up.

"Umm, I need to shower." Sitting back up, I screw my face up at him in humor at the sticky mess now all over my chest.

"No. I don't want you to wash me off you." He's so serious that I'm left confused. He has always been so caring after sex and wanted to treat me like a princess. But now he wants me to stay like this?

"What, you want me to smell like a whore with sex all over me?"

"Victoria! Don't say that."

Wait, what? "So, you can call me that, but I can't? Don't be a hypocrite, Nicholas." How can this man take me from feeling so wrapped up in his spell of pleasure one minute to wanting to rip his balls clean off him the next.

"Because when I say it, you are at a point of no return in sheer ecstasy, and it gets you off. You long for every filthy word from my mouth. But I won't let you degrade yourself when we aren't in that moment."

Pushing off him and standing up, I bend down and grab my clothes. "That makes no fucking sense. Who said you get to make the rules all the time? God, you infuriate me!" I storm off, ignoring him calling me back.

Stomping up the stairs to the shower, I make sure I grab a bra this time, because he doesn't get the pleasure of ogling me again. No wonder my head is so confused. When he's the arrogant asshole, I don't understand what I even see in him.

Turning on the shower, I walk in and let the water pour over my head, when totally unexpectedly, tears start to fall. I don't know what is happening. I don't know what just made me snap. A small voice in my head tells me I know exactly what is wrong, I just don't want to admit it to myself.

I'm falling in love with a man I can't stand most of the time.

Why? Why is this happening?

He is too old for me. We live in such different worlds, and I can never be the woman he needs on his arm. I don't fit that high-society mold. Look at me, I can't even last a day without screaming at him and using words that a proper English lady wouldn't ever let out of her mouth.

And then there is him. He can never open his heart like I know I would need to be happy. He hides the real him, and even when I start to push, he just shuts down. That's not what a soul mate would do. Not that I am looking for a soul mate... or am I?

Leaning my head against the tiles, I hear him walk into the bathroom, but I can't look at him. I don't want him to see the mess I am right now.

But of course, I have no choice. Feeling his arms wrap around me from behind, he pulls me off the wall and back against his chest.

I'm too raw that I just let it all go. My emotions of the last week all start to pour out, and there is nothing I can do to stop it.

"Shh, precious, I've got you." It's the gentlest I have ever heard him speak as he turns me in his arms and wraps me tightly into his chest. The hot water beats down on my back, while my tears are washed down over his heart, ironically. Because that is what has me like this. That muscle in my chest that is beating for him now, but the one I'm crying all over, I don't know if it's even possible of beating for me.

"Please don't cry over me. I'm not worth it."

Raising my head, I look at him. "That's the problem." I let out another sob. "You are! You just won't let anyone see it."

"I should have let you walk away. I'm sorry." He drops his head, not looking at me, but it doesn't stop me. It just makes me cry harder.

"Yes! You should have. But you didn't, and now… now I'm so fucked up over you, and I don't even know why."

"I'll take you home," he says, all while pulling me even tighter against him, which is the opposite than what his words are saying.

"No! That's a cop out. Be a fucking man and start talking. You can't fix everything with sex, you know!" His head snaps up quickly to look at me again. He knows I saw right through that last sexfest in the dining room. Seduction stops me from talking, and he can avoid the hard things in life. And it might have worked with women before me, but this time he is up against his worst nightmare.

"You can't play with my feelings then run away. I won't let you. Get out and dry off. We are having this out now. No sex, no food, no bed, and no other distractions. Just words! I don't care if we are yelling them. I will lock you in the bathroom if that's what it takes to get you to open your mouth and talk to me. Real talk from in here!" I snap, poking his heart and then stepping back from him. I've left him shocked to the point he isn't moving, just staring at me as I step around him and walk out of the shower.

I wrap myself in one of his big fluffy, probably super expensive towels and stand, waiting for him to respond.

"Now, Nicholas." I'm not backing down. My tears have shut off and the anger is rising. He has made me feel the highest of highs and lowest of lows in the last week, and that ends now.

"Yes, I can be a bossy bitch too. Move." I watch him finally shut off the water and walk toward me.

Snapping himself out of the shock, he stands in front of me without shame, wet, naked, and with his cock already standing at attention. Leaning around me, he reaches for his towel and in the deep rasp that makes me weak in the knees, he says, "FYI, the bossy bitch is fucking hot!" He wraps the towel around his waist and storms out of the room, not saying another word.

This is going to get interesting. Who will win the battle of wills?

But more importantly, will it make any difference? Or by the end of the day, will I be packing my bags and walking away? Because I deserve more than to be his plaything, I have more respect for myself than that.

No matter how fucking fantastic the sex is…

Chapter Eighteen

NICHOLAS

S he drives me fucking crazy!

I have never let anyone this close to me before, and I defi-nitely have never fucked anyone like I have Victoria, but it's still not enough for her.

She wants more from me, and I don't know how to say no to her. As infuriating as she is, she is right. I owe her more. I'm opening some major feelings in her that she had no idea what her sexual side was like. I can't just walk away from her when her emotions are at their most vulnerable. That would make me an awful human, and I don't want her to think that of me. I don't care what others think, but Victoria is different.

She is everything!

I don't want to admit it, but I can't deny my feelings. It was an instant attraction that won't let go, and now that I have dragged her in with me, I need to man up like she is demanding.

After I found out about my father, I finally sat down and had a very deep conversation with my mum. It was information I didn't want to know before, because just the thought of him brought so much anger to me, but when I finally let myself be open to hearing about him, I learned how hard he fell for my mother in the first few days. Feelings that were big enough that he was prepared to give up all of this to be with her. To leave his family, fortune, and his home.

Now dressed, I walk downstairs asking myself the same question.

If I needed to give all of this up to keep her, what would be my answer?

I know what it would be, but if I say it out loud, then I become vulnerable, and I just can't do that yet. Too much is at stake.

Standing in the kitchen waiting, my phone starts vibrating with a FaceTime call from Mum. I should ignore it because I know Victoria will be down any moment, but I just can't. Mum will be waking up to the shitstorm that I'm sure is all over social media by now, and I don't want her worrying any more than she already is. I'm concerned about her, and this is just adding to it. And it infuriates me that I can't get on a plane and go home to check on her. No matter how much I push her, she won't tell me if there is something wrong with her. It's frustrating the hell out of me.

As I swipe to answer the call, Victoria's voice is in my head screaming at me that it must be where I get it from.

Christ, now she is in my head chastising me without even being in the room!

"Mum," I say, trying to smile and not let her know what is going on here.

"Richard Nicholas Weston Darby! Why am I finding out on the internet that you have a girlfriend and not from you!"

What is it with the women in my life screaming at me today. For fuck's sake!

But if I'm honest, I was so wrapped up with getting Victoria out of London before she was harassed, I didn't think about telling Mum that part of the story. She knew about the drugs, but at the time, Victoria wasn't in the picture.

Who am I kidding? From the moment she spat her cup of tea over me, she's never not been in the picture.

"Calm down, Mum. It's not what you think." I don't even know what it is, so how do I explain it to Mum? Plus, I don't want to give her false hope. She will have me married and fathering ten children before I even blink.

"What do you mean it's not what I think. I saw the pictures. You are practically eating that poor girl alive in that alley. I can feel the heat from here. You remind me of your father with that stance. So dominant." I can see her mind is back in her memories.

"Nope, do not go there. I've told you before I don't want to hear about my parents' sex life." Taking a seat on the kitchen stool, I look around at a place that normally calms me, but today, I'm not sure anything can settle my inner turmoil.

"Oh, Nic, I wasn't going to give you the details, but you can't deny the lust that is in that picture." As she waits for me to answer, I know I could lie to her, but surprisingly, I don't want to. I need help, and Mum is the only one who truly knows me. She's lived my life of turmoil and supported me through it all, the good and the bad.

"Fair point." My sigh gives away how I'm feeling.

"Talk to me, Nic. Don't let it eat at you. We know what that does to you, and it's not healthy." She is waiting for me to speak, but I don't know what to say. "It's okay to let yourself feel, Nic. You need to stop fearing what will happen if you do."

"I'm not right for her, she deserves more than what I can offer." And that is the bottom line in this whole internal debate. All the money in the world can't fix my fucked-up personality and give her the emotionally stable man she wants.

"I know we aren't talking about lifestyle here, because you could give her the world, but she wants more, doesn't she. She wants you, even the parts you have always been afraid to give."

"Why am I talking to you about this? I hate when you see past my blocks that everyone else backs away from. She is just like you. Drives me so damn wild, pushing like you do." Standing, I start to pace the kitchen.

"Nic, sit down and stop pacing. You need to finally let this go. You are not your father, although in so many ways, you are exactly like him. Strong, demanding, controlling, stubborn, and arrogant at times. But what you won't let anyone see is the softness, kindness, loyalty, and protective love you have been hiding since you were old enough to understand about your father disappearing from you. It's time you let someone in, and the fact that we are even talking about this woman means she is the one who has gotten through that wall."

Why, for once, is my Mum making so much sense?

"I hardly know her," I say, trying to make her understand my turmoil.

"Your father told me he loved me the third day we were together. You Darby men fall hard and fast. And in case your stubborn head has forgotten, I was the furthest thing from the right kind of woman for your dad and his lifestyle. But we worked. Oh God, did we work…"

"Mum… remember the rules," I say, laughing at her with such a smile on her face.

My smile drops as I sober. "That may have been you both, but we fight more than we talk. She has the sassiest mouth on her. She won't back down from anything, and it infuriates me. And when she is backed against a wall, she comes out swinging to protect me, even to the detriment of herself. We will kill each other if I take this any further."

"Oh, I bet the sex is off the charts."

"Fuck me!" Plonking myself back onto the stool, I drop my head into hands after standing the phone up against the fruit bowl. "You did not just imagine my sex life. I can't even deal with you sometimes."

"Sex is natural, Son, and I'm not sure you have heard everything about your father and me in our time together. It was only such a short time, but for me, it was like a lifetime. Sure, you have heard all the great things, but it wasn't like that all the time. We were polar opposites. We fought a lot too, but like they say, opposites attract. He was used to getting everything his own way and wanted all the control. And yes, I did love that at times too, if you get my drift, but there was no way I was putting up with him being such an asshole all the time. We worked at it, and my free spirit calmed his heat when we needed it to. But I never felt as loved and protected as I did when he took me in his arms and stared down any man who even looked sideways at me. We worked in a way that no couple should have, and we would have worked forever if life didn't have other plans for us."

Today has been a lot already and hearing this now after all these years of me believing that their time together was all sunshine and rainbows, it's the catalyst to release all the emotion I've been holding for so long. I can feel tears wanting to break through. I can't let them. Strong men don't cry, but this is the closest I have ever gotten.

"She's young, Mum, just discovering her life. What can an old emotionally stunted man offer her? She deserves more." I quickly pull myself together as I hear a noise behind me. "Anyway, enough of this. Are you doing okay?" I say, trying to change the topic before Victoria enters the room.

My mum laughs at me, knowing what's going on.

"Oh, we aren't finished with this, that's for sure. We will continue it later." And the way Mum's eyes open wide and look like they are about to pop out of her head, I know Victoria is standing behind me.

"Nicholas?" All the anger and feistiness from upstairs is gone in her gentle whisper.

"Oh, dear girl, come closer and say hello. Let me look at you." Mum moves the camera closer to her face like it will help her see more. Which breaks the silence because you can't help but laugh at older people with the way they cope with technology at times.

"Mum, behave." I try to rein her in before she gets out of control.

I turn to see Victoria looking as beautiful as ever, her hair hardly dried and pulled up onto the top of her head in a messy bun, with those few loose curly strands falling down around her face. Her cheeks are a slight shade of pink at meeting my mother like this. She's still in the same yellow flower-patterned sundress that she had on for dinner, that just softly flows over her body. My mother's words are now racing through my head.

Reaching out to her with my arm, she steps forward and into my side as I pull her against my body tightly. I try to show her without saying a word how much I want her here, although she is doubting it so much right now.

"Victoria, this is my nosy mother, Sally. Ignore anything she says about me, it will be all lies," I say, trying to lighten the moment, but I needn't have bothered because Mum is surely going to do that all on her own as her excitement takes over.

"Hi, Sally." Victoria lifts her hand to wave.

"Oh, my Lord, you are so beautiful, I don't know what you are doing with my Nic."

"A question I'm asking myself too." She tries to laugh it off, but I know she is serious. "To be honest, he kidnapped me and brought me here. So, I didn't have much choice." Now she turns to look at me, waiting for a bite.

"You are both ridiculous." I won't take the bait from either of them. I'm slowly running my hand up and down her side, and the perfume she wears is already sending my senses into overdrive.

"I brought Victoria here for a few days to escape the paparazzi. We are going to be working here for the rest of the week."

"Work, what a waste. Enjoy yourselves. You have never taken a girlfriend to the estate before, Nic, don't spend time sitting in front of a computer. Take her riding, or walk the fields like you love, cook her some magical meals. Come to think of it, you've never had a girlfriend at all... so strike work off the list."

"What? You've truly never had a girlfriend before?" Victoria looks down at me, shocked, but I can see things clicking into place in her head. Yes, gorgeous, I'm so fucked up that I haven't gone there with anyone. Until you. And although it started out fake, we are past that now and in no-man's land.

Not wanting to give too much away, I shrug it off. "There have been other women." I say it so offhandedly that both women look at each other and start laughing.

Mum shakes her head. "Yes, women that you have no doubt fucked, but nothing serious!" Victoria is still laughing as my mouth hangs open at my mum's comments.

"Mum! Seriously, I will hang up on you." I can feel Victoria relax in my arm the more she laughs at my mother.

"Well, it's true. You are almost forty and I've never been introduced to a woman while they are with you, and the only woman you have taken to the estate is me, your old-fart mother. So, tell me I'm wrong that Victoria is special." I could kill her right now. She knows exactly what she is doing.

"Oh, she's special all right," I say, earning me a playful slap on my shoulder at trying to make a joke of it.

"Nic…" Damn you, Mum, stop pushing me to a place I don't know how to handle yet.

Looking up into those eyes that get me every time, I can't help but admit, "She's more than special… Victoria is everything." And the truth is out there. Pulling her down onto my lap, I kiss her softly on the lips until she melts into my body.

I almost forget Mum is still there until I hear her. "Awww… finally." It's not much more than a whisper, and for Mum that is saying something.

Feeling Victoria's hand running softly up and down my arm is comforting in a time where I feel so out of control.

"I think it's time I came to London for a visit."

"Yes!" Victoria replies excitedly as I yell at the same time, "No!"

The last thing I need is my mother here making things ten times harder, pushing in where I don't need her, and things are too uncertain here at the moment.

"Someone needs to be there to make sure you don't mess this up," she says. I can already see she is planning it in her head.

"I'm a grown man, I'm sure I can handle my own life." By the looks both Victoria and Mum are giving me, the words out of Victoria's mouth just make me start laughing.

"That's debatable." And that's why she lights my fire. She's never afraid to tell me what she thinks.

"I like you, Victoria. You are just perfect. I can't wait to meet you when I get there." Mum will already be packing her bags as soon as she gets off this call, I can tell. I need to slow this woman down before she turns up on my doorstep. And my life history has me living with a real phobia of her traveling without me, not knowing where she is and how she is getting there and home. If my dad had just told his parents, they would have picked him up and we might still have him today.

"Me too. We have a lot to talk about, I'm sure. And don't let him keep you from me. He's just scared that we'll gang up on him." It's like I'm not even in this conversation anymore, as they start talking about different places that Victoria can take her to see when she visits.

"Fuck, kill me now. I've got no say in this, have I?" I pretend to be annoyed, but really, there is a part of me that will be happy to see my mum and make sure she is okay. And there is an even bigger part of me that wants the two of them to become friends. If this thing with Victoria is ever going to work, they need to fit together in my life. There is no other option.

Finally breaking into the conversation between them that I'm no longer included in, they both stop and smile at me as I tell them, "I'll have Lucy organize a plane for you. There is too much happening this week, but I'll arrange for the week after that. Don't book anything, understood?" Knowing her, she will book some cheap-ass seat in economy that will have her in the air for thirty-five hours with multiple stopovers in some weird-ass place.

"So bossy." Mum looks at me.

"Don't I know it," Victoria mumbles under her breath, but Mum knows exactly what she said, and that's enough to make me embarrassed. It's not something my mum needs to know. But the way Victoria said it makes me relax, knowing that we will be okay.

She's right, we do need to talk, and I need to be honest with her. It's not something I'm keen to do, but she deserves that from me.

"I think it's time I let you both get back to whatever you were doing. And just remember, no work, you need to discover each other first. There is plenty of time for work later."

It all sounds good in theory, but not a day goes past that I'm not working in some capacity, and I can't expect Victoria to just step away from her job. Financially, I doubt she could afford to do that, but careerwise, I would never expect that of her.

"Thanks, Mum, and stop reading the trash on social media. I've told you that before. I will sort this out. Trust me, it will be fine. I'll be in touch."

"No, don't call me, just concentrate on Victoria. I'll talk to Lucy."

Rolling my eyes at her, she knows she has gotten her way.

"Love you, Mum, and thanks for the chat. I mean it." And I do. She has made me look at things in a different light.

"Love you, Nic, and can't wait to hug you both soon." I think she's done and about to hang up when she quickly gets in her last say, just like she always does.

"And don't let him push you away, sweet girl. Push back hard, you are everything he has ever needed."

Before I can say a word, her face has disappeared, and the call is disconnected.

"I love your mum already." Victoria has a smile stretching from one side of her face to the other.

"Ughhh," I groan. "I bet you do!"

I'm screwed, like totally screwed. Once these two are in the same room, there will be no going back. Mum will be planning a wedding, and Victoria will have way too much background information on me.

What have I done.

I sit for a little longer just holding her, trying to tell her I'm sorry without words.

Why is it so hard to let myself be vulnerable? Is it a guy thing, or am I just as fucked up as I feel?

I know it won't last, but holding her like this is so calming. When we are both silent, it's like we allow our hearts to talk and don't let our heads get in the way.

She can feel it too, her breathing soft and slow. Why can't we just stay like this and there would be less tension?

Who am I kidding, we both love the tension and what follows. She can tell me I use sex as a distraction, and she'd be right. But it doesn't take away from how fucking awesome we are together naked.

"She is your world, isn't she." Victoria's soft voice breaks the silence that had wrapped around us, comforting us.

"My mother gave up her life for me. I will always be grateful for the unconditional love she shared and for all the tough times she battled to keep a roof over our heads. I would give her the world if she would let me. But she won't, and I have to respect that, as hard as it is."

"Then she raised you right. Respect is an important trait in any man." It makes me think we were brought up with similar values.

"Thank you," is all I can manage to say in reply.

I lift her off my lap, needing to move somewhere more comfortable. There is no getting out of this, and I know we should talk.

"Go and make yourself comfortable in the lounge room. I'll get us a night cap."

She smiles at me with a sense of sarcasm coming. "Not sure alcohol is a good idea for me, never seems to end well."

I laugh at her as she starts toward the living room. "Agreed, but if you want me to talk, then I sure as shit need it."

"Then bring the bottle," she yells from the hallway, and I can't help but laugh harder because it's not a bad idea.

As I walk into the room lit just with lamplight and see her in the corner of the big cream comfy couch, feet pulled up beneath her and her head leaning back, it has me catching my breath. As much as she turns me on when we are going toe to toe with each other, the sight of her like this, still, quiet, and relaxed, is something I long to see more of.

"I was joking about the bottle," she says, smiling at me as I hand her a glass.

"I wasn't." Pouring a small amount of port into our glasses, then placing the bottle on the coffee table, I take my seat as close as possible to her without sitting on her lap. I need to be touching her.

She sips her port and closes her eyes as it slides down her throat nicely. If there is one thing that I've learned as a chef, it's that the quality of good alcohol makes a world of difference to the taste, as well as how you feel the morning after.

"Your mum sounds like she went through a lot with your father."

She places her hand on my thigh and squeezes with a little pressure, reassuring me that this is a safe space.

But all my panicking brain can think is that she heard our conversation.

I stiffen up. "How much did you hear?" I ask, pinning her with my stare. I don't want any bullshit answer.

"Most of it."

And I want to get up and walk out. Here I was trying to pull together the courage to show her my vulnerable side, but she saw it all anyway. No one has ever been able to strip back my layers like my mother can. Until now.

"Don't shut down on me, Nicholas. Please don't shut me out."

I throw my head back and down the rest of my glass of port, because I don't know what else to do. "Ughhh," I groan, looking up at the ceiling, and finally lower my head back down to look into her eyes. "I'm trying not to, I truly am." I can't be any more honest than that.

"Then let me lead for once. You tell me if I'm wrong."

Yes. Yes, I can do that. If she says the words, I just need to agree.

What is wrong with me that I need this woman to hold my hand on my emotions? If the boys could see me like this, they would have a totally different opinion of me.

"You told me I should have researched you on the internet, but I don't want to know that person. I want to know the real you. This man here. The one who loves and respects his mum. Who would do anything for his friends and everyone who works for him. That I can tell by the way you want to protect the business from a scandal. You don't care what people think of you, just the hotels, because you don't want anyone to lose their jobs. Well, maybe Jocelyn, but you get my vote on that one too."

"My staff work hard, and no matter what their role is in the hotel, at the end of the day, they are doing it to support themselves or someone they love. My mother and grandparents did that their whole lives, and I respect people who work hard like they did." My passion for the people in my business bursts forward as soon as she talks about them.

"I get that. I come from the working class too, and I applaud you for the respect you show them." She pulls on my arm until I'm almost lying on her side, and this time, I'm the one in her arms.

"But the real Nicholas is the man your mum talked about, an asshole because he is scared to feel. Everything she said made so much sense. You want to control me, and I'll only ever admit this to you, but I fucking love being dominated in every way you have thrown at me so far." Taking a breath, she kisses the top of my head and then continues. "But you do know that it is a cover for you. You think if you treat women like that, then no one will ever fall for you. You won't have to open up, and especially, you will never have to feel anything. Except, of course, immense pleasure at getting off while you are in your element. But one day, that will stop being enough, and there won't be anyone here to comfort you in the days that you need them. Like this, when you just want to be soft and not always having to be the one pushing the moment."

"I will never get tired of your body," I slip in, objecting to what she said.

"Of course, that's all you heard." There's frustration in her voice. I can't let her think I don't want her to keep going.

"No, I heard it all, and it's just so close to truth that you must know how hard it is for me to acknowledge." I gulp, wishing I still had the glass of port in my hand. I don't know what to do, and I want to get up and pace, but I can't. *Man up, and finally face your fears.*

"Has it occurred to you that if you can't do it with me, then you may never open up to anyone?"

"Yes," I growl like a child.

"Well, at least we are getting somewhere." She tilts my head up so I am looking at her and can't hide.

"Then what are you afraid of?"

I think about my answer but know I can't do anything but face the truth.

"Falling for you so far that I can't walk away before we get hurt. I don't want to hurt you, Victoria, but I'm not capable of loving you like you deserve. I don't know how."

"Oh, Nicholas, I wish I could make you see how wrong you are.

You told me in Rome that you don't believe in love, but I don't think that's true. I just think you are scared to love."

Maybe she's right.

Because I know that my mother's love for my father was real. I didn't need to see it to feel how real it was for her. It's in the way she talks about him, the look in her eyes and the years of loneliness she has endured because nothing has ever come close to the love she felt with him.

So, I believe in love in some ways, but I have also seen the hurt in her during the quiet moments at night when I was younger and she would hold herself in her bed, with silent tears streaming down her face, crying over what she had lost. Thinking he had just left her and that she wasn't good enough for him. I know I won't survive that kind of hurt. I too lived it my whole life, thinking I wasn't good enough to be loved. I know it was irrational, but the mind is a powerful thing, and if you think something long enough, then it becomes a part of you that you can no longer shift.

And nothing will ever take away the vision of my mother breaking into pieces at my father's grave when she finally came to London to meet my grandfather. Every piece of herself that she had been holding together for all those years crumbled as I held her sobbing for what felt like hours. That is the real pain of true love.

I can't do that. I'm not as strong as she was.

That's why I can't love, because the truth is, I'm not strong enough to survive the loss.

"Love is something that you shouldn't be scared of… but I'm terrified of it," I admit, kissing her on the lips, trying to get her to understand. "And I know I will never get past that." I kiss her again. "I'm broken, and you are perfect. I can't ask you to love a broken man…"

But my heart for the first time in my life is crying out to her… *please, love a broken man. I'm begging you.*

Chapter Nineteen

VICTORIA

Oh, my poor Nicholas. The sadness in his eyes at how broken he feels is so heart-wrenching.

"You aren't broken, you just need to learn that it is okay to open your heart." To me, please open it to me.

My head is telling me I will probably regret this, but I want to go all in with him, because I know that deep inside is the man I could love, without a doubt.

He will push me to the point that I want to kill him daily, but as long as I can come home to this beautiful man, this sensitive loving man, then I'll take all the fire between us day in and day out.

Elouise is going to want to lock me up when she hears what is in my head. She will tell me all the reasons he is wrong for me. The age gap, the lifestyle, the stress levels he drives me to, and pushing aside my dreams. But I think he will be worth it all.

I want to give it a shot to see if we can make this work, as crazy as that sounds.

Now I just need to convince Nicholas that even if he thinks he's broken, which he's not, that it will be okay. He can get past the heavy weight he has carried for way too long.

His laugh surprises me a little. "I tried keeping my heart closed, but you just barged through the door anyway."

"Well, then look out, baby, because you ain't seen nothing yet!" And this is what he needs from me. To acknowledge how this is hard for him, but to give him the tools of comedy and dare I say sex to get himself through to the other side. The gap between us is wide at the moment, but with time, I can fill in from the edges until it is only a small step for him to make it to the other side.

"Why does that frighten the hell out of me but excite me at the same time?" He sighs but in a good way. Nicholas sits up again and looks at me. "I'm in trouble with you, aren't I?" He's half joking but half serious.

"No more trouble than I am with you. I didn't factor you into my life plan, Nicholas Darby, but you came thundering in anyway. I like surprises, but with you, I'm still trying to get over the initial shock of what have I walked into."

"Ditto, beautiful. Fucking ditto." Pulling me to him, his lips are so soft as they take mine. Nothing like the intensity when he is trying to fuck me into submission.

This kiss is him laying himself bare to me, as much as he can so far.

And for now… that's enough.

"Come to bed with me," he says, standing and holding his hand out for me to take.

My brain is worried that he is about to slip back behind the wall and use sex to calm his feelings, but the look on my face must tell a story.

"To sleep, Victoria. I just want to hold you." And relief floods through my body. One, because I want him to step forward, but two, because I don't think my body can take another pounding tonight, and I have yet to know if Nicholas knows any other way to fuck than to take me to pound town.

As I stand and step into his arms, he buries his head into my

In the last two weeks, I have started a new job and hardly worked a day in the office. I can imagine the way Theo must be carrying on about me, which will be hard to cope with when I return. I met a man, spat tea over his expensive suit, and now I'm living in his wealthy estate. I mean, let's not forget the trip on a private jet to Rome and fulfilling a childhood dream of making my wish in the Trevi Fountain. This can't be real; surely tomorrow I will wake up and relive the moment of embarrassment on the train and life will just continue as it was supposed to. Plain, boring, and normal!

The smell of the amazing food that Nicholas is cooking in the kitchen reminds me that I didn't wake up this morning on the train, but instead to some hot billionaire hotel owner and chef between my legs, feasting on what he tells me is his to devour when he wants. How can I argue with that.

I'm not wanted in the kitchen while he is preparing lunch for everyone arriving here around one o'clock. The guys have business to discuss and plans to make that are easier when they are all together. Honestly, though, I think Nicholas needs to see them. He is trying to show how calm he is about this investigation, but I know part of him is nervous. As much as I try to reassure him, I have no idea about the world he lives in, but his friends do, and that is why he needs them too.

He got me to ask Elouise if she could take Friday off work and he would have a car pick her up. I'm pretty sure she just pretended to be sick, but I don't care how she managed it, I just wanted her here. He heard me on the phone to her a few days ago and could tell how much I miss her, and if I'm honest, I need to see her too. The guys might be his lifeline, just as much as she is mine. The phone calls have been full of shock as she listens, yelling when she tells me I'm crazy and should get out of here, to laughing and crying at the stupid things I've done since I've been here.

Who knew that when a horse lifts his tail while you are patting his ass, that means he is about to take a shit. Before Nicholas could tell me to move, the first plop landed on my feet, and I was so shocked I screamed, making the horse take off down the field as I fell sideways into a pile of hot horse shit. Oh yeah, just because I'm with Nicholas, it hasn't stopped me from being a walking disaster. I hope he knows what he has gotten himself into.

My phone hasn't stopped buzzing with messages since Wallace picked Elouise up. She keeps telling me how she feels like a princess, but she should wait until she gets here and sees the house and the three cars parked in the garage. Nicholas has a thing for his Maserati, but of course, also has a Porsche 911 and an Audi R8 lined up beside it. I mean, what the actual fuck. Who owns three luxury cars?! And that's just in this country. I have no idea what he owns worldwide.

The surroundings will be enough to blow her mind, but the guys' arrival will have her head spinning. There should be a rule about that many seriously hot men being allowed in one place at a time. She is normally the calm, sensible friend in this relationship, but I think today will test that well and truly.

She is only about twenty minutes away, and I can feel the excitement building as I walk back inside to check on my man. Yes, it sounds strange but very quickly that's what he has become, and I'll take on anyone who tries to tell me differently.

I'm actually nervous to see the guys again. Last time was so rushed and the world was exploding around us. And although I have spoken to them a few times on video calls, this will be different. It's a more relaxed environment, and I'm bound to fuck something up. That's what I do.

What if they see how wrong I am for Nicholas? They could make life difficult, and the truth is they would be right. I'm wrong for him in so many ways, and when they see it, they could be the voice of reason that makes him see it too.

I hadn't realized that I was standing just inside the kitchen, frozen in thought.

"What's wrong? You look like you have seen a ghost." His deep voice in front of me snaps me out of my contemplation of what will happen today.

"Ahh… nothing." I go up on my toes to kiss his cheek, knowing I need to get out of here before he sees straight through me.

"Bullshit. I'm not blind." Taking me in his arms, he hugs me tightly. I can smell all the mixtures of food on him, and my stomach takes the opportunity to show I'm hungry.

"Your body is vibrating, Victoria. What is going on?" Holding me out in front of him, he inspects my body language, and as per usual, my words just start pouring out, rambling at my finest.

"What if they hate me, then you will hate me. They will see I'm just some girl from a working-class family. Maybe they will think I'm after your money, which I'm not, by the way. I don't want a cent from you, I'd rather be poor than be a money muncher. Oh God, what if they think I had something to do with the drugs? I've never used drugs, or even seen any. I don't know anything about them, but they might think it was me. Is that why they told me to come here, so they could watch me and make sure I don't make a mess of this in the media? 'Trashy London woman sinks her teeth into London's most eligible bachelor.' Fuck, I should leave, or lock myself upstairs so they can't find me. Yes, that's what I'll do…"

"Knees, Victoria." His growl stops my absolute mess of words.

"What?" I ask, confused at what he said.

"On your knees now!" With his hands on my shoulders, he pushes me to the floor, where my body goes willingly. When he gives me a command, my body obeys on instinct.

Looking up into his eyes, I see he is trying to calm me by bringing my attention to him.

"Open your mouth, wide." He pulls his apron from around his waist and pops the button on his shorts. The zipper slides down as my mouth drops open in anticipation.

His cock is out before I have time to blink.

"Take it," he demands as I wrap my lips around his tip and suck it all the way to the back of my throat.

"You need to stop talking crap. Now be a good girl and calm down."

I take a deep breath through my nose as I bury my face into his skin around his cock. His manly scent is all I can think about now.

His hands slide into my hair and start to set a slow torturous rhythm. Not pulling on my hair but instead stroking me softly. I never know what to expect with him, and it's the anticipation that has me buzzing.

"Is this what you want our guests to walk in and see, you on your knees like the good little cock lover you are?" Panic setting in, I shake my head back and forth.

"Then I suggest you finish the job." His hands releasing me, my body takes over.

The electricity running through my body has me attacking him ferociously with my mouth. My hands are on his cock and balls, working every part of him as he starts moaning my name. It's what I want when I'm on my knees, I just want to please him. He shouts my name so loud that I know anyone outside would hear it as he comes down my throat, and it has me wondering who he is actually trying to calm here. Maybe he is as nervous as I am.

Basking in the afterglow of watching him lose his control, I'm happy to just clean him up and redress him, but Nicholas has a different idea. He proves his strength by lifting me from my knees and up onto the kitchen counter, and it has me gasping.

"I will never leave you hanging unless you deserve it." He pushes me backwards so I'm lying on the counter, with a few things flying to the floor that he doesn't seem to care about. Before I can say a word, my mouth falls open, letting out the first moan as I lick the residue of come drool from my lips. He slips his fingers in the side of my panties under my skirt and wastes no time making my body start to quiver.

"Don't take too long, precious, otherwise you will have an audience. Is that what you want?"

"Oh God... no... please, no... come... want to come." And before he can give me permission, he pushes my body to explode on its own. Exactly like he planned. First fucking my mouth and shutting me up, then making me a quivering mess so I am putty in his hands when his friends arrive.

"Mhmm," is all I can say as my body starts to come down from the quick high he took me on.

Leaning over top of me and kissing me so tenderly, I know he needed that release too.

"What was that?" I mumble.

"Stress reliever." He smirks, standing back up, smoothing down my skirt and lifting me to my feet.

"For whom, you or me?"

Tucking himself into his boxers and zipping up, he wraps the apron back around his waist. "Both." He laughs as he kisses me on the top of my head, then turns me facing toward the hallway to the stairs to head up to the bedroom. Swatting me on the ass, he sends me on my way.

"Now go and clean yourself up. No one wants to smell sex at the lunch table."

Groaning at him, I run down the hallway, starting to panic that I need to get upstairs before anyone arrives.

"You are such a jerk!" I yell as I run from him.

And all I can hear from behind me is him laughing a deep chuckle because he knows I'm right. It's what makes him who he is.

Not wasting any time, I feel more put together and calmer as I walk back down the stairs when I hear the first car approach. Looking out the front window before I head back to the kitchen, I see it's Wallace delivering Elouise around to the back entrance where Nicholas likes to enter the house.

Oh my God, she's here!

My steps get quicker, trying to get to her before Nicholas does. She will be so intimidated, and I know exactly how that felt the first time I drove up the long driveway.

I find Nicholas with a smug grin while he is wiping off the counter he just made me explode on.

"Don't say a word," I say as I'm passing him.

"Wouldn't dream of it. Your flushed cheeks say it all."

Bastard! Now that's all I'll be thinking of when the guys arrive, and he knows it.

Wallace opens the car door and smiles at me. "Miss Elouise, delivered all safe and sound for you." He is like a cuddly old grandpa, and I can understand why Nicholas wanted him to stay with him after his grandfather passed away. He is like a link to a past that he missed out on.

Just like I expected, Elouise steps from the car looking totally shellshocked. We have only ever seen places like this on television or in movies. We know they exist in England but never thought we would see one in person. It's like being given a golden ticket to the Willy Wonka factory for kids that grew up where we did.

"Thank you, Wallace," I say, seeing him smiling at her too. He understands. He might work for the Darby family, but it doesn't mean he lives like they do. I make a mental note to get to know more about him once things settle down. If that ever happens.

Taking the few extra steps to where she is still standing next to the car, I pull her forward into the biggest hug I have ever given her. Wallace, now able to close the door, disappears to move the car out of the way before everyone else arrives.

"Lou."

Her arms grasp on to me like her life depends on it. "Tori. What. The. Actual. Fuck." And I can't help but giggle at her.

Pulling back, I let her go from my arms. "I know, right? It's insane, but so, so, beautiful. I'm living in a fairy tale. Well, I hope it's that and not going to turn into a nightmare."

I link my arm in hers and turn toward the house. I want to get her inside and meet Nicholas before everyone else descends on us and chaos breaks out. But as I'm turning, he comes out the door and I hear her whisper under her breath.

"Fuck me dead."

"Oh, he does." I giggle at her words.

"I get it now. His suit last time, yum, but this? I fucking get it." I'm guessing she is referring to his bone-colored shorts hanging low on his hips and the dark charcoal-gray polo collared t-shirt that is molded to his biceps and chest. But for me, it's the bare feet that complete the ensemble. He thinks he is still in Australia where shoes are apparently optional.

His hair is getting longer by the day on top and giving him more of an unkept curly look that is so hot. He told me his hair was blonder when he was in Australia when he saw more sunlight, but I love it just the way it is. Blond highlights in a light brown mop of hair. The stubble on his face is darker than the hair on his head, but

I don't care about the color of it. The feel of it on my thighs is what makes it attractive.

You couldn't really see much of the variations when we first met because he kept his hair short and styled for work. Groomed and tidy, but since we have been here this week, he hasn't once put any product in it, and I love the natural man he is when he lets himself go.

I try to get her feet moving so we don't look like two idiots frozen looking at the hot man. I mean, Nicholas knows I have no class, but I don't want to prove him right.

"Elouise, it's lovely to meet you properly this time and not while I'm carrying a drunk woman into your house at some stupid time of night."

"Hey, in my defense, you insisted on taking me home!"

He leans down and kisses her on the cheek like he knows how important she is to me, so she is important to him too. "Welcome to my home," he says, sweeping his arm around at the surroundings. "Please come inside and I'll get you a drink. I'm sure you could use one after that drive."

"Right, this needs to stop now," I say, snapping my fingers in front of Lou to wake her out of the hypnotized state she's in since he kissed her. "He can be an asshole too, don't let him fool you. Besides, he's mine, so you need to find your own Neanderthal."

That works to bring her back to reality. She swings around to push me with her hand. "Tori, stop it. Don't be a bitch. As if I would go after your man."

Nicholas catches me as I stumble back a step, with her shove being a little harder than she meant because I have embarrassed her.

He whispers into my ear, "Your man, huh? I like the sound of that." And with that, he releases me again and walks toward the door, motioning for us to follow him. Of course, he doesn't enter until we have walked past him. He can still be a gentleman when he wants to be.

Nicholas gets us both an iced tea while I start to show her

around the house and what feels like a million bedrooms and bathrooms.

As we walk into the main bedroom, she stops and grabs my arm. "I don't want a tour of your sex cave."

And of course, I had just taken a sip of my drink and almost choke trying not to spit it out everywhere over the cream rug on the floor.

"Are you serious? Why would you say that?" I gasp, trying to calm my coughing reflex down.

"Because it's true. Don't you dare try to deny he hasn't been tying you up in here and fucking you stupid."

"Hmmm, being tied up," I murmur, placing my finger on my chin like I'm pondering her words. "Haven't tried that one yet."

"Oh my God, I can't be in this room. I bet if I shone one of those black lights in here there would bodily fluids on every surface." She looks at me with all the jealousy I know she is feeling because she has been telling me all week that I'm getting enough for the both of us.

And I haven't even told her the half of it. I can't. I'm still coming to terms with what he has brought out in me that I'm not sure how Lou will cope with it. Before now, I would've said we were both conservative and the few times we have had sex with guys it was always the standard deal. Missionary or on top if we were lucky.

Just thinking about my life before Nicholas makes me squirm. It's like I'm a totally different person, and even though I haven't told her that, I think Lou can tell too. We have been in sync most of our lives since we became friends, so I can't imagine it will be any different now.

"Then if you are worried about that, I suggest you don't shine the black light anywhere else in the house either."

"Who even are you and what have you done with my friend Tori?" she jokes with me, but I think there is part of her that wants the answer to that question.

"Shut up. You know I'm just joking with you… maybe."

"You are not. Your face gives you away every time. And I'm not eating or sitting anywhere until that old man drives me home again."

Backing out of the room, I can't help but keep her going. "You better be talking about Wallace as the old man and not Nicholas; he will poison your food if he hears that. Plus, what makes you think the car is safe territory?"

"I hate you! Only you could spit on some guy, and he ends up being sex on a stick and treating you like a freaking princess in his ivory palace. I just want some man to look sideways at me to make me feel a cheap thrill."

I stop and pull her into the spare room next to Nicholas's room and shut the door. "Don't you settle for that shit. I don't know what the hell is happening to me. He might be hot as fuck, but this is complicated. Like Rubik's cube hard-as-fuck complicated."

Her face drops, and she understands that I'm talking for real now. Not the cotton-candy fluff that the last two weeks has looked like. "Tori, are you okay? I'm serious, should I be worried more than I already am?"

Landing in her arms that she is holding out for me, I know I can't cry because there is no way I'm walking out in front of Nic's friends looking like some pathetic woman who can't handle this life. But just taking the comfort she is offering is what I needed.

"I'm all right, truly." I hold her hands. "It's just a lot, you know. This doesn't happen to people like us."

Lou drags me to the bed and sits us both on the edge. "Talk to me, Tori, and not just the fluffy stuff, like you said. No bullshit. What is going on?"

For the first time since that morning on the train, I spill it all as quickly as I can. I hear the guys are all downstairs now, and Nicholas will come looking for us any moment, but I need my friend. I need to let all my worries out and have someone who is far more rational than me, the person who knows me inside and out, tell me if I'm making the biggest mistake of my life.

"Holy shit! How are you still holding this together?" she asks, dropping my head to her shoulder with the weight of her words.

"Ummm, did you not just hear what I word vomited on you? I'm not. But I'm already in too deep, aren't I."

Both of us breathing deeply, Lou tries to just process my thoughts I have dumped on her.

"Time is irrelevant here, and there is only one question really that needs to be asked," she says, putting her finger under my chin and making me look up into my best friend's eyes so I can't bullshit her in my answer.

"Do you love him? And not the pretend type of first flutters, but like the kind of love that will rip your heart out if he walks away?" She knows. With everything that I just said and how much of an asshole he is, I know it's too late. I'm already gone.

"Yeah, I think I do. So much, that I will take the bad in spades, just to be smothered in all his goodness." As I hold back the tears that are brimming in my eyelids, she pulls her shoulders back and wipes my eyes for me.

"Right! Then you fight for your man, like a woman shopping for a pair of Louboutin shoes at the Boxing Day sales at Harrods."

And this is why she is my best friend. She gets down and dirty in the trenches when I need her. "No bitch gets in our way. Once you have them in your hand, you don't let go."

Laughing at each other, it's exactly what I needed. For her to tell me it's okay. No matter how messy this is, it's still worth it. Nicholas is worth it, and for once, I understand that I'm worth it too.

Besides, no matter how much I tried to tell Lou it was still an option, it's not. I can't let go. It's too late.

I belong to Nicholas, heart and soul.

Chapter Twenty

NICHOLAS

"I love when I don't have to cook," Flynn announces, walking into the kitchen with Forrest and Rem.

"You mean you love eating my food because it's better than when you cook." I lean over the counter where I give the last few touches to the lunch spread I'm about to serve.

Victoria disappeared upstairs with Elouise as soon as she arrived, which didn't surprise me. I know she will need her to navigate through all that has happened. I'm a lot to handle, I know that, and I'm sure I can feel my ears burning at the amount my name and the word asshole are being thrown around up there.

"You wouldn't be half the chef you are without me. Who do you think taught you everything you know!" Flynn takes a spoon and tastes the creamy garlic sauce for the seafood pasta I've been preparing.

"Bullshit," I cough into my hand as we both laugh a little, and he gives me a slap on the back as we share a man hug.

"It'll do." His comment on the sauce has me flipping him the bird because I know it's good, and if it wasn't, he seriously wouldn't let me serve it. No chef wants to eat crap food.

I give Rem and Forrest the same man hug. I don't say it out loud, but damn, it's good to see them.

"Where is the lovely Tori?" Flynn asks, taking a seat on one of the stools and raising his eyebrows up and down just to piss me off.

"Can we at least make it through the first ten minutes of you being here before I want to kill you?" I throw the tea towel in my hand across the island at him.

"Probably not," Forrest replies as he sits next to Flynn.

"You know what will help? If you shut him up with a beer." Rem opens the fridge like he lives here and slides the first bottle across the counter toward Flynn.

"Now we are talking, but you didn't answer my question. Where's Tori?" Flynn twists the top off the bottle and takes his first mouthful.

"Upstairs giving Elouise a tour, which is girl code for hiding away so they can bitch about me." I roll my eyes at them.

"Show me the way, I love a good bitch session. Plus, let me see this friend of hers. I mean, I've seen the security pictures, and damn, she's hot." Flynn's words make the hair on the back of my neck stand up, which is nothing unusual with him.

"Don't even think about it and shut your mouth about the security. Fuck me. I haven't told Victoria everything. I just don't want to freak her out so she panics and runs." And before I can do it myself, Rem hits him around the back of the head.

"Why do I tell you anything? You know the big red letters that are usually plastered all over the files that I send you, that say strictly confidential? Well, that means it stays in this square of silence, dickhead, remember?"

Flynn is still scowling at Rem for the slap on his head and rubbing where it hit. "In case your eyesight is failing you in your old age, this is the square of silence, you twat!" Flynn waves his hand around the kitchen between the four of us.

Forrest cuts him off. "Yes, but with your loud booming voice, the girls are bound to hear you, idiot. I doubt Nic wants Tori or her friend to know we are watching Elouise as well. She doesn't deserve to be pulled into the ridiculousness that is our lives. Tori, maybe because she is attached to him, but Elouise is an innocent bystander." Forrest is always the sensible one.

"Whatever," Flynn grumbles. "Anyway, we need to talk about something." I should be worried when he says those words, but what makes me more concerned is that his face has turned serious, and he gets straight into it before Victoria comes back.

"Let's eat first," I say, trying to delay any bad news, but he won't hear of it.

"You need to take Victoria to the Kindness before Violence charity dinner on Saturday night. The legal and PR department think you are better off continuing as normal to show that you aren't concerned about the investigation. You know, like you have nothing to hide." I can see he is ready for the backlash as I open my mouth.

"Not a chance. No fucking way!" I growl at him as I stand straight upright. I want to pace the room, but I try so hard to hold it together. One, just one day, that's all I wanted for all of us to have a nice peaceful lunch and for everyone to get to know each other.

"I'm not putting her in that position to be talked about and glared at, interrogated and eaten alive by the socialite sharks, and then her face plastered all over the internet. Not happening!" I can't believe he even bothered bringing this up.

There is a reason we are out here and that is to lie low and away from all that drama.

And I'm not going to lie, I love having her to myself. Maybe I will just lock the gates and we will stay here forever, have food shipped in, and there will be no need for clothes, they can always be optional extras.

"Don't you think that's my decision to make?" Victoria's voice coming into the room has me glaring at Flynn that now I have to battle her too.

"No!" I snap, turning from all of them and stirring the pasta, which is just about right and ready to serve.

"Nicholas, I'm not some glass princess you need to protect. Well, maybe from myself half the time, but not from them. I can handle them."

I turn to look at her standing there with that fire that flares when we are about to battle something out. She has no idea how bad "they" can be.

"If she can handle you, then Tori can handle anything." Flynn laughs at his own joke.

I haven't taken my eyes off her, trying to tell her how much I don't want to do this.

Rem adds, "You know I can protect her from the worst of it. We can put extra security on her and make sure one of us will be by her side the whole night." That pushes my buttons even further.

"*I* will protect her! No one else!" And that is when she smiles.

"Great, so we are going. Just one problem—I doubt I have anything here with me to wear to some fancy dinner."

"We will get Lucy to send some dresses out in the morning," I grumble as I start draining the pasta.

"Thank you, and if you think you are going to turn up grumpy like that, I might just ask for a purple dress."

Snapping my head around to look at her, I can feel the steam coming out my ears. She knows I hate the color purple, and now she is just trying to piss me off.

"Don't push me, Victoria!" That smile of victory on her face does me in. If only she understood that it's her that holds all the power in this relationship. I would do anything to make her happy, even if I'm ready to rip someone apart for even suggesting this.

"Right, okay. that's settled. Now, everyone, this is my best friend, Elouise. She is the smarter one in this friendship as you will learn. Lou, this cheeky one is Flynn who I suggest you stay away from, he's trouble with a capital T. His brother Forrest, the gentleman of the group, and Remington who is our stealth man who loves adventure, so they tell me." And she thought she wouldn't fit in.

Victoria has floored all three of them with her accurate descriptions and the way she is in total control of the room, including me.

If only she could see her true strength, because it's sexy as fuck and draws me even further toward her.

"Well, I'm not sure I'm happy with my introduction from this one, who I think will give us more trouble than I ever have, but lovely to meet you, Elouise." Flynn stands up and takes her hand in his and kisses her on the cheek. Oh, Romeo is in the house. Back off, big boy, otherwise Victoria will tear you apart. I have a feeling Lou is off limits at the moment, until Victoria gets to know my friends better. Truth be known, she is probably worried they are like me, and she is barely coping with that.

Elouise giggles at him, and Forrest rolls his eyes at me as he and Rem also stand to say hello.

"Okay, enough of the chest pumping and my girlfriend trying to piss me off. Let's eat." Victoria's eyes burn into me at the use of that word. Plating the food, Flynn is at my side helping, and Forrest ushers the girls to the table.

It's like the old days in the kitchen with Flynn beside me. I miss that. Life was simple then and carefree. Sure, there was stress but nothing like this.

"Girlfriend, huh, how'd that feel coming off your lips?" he asks, nudging me with his shoulder.

"Surprisingly tasty," I reply, chuckling at him trying to get a rise from me.

"Oh, I bet it is." He disappears with the first batch of plates before I can growl at him for his reply.

Thankfully, I know the food will shut him up, but it won't be for long, and that's when the trouble will start.

"That food was amazing." Elouise sits back in her chair next to Victoria, sipping on her wine.

"Thank you. I do miss cooking for more than just myself." I think about the meals with Victoria this week that never seemed to run according to plan. Her hand on my thigh under the table squeezing me tells me she was thinking the same thing.

"Agreed. We used to serve hundreds of people a sitting with skillful ease, and it was a great adrenaline buzz." Flynn's sitting across from Lou, and I can see the same longing in his eyes that I get some days. We both became chefs because we love to cook, and even though I also love my life now, there are some days I still wish to be back in Sydney running a chaotic kitchen.

Victoria reaches for her phone and quickly types something into a note. Something she has been doing a lot this week. I get it, when your mind is racing with ideas, getting them down somewhere is important before they slip away. One thing that phones have become perfect for. At least you can't lose the pieces of paper like what my mum used to write her lists on, then when she was ready to head to the shop, she couldn't find the paper. I bet the same is still happening with her today.

"I can't imagine you two working together in a kitchen without killing each other. Lou and I can barely make an apple pie without a catastrophic explosion happening. I mean, who puts a full crust on the pie? It's a crumble top every day of the week," Victoria says as she throws her hands in the air and of course knocks her wine glass, which I manage to catch before it hits the table. "Oh shit, thanks. You could come in handy in my life."

"Oh yes, definitely what I was put on this earth to do, clean up your messes," I mumble and smile as she keeps going.

"Shit, well then, you're going to be busy." She kisses me on the lips, and not missing a beat, goes back to her conversation about pie.

"I'm right, aren't I, Flynn? Tell me you're a crumble boy." Her attention shifts to him, waiting for his reply to back her up.

A few wines have brought out the confidence in Elouise, and she and Victoria just bounce off each other. It makes me happy I brought her out for the day. I think it's just what Victoria needed.

"There is no way he is a crumble boy, he is a pastry man all the way. Thick and hard, that's how the dessert is supposed to be served." While the girls are talking pie, it's the first time, I've seen Flynn lost for words.

Before he can even answer, Victoria replies for him, "Yes, with cream and ice cream, which just tops off the taste of the crumble."

Forrest looks away, trying to hold it together. Remington is already laughing as he calls the girls out to what they are totally oblivious of.

"We are still talking about pie here, aren't we?" Rem tries to get out between gasping for breath while laughing.

Flynn is still silent, and I can't help but grab my phone and snap a picture. No one will want to forget the day he was struck speechless.

"Wait, what?" Two words that Victoria seems to say frequently. "We are talking about apple pie. What did you think we were talking about?" She looks around the room, and I can see on her face when she starts to get it, as she sees the guys now losing their shit and obviously replays her words back over in her head.

Elouise is now blushing and giggling too.

"Ughh, who are the young ones in this room. Get your heads out of the gutter." But Victoria is now laughing too.

My relationship with my friends is strong and there are plenty of great times, but I didn't realize this was what I was missing. Having the girls here just adds a whole new dimension. Victoria is opening my eyes to a whole new world that I have been avoiding, and each day I start to wonder why just a bit more.

"So, share with the class, Flynn, is your pie pastry all dry, crusty, and flaky?" I tease, unable to help but join in.

"Fuck off, you tosser!" he says, pulling himself back to his usual self. "My pie pastry is smooth, hard, and creamy. Melts in your mouth and every customer's fantasy. My pie has been described as an orgasmic dessert more than once before." Leaning back on his chair, he lifts his hands, clasping them behind his head.

"You had to go there, didn't you," Forrest groans next to him.

"Hey, Nic's girlfriend started it. You can't blame me for joining the conversation," Flynn says, trying to justify himself, but nobody is buying it.

I shake my head. "And thanks to Flynn, I don't feel like dessert now. Girls, please excuse us, we have some work to do, and we will see if we can erase the visions of Flynn's *pastry* from our minds and we can have sweets then." I stand and pull out Victoria's chair for her as she starts to stand.

Flynn's about to speak, but I glare at him. "Don't say another word." And thank God, he listens for once.

"Go be all bossy and important, we can clear these." Victoria starts to stack plates.

"Leave them, beautiful. I'll deal with it later, just relax." I don't know what is going on with me today. I never thought I would call her any term of endearment in front of anyone, but it just feels natural.

From the twinkle in her eye, I can see she is happy to hear it too.

"Don't be silly, we aren't useless, are we, Lou. Just don't tell me these plates are five hundred years old or something like that."

"Like it will make any difference," Eloise says. "I've gone through a whole dinner set since I moved out into my own place, with you coming to visit" She is trying to keep her face straight so we think she is joking, but I actually believe she is serious.

"No, they are only a hundred years old and a limited edition with gold edging that is not made anymore. No need to worry." Watching Victoria's eyes nearly pop out of her head was worth every bit of my joke.

Flynn tuts. "You are full of shit, Nic, these are the same plates I brought at Harrods when we set up my apartment after coming home from Australia. How cruel you are." Trying to make himself look good, Flynn just takes a few plates off the table and starts walking toward the kitchen.

"Bastard," Victoria chides me. "Now get out, all of you, and leave the two of us to talk about you while you are gone."

I lean down and kiss her on the top of the head. I don't doubt that all our ears will be burning.

"You heard the lady," Rem says. "It's her polite way of telling us to fuck off and work. Anyone would think she has already been hanging around Nic or something." He stands, and we all head toward the office where he left his bag as soon as he walked in. I have a full office set up here, but Rem never goes anywhere without his computer. I don't know much about technology, but he is my head of security, so I never question anything he does or says. That's what I pay him for, and it's why I trust him and Broderick with my life and the lives of everyone around me.

We got through all the normal work we had to discuss and left the hard discussion until the end. I already want to punch a hole in the wall.

"So, what you are telling me is that we have no security footage from the hotel, that it just mysteriously disappeared. There are no fingerprints on the drug package, so in theory it could have been me, and there's nothing to confirm the time of night that I was out in the car because the cameras in the garage weren't working. Fucckkkk!" I slam my fist on the table, hard enough that pain radiates up my arm.

"Not exactly. We have street cameras that picked up the car leaving the hotel and at different points along the route to the fountain. Why the hell did you go to the fountain? It doesn't fit with anything. Oh, and of course the security camera footage from there, that is grainy at best but shows you leaving the fountain then coming back ten minutes later, handing something to the homeless man, and you taking something back to the car." Rem is loading pictures onto the three screens on my desk, and I can feel my stomach sinking further with worry, but it's not stopping my anger at the whole thing.

"A blanket! It was just a fucking blanket because he was old and cold. He insisted on me taking the dirty scrap of thread he was using to keep his hands warm as a thank-you. More fool me for not wanting to insult him by throwing it straight in the garbage can nearby."

Forrest places his hand on my shoulder to try to calm me because he can tell I'm about to explode.

"We know, and we will find him. I have men on the ground looking for him, but it wouldn't make a difference in any court because he is not a credible witness. So, we need to work a different angle. I'm not telling you what that is, but you just have to trust

Broderick on this one. That man has never let you down before, and as soon as he has something, we will move."

"What the fuck do you mean?" Forrest yells, pushing me back into my chair and taking on my anger for me. "We are just simple, damn businessmen. We don't live in the world of all this sort of shit."

"Speak for yourself, I'm far from simple," Flynn pipes up from across the table.

"Flynn!" we all growl at him at the same time. But he achieved what he was aiming for—getting our attention.

"Right, now listen up, all of you angry, alpha, testosterone dicks. We need to let Rem and Broderick do their jobs and continue to do ours, which is to keep fucking calm. We have an empire that needs our attention, an acquisition in Florence to complete, two women to keep safe, have every spare set of eyes on Jocelyn the wicked witch, and prepare for the visit next week from Mumma Sally. Now, if that isn't enough to keep you all busy, we also have a charity event tomorrow night to turn up to and schmooze every influential person in that room, including the head of Scotland Yard who I have on good authority will be there, considering his wife is on the charity's board. Show them all that Nic is some decent respectable man who couldn't possibly be guilty of what they are accusing him of, hence why they haven't laid any charges yet. Now I know it's a stretch of the imagination to say he is a nice man, but do your best, people." Flynn grins at his little speech.

I take a deep breath. I can't even deal with everything he just said. All I can think is I know they aren't my drugs, so I just need to trust them like they are telling me. But one thing really jumped out at me.

"Mumma Sally? What the fuck, Flynn?" I try not to laugh at the ridiculous name.

"Ahh, and there he is. Not so growly anymore. Can't let you walk out of this room all grumpy and snarly. You will frighten Elouise away, and we can't have that." He knows how to poke the bear. I'm not sure that's what friends are for, but Flynn loves to rile me up.

"Don't you dare touch her. She is important to Victoria!"

"Yeah, yeah, and Victoria is important to you. I think we all got that memo already. And can I just say, I never thought it would happen, but about fucking time you started to chill out and let a woman into your life." I can't say he's wrong. I'm still worried I'm making a mistake letting her get close, but not because of who she is but more of because of who I am and the baggage I'm bringing with me.

"I'm not convinced he is all in yet. Look at the way his skin is prickling when you talk about commitment." Rem laughs, and I just look at all three of them. I want to tell them to fuck off, but at the end of the day, these guys know me. They might not know the reasons behind why I am like this, but they will have my back regardless. So, I think it's time I start to let them in a little too.

"I'm trying. It's the best I've got." And the shocked look at my reply tells me they all understand how hard that was for me to say out loud. Victoria is not just a woman, she's the only woman. The one who will break me, either by pushing down the walls and making this work, or breaking my heart into pieces, never to be repaired again.

Time will tell, but at least they know to back off and let me try to work through this the best way I can, in my own time, with Victoria right by my side.

"Understood," Flynn says. "Now just one more thing to clear up. Who gets to be Jocelyn's plus-one tomorrow night? I vote Forrest who seems to be the Jocelyn whisperer."

Laughter rings out around the room while Forrest replies to his brother, "I hate you!" with a face that tells him he wants to wrestle him into a head lock like they did as kids.

"I know, but I don't care. I'm ready for dessert. Who's having pie?" Flynn stands up and starts to tidy the files we had on the desk.

"I'm never eating apple pie again because it will make me think of your dick, and that's just wrong!" Forrest looks like he is about to be ill, and to be honest, I'm not sure I'll ever bake apple pie again either.

Shutting down the computers, Rem and Forrest walk out of the office in front of me when Flynn pulls me aside.

"You know I only act like a dickhead to break your tension, don't you? I've got your back, Nic, I've always had it. No matter what happens with this, or with her. I'm here and will fight like hell to protect you. Understood?"

All I can do is grab him with both hands and hug him as tight as I can. We have never said it because we have never needed to, but right now, I need to hear that. More than he will ever understand, I need him.

"Same, brother, same!" Which has him tightening his grip, acknowledging my answer, and then in a split second he is out of my arms and back to the ridiculous cocky Flynn that I love.

"Right, dessert. Oh how I could really go with a little extra cream tonight." He walks away from me, leaving me shaking my head as I close the door on work for tonight.

Not that I can switch off my thoughts or fears, but I'm sure I know a naughty little lady who will help me try later tonight.

Asking Elouise if she would like to come to the charity dinner tonight with us seemed like a good idea to help Victoria with all the nerves. Ones that I'm sure will have her tripping over, spilling drinks, and saying all the wrong things. Not that I care one bit if they happen, but I do worry about how much it would upset her if she was plastered all over the internet over something stupid.

I needed Elouise to understand what she was walking into, being associated with me and everyone around me. I explained how her life will change and may never be her own again, but just like my girlfriend, she told me she didn't give a flying fuck what other people do. She would be there to support her best friend and her best friend's boyfriend. They are two ballsy women, and together, I doubt they would let much get past them.

Victoria was so excited last night when I brought it up just as they were saying goodbye. They then continued the conversation while FaceTiming the whole car ride home that Elouise had with Wallace. *Oh, that poor man,* was all I could think. I bet he hasn't had to put up with that the whole time he has worked for this family, but I have a feeling he will need to get used to having women around him, and crazy ones at that.

Mind you, I am starting to regret agreeing to go to this dinner now. I have been standing in the living room of my city apartment where we decided to get ready, because it is closer to the venue, for the past thirty minutes after I was kicked out of the bedroom so Victoria could get dressed. If I'm going out tonight, then there was no point hiding at the estate until the last minute. Plus, I wanted to show Victoria where I live normally, because I'm hoping she will be spending most of her time here with me going forward.

At one point, I stalked down the hallway and knocked on the door to remind her we would be late if she didn't hurry up, to which I got screamed at to leave and "Don't you dare open the door," and that she would just be five minutes. Looking at my watch, that was fifteen minutes ago, and I'm getting worked up because she knows I hate to be late. I'm about to walk down there and carry her to the car, ready or not, but as I look up from my watch, I hear the soft click of heels coming down the hallway toward me. She has me absolutely stunned by the beautiful vision before me.

"Victoria …" My mouth is dry, and every fiber of my body is on fire.

Standing before me is the woman of my dreams, no matter what she wears, but tonight she is ready to rock the world and arrive in style.

A long, very fitted, black satin dress hugs every one of her curves that I worship daily. It has a split up her right leg that has me salivating at what I would love to do with that access to her body.

The black has her deep red hair shimmering and lighting up her smile. There is a silver necklace full of sparkle around her neck that I want to replace with real diamonds and let the world know she's mine. And her sparkly bag and shoes set off the outfit.

"I didn't think you would want me in purple," she says, her voice so hesitant. She has no idea how stunning she looks or what she is doing to my body.

"Oh, beautiful lady, you are perfect. So perfect."

Walking toward her, I take her hand and slowly turn her in front of me.

"Black is your color, it reminds me of the devil in you. All night I will be reminded of what a bad girl you are and how I will be ready to punish you later for making me hard as stone with your beauty."

Taking her hand, I start to walk to the elevator, mumbling under my breath, "I'm firing Lucy. She's too good at her job. I told her to make you feel beautiful."

"And I do." Victoria starts to giggle as I place my hand on her lower back and walk through the open doors of my private elevator.

"But I didn't tell her to make you look like sin so I have to fight every man in the room tonight. She will pay for this on Monday."

And Victoria will pay for her flirting with me that I know is coming, later tonight.

Let her into your life, my mother said. Well, the pain in my cock tonight will be a reminder of why I always thought it was such a bad idea.

This woman's beauty will kill me before the night is out. That I'm certain of!

Chapter Twenty-One

VICTORIA

"Why do they make these stupid shapewears so tight? I feel like I'm about to pop like a balloon, and it will not be a pretty sight," I whisper to Lou in the back of the limo that Nicholas ordered for tonight. Because how else do you arrive to some big flashy red-carpet affair?

All the guys are with us, since they figured that arriving as a united front would take the heat off Nicholas and me. Lou looks stunning in her navy gown. She asked Lucy for something simple so she wouldn't stand out in the crowd, but there is no way that she paid any attention. The dress is a classic style, with shoestring straps, fitted at the waist, and with a full skirt that falls from there. But with her brown hair and pale English skin, it really makes her beautiful face pop. It's no wonder Flynn can't keep his eyes off her.

"I bet some man invented these things just to torture us, because he knew we would buy anything to try to make ourselves look like all the perfect women out there." Lou is not good at whispering when she is nervous, and the look on Nicholas's face tells me he heard that.

"You are both 'perfect,' and I'll take on anyone who tells you different." His words are straight to the point, and I know he means it by his tone. With no intention of keeping his voice down, the others all stare at both Lou and me.

"Umm, you both look hotter than any of the women who will be in that room." Flynn makes direct eye contact with Lou. I need to watch him. He is a player and totally wrong for her. But then, I would never have thought Nicholas would be right for me either, so maybe I just need to sit back and watch. Not something I'm great at doing. Especially when it comes to Lou and me. We are up in each other's business twenty-four seven, but that's what good friends do, we take care of each other.

Nicholas groans under his breath, clearly making it known he doesn't like Flynn commenting about my looks, but he won't say anything because he wants Lou to feel confident walking into the room.

My hands are sweaty from nerves, but I don't want to let Nicholas know how much I feel like I want to pass out. This is a big thing for him. There are so many reasons I need to make the right impression. He wants to get the public opinion on his side and continue to show that he is a good person, but I know more importantly, he has never stepped out with a woman on his arm that means more to him than he knows how to cope with. Especially with the current drama where he is trying to protect me, his image, and everything around him. The pressure is immense, and it's taking its toll.

I've seen him broody but not like this. Tonight is a lot for him, and I'll be damned if I let him take on my nerves too. *Pull yourself together, Victoria, your man needs you. Don't let him down.*

"Remind me again why we can't have a drink in here? Isn't that the point of these big poncy cars, that the party starts early?" Flynn lifts the lid on the secret fridge that contains a variety of drinks.

"Because I said," is all that Nicholas replies.

"You are being that grumpy, boring boss man already. I hope that doesn't continue all night long." Flynn starts tapping his leg with his hand, and I realize he is just as nervous as Nicholas, he just won't admit it.

"Flynn, surely you have worked out by now that he has done that for me. I'm a mess if I have too much to drink. I fall over, say things I shouldn't, talk with a potty mouth like a drunken sailor, and that's all before the third drink. Do you really want to hang out with me after I start drinking early?" Trying to take the attention off Nicholas is working, with everyone laughing at what I wish was a joke, but sadly, they all know is true.

"Fuck yes, I do. I'll be buying you the first drink. It will be way more entertaining than the rest of the old farts in that room." That he is always looking for a fun night is what I get from Flynn's comments.

"You included?" Lou pipes up, and we all laugh harder.

"Oh, we'll keep you." Rem claps at Lou's comment directed at Flynn. "Anyone who puts the clown over there in his place is welcome in this circus."

"Why is everyone ganging up on me all of a sudden?" Flynn looks a little perplexed.

"Because we can. You make it so easy," Forrest adds in just to make everyone laugh harder. Even Nicholas is starting to join in, although it's not as relaxed a laugh as everyone else's.

The car starts to slow as we pull up out front of The Savoy Hotel. My hand falls to Lou's, and we hang onto each other for dear life. This is so far out of our league that I'm so glad I have her to help calm me. I know she is as anxious as I am, but if anyone will have my back and help me not make a fool of myself, it's her. Nicholas has his own thoughts that will be racing but will be oblivious that for Lou and me, this is more than the drama that is circling him.

I have never felt so prim and proper but totally out of place in my life. I have walked past this hotel but never stepped foot inside it. It's just not somewhere I belong. The grandness of the entrance and all the gold has my body starting to shake involuntarily.

"Breathe, we've got this. We are as good as any toffy-nosed bitches in there. And they're all feeling the pain of these fucking uncomfortable shapewears too," Lou whispers into my ear as the guys are all filing out of the car until there is only us two and Nicholas left.

It's exactly what I need to take my mind off how out of my depth I feel.

"Thanks," I tell her, giving her a hug before she slides out of the car—with Flynn's help, of course.

The deep sigh I hear from Nicholas tells me it's time to go.

As I start to move, he wraps his hand around my waist and pulls me tight against him.

"You don't have to do this. Just say the word and we leave. I'm asking way too much of you." The vulnerability in his voice tells me that he knows the moment we step out there, there is no going back. We will be the most talked about couple in tomorrow's gossip columns like he warned me. But part of me is worried that maybe this is something he isn't sure he wants either. He has been pushed along the merry-go-round since we met because so much has happened so quickly.

He wants me, I don't doubt that.

But is he ready for this? To be all in with me, attached to someone who tests him more than he knows how to cope with? It scares him. His mother's voice is in my head, reminding me that when he tries to run, I have to push back hard, and that's what I intend to do.

"Are you embarrassed to have me as your date?" I ask, knowing exactly what I'm doing.

"No!"

And before he can say another word, I continue, "Right, then get out of this car. I didn't spend three hours trying to look like this just to sit in here all night." I take his hand and bring it to my lips, lightly kissing the top of it but not hard enough to smudge my lipstick or leave an imprint of my lips on his skin. "I've got you, and as long as you've got me, then we can do this." I say it out loud, also trying to convince myself.

"You have no idea how amazing you are." He leans down, kissing my neck as I feel him take a deep breath and absorb the strength he needs from me. I'm shivering all over. His words make me feel special, but I only wish I could believe what he is saying.

Sitting back up, I see his walls come up, and he is ready to handle whatever gets thrown his way tonight.

His stare into my eyes tells me all he can't say in words. Then he steps out of the car, and I know it's time.

I can do this, I repeat over and over again as I step out behind him. He helps me stand then immediately slides his hand into place on my lower back, claiming me so everyone around knows I'm his.

Trying to get my bearings as I stand up straight, I hope that every part of my outfit is still sitting the way it should. I look across at Lou who looks as petrified as I feel. Both of us put on a fake smile, and Nicholas moves us forward toward the doors, as there are a few photographers taking pictures. He must look like someone important with his entourage following behind him. If only the outside world knew the real people walking with us. They are some of the most genuine people I have met, and their wealth means nothing to them. It's just part of what they are, but it does not define them. Otherwise, there's no way I would be walking in on Nicholas's arm tonight. I don't do fake or pretentious, and he is neither of those.

There are a few people in front of us as we walk toward the ballroom doors. One of them is a woman who looks very much like the disco ball dress lady from the bar. Ugh, why didn't I think about all the ex-flings that I will see here tonight? I was so focused on the whole drug allegations, his business associates, and trying to fit into this dress that my brain didn't even get as far as that thought.

And by the look on her face as she spots us, it's not going to be a fun encounter.

Standing at her side is the woman that Flynn took home with him that same night, and they both look like they want to take daggers to Lou and me and make us disappear. Here Nicholas was talking about fighting off all the men tonight, but it will more likely be me fighting off the women.

If they have had sex with my man before, firstly I want to stab them too, but I understand why they want to come back for more.

Well, ladies, back off! He's mine, and I'm doing everything in my power to keep him.

I didn't think I would be that woman, but tonight, I so am.

Turning, I rise up on my toes and kiss him on the lips gently, hooking my arm around his waist.

"Feeling possessive?" There's heat in his smile as he looks at me now.

"Very!" I bite down on my bottom lip and let it pop back out as the heat between us starts simmering.

"Noted." He moves his hand from my lower back to around my waist and pulls me that little bit tighter against him. "You'll be lucky to make it home still in that dress if you keep this up."

I can feel him vibrating in the best possible way.

"Ooh, also noted. I'll make sure I keep reminding you what is waiting underneath this sack I'm wearing." We take a few steps closer to the doors.

"I wish it was a sack, so my cock wouldn't be in so much pain." Our voices are so low that no one else can hear us, making me feel like I'm in my own intimate Nicholas bubble. Somewhere I would love to be able to hide all night.

But of course, glitter ball girl comes crashing into it.

"Nic, so good to see you again." Her voice couldn't have any more flirting in it if she tried. Her breasts are almost falling out of her dress as she pushes them toward him and tries to lean forward to kiss him on the cheek like they are great long-lost friends.

Suddenly my body is pulled backwards, and I feel Lou's hand on my back to save me from falling off balance. I try not to laugh at the burn that Nicholas has just given her by stepping out of her reach, not wanting her touching him in any way. And to be honest, it's so trashy to try to kiss a man who is already wrapped around another woman.

"Simona, nice to see you. Enjoy your evening. Excuse us, it's time for me and my girlfriend to head inside."

Boom, and that is how you do it. I didn't have to say a word. Nicholas made it abundantly clear he is off the market to her and any of her friends that I'm sure she is about to run off and gossip to.

She's not finished, though, still trying to make sure he knows she is pissed that he dumped her that night.

"Oh, that's right, you are that girl Nic picked up out of the gutter the other night when we were together." And the fangs are out, but I won't sit back and take that lightly.

"Yes, that was when my Prince Charming swept me up in his arms and carried me away to his castle. Enjoy the night with your friend." As I wave at her and take a few steps forward, Nicholas takes the hint and happily follows, still firmly holding me close. I can hear both Flynn and Lou behind me sniggering like schoolkids. I didn't want to come off as a bitch before I even got into the place, but she pushed my buttons straight up, and there is no way I'm going to let another woman try to degrade me that way, regardless of who I'm here with.

Why do people have to be so awful while attempting to climb the social ladder? Trying to be anyone other than your true self is a waste of energy.

"I don't know why I bother hiring security. You are scarier than any of Rem's people," Nicholas quickly whispers in my ear as we get closer to the organizers who are greeting people as they enter.

"You're not the only one who will protect what is theirs," I reply through my plastered sweet smile, trying not to look like someone who wants to throat punch that woman.

"Victoria." His low growl in my ear tells me how much he liked that, but he also needs me to stop before he embarrasses himself with an erection he can no longer hide.

"Nicholas, thank you so much for joining us tonight, and of course, for your extremely generous donation." The older man in the black suit in front of us extends his hand to Nicholas. I'm guessing he's in his late seventies or early eighties. Nicholas has to let me go to shake his hand. I miss the warmth of his body instantly, and I want to be back in his arms as soon as I can. I didn't understand how much confidence and strength his touch has given me since we left the car.

"My pleasure, Gordon. I know this was an important charity to my grandfather, along with your friendship," he says, shaking his hand. "Gordon, please meet my girlfriend, Victoria Packer." I hold out my hand to shake his, and he takes it and kisses it like an old-school English gentleman. I start to imagine this is what Nicholas's grandparents would have been like.

Not sure they would be very approving of my display outside the door as a partner for their precious only grandson.

Pushing that thought out of my head, I smile at this gentle man in front of me.

"Victoria, Nicholas didn't tell me he was bringing such a beautiful date with him. I would have insisted they change the tables so you could sit with me. I would be far more interesting than this young man."

"Watch this one, he likes to think he is still young enough to sweep women off their feet." I can hear in his voice how much respect Nicholas has for Gordon.

"How am I doing so far?" His other hand is now patting the top of mine, and I can't help but giggle.

"Let's just say Nicholas should be concerned," I say, which brings out the sweetest laugh in the old man, and I think I have made his night.

"Oh, you flatter me, but keep it coming." Gordon waves his hand in the air, making us all smile. He has flair, I'll give him that, and he's not afraid to use it. "I see you brought the cavalry with you." Leaning closer to Nicholas and lowering his voice, he says, "I don't believe a word of what they are saying. You are a good man. If you need any help, you call me."

My heart melts for this little old man who probably just made Nicholas's night a little more comfortable.

"Thanks, Gordon, I appreciate the support, but let's just worry about this great charity we are here to raise money for." That's the man he is. Doesn't want any fuss or attention, be it good or bad.

"Right, yes, well, you have already given us a very generous head start. Go and have a drink on me and treat the beautiful Miss Victoria and your friends to a lovely evening. Enjoy, and like I said, call me. You'd be surprised about my contacts." Chuckling to himself, he is already moving to the group behind us, and we head into the room that is full of glitz and glamour everywhere I look.

The room is full of men in mostly black suits with the occasional dark charcoal-gray, because you don't want to be too outrageous. Every woman in this room has spent probably my monthly salary on the dress they are wearing and then will never wear it again. I feel a little sick to my stomach at how much Nicholas spent on my dress and shoes, but I doubt he would tell me how much, even if I asked.

People are looking at us, but you wouldn't know that Nicholas is worried about being here. He is walking with such confidence and power in his stride. I should have reminded him that I have shorter legs, a very tight skirt, and ridiculously-high-heeled shoes on. If he doesn't want to peel me off the floor where I have face planted, he needs to slow down a little.

Nicholas acknowledges people with either a simple wave or nod to say hello, but he has no plans to stop until we get to our table that Rem already made sure he knew where it was and who we were sitting with. He didn't want any drama when we got here.

We have one of the prime tables at the front which reminds me that Nicholas is kind of a big deal in the business world. My man is powerful, and it's hot as hell watching him in this kind of environment where he is controlling the room. People want to talk to him, but he chooses who he wants to acknowledge or not. That air of arrogance is something that needs a fine balance to still hold people's respect before you fall into a reputation of being the guy no one wants to deal with. Watching him, he has the balance just right!

If I weren't with him or if circumstances were different, would he be on the other side of the room chatting to people who were trying to catch his attention?

He slides my chair out for me, while Flynn is doing the same for Lou on the other side of me, when out of the corner of my eye I catch a glimpse of someone I never expected to see.

"Tori," he calls from two tables over and starts heading toward us. I hesitate to sit because I would rather be standing so I'm close to Nicholas. I have a feeling this could get tricky.

"Theo, what are you doing here?" I can feel everyone around me tensing, wondering who this random man is.

Before I even have a chance to say anything, he wraps his arms around me and pulls me away from Nicholas.

Shit, this isn't good. Tonight, of all nights, no one needs to poke the bear next to me.

Quickly pushing out of his hug, I take Nicholas's hand into mine straight away, giving it a fast squeeze of reassurance and trying to explain who he is.

"Everyone, this is Theo Cheston that I work with at York and Webb. Theo, this is my boyfriend Nicholas, Elouise, my friend I told you about, Flynn, Forrest, and Remington."

"Girl, who are you kidding, you work with me? I have hardly seen you since the day you started. Boyfriend, huh, you work fast, from client to this," he says, waving his hand in front of us.

"Steady," I hear Forrest say, now standing beside Nicholas, and see his hand wrapping around Nicholas's arm.

Theo has obviously been drinking before he arrived because he is already in the party mood. Just like the night we went for work drinks, he wants to be the center of attention. I'm just not sure this is the right sort of event for his kind of vibe.

I need to defuse this situation before it escalates further.

Totally ignoring his insult insinuating I'm sleeping my way up the ladder for a job, I change the topic. "What are you doing at this charity event, do you support this great cause too?" My voice gives away how uncomfortable I'm feeling, with the way it's higher pitched than normal.

Oblivious to the fact he isn't welcome here, Theo is still trying to take me by the hand to talk privately, which I manage to avoid.

"Don't be silly." At the last minute, he changes his words when I'm guessing he sees the look on my boyfriend's face. "I mean, it's a great cause, but no, I'm here on my parents' money. They buy the tickets so they can say they are doing something good for the 'poor' people in the country, and I get the benefit of the good food and free drinks. And of course, all these gorgeous women around that I can then find a date for later tonight."

This is exactly why I worked out after a few days at my job that I needed to distance myself from him. Theo is a complete and utter ass!

I don't even have to answer because Lou decided it was her time to step up into the conversation. "I don't know you, but in a way I'm glad. Anyone who demeans the importance of a charity event by just using it as a Tinder date meet-up is no one I would like to spend time with. You might work with Tori, but that doesn't mean she has to socialize with you or your pathetic attitude, so off you go, back to your free food and drink."

So much for not creating a scene here tonight.

"Wow, I'm guessing since you lifted your skirt for Mr. Darby here, you are too good for your work friends now. These ones seem soooo nice too…"

"Enough! Leave!" Nicholas steps forward and pushes me behind him, but Rem puts himself between Theo and Nicholas.

"You heard the man. I think this conversation is over for the night, and may I suggest you slow down on those free drinks." Placing his hands on Theo's shoulders, he turns him back in the direction of his table and starts to walk him back where he came from.

"I'm sorry." My voice is a little wobbly as Nicholas turns and faces me again.

"Don't be." He wraps me in his arms and all feels right in the world for a split second. "None of that is on you. He'll be lucky if I don't get his ass fired."

"Shit, no, please don't interfere in my job. I can handle him." I can only imagine what Theo has already been saying around the office, when they told them I wasn't coming back in this week. I mean, I'm surprised it's not my ass they want to fire. I'm supposed to be covering for my boss, and I'm not even there to do that. What a mess this whole situation has become.

"Not sure you could get him fired if you tried," Forrest informs us. "His parents own half the shares in York and Webb. He is Warren Webb's stepson." I should be concerned by how he knows this, but it's obvious they have done a full background check on me and anyone associated with me. It makes sense, considering what has been happening. So the horror I saw on their faces when Theo walked up was because they already knew who he was.

"What the fuck." I can't help dropping the F-word, even though I was trying so hard to be a proper lady for the night. I slap my hand over my mouth as it comes out, I look apologetically up at Nicholas who is finally smiling again.

"And there is my girl. Saying it like it is." He guides me to my seat finally, and as I slide into it and Lou beside me, she can tell I'm in shellshock.

"So why am I his boss and everyone in the office makes jokes about him?" I ask. I'm so confused.

"Obviously because you are smarter than him, and he has been given a token job to keep him out of the parents' hair." Lou shuffles in her seat, trying to get comfortable and reaching for the glass of water that Forrest started pouring for everyone.

Things start clicking into place now, thinking back to what he was like those first few days. He will try anything to get a leg up in the company to please his parents but doesn't want to have to work for it. He is all talk and no action.

"I think I need a drink a lot stronger than water," I groan. "I mean, who drinks water anyway, you know what fish do in that?" Nicholas looks at me with the eyes that tell me he is worried to ask. "They shit in it. So, we are all drinking fish shit, people. Now if that doesn't make you want to take a shot of tequila, I'd be surprised." My anxiety about the night that I was keeping under control has totally broken free and my rambling has started.

"What the hell is in that head of yours?" Flynn asks. "They think I'm crazy, but woman, you beat me hands down." He shakes his head at my confession. "You're right, I think we all need a shot to start the night. Things can only get better from here, surely."

I wince. "Now you've done it, put the hex on us. Look out, the night is about to go pear-shaped, and it's Flynn's fault."

"It's always Flynn's fault, that's a given." Forrest takes a seat on the other side of Nicholas.

Rem returns to the table and gives Nicholas the chin lift, letting him know he has sorted out our little interruption.

"What did I miss?" he asks as he sits next to Flynn.

"Just Flynn jinxing us that the night can't get any worse," I proudly announce to him as Flynn gives me the death stare in a fun way.

"Christ, how can it get worse than that dickhead?"

No sooner have the words left Remington's lips, and we all work it out.

"Good evening, everyone. Where am I sitting?"

"Jocelyn." Nicholas stands like the gentleman he is and points to the seat that Forrest is also now up and pulling out next to him.

Oh, just light the fireworks now, because it won't take long for the spectacle to begin.

Where's that alcohol? I think I'll need more than one shot!

Chapter Twenty-Two

NICHOLAS

When Rem told me we should have Jocelyn at this dinner, I almost choked. I have stood her down at work and taken all access away from her, and now he wants me to sit here with her tonight and pretend we are all one big happy family.

It's bullshit!

To me we are sending the wrong message to her. I want her gone, not letting her think that her behavior has been forgiven.

She has been undermining me for years, and the last straw was her trying to get the board to dismiss me with a vote of no confidence. My grandfather would be devastated to see it has come to this. Even when he and his brother, Jocelyn's grandfather, decided they couldn't work together, they just amicably split. There was no backstabbing. Money changed hands, and it was done.

Instead, I'm working with a distant relative who I don't trust one little bit!

She is holding secrets, I can tell, and is working behind my back, putting doubt in people's minds on whether I can successfully run this company. Even though I've been doing it for years.

My distrust has me suspicious about these drugs planted in my car, considering it was at the same time a random photographer managed to be there at that moment I lost my restraint and chose to kiss Victoria. How did they even know I was in Rome with a woman? It was such a last-minute decision to take Victoria that only my office knew. Information Jocelyn would have had access to, being on the executive staff.

But the thing that is nagging at me the most is if I find out that she has anything to do with this drug suspicion hanging over me, I will more than fire her—I will destroy her.

I have known hate before; I've lived most of my life with it. Sadly, it was aimed at a person who didn't deserve it, and I think that eats at me more, knowing I felt that way for so long about a person who was just trying to love my mum and paid the price for it.

All that aside, the way I feel about Jocelyn right now is right up there with that level of hate.

From the first moment I met her, she had it in for me. That is the stupid part of this war between us that has been festering for years. If she had accepted me and talked to me in the beginning, I think we could have made a great team. She knew this business, inside and out, from her years of working with my grandfather. But instead of doing that, she let jealousy and hatred for me get in the way of staying involved in a company that she had assumed would always be hers.

Her grandfather was the brother that my grandfather started the business with, but that was so many years ago that he sold out his shares, and way before she was even born. Darby Hotels was never hers to inherit, but my grandfather was the kind of man who brought her into the fold because she was family, and he wanted some connection after losing my father. I would have given her a share eventually, we could have done this together, but she was never born to be a team player, and I can't work like that.

I might be the person whose name is above the door on this business, but I couldn't do it without the men around this table. We are a team, and they know what they mean to me. I have never hidden my appreciation from them, and as much as we are constantly talking shit at each other, it's the best kind of banter because it is done in good fun. To be honest, we wouldn't be the friends we are if we took life too seriously. It's just not who we are.

"Thank you for allowing me to be here tonight," Jocelyn replies to me as she takes her seat next to Forrest.

I'm grinding my teeth, trying to be nice to her. "Let's just try to be civil to each other and get through the night without any drama." I can feel Victoria's hand on my lap, trying to reassure me that I can do this. I can be a respectable man and not make a scene. Hell, I managed to get through the last fifteen minutes without punching that dickhead, when all I wanted to do was take him outside and teach him a lesson for speaking to Victoria like that.

If I can contain that anger, then surely, I can cope with the viper on the other side of the table. To be honest, she is probably more scared of Victoria than me, and I can't blame her. The way she put her in her place that day in the boardroom had me in awe, and that was before we even really knew each other.

"I'm not here to talk about what you did. I'm here to support something that was important to my great uncle. I haven't missed one of these dinners since the charity was started. He invited me every year, and I thank you for honoring that." There is something about her that doesn't sit right with me, and I can't work out what it is. Maybe Rem was right in bringing her here tonight. Her not being in the office, we don't really know what she is up to.

Now I feel a little guilty because our invitation for her tonight had nothing to do with honoring my grandfather and her relationship but more about us not trusting her. I just nod and don't say anything, that way I'm not lying to her.

"Drinks." Flynn places the drinks tray with the shots on it on the table and the waiter behind him has another tray full of beers and gin and tonics for the girls. Flynn is good, only knowing Victoria a short time, but he already knows her drink order, which means I need to watch these two. I have a feeling there is a very firm friendship forming between them, and that can only result in bad news for me. Two against one in arguments or votes on the ridiculous things, like where we go for dinner, means I will always lose, and we can't have that.

"I don't know if this is a smart idea but bottoms up." Victoria holds her shot glass up for all of us to clink with each other.

"Tequila is never a good idea, but here we are," Forrest comments with strain on his face. I know he is the serious one in the group, and it's probably not fair how we have stuck him with Joce-lyn, but he seems to manage her better than any of us can. I wonder if it's a skill he learned growing up with Flynn and keeping him from derailing from stupidity.

I don't think I've ever really seen Forrest completely let go, and I think it's time we rectify that. He shouldn't have to be the babysitter for us all the time. Tonight is not the night to test the theory, but one night when all this is over, I think a good night of fine food and drinking, followed by everyone sleeping over at the estate will be a good way to celebrate.

"Can't say tequila is my poison of choice, but it will do," I say as I lick the salt off my hand and suck on the lime.

With everyone finally seated, the entrees already served, and the conversation light around the table, Jocelyn is surprisingly quiet, and Victoria and Flynn are, as to be expected, talking non-stop. I know it's a nervous thing, but she has no reason to be. I might be biased, but she is easily the most beautiful woman in the room. I could feel all the eyes on her as we entered, and while she thought that was about me and the accusations, it wasn't. It was definitely all her.

Gordon takes the stage, and a hushed silence now falls over the room. He starts welcoming everyone and explaining the core values of the charity and what it does.

"Kindness before Violence has supported so many children, and we know that by supporting them after they have grown up in a domestic violence environment, they are far less likely to carry that violence on through their own adult life. With the programs, hous-ing, and financial support we have in place for these children and parents or carers, they can begin to live a normal, calmer life and finally feel like they have a safe place. Everyone should have a safe place." His passion for this is evident in the tone of his voice.

I understand why my grandparents both thought this was a wonderful idea and why I continue to pour money into it after their passing. I grew up in a tough environment, but no matter what was happening around us, I always felt safe and loved. Every child deserves that.

"So please give a big round of applause for Mr. Nicholas Darby of Darby Hotels who has already kicked off the night with his huge donation of two hundred and fifty thousand pounds."

Obviously, he has forgotten I like to give anonymously, but it's too late now. Everyone gasps and cheers, but the biggest gasp of all is from the woman beside me.

"Holy shit, Nicholas." I can't help but laugh at her. She really has no idea how much I'm worth, and it's been refreshing.

The alcohol from her second gin and tonic is kicking in, and I'm just glad she is containing her volume. "How rich are you?" I'm not bothered she asks because I love the innocence of the question.

"Filthy rich," I lean down and whisper in her ear.

I feel her shiver as I lay my arm across her shoulder and sit back up straighter.

"Figures, everything about you is filthy." Her heated smile gives away what she is already thinking about, and it's not my money.

"I don't see a problem with that, do you?" I say to tease her a little.

"You know I don't, and stop looking at me like that. We have a long night to get through, and it's not fair if I'm sitting in wet under-wear all night." Oh yes, she is loosening up the more she drinks.

"Challenge accepted then." And the burn that is rising between us already has me thinking about how early we can get out of here.

Unfortunately, the more drinks Victoria has means that everyone else is on the same round too. Jocelyn included.

"Wonder where all the money comes from to splash around and look good. Maybe has something to do with the side hustle," I hear her mumble across the table, and Forrest immediately tries to get her to shut her mouth.

"Ignore her, she is baiting you," Victoria says under her breath to me.

"Seems to be a common theme of the night. First that dick from your work, now her. I'm starting to regret coming," I mutter, staring down Jocelyn as she looks at me with that bit of viper in her. Oh, she is brewing for a fight, I can feel it.

"Whoa! Steady on there, I never regret coming." Victoria's little giggle pulls me back to her and once again averts me from wanting to chastise Jocelyn.

"No, I'm sure you don't, but if you don't behave yourself, you might regret it when I won't let you come later." Softly, I push her soft curls off her neck, then kiss it so tenderly.

"Don't be cruel," she moans on a whisper.

"Then behave." Gripping her thigh so she knows I mean business, her cheeks flush up nicely, and I know we are going to be enjoying each other later tonight.

The speeches wrap up, and I make sure there haven't been any more drinks served. We don't need to put more fuel on this fire. I watch as Jocelyn takes her phone from her purse, answering a call as she stands and leaves the table, but she still hasn't said a word to whoever it is yet.

"She just looks evil," Lou declares her thoughts to the table.

"Definitely the Wicked Witch of the West," Victoria says. "We can only hope one of the hotels lands on her and squishes her too, then I'll happily steal her sparkly red shoes." Victoria is off on a tangent again, but I'm starting to understand that's just her.

"I don't think she is that bad," Forrest says. "Just a little misjudged at times, and maybe a spoilt child who is used to getting what she wants. So, when she doesn't get her way, there are repercussions for us all." He must see something in her that none of us manage to see.

I don't know what, but he has never been on the same "let's all hate Jocelyn" team as the rest of us.

"Well, maybe we should give her a set of her own blocks to play with and then she won't want what everyone else has," Victoria's quick wit cuts in again.

"Not a chance, she'd just use them as weapons to throw at other people," Lou says, snickering. "Some kids just don't play well with others. Sounds like half the pretentious snotty kids in my class. The joy of teaching at a private school." The girls laugh at the vision we all have of Jocelyn throwing a two-year-old tantrum, which is effectively what she did in the boardroom last week.

Lou whispers something into Victoria's ear, and they both nod and reach for their handbags that are on the table. Already guessing where they are headed, I just grin at them as they excuse themselves from the table. The usual trip to the toilet where women have to take a friend always makes me laugh. The last thing I need is a friend to hold my hand when I need to pull my cock out.

"What do you think is going on with Jocelyn? She's been quiet, then that comment out of nowhere. She looks more unstable than normal." Flynn gives me a concerned look.

"Yeah, I'm worried she is about to let loose, and I don't want it happening here. If she is going to finally throw her cards on the table, I want it to be in private."

I sit in silence, just trying to settle my anger that is building. Why do I have to navigate all this shit? Plus, I'm dragging Victoria down into it too. I need some air. Standing quickly, I push my chair back, and both Flynn and Rem stand too. I wave them off; I just need space. The longer the night goes on, the more I feel like the world is closing in around me. First watching Victoria having to deal with Simona, then Theo who I wanted to punch his lights out for the way he spoke to her, then Jocelyn, and that's on top of everything else that is happening. Drug accusations, attempts to be thrown out of my own company, and something is going on with my mother, but I have no idea what since she is so far away, and I can't leave the frigging country to check on her.

I've never had a problem with feeling anxious, but all this is pushing me into a space I don't like being in.

I walk back out the doors to the ballroom and down a corridor I don't even know where it leads. Twisting and turning, I just want to be away from people, in silence, to breathe. Turning the corner, I've found myself in a small quiet hall that has a nice striped cloth-covered bench to sit on. Normally I would be up pacing, but this time I just want to sit.

My thoughts are racing. I might have all the support in the world, but what if I can't prove those drugs aren't mine? I can't go to jail for something I didn't do, but what if I do? I'll lose everything. The business will crumble around me, the respect for the family name, and Victoria. If you had asked me when the police first arrived if that was the case, I would have said she wasn't even on my radar, but now, it's one of the biggest things that have my heart beating hard with concern for her. I feel like I'm being backed into a corner at the moment, and the hardest part is that I don't know who's doing it. It's hard to fight an unknown adversary.

Resting my head in my hands and rubbing my face, I know I need to snap out of this. I'm stronger than that, and everyone is relying on me. It's my job to protect them all, not sit back and let others protect me. The picture of my father that I have on my mantelpiece above the fireplace at the estate house comes into my vision. That was what he did. He chose to change his life to protect my mother, because he thought that she didn't deserve to be pressured to fit into his world. It didn't turn out the way he planned, but still, his intention was what I can feel flooding through my veins. The built-in need to protect the ones I love. And although I'm not ready to admit it to her or anyone, I know deep down I've already fallen in love with Victoria, and she doesn't deserve a life like this, with drama hanging over her all the time.

I pull my phone from my pocket. I'm done waiting.

"Aren't you supposed to be enjoying a lovely evening of food and music with your girlfriend?" Broderick's voice comes through my phone.

"I wish! Instead, I'm sitting in some hallway trying to breathe before I lose all sensibility and do something stupid. I want answers, and I want them now. I don't care what you have to do. I know I said don't do anything illegal, but now I'm telling you to do whatever you need and just get it done!"

"When will you learn to trust me? I ignored everything you said about pussyfooting around this. I'm doing it my way, and you just sit fucking tight. I'm close, Nic, hold on and don't blow it up before I can nail them." There is no friendly tone to his voice, straight to the point, and it's what makes me stop and listen.

"Them... so you think there is more than one person involved?" I stand because the wallowing I was doing a moment ago is long gone, and my pissed-off energy is back.

"I know there is. I just need to connect everything. Hold tight. I told you after that night in Sydney that your father was a friend of mine, and the moment I found you, I would protect you for him. I owed him that, and your grandfather too. They took me in when I needed someone to have my back. And I've been making sure I've had your family's back ever since. Breathe, I've got you, son." I can feel his voice seeping through my muscles and taking some of the anxiety with it.

Broderick is the closest thing to a father I have ever had, and a man I never knew I needed until I met him four years ago.

"Thanks for everything." My words get stuck in my throat from the emotion of being able to let my guard down even for just a small moment.

"Always." He knows what I mean and what I can't say in more words than that, but his one-word reply tells me he understands.

"Now get back inside and wrap your arms around that girl-friend. No way I'd be letting her out of my sight in a room full of old men. They're like vultures." It brings a laugh out of me, because he is pretty accurate.

"Yeah, yeah. Call me as soon as you have something," I say, starting back toward the ballroom.

"You'll be the first to know." Then the sound of silence in my ear tells me the call has ended. Sliding my phone back into my jacket pocket, I feel stronger than when I walked out here.

Striding down the winding corridor that I had slinked away into, I can hear familiar voices ahead from a side corridor. Stopping just before it and leaning back into a recessed doorway, the words I hear burn me up instantly.

"He might think he can buy his way out of the drug charges, but if I can't get him, I will destroy that little toy bitch he has on his arm, and it will hurt him just as much. Nobody speaks to me like that. She had no right to even be in that boardroom." Jocelyn's voice is one that haunts me, and there is no question it's her talking.

"You can go wherever you like when you are fucking the big boss," a second voice says, and I recognize it as that guy Theo. "Don't worry, I will set her up nicely to fall when I talk with my step-father. I'm sure he won't want the company name pulled through the mud with one of his staff sleeping with a client. Especially a client that has pending drug charges hanging over his head. That job should have been mine anyway, so the sooner I get rid of her the better." His words are a bit slurred, and he obviously ignored Rem's suggestion of easing up on the drinking.

"Between the both of us, she will never work in this town again or the industry. The only rebranding she will be doing will be of her own image." Fucking bitch, I knew she was quiet and up to some-thing tonight. There is no way she would have taken me repri-manding her without a fight. But I wasn't expecting she would attack Victoria. If she wants a fight, then come at me and leave her out of it.

"Did you bring my packet?" Jocelyn's voice is a little quieter now, and the shock of what I think she is talking about falls over me. Surely not, I would have suspected something by now.

"Have you got my money? I'm not a charity. My trust fund is big but not big enough." I want to charge around the corner and catch them both in the middle of what I suspect is a drug deal, but I can't be caught anywhere near this. Two against one, they could twist things to look like I was somehow involved.

"Little prick, you have more money than I will ever have thanks to the jerk who stole my life. So much for family, he doesn't give a shit about me." The bitterness in her voice is sharp.

"Oh, suck it up, princess. If it wasn't for him, I would have fucked her that first night I took her for work drinks at the club, but he stepped in and ruined it. The drugs I put in her drink were just starting to take hold, but he picked her up and took her away. If I took her home, I would have had the naked pictures I needed to blackmail her to take all the credit for her work and get the promotion I deserve. The bitch of a boss I tried to get before her took off on leave and hasn't returned. I got screwed over. He owes us both, and we will make him pay for taking what's ours. I hate pricks who get everything handed to them on a platter. Now get the fuck out of here before they see you with me. I don't want to have anyone sniffing around my operations because you are fucking sloppy."

"Listen here, you little shit. I was in this world, running these hotels, long before you were out of nappies, so shut your mouth and make sure you have my next package when I message. And if anyone asks me, I don't know any lowlife that sells drugs, I've never touched a pill in my life."

His scoff and the sound of movement has me pressing myself as hard as I can back into the alcove and not breathing until they have turned the corner and continued down the corridor away from me, separately, turning in different directions at the next intersection of hallways.

I press my phone hard to my ear instantly. I'm so close to exploding.

"Car to the front doors now!" I growl, before hanging up and storming into the ballroom. Not looking sideways at anyone, I just zone in on Victoria and the rest of the table. Thankfully Jocelyn hasn't made it back to the table yet.

"We are leaving. Now!" I hold my hand out to Victoria, and thankfully she doesn't even hesitate. "Flynn, get Lou out of here, and you two don't let that bitch out of your sight for the rest of the night. I will fill you in later. I can't be here."

Almost dragging Victoria through the room toward the front door, I know she must be worried what has made me snap, but I can't say a word here. I can't trust anyone, plus once I open my mouth then there won't be any stopping my anger from escaping.

If they touch her in any way, then there is no stopping me. He already tried to fucking drug her. What the fuck!

I should have beat the shit out of him when I had the chance earlier tonight. Thinking back to how out of it she seemed that night at the bar, being drugged explains her sound sleeping in the car and how she couldn't remember much the next day. I'm going to nail this guy to the fucking wall. He has no idea who he has just taken on. Nobody messes with the people I love!

I open the car door before the driver even has time to get out of the driver's seat as he pulls the car to a stop. Ushering her in and following her, I slam the door and tell the driver to take us back to the apartment.

I can't touch her, otherwise I know I will be too rough. I need to take my anger out on something, and Victoria will push me into trying to release the stress on her instead. It's not happening. There is a difference between domination in sex that is fun, and losing control to the point that she gets hurt in some way. I've never been this furious around a woman, so I don't want her to see me like this.

"Nicholas." Her voice tells me she is scared, and I can't explain to her what has happened. I need to tell Broderick, but I can't do that when I'm with her.

"Fuck!" I yell, thumping my fist into the seat beside me.

"Talk to me, don't shut me out," she begs me, but I can't, I just can't.

"Not now." I take her hand in mine to try to reassure her that it's nothing to do with her. "Just give me time."

Nodding at me, she won't let go of my hand, needing the connection with me to know she will be okay. To be honest, I need the connection too, but for me it is to stop me from exploding.

The rest of the car ride is made in silence, and as we pull up to the apartment building, I hand her the key.

"Go to bed. I will be home later." My words are blunt and with no emotion.

"What, why?" I can see tears in her eyes, and she has every right to be upset. I'm acting like the asshole she knows me to be, but this time it's worse, and I can't stop it.

"Just do it, Victoria!" And my rudeness is enough that she turns and get out of the car, marching in through the open door that the doorman is holding for her. I wait until I see her enter my private elevator and then I tell the driver to leave and take me to my office.

I need to be alone.

Chapter Twenty-Three

VICTORIA

I love him, I know I do, and it's crazy because I only just met him. And I know love is supposed to conquer everything, but it doesn't.

Can I live like this? One moment in the lust-driven paradise where he is worshiping me like forbidden fruit. Then the next minute, it's like I'm in the dark of a cupboard where the door has been shut on me, not knowing what the hell is happening, scared and so confused.

This isn't what love should be.

I might not have age or experience on my side, but I know emotions, and this is not how good ones should feel, rising and falling more times in a day than a rollercoaster.

I'm standing in the bedroom with all my things scattered around me, but in his space, I feel like an intruder, and I can't take it any longer.

I know he will be gone for a while. He was not like normal, worse than I have ever seen him before. It wasn't just anger, there was more. He had shut down. The wall that I had pushed so hard to get through was back up, and it felt thicker than before.

He has baggage, don't we all in life, but I don't think I can help carry his if he won't let me in. His mum was right about him pushing me away, but I'm not sure she understands the extent of this broken man. He needs help from more than just me, professional help from someone who can pull back the layers of anger and abandonment that clouds every step he makes in life. I think carrying these thoughts all his life has robbed him of the chance to learn how to feel. He mentally and physically doesn't know how to receive love or how to reciprocate it when it's right there in front of him.

I was fooling myself if I didn't think he would run again. Deep down I knew he would hurt me, and I stupidly thought I could push through that and prove to him that I was worth the hurt we were both feeling.

That I could fix him.

But I was wrong.

As much as I can now see he is incapable of love, I also don't think he feels hurt like I am riddled with right now. How can two weeks with someone feel like a lifetime when your heart is beginning to shatter?

I won't stay, I can't.

He might not think it, but I am worth more than this.

I deserve the respect of a man who gives himself to me without guards up. I deserve everything without conditions.

The tears that have been pouring down my face since I stepped into the elevator are drying up. I will not give him the power to do this to me.

When I was growing up, through high school, I would remind myself often that I was strong and I wouldn't let anyone pull me down. I went through the normal self-doubt about how I looked and who I was, but I was determined that no one would ever make me feel less than I could be. And although Nicholas has never said or done anything to push me down, his actions are forcing me into a toxic place where no one should be. Where I am accepting that it is okay to love through the hurt. It has to stop, and the only one who can do that is me.

I know it's time to do what I should have done after Rome—walk away and protect my heart. I scoop up all the pieces of my heart, lock them away, and slowly when the time is right, I will put them back together.

I strip off this dress that I had been fantasizing all night, about how I couldn't wait for it to fall from Nicholas's hands to the floor and all that would follow. Instead, I lay it gently on his bed along with the shoes and jewelry that all belong to him. I won't need it where I'm going.

I collect my small number of things and leave all the expensive makeup, perfume, and beauty products that he had delivered here today. I can't take them. This world is not for me, and in a way, all these gifts feel like they are tarnished by what money brings. I have finally discovered that money doesn't buy happiness like we all believe. To Nicholas, all it has brought him is loneliness and sadness.

Is it worth it? I hope he can see the answer is no.

Taking one last look in the apartment that I never even got to stay the night in, I take a deep breath. I can feel Nicholas all around me, and I want to take part of him with me.

Who am I kidding, every part of me has Nicholas burned into it. There will never be a moment he won't be with me. I may be walking away from the physical, but his soul is buried so deep inside me that I know I will never let it go. Thoughts of his mother, a woman I'll never get to meet in person, makes me sad that this is how she lived her life. Finding your soul mate and losing him again so quickly is a pain Sally has carried her whole life. Hopefully I will have her strength to move on like she did.

I know what I need to do, and I can't waste any more time. Pressing the elevator button, the doors open, and I step inside, closing my eyes as the doors close again. Drawing on every bit of strength I can muster, I walk away.

"He just dumped you at his place and left? Not giving you a reason." Lou is standing in my bedroom as I throw clothes into a bag.

"That would involve talking to me, and that's a skill he seriously lacks sometimes. He probably planned on coming home and fucking his problems out on me, but not this time. That's not healthy. He needs to work his shit out, and I'm not going to be his personal 'sex' therapist for him to release whatever is ailing him. Not a sex therapist in the true sense, because Lordy, he doesn't have any problems in that department, but someone that can make him understand that sex doesn't fix everything."

"Flynn wouldn't tell me what was happening, but I think it was because he genuinely didn't know. Men!" She flops down onto my bed still in her dress and fully put together. I, on the other hand, am standing here in blue jeans, a white t-shirt, runners, and all traces of the night wiped from my face. My pale skin is on show and my eyes are puffy from crying, giving away the real me. My hair is brushed out and pulled back in a ponytail to keep it under control and out of my eyes.

"So, I'm guessing by the clothes in the bag that you are going to come and stay with me for a few days until this settles down. I can be the gatekeeper, and when he comes looking for you, which he will, I'll happily tell him to fuck off." Lou sits up and looks at me, but with the look I'm giving her, I can tell she is starting to worry.

"Tori… what's the bag for?"

"I'm leaving tonight on the Eurostar to Paris, then I'll see where I go from there."

Elouise jumps up from the bed in an impressive move since she's still all dressed up. "No, you're not! Don't be ridiculous. Sit your ass on that bed and calm the fuck down. You don't even know how to travel except in a private plane where you're wined, dined, and fucked in style."

"Lou!"

"What, it's true. You complained you were worried he would run, and now that's exactly what you're doing. You don't have the money to just quit a dream job and take off to who knows where." With her hands on my shoulders, she pushes me to sit down.

I look up at her. "Dream job, yeah, right! Working with Theo!" I get agitated just thinking about the dick and the way he treated me tonight. "I will never be able to go back there, because he will always act that way, and Daddy will never sack him for his behavior, so that dream job went up in flames earlier tonight." Pushing back up off the bed, I grab more clean underwear from my drawer, shoving it in my bag.

Lou is right, I don't have a lot of money, but I have enough. I can stay in hostels until I can pick up some waitressing or a job somewhere doing anything. But I know I can't stay here. I need to get away from him, otherwise I will give in, and tomorrow night I will be back in his bed again. And that's a thought I can't even think about now.

"So, get another job." Lou is getting upset. I can see it in her body language that she is starting to realize I'm serious.

"I need to do this. You know I have always dreamed of traveling one day. Well, it's just happening sooner than I thought. I have to do this. Shit, I was ready to give up my dreams for this man. Someone who can't share himself fully with me. I don't want to be that woman who looks back on her life and regrets something."

I can't tell her that I already know the thing I will most likely regret will actually be walking away from Nicholas, because if I say that out loud, it will be the final straw and break me.

"I thought you loved him." Her voice is barely more than a whisper.

"I do, and that is why I need to do this." Zipping up my bag, I take my passport from my top drawer. I can't believe that I'm about to use it for a second time in two weeks. It sat in this drawer so long, waiting for me to take a leap.

"When is your train?" The tears are already falling from her eyes.

"I have fifteen minutes to make it back to the station to get the train that will get me into London, with only twenty minutes to spare to make it to the last Paris train of the night. I've already got a ticket online. Now get up and hug me."

Pulling her into my arms and letting all my fears show, I hug her like my life depends on it.

"Stay safe. And if you don't send me multiple proof-of-life pictures a day, I will hunt you down, woman." We are both crying now, and it's messy, rambling words between us that we are both trying to say in hurry.

"I have to go." Pulling back from her, I take a look at the person who always stops me from doing stupid things, and I know she wants to do it again right now but won't. "I'll be back, I promise." I grab her for one last embrace and then pick up my bag, swinging it onto my shoulder, nearly knocking myself over with the weight of it since I have packed way too much. Lou has a key to my house, and I know without even asking that she will clean out the fridge, water my plants, and keep it like a shrine, begging every day that I will be home soon.

"Promise you won't talk to any other weird man on the train," she says, trying to break the tears with a joke.

"Only if you promise to stay away from Flynn. These rich boys don't play fair with your heart. Take it from me." I'm about to break down, and I find myself turning and almost running out of the house down the street toward the station. I need air to hold myself together.

Sitting back in the train seat, my bag beside me, the reality of what I'm about to do hits me.

Nicholas is going to hate me, but maybe that's what we both need. Anger is his go-to emotion. I need him to leave me alone until I can learn to feel any emotion again that doesn't involve him.

Nothing unusual for me to be running late, I push myself to make it down the platform and catch the Paris train by barely one minute before the announcement comes over the speakers that we are about to depart.

Sending the last picture of me on English soil for a while to Lou, I ask her to give the message to Nicholas that I'm sorry, before I shut down my phone. I know it won't be long before it starts blowing up with calls and messages from him, and I can't cope with that just yet. Who knows, maybe I will never be able to, but my new motto is, one day at a time.

It's as much as my brain can cope with.

Laying my head back on the seat, I close my eyes, but I know I won't sleep. Instead, the vision of Nicholas standing above me as I worship him on my knees is on replay in my head.

God, what have I done!

NICHOLAS

I knew walking into my office that Broderick would be there.

The moment I messaged him that I needed him, it was a given that he would drop everything and respond to my SOS.

"He fucking drugged her! I want him to pay. I'll beat the ever-living shit out of him myself if I have to, but he will pay." Picking up the statue on the coffee table in my office, I throw it at the wall, smashing it into a million pieces, but it doesn't make me feel any better. I've been angry for one reason or another my whole life, but that's nothing compared to the rage in me right now.

The woman I love has been violated without even knowing it, and now they are teaming up against her to ruin her career and life, all because she is associated with me. Why is this even happening?

"Slow down and tell me everything. Every single word. I need it all." Broderick is sitting at my desk and logged into my computer, taking notes as I yell in rage all that I heard.

"I want Jocelyn fired and all association with this business and the family name severed immediately. Victoria is not her punching bag because she didn't get out of life what she wanted. I'll protect Victoria with my whole being if I need to, and if that means killing them both, then I'll happily sit in jail for the rest of my life."

"Right, stop that shit now! You are not touching anyone, and you definitely aren't going to jail for violence, or any made-up drugs charges. Are you listening to me?" Before I have time to reply, he is in my face and has my shoulders in a firm grip to stop me from continuing to spiral.

"Do you love her?" He stares at me, waiting for my answer.

"Why?"

"Do. You. Love. Her?" he repeats slowly but firmly to me.

"Yes! All right, yes, more than I know what do with." His hands loosen on my shoulders, and a small smile appears on his face.

"Then we protect her, and we make sure they pay, but never, I repeat *never* do we resort to violence! We are smarter than that. Understood?" With his forehead on mine and his face so close, I can feel him boring the words into my soul.

He's right, like always. I'm not a violent man, and I won't let them change that.

But I will get them, that I can guarantee.

I walk away from him and to the window, needing to keep breathing and bring myself back to the man that Victoria needs and hopefully still wants at the end of this.

Broderick is on the phone, and I can hear him talking and typing. Tuning him out, I am already coming off the anger rush, and my body knows where it wants to be. Home wrapped around my Victoria and groveling for my behavior earlier. I shouldn't have done what I did, but I don't want her to freak out about what they are planning. That's my job.

I know he has been on and off a few calls, but finally Broderick is at my side again and looking out the window with me.

"She's gone, Nic." I'm not surprised, but I need to get to her and explain.

"Get me the car," I say, starting toward the door.

"No," he demands in a voice that makes me stop.

"I'm the boss here, get me the fucking car now!" I storm at him, about to lose my temper that I have been trying to calm down for the last twenty minutes.

"You need to let her go. If she loves you, like we both know she does, you won't lose her."

"No, I need to find her. Now, I can't… what if something happens, she can't leave me. Not again… I can't lose someone I love…" Years of heartache and panic are rushing through me, and I can feel myself going weak. When I need every scrap of adrenaline,

326

I lose the fight instead, and my body gives in. The world around me is spinning, and I can't breathe.

Blackness closes in, and my rage is all I feel in a strange way, surging through my body as I start to fall. I have never felt panic of this scale, but now I understand how powerful the mind is.

My fear of love is small compared to my biggest fear that is hitting me at full speed.

The fear of losing her.

I feel weak and stupid as Broderick talks to Rem on the phone. He managed to catch me as I fell and got me onto the couch where I'm still sweating and trying to push myself up.

"I swear to God if you try to move, I will tie you down. Stay!" Broderick says, pointing at me while Rem is talking in his ear.

"I'm not a fucking dog!" I yell as I push up to a seated position, but the way my head is still spinning, I know I need to stay here for a minute until the world rights itself.

"Got it. See you soon." Ending the call, Broderick sits back in front of me on the coffee table that is now minus one expensive statue.

"We have a man on her, she just got back on the train heading for London with a bag. She is safe." Before I can even attempt to get up, his hands are on my knees. "We aren't sure where she is headed, but I don't think it's back to your place. Otherwise, she never would have left."

"I want a woman too."

Broderick looks at me, confused.

"I want a woman security guard with her. I don't want her alone, not for one moment." And I mean it. I don't think she is in danger from those two idiots trying to destroy her reputation, because they don't have enough brains between them to organize something so sophisticated, but I don't want to lose sight of her, it's as simple as that. A woman guard is not restricted about where she can follow her.

"Okay, okay, I'll get Rem on it. Flynn dropped Lou to Victoria's house, and her guard just reported she is walking back the few streets to her own home, and she's been crying, makeup all over her face."

It's the words that confirm what I suspected. She isn't on her way back to me.

"I know you don't want to hear this, but we actually think Victoria is doing you a favor. If she is out of the picture, we can deal with this drug problem without having to fight the side battle of these two spoilt children. And from now on, there will be mandatory drug screening of all staff. I don't know what Jocelyn's on or how often she is taking them, but maybe it explains a bit of her hostile attitude. Either withdrawal when she is at work, or it is something that brings out the worst in her. Something we will eventually get to the bottom of."

"I don't give a fuck what she's on. She will never work another day in a Darby business. Period! If she wants to screw up her life, that's on her, but she's not taking me down with her." I take another sip of water from the bottle that Broderick got me as I come out of my fog.

"Agreed. Now we need to get you home. Rest is what will be best while we sort this out."

He has to be kidding if he thinks I can sleep knowing that Victoria is leaving me, and I can't do a damn thing about it.

As I stand and walk with him to the elevator, he throws the words at me that make we want to run too.

"Oh, and I can confirm your mum is on her flight and will land here early Monday morning."

"Shit, get ready to watch a sixty-year-old woman want to kill her son when she arrives." Running my hands through my hair, I can feel the disappointment already that she will try to hide when she arrives. She and Victoria connected in that first initial call, and Mum will have been planning a wedding in her mind and counting future grandkids. "The women in my life drive me batshit crazy!"

The elevator doors start sliding closed, and I'm put in my place by his fatherly voice. "Don't speak about your mother like that, she deserves your respect."

"And she has it, but it won't stop her from ranting at me how much I fucked up by losing Victoria."

The silence as we descend is broken as we reach the ground floor. "Not yet, son. I told you we aren't letting her go, just giving her a bit of space… for now."

And that gives me the tiniest splinter of hope.

The last two weeks have been the worst of my life, with my mum being here, trying to mother me to death and fix my broken heart. She forgets I'm not six anymore where she needs to fix a scraped knee. Don't get me wrong, that first hug from her when she arrived, I needed more than I realized, but now, I'm in full asshole mode and just want to be left alone. Even the guys have worked out they should stay clear of me unless I want to see them.

I think Mum finally got the message when she arrived at my office this afternoon unannounced while I was in a meeting with Broderick. He was in the middle of calming me down and telling me to be patient with the case. He seems to be positive that things are about to change soon, and all will be resolved. I wanted to push him further because I think he is hiding something from me, but with Mum here, I let it go for now.

Mum wanted to make plans for Friday-night dinner, but that's the last thing I want. What I really need is to sink myself deep inside Victoria and not let her go. But that is a long way from happening and my greatest fear is that it may never.

Broderick took Mum out for a drink, saving me from saying something I would regret later. At least one thing that has helped me to settle somewhat is having her finally tell me what the hell is going on with her. I had visions of terrible things, and although I'm still concerned, it wasn't what I was expecting. She has been diagnosed with diabetes, and the day she forgot the handbrake on the car and let it roll into a tree was when she finally accepted she needed to get serious with what the doctors were telling her. So, watching her sugar levels is a constant thing until we get her stable, and she hates the insulin injections, but there are worse things in life. This I can handle, and although she tells me it may as well be death if she isn't allowed to eat chocolate or my desserts, I make her follow her diet. I reassured her that I will find a way for her to still be spoiled with good food, but not the type that will kill her. Stubborn woman!

Knowing she needed to eat, Broderick's timing was perfect, and I know he is all over what is going on with her. He knew before I did that something wasn't right, admitting he took a quick trip to Australia to check on her without me knowing. At first, I was so angry that he didn't tell me, but I understood once he reminded me that it wasn't his news to tell but that she is always safe, he makes sure of it. It seems he has taken a personal interest in her, and if I had more mental space I would question why, but I just don't right now. That can be for another time.

After they left my office, instead of heading out to the estate for the weekend where I just want to be left alone, I have spent the last thirty minutes sitting in an interview room down in the police station with my lawyer, after receiving a phone call that I was required for more discussions. Although I think the word they meant to use was questioning, which to me means interrogation.

The door opens and the original two officers we spoke to enter the room with absolutely no expression on their faces. This can't be serious, otherwise surely, they just would have turned up at my office and charged me, carting me away in handcuffs. Oh, wouldn't that be a sight for the paparazzi who camp outside my offices. They think I don't know they are there, but the same guy sitting in the same seat every day, all day, at the café across the street is a little obvious.

All I can think about as they sit down and start rustling through papers is Victoria and how I'm glad she isn't here if this goes sideways quickly.

The last update I had from Broderick is that she is working in a café near the Eiffel Tower that is a popular spot for expat Australians. Quite ironic really, maybe she misses my accent, which

I'm clinging on to hope that it's that. But realistically, it's probably that they had a job opening and she needed money. I hate that she is staying in a backpackers' hostel, but Broderick keeps telling me I need to stay out of this and let her live her dream adventure. That coming from a man I've never seen with a woman the whole time I've known him. This staying away and not interfering is torture.

I haven't messaged, called, or reached out to her in any way because I know she doesn't want me to, and I'm trying to respect that. I know if I sent a message and it went unanswered then it would break me more than I already am. I have to let her do this her way, as hard as that is for me.

But maybe that's the point. I need to learn something from all of this, in more ways than one. Which was made abundantly clear when Flynn arrived the morning after the charity dinner with Elouise, and she left nothing unsaid about what she thought of me and what had gone down with Victoria. I tell you, those two women together are a force to be reckoned with. She didn't hold back, and for a little woman, she packs a punch. I could see the smirk on Flynn's face but know he didn't disagree with some of the things she was saying. Including that I needed to talk to someone to finally get past my inability to treat a woman the way I should. I don't know how much Victoria told her about me or if it was Flynn, but she seemed to know enough to be reading me well.

Walking in to see Dr. Mist for the first session was probably one of the hardest things I have done. Hearing the words from her, like vulnerability, feelings, and trust are ones that always make me want to shut everything out, but I'm trying. I'm a long way from being a man who can stand in front of Victoria and tell her how I truly feel, but with time, I want to be. And to do that I need to get myself right first. A version of the man that will never make Victoria run again.

In the meantime, I'm still dealing with this shit, and that's part of the problem. No one seems to be in a hurry to sort out the mess except me.

"Sorry for the delay. Mr. Weston Darby." The officer across from me looks at me with his hands clasped on the desk in front of him.

It's not very often I hear my full name, and it still sounds strange

331

after being a Weston most of my life, but now I couldn't be prouder of the addition of the Darby name to mine. Mum told me I could have dropped the Weston name, but I would never have done that. I kept it out of respect for my mum and for my pop and nan who gave everything they had to help raise me. I will never turn my back on that sacrifice and love from all three of them.

"There has been a development overnight in the case against you."

My heart stops with a thud in my chest, the way he says case against me. The last I heard I was just a person of interest.

Trying to control my breathing, I ask the questions that I'm not sure I really want to know the answer to. "What developments, and since when is there a case against me?"

"I'll ask the questions, Mr. Weston Darby, I just suggest you answer them." What I wouldn't give to be able to reach across the table and punch that smugness off his face, but as Broderick has constantly reminded the last few days, violence is not an answer. I'm sure it would feel fucking satisfying, though.

"Then start asking them and stop wasting my time." The aggression in my voice is not going to help my cause here.

Good one, Nicholas, piss off the man who has the power to lock you up.

Not sure that therapy is working just yet.

Chapter Twenty-Four

NICHOLAS

"We had an anonymous tip that one of your employees was found beaten pretty badly last night in the alley next to Bar Diamond. Is this a bar you frequent regularly?"

"Who?" I spit out before he'd even finished his question.

"Answer the question," he replies as my mind is running wild. What else could go wrong?

"Yes, I drink there sometimes, but not last night. In fact, I haven't been there in over a month." Mainly because I can't bring myself to go back. The last time I was there was the night I took Victoria home. The day my life changed forever. "Now tell me who is hurt, and are they okay?" I don't know everyone who works for me, but that doesn't even matter. If they are one of my employees, then I need to take care of them.

"He is currently in the hospital, and the reports are he is recovering well. His name is Laurence Wetherington."

"Christ, what happened?" The last I knew he was in Rome finishing off the last of the repairs and making sure the hotel was back fully functioning. What was he even doing there in that bar? I've never seen him there, and it's just not the kind of place I can imagine him frequenting. He's more a pub-and-beer kind of guy.

"We are still piecing it together, but security footage shows him arguing with a woman that we haven't been able to identify yet, and then after she leaves, there are three men who step into the frame, one a younger man and two others who jump Laurence and start to beat him."

My stomach drops. He never stood a chance against three men.

"Have you identified any of the men at all?" My lawyer asks the question that was on the tip of my tongue.

"We have the younger man, Theodore Cheston, who stood and watched them, on drug possession, and after interviewing Laurence, it appears he was accused of owing this young man money for drugs, which Laurence firmly denies."

The muscles in my body are tense and fury races through them. "Show me the footage!" Demanding they show me is probably not the best idea, but I can't hold back. I know who the woman is without even needing to see it.

"I think you forget who you are in this room, sir," Sergeant Collins reprimands me.

"What my client means is if you show him, he thinks he may know who the woman is." My lawyer Phillip has likely guessed who I'm thinking it might be, but we need to see it to be sure.

The two officers whisper between themselves and finally agree to it, with one of them spinning the laptop around.

The video quality and angle, like all security camera footage, is not great, but I know as soon as she steps into the picture, it's Jocelyn. The way she stands, and the handbag that is on her shoulder is one she carries every day in the office. Some designer brand that almost feels like she is making sure the rest of the staff knows she has money. Although in this footage she looks less put together, and I think the last few weeks have taken a toll on her. It took the wind out of her sails when Victoria disappeared, and she didn't have anyone to use as her fodder to feed to the gossip rags.

"Jocelyn Darby. My distant cousin and a former employee. Check the club footage and find a front-facing image and I'll confirm it for you."

"Why would she be with a drug dealer and his cronies in an alley with another of your employees?"

"Isn't that your job to find out? But I'll tell you this, Laurence was in Rome the night the drugs were found in my Maserati, and those two, Theo and Jocelyn, have a history of trying to attack both myself and my girlfriend. So, I suggest you start piecing things together and finally work out that I have no more questions to answer. There is something going down here between the three of them, and like I have tried to tell you all along, I have had nothing to fucking do with the drugs found in my car." Phillip puts his hand on my shoulder to try to calm me down, but it has no effect.

"What Mr. Weston Darby is trying to say is we would be happy to help with your inquiries into this mess and look forward to you confirming the woman's identity and the connection between the three of them."

It's all falling into place in my head, but I need them to finish this once and for all. I have no idea what the relationship between Jocelyn and Laurence is, but it's no coincidence that the woman who despises me the most in this world and is a drug addict, is in an alleyway with my employee who was in Rome that night, and he then gets beat up for owing her drug dealer money.

Phillip takes over the discussion, and I just answer where I need to. We finally leave the station a few hours later and are told they will speak to me again as soon as they have confirmed everything. I have told them everything I know, including the discussion I over-head between Theo and Jocelyn at the charity function.

At last, I slip into my Porsche, after what feels like a day that has gone on for eternity, and I start the drive out to the estate. There is a lightness hovering over me, something I won't allow myself to truly feel until this is all settled. Nothing has been proven yet, but I can feel that we are close.

Broderick and Rem have been telling me for a while to sit tight and wait. Things were happening behind the scenes, and they were close. They knew that something would come eventually, and now I think I know who the anonymous tip to the police was from. They have been piecing everything together, and I trust that the police can now see what's right in front of them, thanks to my team who have made sure they do.

They have tracked down a drug dealer in Rome that sold the methamphetamine to a man with an English accent who was talking about using the drugs for revenge, but they haven't gotten a physical description out of him for who the customer was. Not that Laurence would have used his real name anyway. There is footage of the deal happening, in the alley just up from the hotel, ironically the one I stepped into and kissed Victoria for the first time. I hate that they have tainted it with something like this. The guy can be seen with a hood over his head, a baseball cap on, dark glasses, and the police can't seem to identify him. However, now they may have a chance of finding the disguise at Laurence's place because he is probably stupid enough to have kept them, and then things will fall into place.

I still can't process why he would do this to me. I thought we had a great relationship, and he is good at his job. I've never had any problems with him, or so I thought. My life has been so upside down, I've given up trying to work out any of it lately.

I asked Mum to stay in the apartment in London this weekend and have arranged for tickets to different musicals in the West End. Wallace will drive her around, and she can shop to her heart's content with my card, even though I know she won't. Broderick will watch over her, which makes me feel better, and he wanted to be the one to do it in person rather than assign a guard. In a way it makes me feel better, as I trust him, and he assures me he can work while she is in the shows, so things will still get sorted.

I just need time on my own, something I haven't had since Mum got here, and truly, I don't think I have taken the time to just let out the hurt and sadness of feeling so bad for what I put Victoria through. I don't care how fucked up I feel, but it's what she is going through, because of me, that kills me.

Walking into our bedroom, which is what I call this room now, my heart physically hurts. I avoided love for so long, and then this little redhead came storming into my life and there was no way I could ignore it any longer. Her fire and attitude were what grabbed me, and I knew I couldn't let her go. For the first time in my life someone called me out on my bullshit and pushed me in a way I had never been pushed before. But once I brought her here, we finally found that there was so much more between us. The intimacy we share, I crave that just as much as the way we connect through our bodies when she submits fully to my need for control. She knows what I desire, and we found a place that we both can finally feel set free in the way we share our passion.

Watching Victoria submit to me is what allows me to breathe. She gives me life in a way I can't describe. I want that again, here in our room, totally stripped bare and not just physically. I'll give her my whole being like she deserves.

But not yet. This needs to be finally settled.

And we both need to be ready.

I have to work on myself, something I can admit in the stillness of this room, so that when I finally lay her down on this bed and find my home inside her, I will never let her down again.

Oh, my beautiful girl, how I miss you.

As I lay my head on her pillow that still has the faint hint of her scent lingering, tears start to fall. In the quiet of my home, I let go.

I finally let it all go.

VICTORIA

It's been three months since I left London, and although my heart aches to go home, it's not to the city that I miss... but for my Nicholas.

I thought traveling would heal my pain, but instead, all I have done is learn to tolerate the loneliness, while enjoying the places I have visited and the people I have met.

I don't think I ever would have done this if I wasn't pushed to leave. My dreams were big, but I don't know if I would have taken that leap for a long time yet. There would always be an excuse as to why I couldn't go. I liked the security of my life, but that changed in an instant the day I met Nicholas.

Running from him was the worst night of my life, and I cried the whole train ride to Paris, so much so that the older lady that was three seats down from me got up and offered me some tissues, probably to shut me up. I wish I was a quiet crier, but let's be honest, I'm not quiet in anything I do. It's always dramatized, and that night was no different.

I have an alert set up for him on my phone's browser, so I would know any good or bad news that was happening in his life. If I thought he needed me, there is nothing that would have kept me away. But instead, things have been quiet on the web, and that worries me more. He's been hiding, and I hate that for him, because it tells me he is as affected by all this as I am.

I long for any updates from Lou. She hasn't been dating Flynn, but they have stayed in touch, and she makes sure she gets any news she can for me. Her anger at Nicholas for what happened is overshadowed by how much she understands he means to me, so she continues to push Flynn for answers.

Nicholas shocked me when I finally turned on my phone the day after I left. There was not one single missed call from him, no text messages or fired-up voicemails where that deep voice of his was yelling at me to get home immediately. I lay at night in bed, sometimes wishing there had been, just so I could replay them and hear his voice, the one that makes me go weak at the knees and tingle all over. But the more I think about it, he did what I should have known he would do all along when dealing with emotions.

He shut me out in true Nicholas style.

It never made the gossip columns that his case was resolved, but Lou told me that he had his name cleared of the drug charges, not that I ever had any doubt that it would happen eventually.

I was shocked to hear it was Laurence, his builder, that had set him up. The poor man had become caught up with Jocelyn, and he was trying to win her love. He was never going to be good enough for her, just being a builder in her eyes and not some corporate high-flyer, but she used him for sex and information on what was happening in the company. The poor man was under her spell, loving her and not realizing it wasn't returned the same way. So he thought if he set Nicholas up, it would win her over, once and for all, and she would take control of the company they both believed should have been hers all along.

The sad part of the whole story was that he did it all on his own. There was no evidence of her involvement, so when everything fell apart for him, she hung him out to dry. She was the one who owed money to Theo, the disgusting little drug dealer that he turned out to be. Laurence was trying to help her defend herself against Theo, while begging her to stop using drugs. It was a tragic love story in the end. Laurence and Theo were both charged, but the woman at the center of it all walked away with nothing but a bad reputation which will disappear when some other scandal is more interesting, because that's just life.

The only thing for certain is that she is no longer part of Nicholas's life, and that makes me happy.

My passport is starting to look like I dreamed of when I was a little girl, where it tells a story of my adventures. The journal I always knew I would write, however, is not like I imagined it would be but is more a book full of my thoughts I wish I could share with Nicholas of everything I see. What the food is like and how much he would long for tastes and smells of the little street restaurants that are the true secrets of the countries I've visited.

Next week it's Christmas, and I miss my family and Lou, but I know where I am going to be instead of home. If I can't be in London, where I long to be in his arms, then I will be in the only other place I feel close to Nicholas—Rome.

That first day we spent together, walking, holding hands, seeing the sights. It was the place where he finally gave into his intense desire and kissed me in a way that told me right then and there that there was no turning back. I was his, he just needed to take me.

When I arrived in Rome on the train, I felt so emotional that I needed some comfort. There was one place I knew that I could afford to eat, and it was Pepe's Place where Nicholas and I ate that night. We laughed as we enjoyed each other's company, learning small amounts about each other, with what he was willing to share. It's Nicholas's favorite restaurant in Rome. Sitting at a table outside on the patio, I can see his hotel and just dream of him, because there is no way I can afford a room there for the night. It was a world that I briefly lived in, but alas, it wasn't for my budget.

Partway through the night while I was sipping on the one glass of wine I had allowed myself, Angelina and Pepe appeared out of the kitchen to say hello. Angelina had noticed me from the kitchen and came rushing out to hug me. A few broken words in English later and they had insisted that I stay in the little apartment above the restaurant for a few nights. It was their daughter's place, but she had gone to visit her boyfriend's family in Sicily for Christmas, so it was empty. It felt strange, but I wasn't about to let free accommodation pass me by when my funds were running low. I needed to pick up some more work, and I would after Christmas, but for now I just wanted to be here and to soak it all up. To reinvigorate my soul so I can push forward again, living on my memories of my man.

I have spent today on the bus we traveled on, taking photos and taking the time to write in my journal at each stop. My words are full of what I see around me, combined with how I feel deep inside. I wish I had met Sally before I left London because I feel like we would have a lot in common now. She would understand the words and fears that I write down often, questioning how I felt in those few weeks. Were my feelings real, and how was it possible to fall so hard so fast? Maybe it was all one-sided and I truly was just a plaything to him like I worried in the beginning.

Some nights it makes it hard to sleep with worry. But when I close my eyes, I can remember his touch and the way he made me feel treasured, even in the times he totally controlled me in the best possible way. Never did he make me think he wasn't genuine. But probably the most telling memory of how real we were together was the fear in his eyes when I made him feel something intense. Not just any feelings but to really feel something for me, deep in his soul.

That was when I knew I had him. He was mine then.

I just hope after my decision to leave, that he still is now.

I've left my last stop of the day to be the Trevi Fountain because I know it will be full of emotions for me. I never told him what I wished for that day we visited here together, but he made it come true anyway. Wishing to find love was a wasted wish when he was already standing right in front of me.

Standing here again, but sadly alone this time, it just doesn't feel the same. Instead, I take the time to sit here and truly take in my surroundings. I was so overwhelmed last time with Nicholas beside me and sparks that had been zinging all day, that I didn't appreciate the beauty.

Watching people come and go, both young and old, throwing their coins and making their wishes is comforting to me. I hope that they, too, have their dreams come true.

I have been twirling and rubbing the coin in my hand since I sat down here, just wondering what I should wish for this time. Nicholas gave me two coins to pick from that first day to throw over my shoulder. I tried to give one back to him, but he insisted I keep it because it might come in handy one day. Both were Australian fifty-cent pieces that are an odd shape, that he later explained were a dodecagonal shape, twelve-sided. It's a coin with sharp edges, a lot like Nicholas's personality, so he thought they suited him, which has me smiling now at that thought. I asked him why he knew that useless piece of information about the name, which he informed me was one of the few facts he remembered learning at school, and then I wanted to know what made him keep them in his wallet. I thought it gave an insight into who he was when he answered in a quiet voice, like he was giving out a secret about himself, that he always wanted to keep a piece of home with him.

I loved that money hasn't changed him and there is a soft side hiding inside that hopefully he will learn to let out more often.

The coin was still in the plastic sleeve with my passport where I placed it when we got home from Rome. So, I have been carrying this piece of him, my home, with me on my travels this time too.

I didn't think I would ever part with it, but being back in Rome for a few days and now here in this spot, I've realized you can't live in the past. Memories bring comfort, but they won't help me grow. I have to let go of him to move forward, and this coin is a symbol of the hold he has over me still. I'm not the woman I was when we first met, and that is because of him. He made me discover parts of myself I never knew existed, but he also pushed me to walk away so I could grow. I know that now. If I hadn't left, we would have eventually exploded apart in spectacular fashion, because we weren't ready. I can't blame him, we both had paths to travel, in totally different directions, and I'm glad that I didn't push aside my dreams to travel, that have now led me here.

It's time for me to make my wish and move forward.

The daylight has started to vanish and the cool of nightfall has crept up on me, which means there are now fewer people around. It's perfect. The quiet of just a few voices instead of the loudness of the crowd before is so much more calming as I stand with my back to the fountain.

Closing my eyes, I grapple with the words in my head. I try to change my wish at the last minute, but I keep coming back to the same words. The universe is telling me that it's the only wish I have inside me, so why am I changing it?

I rub my thumb over and over the coin in my fingers, across the pointy edges that I just can't seem to let go. Taking a deep breath, I say the same words I said that first day, just this time with a few extra words to give more truth to them.

"I wish for a lifetime of messy, soul-gripping, deep, dominating love."

And as I raise my hand toward my shoulder, with tears rolling down my face, a strong hand grasps mine, and before I can open my eyes, the words I have longed to hear awaken my heart again. "I'm yours, heart, body, and soul, and nothing in between us."

He pulls me into his arms so quickly I'm struggling to breathe in the best possible way. "I didn't believe in love until you. You made me love you, Victoria, and now I can't live without you. Make *us* your forever wish."

The tears are now flowing freely, and without needing to say a word, I again lift my hand, with his wrapped around my wrist, and close my eyes as I throw the coin over my shoulder, telling him out loud, "I love you, forever," knowing that my dream has already been answered.

His lips are on mine, with the roughness and intense longing I missed, because soft and gentle is not our way of doing this. He claims me all over again, and I know we are both remembering what the taste of our crazy is like. He doesn't care who's around us, because he's telling me what I already knew. I'm his, and I have always been his.

Breaking apart, he takes my face in his hands and holds me so close. The seriousness is radiating from him. "I'm never letting you go again. Please forgive me, Victoria, and I promise you, this will all have been been worth it." His eyes are not like I imagined they would be when he finally said these words. He has lost the panic, and all I see now is a longing to be loved.

Kissing me again, he drops his arms to wrap me up and hold me close. He has always needed touch to allow himself to be vulnerable.

"I knew you would come for me, but what took you so long?" I ask, laying my head onto his chest. I hear the familiar sound of his heart thumping just for me.

His deep laugh radiates through his body, and before I know what's happening, my feet are off the ground and he is twirling me around.

"How did you know?" Slowly, he places me back on my feet.

"Because there was no way you would let me go that easily. You've known where I was the whole time, haven't you?" I say, calling him out on the two guards who have been following me across Europe.

"You're mine, and I wasn't about to let anyone hurt you. You have to know it comes from a place of love."

"You poor, controlling man. These last three months must have just about killed you."

"You have no fucking idea, and you will never leave my side again." There is that growly tone in his voice that I have desperately missed. "But I knew I had to let you do it your way. I couldn't clip your wings. You needed to fly, but can you please come home now? I miss you, beautiful." I can see the change in him, the way he is so freely laying his heart out for me to hold.

"Home is wherever you are, so take me home." I gently kiss him on the lips with all the truth behind my words.

His shoulders drop with relief after the stress he was feeling, worry that maybe my answer may have been different. I will travel again, that I have no doubt, but in a little bit more style and never alone.

"Thank fuck for that, because I'm not ready to share you yet, so home is in my bed with me and where I will not be letting you leave for days, and even then, you might be lucky if I let you wear clothes out of the bed." And there he is, my controlling man who is about to punish me for leaving him on his own.

"Promises, promises, from an old man. Are you sure you have enough stamina for that?" I can't help giggling because I know pushing him is only going to bring me the most intense pleasure.

"All the words in the world won't save you from what I'm about to do to your body. And just so you know, I remember how begging looks so good on you."

He slides his arm around my shoulder, guiding me toward where I imagine he has the car parked. This man likes to travel in style and enjoys the luxury his life allows him.

There is so much I could say about his comment, but I don't, because the truth is, I can't wait for him to force me into letting go.

"I'm confused," I say, looking across to Nicholas in the driver's seat as he just smiles and continues driving past the hotel, where I imagined we would naturally be staying.

"I meant what I said. I'm not ready to share you yet, and I don't want you to feel any hesitation that may be lingering from our last visit to Rome and that the same thing may happen again. I promise that will never happen again, but I need to prove to you that I am worthy of your love, and for that we need time. Time to talk, time to make love…" He looks at me with such heat in his eyes.

344

"And time to fuck? Please tell me you haven't changed that much while I was gone. I kind of loved the way you fuck me... hard and dirty." I can feel the heat in my cheeks at my honesty.

"Oh, that part of me will never change, because whenever I am near you, I want to do bad things to you... very, very bad things."

"How long until we get to this hideaway you have planned for me? Because suddenly I'm hungry, and I can tell you it's not for food." I slide my hand over his cock that is already hard and ready to get reacquainted.

"Not soon enough!" he growls, pushing his foot down harder on the accelerator. My body is thrown back into the seat, and all I can do is smile at his desperation.

"I agree," I purr, still torturing him with my hand and feeling my body dampen with anticipation.

There isn't even any time to notice the surrounds of the Italian villa that we have arrived at in the dark. As soon as the car pulls to a stop, Nicholas is out and around the car, pulling me by the hand from my seat.

"In a hurry?" I giggle as he brings his arm under my legs and sweeps me up off the ground. Carrying me inside, he heads straight through what appears to be the living area, up a flight of stairs, and into a room that has two glass doors open onto a balcony, the breeze making the white sheer curtains sway.

He sets me down on my feet and commands, "Strip." His stern voice echoes through the quiet of the night as he disappears into what looks like a bathroom.

I can't get my clothes off quick enough, now standing naked in front of the open doors and smelling the salty air. The sign we drove past tells me we are somewhere on the Amalfi coast, but I don't care one bit. We could be anywhere in the world, as long as I'm with the man I love and feeling his love returned just as intensely.

I turn to look back into the room at the candles, now lit, and the soft glow lets me see all of him. He's naked, with every muscle on show, and his erection is so intense the pain is written all over his face.

"On your knees where you belong, Victoria."

As he walks toward me with the confident stride I've missed, I drop to the floor with pleasure.

"Open your mouth and suck me like the dirty little thing you are."

I open my lips wide, and he slides his tight engorged cock inside. My moan tells him how much I have missed him.

Welcome home, my beautiful asshole.

Epilogue

VICTORIA

The days that followed that first night at the villa, Nicholas proved his point when he had said he was going to punish me. And the whole time I kept trying to think of things to do wrong so he would continue to punish his naughty girl even more. We didn't leave the bed unless it was a necessity, and I still haven't had one item of clothing on since we arrived.

On the balcony we have a hot tub that is shielded from anyone's view, and every night he takes me out there to relax in the bubbles, but only after he has fucked me in so many different ways, each one taking me to new highs and places I didn't know I wanted to go.

But the main thing we did was what we should have done in the first few days after we met. We talked and talked and talked. And I understand more now why it was so hard for Nicholas to open up to me at first. Pushing him to do it had only made things worse. His therapist explained to him that carrying such hatred toward his father for most of his life, and then finding out things were never as they seemed, had totally rocked his world. His subconscious was warring with itself, trying to turn his hate into a place of love and admiration, all the while not beating himself up for hating someone who didn't deserve it. I think all of that mixed in with sadness and a massive change in his life circumstances led him to shut himself off to everyone, including himself.

When we met, feelings started to bubble away under the surface, and he didn't know how to cope with it. It resulted in the push and pull that ignited our passion but couldn't give us enough stable ground to base a serious relationship on.

As hard as it was for both of us, me leaving and severing all contact with him was the best weapon I had, to make him take action to help himself deal with years of hurt.

He finally understood that to let love in, first he had to let go of the hate.

I'm sitting out on the balcony when I hear Nicholas come up behind me. He was on a phone call with Broderick that sounded intense and had been going for a while. I don't want to intrude on Nicholas's work life in any way. We have been locked away from the world for a few days, but it would be naïve of me to think that it can continue that way forever. My boyfriend—which is still hard to let sink in, knowing it's for real this time—is a high-powered man, and Christmas is one of the busiest times of the year for the hotels.

"You're dressed. I'm not sure I allowed that." Kissing me on the cheek, he sits down in one of the chairs next to me. He is dressed too, but barely. Gray trackpants and a long-sleeve linen shirt that is still open down the front, giving me the perfect view. And of course, no shoes. What is with these Australian men and bare feet? Although, I must admit, it's a hot look.

"It's too cold to sit out here naked and not in the hot tub. So, give me a bit of leeway, mister. Besides, you are dressed too." Reaching out, I take his hand as he smiles, looking out at the view. "Everything okay with work?"

"Mhmm," he murmurs, clasping my hand tighter. "But it wasn't about work."

"Oookkkaaayyy?" He looks like the cat that ate the canary. "Want to share?"

He takes a moment because I can tell he is still digesting the phone call. "Brokerick called to ask my permission to date my mother."

"Holy shit, what the hell have I missed? You better start talking, and don't leave out any of the details." I jump up from my seat and sit in his lap, curling up like a kitten.

"Damn women and their gossip, wanting to know everything. I don't know all the details, only that he has been her guard while she was in London, and I have a feeling that they've been talking since he came to Australia to find us." He laughs at me, because he can tell I want more than that.

"How closely was he guarding her? I can't believe this all happened while I was gone, and I haven't even met her face to face yet. Wait, what did you tell him? You better not have scared him off, that woman deserves happiness. Nicholas, don't leave me hanging!" My squeal of excitement gives away how exciting this sounds for Sally.

"Steady on there. Firstly, I don't want to know how close they have been. This is my mother we are talking about. And secondly, I did what any son would do, I told him that's her decision to make, but if he hurts her in the slightest, I will personally kill him with my bare hands. Is that good enough?"

Snuggling down into his neck, I say, "Perfect, that's what I would have said too."

His deep laugh makes his chest shake. "Glad you approve."

"But just one question. She lives in Sydney, and he lives in London; how will that work?"

"No idea, that's for them to work out, but I have a sneaking suspicion it's time to buy a private jet of my own."

"How much money do you have? Seriously. Who just ducks out to the shop and buys a private jet." I look up at him because I can feel his body tense up a bit with my offhanded comments.

"You need to understand, I have more money than I can spend in a lifetime or ten. That doesn't mean I flaunt it or spend it unwisely, but if I want to spoil the people in my life then I will. So, listen up and listen hard. The private jet is so you can travel. I want to show you the world like you always planned. If you want to travel on your own, then you take the plane and your guards and do that. Will I hate it? Abso-fucking-lutely, but will I stop you? Never. I don't want you sleeping in backpackers' hostels or dodgy motels. That stops right now! You will stay in my hotels or an equivalent five-star one. You have just about killed me the last few months, thinking about you sleeping in insect-infested beds, where there is probably more sperm on the mattress than in a sperm bank.

"I want us to travel and make memories, but I'm not stupid enough to ignore your stubborn independence. I've learnt that lesson, plus my mother dressed me down for not respecting you and letting you live your life without me hovering when she found out I was trailing you across Europe." He rolls his eyes at me. I can just imagine Sally letting him have it when she arrived to find I was gone.

When I shift on his lap so I'm straddling him, I have his full attention. "I have an idea. We can travel your way, in full luxury as Nicholas and Victoria, and live your fancy life of private jets, fast cars, and five-star hotels. But once a year you have to travel with me as Nic and Tori, on a trip I plan and pay for, and you will have no input into where we stay or how we get there. And before you answer, Nicholas, this is non-negotiable." Taking his face in my hands, I kiss him before he can retaliate with a negative answer.

"Then you better have a high-paying job, because I'm not a cheap date, you know, and it costs a lot to hire my private jet and stay in one of my hotels… and that, my bossy girlfriend, is my non-negotiable deal."

"We'll see. I can be very persuasive when I need to be." I loosen the tie on the big fluffy robe I have on and reveal my cold nipples that are longing to be warmed up.

"So can I…" He takes my nipple into his mouth and laves it with his tongue, while the other is in his hand being gripped hard.

What was I thinking?! I'll never win a battle with him if I'm trying to use sex as my persuasion tool.

He will always guide me in the most dominating way to where he wants me, and I wouldn't have it any other way.

NICHOLAS

The days leading up to flying to Rome to get my girl were gut-wrenching.

I had dealt with all the drug-charge drama and made sure I buried Jocelyn so far down in this industry that she will never work in a luxury hotel again. She may not have been charged with anything, but her wicked ways and manipulation of Laurence meant that I couldn't stand back and let her walk free.

Broderick let a few stories get leaked to the media on how we had terminated her from the company and severed all family ties due to drug use, all hypothetical, of course. But then there was some mystery security footage that my team had managed to track down that might have then been leaked to corroborate the stories a few weeks later.

The last I heard—because you can guarantee I have someone watching her and will continue to until I don't feel the need—was that she was working at a small pub in Scotland and living upstairs above her workplace. Her family had cut off her trust fund, and of course, she had been blowing her own money for years on feeding her drug habit. It still shocks me how she hid it from me that well, but as Flynn reminded me, I always look for the good in people, even when they are terrible people. That is why I kept her employed all those years; I kept giving her one last chance, way too many times.

Theo's stepfather, Warren Webb, contacted me when he heard the full story of what had happened at the club, when Theo drugged Victoria, and he assured me that Theo will never step foot in York and Webb Design and that her job will be there when she returns, no matter how long it takes. I didn't give him any answer, because to be honest, that's not my decision to make, but I know she won't be going back if I have any say.

I'm not sure how I will tell Victoria about the drugs in her drink, because she will feel violated, but she has a right to know. I just need to remember that I can be angry for her, but it was her body, not mine. She has the right to feel what she needs to and take the actions she feels are necessary. Nothing can be done now, it is my word against his, but still, it is her decision to make.

Warren also told me that the reason Gwenda Francis had taken extended leave when Victoria started was because Theo had convinced her to take party drugs one night while out at the Friday-night staff drinks, making sure he filmed her without her knowledge, and then he threatened to make the videos public if she didn't help him get a promotion by giving him the bigger clients. When he found out that Victoria was hired, he started pushing Gwenda harder, and she panicked and took a leave. He was a nasty piece of work, hiding behind a bubbly little man who was craving attention. It's good that he was charged and is now awaiting sentencing on all his charges, that escalated to more serious ones once he was arrested. There was more evidence on his computer that showed his drug operation to be bigger than a side hustle.

Once I got through all of that and life started calming down, all I wanted was to be with Victoria, but I knew I had to wait, and when she was ready there would be a sign. I didn't know what that would be, but as soon as I got the message she had arrived in Rome and was at Pepe's, I packed my bags and was on the move. Much to the amusement of Flynn, Rem, and Forrest. I called Pepe on the way to the airport and asked him to hold her there somehow until I could get there. That was when he suggested his daughter's apartment for her to stay, which I tried to compensate him for once I arrived, but he refused. We finally settled on a vacation for him and Angelina in one of my hotels anywhere they wanted to go.

Going to Rome was like she was calling to me to come for her, and I wasn't waiting a moment longer. My therapist tried to tell me I should wait until she came home to me, but that was bullshit, and for the first time in my life, like my mother always said, the universe will send you a sign, and I knew Rome was my sign that she missed me.

Standing to the side, I watched her at the fountain have an internal debate about what she was about to do. It had my heart racing, and the moment she stood and walked toward the fountain and turned her back, I was there and doing what I should have done a long time ago—I grew some balls and told her I loved her. I had never felt it before in my life, and I wasn't letting her go. Just like my mother and father's souls found each other and discovered instantly that they belonged together, Victoria and I were the same, but we just let all the other crap get in the way.

I had my villa stocked with food and her bag taken there during the day, and although my mother told me it was kidnapping, I reminded her I was just doing what she told me and finding a place for us to talk… among other things.

One of the things my grandfather did well was buy properties, not just hotels. He had no one to share his wealth with, so he just kept investing it and also donated a generous amount to charity, but he never took too much credit for it. We have a company called the ARD Foundation that was named after my grandmother Aileen and my father Richard Darby, without listing their names. Every year my grandfather made anonymous donations to worthy causes. I have continued that since I took over, and the only people who know it is me are the guys who I trust everything with, plus my mother, who I now get to help me with picking where the money should be spent.

We have been in the villa for a few days now, and tomorrow is Christmas Day. I promised my mum a proper family Christmas this year, so she and Broderick, the guys, and Elouise are all at the hotel waiting for us to arrive tonight to surprise Victoria. But before we leave, there is one last discussion I need to have with her before we leave the privacy of the villa, where we can yell and scream at each other until we sort out where we stand going forward.

This morning's round of sex on the balcony in the cold wore her out, and I'm not sad about that at all. The more sex we have, the calmer Victoria is, and that is how I like to see her. The vision in front of me, her lying in my king-size bed, wrapped in the warm cream-colored blankets and her red hair spread all over the pillow, is one I will never get tired of. I don't want to wake her, but we need to talk before we go back to Rome.

As I run my finger down the side of her face, her nose starts to twitch, and I can tell she is close to waking. Leaning down and kissing her softly, her lips start to respond, and her soft moan tells me she is responding to my touch.

"Wake up, beautiful," I whisper, kissing her forehead and then both her cheeks before going back to her mouth. Her lips are like a magnet for mine.

"Just because you don't sleep, don't be mean and wake me." Stretching her hands above her head, her eyes finally open, and I see that she is coherent enough for this.

"We need to talk, and then I have a surprise for you."

She sits up in the bed, and her eyes are now wide open and have a sparkle in them. "Ooh, I love surprises. Tell me, tell me." I can't help but laugh at her childlike tendencies sometimes. She can be a hard-ass bitch in business or when she is protecting me, but I love that she can also be so light and fun too. She balances her life like my mum in some ways. She doesn't let anything get the better of her to dull her spirit.

"I need to ask you something that is unresolved between us first. But before you panic, just hear me out."

The fun in her eyes has gone and the worried look is there, and I hate that, but we need to do this.

"Did you come up with the new branding for the hotels?" I know it's a weird way to start, but I'm curious what she will say.

There's a confused look on her face as she thinks about what she is going to say. "I'm not sure if I should be worried why you are randomly asking this, but yes, I knew within a few days of being at the estate what I would pitch to you when the time came."

"Good, then let's have it. I don't need some big fancy presentation, I just want to know from your heart what you think."

She takes a deep breath, clearly nervous, but she doesn't need to be. No matter what she says, it won't change how I feel about her.

"When I spent time with you in the hotel in Rome and got to know you, the real you at the estate, there was no denying what I thought you should do. I think you are going about this the wrong way. Your family name is important to you and has finally given you a link to a family you didn't have the honor of knowing. Sure, let's modernize the look of hotels and the way we market them. Look to target the younger crowd that I think you have been missing out on up until now, and I can suggest ways to do that. But Nicholas, you spent your whole life trying to find who you were. Now that you have found that, don't bury it. Like I said in the beginning, shorten the name, so instead of The Darby Hotel chain, just call them The Darby. Be proud of that name and heritage, don't ever lose it, because I fear you will lose yourself again too."

Looking at me so tentatively, I know she is nervous for my reaction, and this is not the place I thought she would be giving the presentation to me, but in all honesty, it's perfect. She has stripped back the layers of me perfectly, and everything she just said is true. The big well-known hotels don't change their name and are short and to the point. The Savoy, The Ritz, everyone knows them. My job as the head of the family is to make sure everyone knows the Darby name too.

"You know, you didn't need to get naked to hook me with your pitch." Pushing her back onto the bed, I hover above her. "You are the only person who truly knows me, probably better than I know myself. It's perfect, just like you. I love it, but just in case you're worried, not as much as I love you." I kiss her in a way that she will understand how much it means to me that she put so much thought into how important the business is to me and who I am as a person.

"Great, now what's my surprise?" she says, breaking from my kiss to move onto the next thing. That's Victoria's mind for you, always moving at a fast speed.

"I'm not finished yet. There is one last thing I need to ask you." I don't want to drag this out. "Will you come and work for me? Actually, *with* me, not for me. I want us to build the hotels together, and I know that for every day we argue through every little decision we make, we will have made the best decision for everyone. You push me to think, and you won't back down when you believe I'm wrong—which is never, I might add. But what I'm saying is I want to spend my days arguing with you so that I spend my nights loving you."

"What if we break up again? We are only just beginning." Oh, my sweet girl, I don't think I have made myself clear enough.

"Victoria, I am never, ever letting you go again. You are right, this is the beginning of the rest of our lives together. And when we get back to London, I want to meet your parents, because I am doing this the right way. I want to ask for their permission to lock their daughter up in my tower for the rest of her life so I can worship her body and make her do dirty things with me."

Her voice is barely a whisper. "Do you mean marriage?"

"Oh, I mean I will be doing lots of things to you and with you, and marriage is one of them, along with me finally taking that ass of yours. You will spend the rest of your life begging me for more of whatever I choose. And we will both love every minute of it."

Tears start falling down her cheeks, but her smile tells me they are happy tears. "You told me that day on the train when I met you, that you hoped it was the start of whatever amazing thing I wanted to happen." I swipe the tears from her face with my thumb. "You forgot to tell me I was looking at that amazing thing, and that was you."

Kissing her tenderly on the lips, she pulls away for one last word.

"I love you, Richard Nicholas Weston Darby, but I'm not sure I can work with you. We will kill each other on the first day."

Her little giggle tells me that wasn't a no.

"That's what I'm counting on, Victoria. I fucking love fighting with you, because you know the make-up sex is going to rock your world!" Just the way you have rocked mine from that first morning I laid eyes on you.

Who knew I needed this much crazy in my life, but I will thank the universe and my father every day for bringing me just who I needed.

My beautiful and crazy Victoria.

Read on for a sneak peak of *Gorgeous Gyno* from *The Chicago Boys* series

Also by Karen Deen

Gorgeous Gyno

Private Pilot

Naughty Neuro

Lovable Lawyer

The Chicago Boys Box Set (above 4 books in one set)

The Chicago Boys - NYE in New York City (Novella)

That Day

Better Day

Defining Us

Love's Wall

Love's Dance

Love's Hiding

Love's Fun

Love's Hot

Time for Love Box Set (All *Love's* books in one set)

GORGEOUS
Gyno

KAREN DEEN

Chapter One

MATILDA

Today has disaster written all over it.

Five fifty-seven am and already I have three emails that have the potential to derail tonight's function. Why do people insist on being so disorganized? Truly, it's not that hard.

Have a diary, use your phone, write it down, order the stock – whatever it takes. Either way, don't fuck my order up! I shouldn't have to use my grown-up words before six am on a weekday. Seriously!

I'm standing in the shower with hot water streaming down my body. I feel like I'm about to draw blood with how hard I'm scrubbing my scalp, while I'm thinking about solutions for my problems. It's what I'm good at. Not the hair-pulling but the problem-solving in a crisis. A professional event planner has many sneaky tricks up her sleeve. I just happen to have them up my sleeve, in my pockets, and hiding in my shoes. As a last resort, I pull them out of my ass.

I need to get into the office to find a new supplier that can have nine hundred mint-green cloth serviettes delivered to the hotel by lunchtime today. You would think this is trivial in the world. However, if tonight's event is not perfect, it could be the difference between my dream penthouse apartment or the shoebox I'm living in now. I'll be damned if mint napkins are the deciding factor. Why can't Lucia just settle for white? Oh, that's right, because she is about as easy to please as a child waiting for food. No matter what you say, they complain until they get what they want. Lucia is a nice lady, I'm sure, when she's not being my client from hell.

Standing in the bathroom, foot on the side of the bath, stretching my stockings on, I sneak a glance in the mirror. I hate looking at myself. Who wants to look at their fat rolls and butt dimples. Not me! I should get rid of the mirror and then I wouldn't have to cringe every time I see it. Maybe in that penthouse I'm seeing in my future, there will be a personal trainer and chef included.

Yes! Let's put that in the picture. Need to add that to my vision board. I already have the personal driver posted up on my board—of course, he's sizzling hot. The trains and taxis got old about seven years ago. Well, maybe six years and eleven months. The first month I moved to Chicago I loved it. The hustle and bustle, such a change from the country town I grew up in. Trains running on raised platforms instead of the ground, the amount of taxis that seemed to be in the thousands compared to three that were run by the McKinnon family. Now all the extra time you lose in traffic every day is so frustrating, it's hard to make up in a busy schedule.

I slip my pencil skirt up over my hips, zip up and turn side to side. Happy with my outfit, I slide my suit jacket on, and then I do the last thing, putting on lipstick. Time to take on the world for another day. As stressful as it is and how often I will complain about things going wrong, I love my life. With a passion. Working with my best friend in our own business is the best leap of faith we took together. Leaving our childhood hometown of Williamsport, we were seeking adventure. The new beginning we both needed. It didn't quite start how I thought. Those first few months were tough. I really struggled, but I just didn't feel like I could go home anymore because the feeling of being happy there had changed thanks to my ex-boyfriend. Lucky I had Fleur to get me through that time.

Fleur and I met in preschool. She was busy setting up her toy kitchen in the classroom when I walked in. I say hers, because one of the boys tried to tell her how to arrange it and her look stopped him in his tracks. I remember thinking, he has no idea. I would set it up just how she did. It made perfect sense. I knew we were right. Well, that was what we agreed on and bonded over our PB&J sandwich. That and our OCD behavior, of being painfully pedantic. Sometimes it meant we butted heads being so similar, but not often. We have been inseparable ever since that first day.

We used to lay in the hammock in my parents' backyard while growing up. Dreaming of the adventures we were going to have together. We may as well have been sisters. Our moms always said we were joined at the hip. Which was fine until boys came into the picture. They didn't understand us wanting to spend so much time together. Of course, that changed when our hormones kicked in. Boys became important in our lives, but we never lost our closeness. We have each other's backs no matter what. Still today, she is that one person I will trust with my life is my partner in crime, my bestie.

Leaning my head on the back wall of the elevator as it descends, my mind is already running through my checklist of things I need to tackle the moment I walk into the office. That pre-event anxiety is starting to surface. It's not bad anxiety. It's the kick of adrenaline I use to get me moving. It focuses me and blocks out the rest of the world. The only thing that exists is the job I'm working on. From the moment we started up our business of planning high-end events, we have been working so hard, day and night. It feels like we haven't had time to breathe yet. The point we have been aiming for is so close we can feel it. Being shortlisted for a major contract is such a huge achievement and acknowledgement of our business. Tapping my head, I say to myself, "touch wood". So far, we've never had any disaster functions that we haven't been able to turn around to a success on the day. I put it down to the way Fleur and I work together. We have this mental connection. Not even having to talk, we know what the other is thinking and do it before the other person asks. It's just a perfect combination.

Let's hope that connection is working today.

Walking through the foyer, phone in hand, it chimes. I was in the middle of checking how close my Uber is, but the words in front of my eyes stop me dead in my tracks.

Fleur: *Tonight's guest speaker woke up vomiting – CANCELLED!!!*

"Fuck!" There is no other word needed.

I hear from behind me, "Pardon me, young lady." Shit, it's Mrs. Johnson. My old-fashioned conscience. I have no idea how she seems to pop up at the most random times. I don't even need to turn around and look at her. What confuses me is why she is in the foyer at six forty-five in the morning. When I'm eighty-two years of age, there is no way I'll be up this early.

"Sorry, Mrs. Johnson. I will drop in my dollar for the swear jar tomorrow," I mumble as I'm madly typing back to Fleur.

"See that you do, missy. Otherwise I will chase you down, and you know I'm not joking." I hear her laughing as she shuffles on her way towards the front doors. I'm sure everyone in this building is paying for her nursing home when they finally get her to move there. I don't swear that often—well, I tell myself that in my head, anyway. It just seems Mrs. Johnson manages to be around, every time I curse.

"Got to run, Mrs. Johnson. I will pop in tomorrow," I call out, heading out the front doors. Part of me feels for her. I think the swear jar is more about getting people to call in to visit her apart-ment. Her husband passed away six months after I moved in. He was a beautiful old man. She misses him terribly and gets quite lonely. She's been adopted by everyone in the building as our stand-in Nana whether we like it or not. Although she is still stuck in the previous century, she has a big heart and just wants to feel like she has a reason to get up every day and live her life.

My ride into work allows me to get a few emails sorted, at the same time I'm thinking on how I'm going to solve the guest speaker problem. Fleur is on the food organization for this one, and I am on everything else. It's the way we work it. Whoever is on food is rostered on for the actual event. If I can get through today, then tonight I get to relax. As much as you can relax when you are a control freak and you aren't there. We need to split the work this way, otherwise we'd never get a day or night off.

The event is for the 'End of the Cycle' program. It's a great organization that helps stop the cycle of poverty and poor education in families. Trying to help the parents learn to budget and get the kids in school and learning. A joint effort to give the next generation a fighting chance of living the life they dream about.

Maybe if I call the CEO, they'll have someone who has been through the program or somehow associated with the mentoring that can give a firsthand account of what it means to the families. Next email on my list. Another skill I have learned: Delegation makes things happen. I can't do it all, and even with Fleur, we need to coordinate with others to make things proceed quickly.

As usual, Thursday morning traffic is slow even at this time of the day. We are crawling at a snail's pace. I could get out and walk faster than this. I contemplate it, but with the summer heat, I know even at this time of the morning, I'd end up a sweaty mess. That is not the look I need when I'm trying to present like the woman in charge. Even if you have no idea what you're doing, you need people to believe you do. Smoke and mirrors, the illusion is part of the performance.

My phone is pinging constantly as I approach the front of the office building. We chose the location in the beginning because it was central to all the big function spaces in the city. Being new to the city, we didn't factor in how busy it is here. Yet the convenience of being so close far outweighs the traffic hassles.

Hustling down the hall, I push open the door of our office.

'FLEURTILLY'.

It still gives me goosebumps seeing our dream name on the door. The one we thought of all those years ago in that hammock. Even more exciting is that it's all ours. No answering to anyone else. We have worked hard, and this is our reward.

The noise in the office tells me Fleur already has everything turned on and is yelling down the phone at someone. Surely, we can't have another disaster even before my first morning coffee.

"What the hell, Scott. I warned you not to go out and party too hard yesterday. Have you even been to bed yet? What the hell are you thinking, or have the drugs just stopped that peanut brain from even working?! You were already on your last warning. Find someone who will put up with your crap. Your job here is terminated, effective immediately." Fleur's office phone bangs down on her desk loud enough I can hear her from across the hall.

"Well, you told him, didn't you? Now who the hell is going to run the waiters tonight?" I ask, walking in to find her sitting at her desk, leaning back in her chair, eyes closed and hands behind her head.

"I know, I know. I should have made him get his sorry ass in and work tonight and then fired him. My bad. I'll fix it, don't worry. Maybe it's time to promote TJ. He's been doing a great job, and I'm sure he's been pretty much doing Scott's job for him anyway."

To be honest, I think she's right. We've suspected for a while that Scott, one of our managers, has been partying harder than just a few drinks with friends. He's become unreliable which is unlike him. Even when he's at work, he's not himself. I tried to talk to him about it and was shut down. Unfortunately, our reputation is too important to risk him screwing up a job because he's high. He's had enough warnings. His loss.

"You fix that, and I'll find a new speaker. Oh, and 900 stupid mint-green napkins. Seriously. Let's hope the morning improves." I turn to walk out of her office and call over my shoulder, "By the way, good morning. Let today be awesome." I smile, waiting for her response.

"As awesome as we are. I see your Good Morning and I raise you a peaceful day and a drama-free evening. Your turn for coffee, woman." And so, our average workday swings into action.

By eleven-thirty, our day is still sliding towards the shit end of the scale. We have had two staff call in sick with the stupid vomiting bug. Lucia has called me a total of thirty-seven times with stupid questions. While I talk through my teeth trying to be polite, I wonder why she's hired event planners when she wants to micromanage everything.

My phone pressed to my ear, Fleur comes in and puts her hand up to high-five me. Thank god, that means she has solved her issues and we are staffed ready to go tonight. It's just my speaker problem, and then we will have jumped the shit pile and be back on our way to the flowers and sunshine.

"Fleurtilly, you are speaking with Matilda." I pause momentarily. "Hello, Mr. Drummond, how are you this morning?" I have my sweet business voice on, looking at Fleur holding her breath for my answer.

"That's great, yes, I'm having a good day too." I roll my eyes at my partner standing in front of me making stupid faces. "Thank you for calling me back. I was just wondering how you went with finding another speaker for this evening's event." I pause while he responds. I try not to show any reaction to keep Fleur guessing what he's saying. "Okay, thank you for looking into it for me. I hope you enjoy tonight. Goodbye." Slowly I put the phone down.

"Tilly, for god's sake, tell me!" She is yelling at me as I slowly stand up and then start the happy dance and high-five her back.

"We have ourselves a pilot who mentors the boys and girls in the program. He was happy to step in last-minute. Mr. Drummond is going to confirm with him now that he has let us know." We both reach out for a hug, still carrying on when Deven interrupts with his normal gusto.

"Is he single, how old, height, and which team is he batting for?" He stands leaning against the doorway, waiting for us to settle down and pay him any attention.

"I already called dibs, Dev. If he is hot, single, and in his thirties then back off, pretty boy. Even if he bats for your team, I bet I can persuade him to change sides." Fleur walks towards him and wraps him in a hug. "Morning, sunshine. How was last night?"

"Let's just say there won't be a second date. He turned up late, kept looking at his phone the whole time, and doesn't drink. Like, not at all. No alcohol. Who even does that? That's a no from me!" We're all laughing now while I start shutting down my computer and pack my briefcase, ready to head over to the function at McCormick Place.

"While I'd love to stay and chat with you girls," I say, making Deven roll his eyes at me, "I have to get moving. Things to do, a function to get finished, so I can go home and put my feet up." I pick up my phone and bag, giving them both a peck on the cheek. "See you both over there later. On my phone if needed." I start hurrying down the corridor to the elevator. I debated calling a car but figured a taxi will be quicker at this time of the day. Just before the lunchtime rush, the doorman should be able to flag one down for me.

Rushing out of the elevator, I see a taxi pulled up to the curb letting someone off. I want to grab it before it takes off again. Cecil the doorman sees me in full high-heeled jog and opens the door knowing what I'm trying to do. He's calling out to the taxi to wait as I come past him, focused on the open door the previous passenger is closing.

"Wait, please…" I call as I run straight into a solid wall of chest. Arms grab me as I'm stumbling sideways. Shit. Please don't let this hurt.

Just as my world is tilting sideways, I'm coming back upright to a white tank top, tight and wet with sweat. So close to my face I can smell the male pheromones and feel the heat on my cheeks radiating from his body.

"Christ, I'm so sorry. Are you okay, gorgeous?" That voice, low, breathy, and a little startled. I'm not game to look up and see the face of this wall of solid abs. "You just came out that door like there's someone chasing you. I couldn't stop in time." His hands start to push me backwards a little so he can see more of me.

"Talk to me, please. Are you okay? I'm so sorry I frightened you. Luckily I stopped you from hitting the deck."

Taking a big breath to pull myself back in control, I slowly follow up his sweaty chest to look at the man the voice is coming from. The sun is behind him so I can't make his face out from the glare. I want to step back to take a better look when I hear the taxi driver yelling at me.

"Are you getting in, lady, or not?" he barks out of the driver's seat.

Damn, I need to get moving.

"Thank you. I'm sorry I ran in front of you. Sorry, I have to go." I start to turn to move to the taxi, yet he hasn't let me go.

"I'm the one who's sorry. Just glad you're okay. Have a good day, gorgeous." He guides me to the back seat of the taxi and closes the door for me after I slide in, then taps the roof to let the driver know he's good to go. As we pull away from the curb, I see his smile of beautiful white teeth as he turns and keeps jogging down the sidewalk. My heart is still pounding, my head is still trying to process what the hell just happened. Can today get any crazier?

GRAYSON

'I'm just a hunk, a hunk of burning love
Just a hunk, a hunk of burning love'
Crap!
What the hell!

I reach out to grab her before I bowl her over and smash her to the ground. Stopping my feet dead in the middle of running takes all the strength I have in my legs. We sway slightly, but I manage to pull her back towards me to stand her back up. Where did this woman come from? Looking down at the top of her head, I can't tell if she's okay or not.

She's not moving or saying anything. It's like she's frozen still. I think I've scared her so much she's in shock.

She's not answering me, so I try to pull her out a little more so I can see her face.

Well, hello my little gorgeous one.

The sun is shining brightly on her face that lights her up with a glow. She's squinting, having trouble seeing me. She opens her mouth to finally talk. I'm ready for her to rip into me for running into her. Yet all I get is sorry and she's trying to escape my grasp. The taxi driver gives her the hurry along. I'd love to make sure she's really okay, but I seem to be holding her up. I help her to the taxi and within seconds she's pulling away from me, turning and watching me from the back window of the cab.

Well, that gave today a new interesting twist.

One gorgeous woman almost falling at my feet. Before I could even settle my breathing from running, I blink, and she's gone. Almost like a little figment of my imagination.

One part I certainly didn't imagine is how freaking beautiful she looked.

I take off running towards Dunbar Park and the basketball court where the guys are waiting for me. Elvis is pumping out more rock in my earbuds and my feet pound the pavement in time with his hip thrusts. I'm a huge Elvis fan, my music tastes stuck in the sixties. There is nothing like the smooth melodic tones of the King. My mom listened to him on her old vinyl records, and we would dance around the kitchen while Dad was at work. I think she was brainwashing me. It totally worked. Although I love all sorts of music, Elvis will always be at the top of my playlist.

"Oh, here's Doctor Dreamy. What, some damsel in distress you couldn't walk away from?" The basketball lands with a thud in the center of my chest from Tate.

"Like you can talk, oh godly one. The surgeon that every nurse in the hospital is either dreaming about fucking, or how she can stab needles in you after she's been fucked over by you." Smacking him on the back as I join the boys on the court, Lex and Mason burst out laughing.

"Welcome to the game, doctors. Sucks you're on the same team today, doesn't it? Less bitching and more bouncing. Let's get this game started. I'm due in court at three and the judge already hates me, so being late won't go well," Lex yelled as he started backing down the court ready to mark and stop us scoring a basket.

"Let me guess, she hates you because you slept with her," I yell back.

"Nope, but I may have spent a night with her daughter, who I had no idea lives with her mother the judge."

"Holy shit, that's the funniest thing I've heard today." Mason throws his head back, laughing out loud. "That story is status-worthy."

"You put one word of that on social media and I won't be the one in court trying to get you out on bail, I'll be there defending why I beat you to a pulp, gossip boy. Now get over here and help me whip the asses off these glamour boys." Lex glares at Mason.

"Like they even have a chance. Bring it, boys." He waves at me to come at him.

Game on, gentlemen.

My watch starts buzzing to tell us time's up in the game. We're all on such tight work schedules that we squeeze in this basketball game together once a week. These guys are my family, well, the kind of family you love one minute and want to kill the next. We've been friends since meeting at Brother Rice High School for Boys, where we all ended up in the same class on the first day. Not sure what the teachers were thinking after the first week when we had bonded and were already making pains of ourselves. Not sure how many times our parents were requested for a 'talk' with the headmaster, but it was more often than is normal, I'm sure. It didn't matter we all went to separate universities or worked in different professions. We had already formed that lifelong friendship that won't ever break.

Sweat dripping off all of us, I'm gulping down water from the water fountain. Not too much, otherwise I'll end up with a muscle cramp by the time I run back to the hospital.

"Right, who's free tonight?" Mason is reading his phone with a blank look on his face.

"I'm up for a drink, I'm off-shift tonight," Tate pipes up as I grin and second him that I'm off too. It doesn't happen often that we all have a night off together. The joys of being a doctor in a hospital.

"I can't, I'm attending a charity dinner. It's for that charity you mentor for, Mason," Lex replies.

"Well, that's perfect. Gray, you are my plus one, and Tate, your date is Lex. I'm now the guest speaker for the night. So, you can all come and listen to the best talk you have witnessed all year. Prepare to be amazed." He brushes each of his shoulders with his hands, trying to show us how impressive he is.

We all moan simultaneously at him.

"Thanks for the support, cock suckers. My memory is long." He huffs a little as he types away a reply on his phone.

Mason is a pilot who spent four years in the military, before he was discharged, struggling with the things he saw. He started to work in the commercial sector but then was picked up by a private charter company. He's perfect for that sort of role. He has the smoothness, wit, and intelligence to mingle with anyone, no matter who they are. He's had great stories of different passengers over the years and places he's flown.

"Why in god's name would anyone think you were interesting enough to talk for more than five minutes. You can't even make that time limit for sex," I say, waiting for the reaction.

"Oh, you are all so fucking funny, aren't you. I'm talking about my role in mentoring kids to reach for their dream jobs no matter how big that dream is." The look on his face tells me he takes this seriously.

"Jokes aside, man, that's a great thing you do. If you can dream it, you can reach it. If you make a difference in one kid's life, then it's worth it." We all stop with the ribbing and start to work out tonight's details. We agree to meet at a bar first for a drink and head to the dinner together. My second alarm on my watch starts up. We all know what that means.

Parting ways, Mason yells over his shoulder to us all, "By the way, it's black tie."

I inwardly groan as I pick up my pace into a steady jog again. I hate wearing a tie. It reminds me of high school wearing one every day. If I can avoid it now, I do. Unfortunately, most of these charity dinners you need to dress to impress. You also need to have your wallet full to hand over a donation. I'm lucky, I've never lived without the luxury of money, so I'm happy to help others where I can.

Running down Michigan Avenue, I can see Mercy Hospital in the distance standing tall and proud. It's my home away from home. This is the place I spend the majority of my waking hours, working, along with some of my sleeping hours too. My heart beats happily in this place. Looking after people and saving lives is the highest rush you can experience in life. With that comes rough days, but you just hope the good outweighs the bad most of the time.

That's why I run and try not to miss the workouts with the boys.

You need to clear the head to stay focused. The patients need the best of us every single time. Tate works with me at Mercy which makes for fun days and nights when we're on shift together. He didn't run with me today as he's in his consult rooms and not on shift at the hospital.

I love summer in Chicago, except, just not this heat in the middle of the day when I'm running and sweating my ass off. It also means the hospital struggles with all the extra caseload we get. Heat stroke in the elderly is an issue, especially if they can't afford the cool air at home. The hospital is the best thing they have for relief. My smart watch tells me it's eighty-six degrees Fahrenheit, but it feels hotter with the humidity.

I don't get the extra caseload, since I don't work in emergency. That's Tate's problem. He's a neurosurgeon who takes on the emergency cases as they arrive in the ER. Super intense, high-pressure work. Not my idea of fun. I had my years of that role, and I'm happy where I am now.

Coming through the front doors of the hospital, I feel the cool air hit me, while the eyes of the nursing staff at the check-in desk follow me to the elevator. The single ones are ready to pounce as soon as you give them any indication you might be interested. Tate takes full advantage of that. Me, not so much. When you're an intern, it seems like a candy shop of all these women who want to claim the fresh meat. The men are just as bad with the new female nurses.

We work in a high-pressure environment, working long hours and not seeing much daylight at times. You need to find a release. That's how I justified it, when I was the intern. I remember walking into a storeroom in my first year as an intern, finding my boss at the time, Leanne, and she was naked from the waist down being fucked against the wall by one of the male nurses. Now I am a qualified doctor who should hold an upstanding position in society, so I rarely get involved in the hospital dating scene anymore.

Fuck, who am I kidding? That's not the reason. It's the fact I got burnt a few years ago by a clinger who tried to get me fired when I tried to move on. Not going down that path again. Don't mix work and play, they say—well, I say. Tate hasn't quite learned that lesson yet. Especially the new batch of interns he gets on rotation every six months. He is a regular man-whore.

Am I a little jealous? Maybe just a tad. Both me and my little friend, who's firming up just thinking about getting ready for some action. It's been a bit of a dry spell. I think it's time to fix that.

Pity my date for tonight, Mason, is not even close to what I'm thinking about.

My cock totally loses interest now in the conversation again.

Can't say I blame him.

Just then the enchanting woman from today comes to mind and my cock is back in the game. I wish I knew who she was.

Now this afternoon's rounds could be interesting if my scrubs are tenting with a hard-on.

The joys of being a large man, if you get my drift.

There's no place to hide him.

Acknowledgments

This is the part where I get to tell you all how amazing you all are, and I'm not sure words can truly express how grateful I am for each and every one of you.

I started writing with the dream that one day someone would read my words and enjoy my stories, and now here we are thirteen books later and writing has become my life. But none of that would have been possible without you all, my beautiful readers. You continue to encourage me by reading my books and supporting my journey.

Thank you for making my dream come true, I will always be eternally grateful.

But none of this would be possible without the wonderful team of people I have all around me, never behind me, always standing beside me.

I am truly blessed to have my beautiful PA Lee working with me. She works so freaking hard to make sure everything is running smoothly at all times. I'm sure every time I message her, or call her and say, "I've had a thought," that she wants to run far away. Instead, before I know it, she has it sorted and far better than I ever could have done it. I could write a whole book on how fantastic she is if she would let me. Love you to bits, Lee, and I'm so grateful to be doing this life with you.

To my beta readers, this book would not have been possible without your support and encouragement that I was on the right track. You girls keep me honest, and I can't thank you enough.

My editor at Contagious Edits is the most patient and amazing woman ever! Full stop, end of story. Nothing more I can say other than, thank you so much for all you do for me. I would truly be lost without you.

Linda and the team at Foreword PR and Sarah at The Book Cover Boutique have been with me forever. Thank you to you both for all that you do for me.

In the last twelve months I made a massive decision to leave my role of being an accountant after thirty-two years. I am now living my dream every single day, and I couldn't be happier. My husband Michael, son Josh, and daughters Caitlin and Aimee have been the greatest support, encouraging me to follow my dream. I could never have done this without them. I love you for eternity my gorgeous family.

Thank you all for reading and loving Nicholas and Victoria as much as I do. Not all love is easy and perfect, but more like Nic and Tori, it's messy, painful, and the most amazing thing that will ever happen to you.

Never be afraid to open your heart to love, no matter how messy it can be.

See you between the pages.

Karen xx

Printed in Great Britain
by Amazon

33177257R00219